Also by

CW01024508

THE COLOR SERIES

Red Night: Xavier's Delight (Book 1)

Blue Film (Book 2)

White Hole (Book 3)

STANDALONE

The Wrong Man

THE COMPASS SERIES

Beastly Armory (Book 1)

Rawest Venom (Book 2)

Southpaw Slots (Book 3)

Anorthic Anarchy (Book 4)

Full list on Amazon author's page:

http://amazon.com/author/kittykingauthor

THE COMPASS SERIES

BEASTLY ARMORY

BOOK ONE

KITTY KING

Copyright © 2023 by Kitty King

All rights reserved.

No part of this book may be reproduced in any form or by any electronic or mechanical means, including information storage and retrieval systems, without written permission from the author, except for the use of brief quotations in a book review.

For information contact: http://authorkittyking.com

Editing by Nice Girl Naughty Edits

Cover design by Books and Moods

ASIN: B0CGVM12J7 (eBook)

ISBN: 979-8-9880503-6-0 (Paperback)

First Edition: January 2024

10 9 8 7 6 5 4 3 2 1

To those who like a little sex with their blood.

STRAUSS

"Through Force Go Forth from the North"

Vladimir Vincent, II   Alyona Romanova

VLADIMIR VINCENT, III

Right hand:	Sevastian Romanov
Lead tank:	Sergei Antonov
Secondary tank:	Karol Morozov
Lackie:	Petre Nikolev
Spies:	Halcyon & Lark
Hacker:	

COLORS: RED AND BLACK
SIGIL: RED BULL
GOVERNMENT AND TRADE
LEADERS, RULERS, AND ARISTOCRACY

VON DOVISH

"Sly Eyes Skulk the West in Jest"

Franklin Donaldson   Yvette Eflene Fleur

CALUM DONALDSON   Livia Anne

Right hand:	Nick Jordan
Lead tank:	Armel Lenox
Secondary tank:	Jordain Bellarose
Lackie:	Rainier Moulin
Spies:	Alpha, Delta, & Foxtrot
Hacker:	Echoes and Hostile

COLORS: BLUE AND SILVER
SIGIL: BLUE FOX
HALLUCINOGENS AND TECHNOLOGY
CUNNING, SHADOWY, INTELLIGENT

Municipality of
GNARLED PINE HOLLOW

FREIDENBERG

"The Den of the Beast Lies in the East"

Gerald Leon — Mari Lynn Schroft

MAXIMILLIAN LEON — Arianna Bridgette

Right hand:	Markus Schultz
Lead tank:	Jakob Kobb
Secondary tank:	Adal Derichs
Lackie:	Klemens Holland
Spies:	Aries, Egon, and Gemini
Hacker:	Skipper

COLORS: BLACK AND GOLD
SIGIL: BLACK BEAR
ARMS & AMMUNITIONS
LOYALTY, BRAVERY, & HONESTY

DONOVAN

"With Howls from the Pack the South Attacks"

Ambrose McClelland — Collette Murphy

ASA MCCLELLAND — Ashley Ambrose

Right hand:	
Lead tank:	
Secondary tank:	
Lackie:	
Spies:	
Hacker:	

COLORS: WHITE AND BLACK
SIGIL: WHITE WOLF
CASINOS AND ADULT ENTERTAINMENT
INITIATIVE, DETERMINATION, & FEROCITY

Author's Note

This book is very dark and contains adult themes.

If you don't have content problems, just skip the content warning list because it contains a ton of spoilers.

If you are worried, you can find it on my website at authorkittyking.com/warnings.

Does this have a happy ending?
Yes. Yes? I'll go with **yes**.
Remember: *it's always darkest before the dawn.*

One

MAXIMILLIAN

Darkness creeps like a noxious cloud around the Barracuda as it rolls up to the rusted iron fence. There are no streetlights along the lane, the only light a full moon casting ominous shadows behind twisted branches highlighting a haze of fog clinging to the old gatehouse. It's long since been abandoned.

I figured he would be watching, waiting for my return. Arriving in the dead of night under an onyx safety blanket robbed him of the satisfaction. Pitch black is the time people call it. And the sticky ink of the sky feels as if it has invaded my soul.

It's good to be home.

Arianna stirs in the passenger seat as I slow the car for the bump leading into the driveway. She's been asleep for the last three hours. The headlights are off, but I don't dare cut the engine.

"We're here," I tell her.

Arms reaching up into a V, like she's back in her cheerleading days, she stretches her torso against the passenger seat. Her voice is crisp when she asks, "What time is it?" Long brown locks trickle over her face as she leans forward to check her phone.

"It's 3 a.m."

"Ugh! Geez, Maxi. You *would* get us here in the middle of the night."

A frown forms on my lips at my little sister's annoying pet name. "It's safest this way..." Softer, I murmur, "And I didn't have much of a choice." Peering through the blackened windows, I park in front of the bloodstone raging bear monogrammed gates. They've been closed for years. With the air of command, I say, "You need to stay down until we get to the house."

The entire reason for showing up now is to protect my sister from prying eyes. Fortunately, the old cameras on every eastern city street corner sit defunct and derelict, a sober reminder of the destruction our family left behind. Taking the deserted country roads into town, I'd sneaked under the radars without much of a plan of first attack. The threat of authorities back in the city we left caused me to burn all the gas we had without stopping for a rest. Not that East Side has much of anything left to stop for. It wasn't supposed to happen this way, but here we are.

"Fine by me." Tossing her pink fuzzy blanket over her head, she curls her skinny legs up underneath her, blissfully unaware of the changes about to take place in our lives. The scant apartment on the wrong side of the tracks we shared the last four years was sobering enough for Arianna, but once our parents' money ran out, we were left with ramen noodles and overdraft fees. And blood on my hands. Venturing into this, our new world, may terrify her.

It's been too long to remember how cold it can get in this valley, but the reminder slaps me across the face as I step out of the vehicle. Cobbles crunch beneath my careful steps toward the fence while I secure my gaze on the horizon, studying the shadows for any movement. Only the bare trees wave in the distance. No guard sits on duty anymore. Our staff has long since been taken care of, or fled to a new town, if they were lucky.

The tarnished padlock is almost entirely corroded, but the centuries-old key left in my parents' safe deposit box still works. Once slotted in the hole, it nearly twists clear off, but with a few careful tugs, the heavy weight of it drops into my open hand. With a good deal of effort, the heavy gates give, then swing open with tortured groans, angry to be disturbed from their slumber.

Jumping back into my muscle car, I maneuver the tires carefully over the disrupted pavement. Each crevice has as many weeds growing through it as the lawn. I don't stop to close the gates. It's best to leave an escape route.

He knows; I'm sure he knows I'm back. He'll be expecting us.

Images from my childhood invade my vision as we approach the manor over the long drive. Fishing on warm summer days in the pond. Making a secret fort in the large maple in the woods. Playing tag with Ace through the stale manor halls. Hide-and-seek in the gritty cellars with Cal... *Livia*. My Livia.

Over the dried watering hole, the worn wooden swing now hangs by a twine thread from my favorite oak. It sways in the gusts as if taunting me, leaving no doubt that any happy times have been left behind.

A colossal, foreboding shadow looms in front of us. The sinewy clouds part, allowing the moonlight to illuminate the brick-and-stone turrets hanging onto a collapsing roof. It's in worse shape than I thought it would be, and at the sight of its dereliction, a heavy sigh deflates my chest. Hopefully, we won't have to sleep with the raccoons tonight. I've had worse arrangements, though. Rodents are safer than what may lie in wait for us behind those walls.

"Oh, it looks scarier than I remember," Arianna says. The upholstery creaks as she scans the area through the misty glass. She was too young to fully know the place, our parents having taken us far away from Gnarled Pine Hollow when I was just eight and she was four.

"We'll get it fixed. Markus said—"

"Markus says a lot of things." Arianna's eyes snap to my own, their narrowing visible by the glowing lights of the console.

She's right. Markus talks a bigger game than a fisherman with a lost catch. But he is the only person in the world, other than my little sister, who I trust. He was my father's right-hand man, and now my new hype man.

Despite his reticence in our return, he wants the best for the clan. Always there for us, he'd ventured outside Gnarled Pine enough times to keep me abreast of important happenings within the city, and for the last several years, reluctantly aided my homecoming.

"Let's head in." Opening the trunk, our overnight bags fit easily over my broad shoulders as my sister gets out of the vehicle, her hair tangling in a gust of autumn air. She slams her door closed. "Not too loud, Ari." Scanning the forest's edge for a disruption in the light, I instinctively reach for the piece tucked into the small of my back. "He could be here."

At my warning, her head darts around aimlessly. Arianna has no concept of self-preservation, nor has she needed it. She's had me. I've been her protector and sole parent since she was sixteen. Wrapping her blanket around her little body, she scurries to the front door.

Deep within the pocket of my jeans is the shiny, unused key that had also been waiting for me in the bank box for the last eight years. Papa wouldn't have wanted this. He'd hate that we were here. But he's dead. And I need to do what's best for our legacy. Returning to Freidenberg Manor to reclaim our family lands is the first step.

After preparing the people of East Side for a war, taking down Vladimir Strauss will be my last.

The heavy, dark wood front door opens with a menacing creak. There's no power, but the house lived without it for over a century. Turning on my pocket flashlight, I find a wall torch and light the tallow taper with a flick of my Zippo. It crackles as it burns the dust from its wick. My sister's prominent cheekbones appear hauntingly gaunt behind the dancing flame when I hand her the chamberstick.

"It stinks in here. Like mildew." She sneezes.

"Well, we'll clean it up... It's home, Ari." When I glance down, her huge brown eyes fill with tears. She pins herself to my side, and my arm capes protectively around her shoulders.

"Home." She sniffs. "Thank you, Max."

"I got you. I'll take care of you. Told you I would."

She's never had a real home before, living at school and then with me in various shanties over the last few years. Trying to keep us afloat, I had to fight, even do things I wasn't proud of, things that would make Mama and Papa ache with disappointment. This place brought me comfort. A vague recollection of belonging and safety lives among the empty halls. Before I achieve my final goal, I want to give her that feeling, too.

The entry opens into a narrow passageway, which has one step down into a massive two-story living room. The furniture is the same, but I don't stop to consider it. Not at this hour. After driving all day, I need some rest, even if that's with some owls or mice. Stepping through the room, my boots stick in soft mud, evidence of this area having received most of nature's wrath: leaves, twigs, water...all pooled onto the sunken floor.

Left untouched by the elements, the creepy pipe organ stands erect, towering over the room. I always hated that thing; its dissonant tones remind me of my harsh grandfather. Once, while our parents were away on vacation, he monitored the estate. If I made an error on my lessons, he would force me to stand with my back against the wall, balancing a ruler on one finger while he played some horrific tunes. Any time the ruler faltered, he would use it to smack my face.

Meandering through the room until we reach the staircase, I wave off Ari so I can go first, making sure it's steady enough for my weight. Skilled craftsmen built the solid steps hundreds of years ago. Despite the squeaks protesting my arrival, the wood has held up. I test each one with my foot before putting my full body onto them and carefully make my way to the second story.

At the top, I turn toward the right hallway without any thought. The door resting in a darkened alcove swings open wildly when I twist the brass knob to my old bedroom. Everything is just the way it was before. Blue checked duvet. Cowboys on the walls. A basketball hoop hanging from the closet door. Even my clothes are piled in the corner from the night we dashed away.

There are no animals, but the stench of rot is ripe. The bedding is chill and damp. Everything in the house has given up, clearly not expecting my return. Dropping my luggage on the hardwood, I pull out my sleeping bag and lay it out over the bed, too tired to deal with the mess tonight.

"Mine's perfect!" Arianna yells from down the hall.

We shared a bathroom all those years ago. Strolling through it, I notice how bare, but clean, it remains. Startling at my own reflection in the mirror, I'm amazed at how much the image has changed since the last time I was here. My black hair is a disheveled mess from running my fingers through it repeatedly, and the dark circles under my eyes match their color.

What was her name? Mrs. Molly, that was it. She kept everything tidy, scolding me for spraying toothpaste on the sink or dribbling urine next to the toilet. Her breath smelled like coffee. I only heard her laugh once when the butler tripped on the hall runner and fell into a lemon pie Cook had made for his birthday. Other than Papa and Mama, she and our governess were the only ones allowed to discipline "Master Freidenberg." I don't think Papa would have approved of Grandfather's punishments if he had known about them.

Entering Ari's room, my eyes are assaulted by Pepto pink when I swing my flashlight around. Pink walls, furniture, bedding, rugs...It's very *her*.

"My dollhouse is still here!" She rises from behind the tall Victorian model, a happy replica of the foreboding structure we stand in, holding out one of her toys. Her white teeth shine in the light. I haven't seen her this happy in a long time. She looks just like she did that Christmas when Papa pulled off the bow for her, as if twenty years have passed with a flash of her smile.

"Are you going to play with that tonight?" My hand clutches her soft comforter. It's dry. I set her bag on the floor next to the canopied four-poster bed.

"No, silly. I'm going back to sleep." She eyes the open curtains, stepping back from the row of windows facing the front lawn. Hugging her middle with both arms, she asks, "You'll be just across the hall, right?"

"Yeah, I'll be a few steps away." Sliding out my Glock from my back, I check the chamber. One in. "You're safe. Just holler if you need me." In two steps, I cross over to her and plant a small kiss on my little sister's forehead. I give it thirty minutes before she's trying to sleep in my room, just like when we were kids. She always had nightmares about bulls rushing to gore her. No idea where she had seen something like that before.

Thinking about all the tasks that need completion in the morning, it doesn't take me long to fall into a deep trance. My warmth encapsulated by the cocoon of my sleeping bag, I dream of my mother's comforting hugs and my father's laughing smile—things I haven't experienced in years. Not since the day before they were murdered.

Startling awake, an arm snakes itself tightly around my middle. Slowly, my hand slips under the pillow, fingers feeling for my gun. Peeking one eye open, I see Ari nestling against me. Whenever things would change in our lives, when we'd have to leave in a hurry to make it to a new place in the middle of the night, she'd come find me after tossing and turning, afraid to sleep alone.

I sleep like the dead because I'm already half-way there.

Easing out from under her, I'm careful to let her rest. As I shuffle to the front door, I survey the damages. Daylight exposes years of neglect. My focus is on what once was and what will be again. This is a challenge, but nothing will stop me from my mission.

I'm home. And there's something powerful about being where you're supposed to be.

The morning air is clean and refreshes my lungs from the damp musk inside. Hazy light bathes the circular drive that once held a working fountain, now left in a crumbling concrete pile. At the base is a tarnished copper plaque emblazoned with my great-great-great-grandfather's name. Fishing my cock out of my jeans, I piss all over it, then spray the ruins and some wild shrubs as well.

"Mine."

"If you only had to spill urine to claim it." A chuckle rumbles from around the other side of the rubble, and my hand draws my handgun in a flash. "Down, son. It's me."

Markus's ruddy face greets me with three days of white scruff and bloodshot eyes. He's still wearing his old red flannel shirt I remember from the last time I saw him, his familiar presence soothing my inner turmoil. Zipping up, I reach out to embrace him. "Hey."

"Hello, boy. I would say I'm glad to see you, but I'm not." He surveys the house. "Not here anyway." His overweight body backs up to stand at an arm's length. Light eyes take me in behind their thick glasses, scanning my assuredness. Placing a hand on my shoulder, he asks, "I can't talk you out of this?"

"No."

He nods soberly. "That was my last try." Before letting go of me, he pats my shoulder with fatherly affection. "Let's get started, then."

We walk side by side to the front door.

Markus has made his concerns about us quite evident with his protests. He worries about us, as he should. His family has been tied to mine since the dawn of the legends. But this land is my homeland. It's where I belong. My ancestors' blood was shed here, and my bones will decay in the soil amongst their remnants. Arianna will marry a son of a mobster and bare his children, and I suppose I have to find some mafia princess to knock up with a son to take my place. It's just the way things have always been in the city.

In the dark wood paneled entry, Markus whistles loud and long. "Wow. It *is* in terrible shape. I got Jakob Kobb coming. He's setting up a construction crew. Adal Derichs will oversee the security."

"And you trust them?"

"I wouldn't be here otherwise." Markus narrows his eyes under a pair of wiry gray eyebrows. I know he wouldn't. He'd be dead if he didn't trust them. One got put in the ground for trusting the wrong people in Gnarled Pine Hollow.

The problem is, I don't trust anyone, except Arianna and Markus. I hate giving up control to anyone. It's always better if I do the job myself. Then at least I'll know it's done right. And without getting stabbed in the back.

The kitchen is laid with the same intricate ceramic tiles on the floor and faded green cabinets I remember from all those years ago. Arianna stands dressed in a pink silk robe and slippers with little puffs on them, rummaging through an old icebox. "There's nothing to eat."

"Arianna, there's no power."

She giggles. I shake my head when I realize she's teasing me.

"We'll get it working again, sweetie." Markus hugs her with an arm wrapped over her narrow shoulders while I watch where he puts his hands. "Should be on sometime today. I called the electric company about it last week." He tugs my little sister toward the kitchen table, and we sit together. The last time I was in this chair, my feet didn't hit the ground, and I reminisce about Cook giving me pancakes for my birthday breakfasts.

Now, I'm man of the estate and need to get down to business. "Okay, who do we have left?" I ask Markus.

"Jakob is helping me. He will take care of you...*both*." He shoots a warning look at Arianna, and her nose crinkles in reply. She won't like having a guard. I'm the only person she trusts. "Adal Derichs is his right-hand man. He'll organize your security team while Jakob will head up the reconstruction."

"What about—"

"Skipper and Aries. And that's all you need to know."

My hacker and spy, Markus's informants. At least he has people. I briefly wonder if they are left over from loyal eastern associates over the long centuries, but before I can ask, Markus interrupts my thought. "Yes, they're all from the old families. You have to trust me, Max. You have to trust somebody. You can't do this alone." Taking off his glasses, he produces a white handkerchief from his shirt pocket to wipe them clean.

What does he know about trust? I have lived in hiding with an assumed name from the age of eight until twenty. For the last eight years, I have met resistance, to outright danger at every step in my plan to return to our land. *My* rightful land. It's been a daily struggle, and I did it all *on my own*.

I know my father didn't want this life for me, to take my place as the King Consort of the East, sitting on the Senate of Gnarled Pine Hollow's sham government. But once my parents were dead, there was nothing left to hold me back from reclaiming what was mine. They may not have cared about our legacy, but I do. I have thought about it every time I remembered happy childhood memories among the cattails. Coming back is like an act of vengeance against Strauss himself. But true retribution won't happen until he's six feet under. And I want to be the one to take him there.

"Thanks for everything," I say, instead of telling him to fuck off. Papa wouldn't appreciate me disrespecting his best friend. So far, Markus has done everything I've asked of him, even if he didn't want to. Delegating tasks is hard for me, but I'll see how he performs. If it's not up to par, I'll take over. "Will they have *any* weapons?"

Markus looks at the glass tabletop, his solemn face reflected through the dusty surface. "They have a few."

My lips tighten into a grimace. And therein lies the problem. What good is my security team without guns? Sure, Strauss has sat dormant only because the people hold no threat against him as it stands, but how long until he senses resistance?

Markus narrows his eyes at me. "So tonight—"

"Tonight, I'm hitting up the Ace Hole."

Markus's jaw drops. He swallows and clears his throat before saying, "You realize that's closed now. It's—"

"Whatever Strauss renamed it when he stole it from Ace a few years ago. I know, you told me."

"It's the Crimson Angel, and it's not a bar anymore. It's a..." Markus glances at Arianna, who hangs onto every word we speak. Her brown eyes sparkle as they dart back and forth between us.

"I know what it is," I tell him quietly.

"But walking in there could be a death sentence. You'll take Jakob."

Narrowing one eye at him, I shake my head. Sometimes he still sees me as a little boy. "Markus, what have I been doing these last eight years? Sitting on my ass? No. I've been training. Fighting. *Shooting.* I've been to prison, for fuck's sake. I don't need Jakob to accompany me to a... club."

"What kind of club?" Arianna's innocent face lights up with her question.

"None of your concern." Hiking a thumb toward the door, I instruct her, "Go upstairs and get dressed. Men will be coming over to start working on the house." Without an argument, she does as she's told. I watch her leave and make sure she's gone before turning back to

Markus. His gray brows dance with worry. "Make sure no one touches her."

He nods. "I understand, but it's going to be tough, Max. She's an exceedingly beautiful girl. They all have their instructions not to even look at her. It's why I picked Jakob. Please, reconsider taking him with you tonight—"

"I can take care of myself." The chair squeaks as I push it back, then stand and brush past Markus, leaving him to organize the rest of the day.

Two

MAXIMILIAN

By that evening, the manor has power and water. Markus has arranged for a housekeeper to arrive tomorrow and staff by the end of the week. How I will pay everyone's salaries is another day's problem. Hopefully, my new employees can be patient until I get our rightful properties back. If they can wait, I can do it. Nothing will stop me.

Donning a suit for my first task, I undo the top two buttons of my black dress shirt. One bullet sits in the chamber of my Glock's magazine, and I run the polishing cloth over the barrel before tucking it into the holster beneath my gray suit jacket. Brass knuckles weigh down my dress pants. The Cold Steel SRK fits snuggly inside my waistband. Condoms in the wallet. I'm locked and loaded.

Cheap cars fill the small parking lot, as if this is the only place of entertainment for miles around. Ironically, the joint is in the basement of an old Gothic church, with a derelict cemetery housing Asa Donovan's ancestors squatting next to the stone structure. I wonder how pissed Ace must be to have lost this place a few years ago, likely in a rigged gambling match. I'd heard the rumors from Markus or my work associates over the years: Ace's nickname had become a mockery as his luck drained along with his money.

Looming over me is the lofty bell tower, looking like it's ready to give me a lecture on bad behavior. Ace and I would sneak up the rickety wooden steps and hide in the belfry to avoid Sunday school. We tried to shoot spit wads through straws at churchgoers as they entered the chapel far below us, but Mama would find us before we rained down too much terror. If she could see me now, she'd tsk until her cheeks sunk in.

Opening the heavy wooden doors, the vestibule washes an old wet smell over me, casting childhood memories back into my vision that I'm quickly snapped out of as I make my way into the tall nave. Shaking my head in disgust, I walk down a carpeted aisle to get to the side door leading downstairs. An iron archway stands at the altar, set up for an autumn ceremony. Strauss has turned the upstairs into a wedding venue. Nothing he does surprises me anymore.

Catacombs lurk as a sub-basement beneath the lounge. While our parents held secret meetings there, Ace and I would crouch behind the coffins, and whenever Cal would gain enough courage to come find us, we'd jump out and scare him. He'd get so mad; he wouldn't talk to us for a week. Then Livia would kick our

17

shins in until we apologized to her brother. Everything looks completely different now.

The steps are doubly wide and lead to a circular landing room in the basement. All the walls are still stone, but not moldy and weeping. It looks clean, brighter than I remember, though the room is lit mainly by candle-light. My feet almost slide on a velvety red rug as I trip into a small table with a large bouquet of white flowers. Like this isn't some dirty brothel. Without thinking, I reach out and rub a petal of a lily to see if it's real. At least something in here is fresh.

All the black wooden doors surrounding the room are closed. Rotating, I check for any labels to see where I should head for a drink. Just as my pulse thuds harshly with the sense of being trapped, a woman emerges from a skinny door beneath the stairs. The first thing I notice is her exorbitant cleavage and wide, curved hips. My dick thickens in my dress pants as she sways toward me. Her dark skin sparkles in the dim light of the room like she's wearing glitter. Black hair twists in intricate braids on top of her head and her thick lips smile briefly at the sight of me. Strauss certainly knows how to pick them.

"Need a room or the bar?" A deep, sultry voice resonates through the empty air. Deep-set brown eyes linger on my chest, then drop lower as she scans my body.

"Both, but I'll start with the bar."

Turning in a graceful motion, she walks in front of me, her stiletto leather heels making temporary holes in the rug. Her ass is one of the best I've encountered in a while. "This way." With a flick of her fingers, she motions to a door on our left.

Purposefully returning my focus to the strategy I'd set for the night, my hand rubs at my stubble, trying to get my mind off the goods on display. The plan is to be seen here, to make some waves and possibly serve up a Molotov cocktail, but I think I'll hit up a room before I tear the place down. It's been a few weeks and I need to fuck.

She knocks three slow raps on the door, which is opened by a large man, dark shades covering his eyes. The seductress waves me in with her long arm. As I brush past him, the bouncer doesn't even pat me down, so I confidently stroll straight to the bar. That must mean everyone here is packing. Knowing that makes me feel safer, relaxing enough to order a tall pint of tap beer from the well-built bartender. He nods with a smile and eye-fucks me, but I turn my head, uninterested in what he's got to offer. I'll use him to spread some information, however.

A one-step stage and a grand piano, unoccupied tonight, update the lounge area. Mismatched chairs line little tables, with small candles flickering light in the darkness for a romantic atmosphere. The place is almost empty for a Monday night, or perhaps the other rooms are crowded. My ears buzz from the red fluorescent sign blaring Strauss's sigil, hanging proudly behind the barkeep. Its bull horns bore holes into my outwardly calm demeanor.

Squeezing my eyes shut, I scratch at my temple,

willing my temper down. If I can maintain control, I'll light the curtains upstairs on fire before I walk out. Every indication of Strauss irks me, but before I can act on any homicidal thoughts, the bartender sets a glass in front of me.

"You're new."

A sip of the cold hop soothes my irritation. "I'm old."

"You don't look old to me," he says with a coy smile. He's flirting with me.

"Freidenberg."

His grin turns into an open-mouthed gape and a slight turn of his head as curiosity has rendered him momentarily speechless. "Haven't heard that name in a long time. Not since I was a kid."

"I'm sure you haven't, but I'm back. Let it be known." If Strauss didn't already know, he certainly will now. I need to meet with him and what better way than to fuck up his establishment. He wouldn't chance hurting his Northerners at the risk of losing their loyalty. The Strausses have a long history of keeping up the charade of caring consort. People like those hanging in this dungeon tonight like to be fooled by it. Probably gives them some type of sadistic hope that things will improve in their lives if they just put their faith in him one more time.

Looking toward the end of the bar, a lithe blonde woman slips onto a stool while glancing in my direction. Bright green eyes catch the glow of the lights behind the liquor shelves, her puffy mouth painted to match her nails. She's put on a good show tonight and my dick seems interested.

"Scotch on the rocks, please," she says to the bartender, who now is too afraid to speak to me. Lifting one corner of her pink lips, she blinks as she asks me, "You here for a room?"

"With you? Yes." She's a bit older, maybe in her late thirties, but she's enticing. As she turns more toward me, her long, fine strands wisp across her bare shoulder. The tightness of her emerald silk dress lets me know she's bendable. Before I can ask her to grab her drink to go, a tall, but skinny guy approaches her from behind and slides a hand along the small of her back. His eyes crinkle at the corners as he spots me.

"I'm Janna. This is Duke." She leans back into the man's chest.

"Sup, man." Duke nods at me, his light brown hair falling over his forehead when he does. Shoving it back with an open palm, an expensive gold watch peeks out as his black dress coat sleeve rides up.

"Hey. I'm Max." Despite their obvious money, they don't look to be Strauss's people. Perhaps Ace's. Definitely not Calum's—I don't smell a hint of patchouli.

"Want to join us?" Duke asks.

After taking another drink from my pint, I point back and forth between the two with the hand holding my glass. "You're together?"

Duke nods. "Yeah, but there'll be someone else coming along. Foursome?"

"There she is!" Janna stands, abandoning her Scotch to hug a woman outfitted in black leather pants and a bustier showcasing a fabulous set of tits. The ass of the seductress that led me to the bar has nothing on this woman's; this one is going to make me come before I stick my dick inside it. Her black hair has been shaved on the sides, styled into a tall mohawk that falls down her back.

The woman's back muscles flex with her embrace, causing the inked angel wings along each shoulder to flutter. Her arms, chest, and neck are also dotted with tats. As she turns the side of her face to take me in halfheartedly, the dim candlelight reflects several piercings in her face and a series of hoops through her ears.

"You ready?" she asks Janna.

"Dove, this is Max. He's joining us, right Max?"

Dove and I lock eyes, and for the first time since I was a child, I can see a future. Maybe I will live past twenty-eight if it means entangling myself with her. A corner of her lips threatens to lift, twitching momentarily as she gazes at me. My face freezes in awe. Time no longer exists, or perhaps all times merge into one until her lashes flutter and I return to our present reality.

Swallowing roughly, I find my voice to answer emphatically, "Yep." Breaking the hold Dove's eyes had on me, I stand with the others.

"Let's finish our drinks, shall we?" Duke points to an empty table near the stage.

Light jazz filters through a tinny speaker near the lounge area as we take our seats. Not even being casual about it, my head keeps turning toward Dove as if she holds a leash to tug me around. Each time I take a glance at the dark goddess, her eyes dart away like she had just been looking at me.

"You come here often?" I ask to the group, but direct my question to Dove. Maybe I can get some inside intel about where to lay some pipe bombs.

Dove's head dips as a cute snort flashes through her nose. Shaking it off, her black mohawk tail glimmers like a starless night when she sits upright again.

Janna's perfectly outlined lips spread wide. "We've met here a few times now. Duke and I come here regularly."

"How about you?" Since she wouldn't answer the first time, my eyes stare Dove down, so she has to answer.

A suited waiter sets a tall champagne flute in front of her. It's not just an ordinary pour of the bubbly; this one has gold sugar around the rim and raspberries at the bottom. Ignoring my question completely, Dove presses the flute to her lips and sips, her honey-colored eyes sticking to mine. As she pokes out her tongue, a flash of an amethyst jeweled ring entrances me. Swirling the gem around the rim to gather the sugar crystals, she causes the glass to sing a high-pitched tune. The vibrations of the sound go straight to my balls. Biting my bottom lip, I contain the groan threatening to escape.

She's a badass bitch. I want to conquer her. Fuck the shit out of her until she surrenders. Make her submit to my dick alone.

A chuckle from Duke interrupts my trance. "Dove has many talents."

Dove sits back in her chair and sloshes down her drink with a smirk on her full, pouty lips. Her shoulders

shake subtly, as if she's laughing at me. I take that opportunity to finish my beer.

"What?" I ask her with a slight smile.

She shrugs one shoulder. I want her.

"It looks like we're ready to go?" Janna says. She
points us to a door in the back of the room, which leads to
a dimly lit hall. Dove ambles next to me, her eyes traveling up my arm to my face as we walk. Neither of us can
look away from each other. Clearly, she's as interested in
me as I am her, and my skin tingles with anticipation of
being inside her.

Midway down the narrow stone passage is a black
wooden door. A white sign bolted to it reads "Unoccupied," and Janna slides a panel to the side to read the
opposite before holding it open. Inside, the room is
covered with more shades of red. A flat, circular bed is
draped in a sheet that makes me feel sorry for the poor
souls who have to clean up after the patrons. There's a
plush red velvet loveseat with one arm and various
chains, ties, and whips that hang on the walls.

I've never had sex with three people at the same time.
Two women, sure, but not in these types of environ-
ments. Before I can ask what the game plan is, Dove
turns to me and thrusts something rubbery into my palm.
It's a clear butt plug with a blue jewel on the end.

"Hold this for me?" she asks with a glint in her eyes.
Her voice is sultry, and my mouth wants to eat the sound
just to get a taste of her.

Janna and Duke embrace and chuckle while their
eyes roam over the two of us.

"You need help putting it in?" I say with a tilt of my head, letting her know I'll dish it out as much as I take it.

Dove turns on her heeled boot and her pert ass bounces with every step toward a shelf for some lube. When she returns, she slaps the bottle into my free palm. "Sure, tiger. Help me out." At the nickname, my brow twitches. Some feeling of old recognition enters my mind, but I push it aside when she undoes her pants with a flourish.

Standing there like a statue with the lube in one hand and a butt plug in the other, my eyes trail down her body as she lowers the leather to the ground, revealing a lacy, black thong. Glancing over, Janna and Duke lounge on the loveseat, taking in the show together. The siren in front of me draws my attention again, fully bending at the hips with her legs spread wide, shaking her ass a little after dropping her thong.

Oh, fuck. That groan I'd been holding back escapes as I spot a diamond piercing her clit hood. Her pussy lips are absolute perfection, as is her tight little pink asshole. I must spend too long staring at her amazing body because she flips her head around and says, "You gonna stand there all day or stick it in me?"

Dove isn't shy. Like a wild mustang, I'm going to get her used to my presence, then groom, harness, and tame her. She has no idea. It's been a while since I had one that put up a fight and I am thoroughly looking forward to it.

Flipping the cap off the lube, I squirt some liquid all over the clear plug, then toss the bottle aside. Gripping her smooth skinned hip, I place the tip on her tight hole and swirl it around. She moans, which makes my dick fill with need at the sound of her pleasure. The heat of her skin on my palm makes me want to touch all of her, memorize every inch just by the feel of my hands. Slowly gliding the end of the plug inside, I spin it gently, her thighs quivering at the sensation.

"You like that, Duke?" Dove says, tossing a teasing look at the couple.

In between making out, Duke peeks up from Janna's neck. "That's so hot, Dove. Can't wait to feel it inside you."

The fuck? We trading partners? Before I can say anything, Dove's eyes snap to mine, crinkling at the edges with mischievousness.

As I pull her closer to me and push the plug farther inside, all I can think about is plunging into her. The dim lights in the room make the wetness coating her pussy lips shine, calling to me, causing my cock to throb.

Taking my time with every inch so I don't have to let go of her silky skin, she eventually gets impatient and presses back against the toy until it sits fully inside her. She wiggles slightly, causing the jewel's facets to dance, then stands to face me. Patting my chest with both hands, she winks at me. "Good job, champ."

I'm stunned. Before I can grab her and fuck her into next week, Janna and Duke stand and step between us. Janna slides her hands over my shoulders and removes my jacket in a smooth motion, tossing it on a table nearby. Duke watches us with heat steaming behind his eyes. He slings his arm around Dove's waist and kisses her passionately, holding her by the back of the neck as she seems to stiffen slightly in his hold.

"You know I love it when you wear that thing for me." Duke pokes at Dove's plug with a finger, then smacks her ass cheek.

The gesture irritates me, but Janna distracts me with her long, delicate fingers. She takes her time unbuttoning, then untucking my shirt, belt, and pants while I reach behind and unzip her dress. Tilting her squared chin up, I briefly taste her while still staring at Dove, who briefly gives us a glance. Janna tastes like cotton candy, but my mind is still on what flavor my dark temptress might possess.

Janna backs me toward the sofa with a soft touch. Sitting, I spread my arms wide across the back. She kneels and settles between my open knees. The crotch of my trousers lays open, and my hard cock bobs out when she lowers my boxer briefs. I've been ready to go ever since I got a glimpse of Dove's perfectly round ass now being groped by Duke.

She licks the tip of my cock, then the shaft, before suckling my balls. My head dips back for a moment with the pleasure of the sensation. Her fingernail grazes my taint, sending a shiver up my spine. *Fuck*, she's good.

My eyes drift over to where Dove takes off her bustier, then helps Duke undress. I should be turned on by the woman sucking my cock, but instead I watch Dove crawl seductively over to us. *Holy shit.* The sight of her graceful, cat-like movements makes me leak into Janna's mouth.

As she makes her way over to us, I notice her tongue, clit, eyebrow, nose, and ears aren't the only things pierced. Silver metal bars decorate each hard nipple, her heavy breasts swinging with every shift of her hips. Licking my lips, I think about sucking on each and what they must feel like against my tongue, what her perfect chest would look like coated with my cum. Maybe even to take my knife and make some little cuts. Just to watch the red of her mix with my white.

Duke sits next to me, our knees touching. Hoping my hot bitch switches with Janna, I'm disappointed when she squats in front of Duke. The sight of her being so submissive, willing to sacrifice her mouth at the altar of a cock, has my stomach tightening. My hands resting on my lap itch to encircle her neck. Then squeeze until she gives in to me.

"Does he taste good, baby?" Duke asks Janna, eyeing her job as Dove settles her thick lips over the head of his cock.

Janna moans in agreement and meets his eyes. The tones send waves of pleasure along my spine.

"I love watching you suck dick." Duke strokes a hand through Dove's black hair, then thumbs her cheek as if he's into her. Squelching the impulse to break all his fingers, I dig my palms into my thighs.

Despite Janna working me deliciously, I try to make Dove look at me, wanting to memorize the colors in her eyes. Light brown? Green? Hazel? She's looking at Duke, though. When Janna starts pumping me harder, trying to make me come, I grip her hair to slow her down. She sits back and wipes her mouth with her delicate hand.

"Sorry," she says with a little smile. I lift one side of my lips in a reply, then gently stroke myself, willing my balls to calm down before I explode all over these girls' faces.

Dove looks over at my cock. I'm well-endowed, thick compared to Duke. She reaches over and grasps my shaft to tug gently, while Janna gets back to tangling with my tip. My abdomen tenses, and I grunt involuntarily. Dove's hand is tight around me, sending hot electric shocks straight to my testicles. Angling my hips, I push toward her, hoping she'll take the invitation to suckle on me.

Those champagne-colored eyes finally greet me again, and I'm transported to another dimension. No idea why I'm so drawn to this woman, but I can't wait to put my dick inside her. I almost come watching her scan my body along with the pressure that Janna's putting on my cock, the two women working me perfectly in sync. Dove's bottom lip gets trapped under her teeth as she stares at Janna sucking me off.

"You hungry?" I ask her, nodding my head to my crotch.

One of Dove's lids narrows at me, the opposite dark brow arching as she smirks.

Just as I think about pulling Janna off and shoving Dove's face onto my length, Duke stands and nods at Dove to move to the bed. "I'm ready to fuck," he tells her.

"Give it to her good, D," Janna says.

Dove crawls away, showcasing her ass dressed in the blue gem, and pussy lips ripe with need, ready to be mounted. *Ugh!* I sigh heavily as the diamond glimmers in her clit. This woman is perfect. It takes every ounce of self-control not to jump off the sofa to get a taste of her cunt. My little bitch's body is *slammin'*. I want inside it. I want to break it. Cut it open and see what's inside. Instead, it seems this couple we're with wants to fuck other people... Somehow, I need to maneuver my way to my mare.

Gripping Janna's blonde locks, I pull her face up to mine. "Come here." I guide her over to the bed and lay her down beside Duke and Dove. While I take the opportunity to shed my pants, Dove scoots to lie between the couple, her back to Duke. She suckles on Janna's large pink nipple while staring into her eyes.

"Ugh! The sight of you two together is so hot. Give me those lips," Duke says to his girlfriend.

Janna reaches to kiss him over Dove's head. Duke rubbers up and slides inside Dove while spooning her. Holding back a frustrated growl, I situate myself between Janna's legs. Grabbing a condom from my wallet, I rip it open with my teeth, then roll it on.

"Oh, fuck! That feels good." Dove stops nursing long enough to glance back at Duke. I could show her what "good" actually feels like. Hopefully, Duke hurries with her, so I can take a turn. Maybe we could both fit. I could take the place of that plug, or maybe she'll want both of us in her cunt.

"Are you going to let him fuck you, baby?" Duke nods in my direction.

Janna asks, "Do you want to see that, Dukey?"

"Fuck yeah. I'd love to watch him wreck your pussy."

Janna strokes Dove's hair as I separate her knees, then push inside her. It's warm, wet, and comfortable, but her tunnel is too short for my taste. The pussy I want is occupied. Janna moans, then screams when I thrust deeper inside her.

"Duke! He's so fucking big!"

Duke gives me a smile from behind my girl's mohawk, appreciating me pleasuring his woman so well. "Yeah? I'd like to give it a go." He winks at me. All I can think about is the dark-haired beauty now sucking the lips of my partner. The two women fondle each other desperately as our cocks rampage inside them, little whimpers of pleasure escaping into each other's mouths.

Needing to change things up, I slip out of Janna and tap her. "Flip over." She does, then Duke pulls out of Dove. Fuck, he's hogging her. I think about stopping and just grabbing my knife to slit his throat before taking both women. That would ruffle some feathers in Strauss's club. But that may scare off my little filly.

Before I can act on the impulse, Duke gets up on all fours and leans his face right over Janna's ass, resting his cheek there. "You like his cock, baby? Uh, I love watching it pump into you." Janna moans in affirmation as I thrust harder.

Dove gets off the bed and slinks by me, letting her

long fingernails scratch my bare back as she walks past. Letting go of Janna's hips, I snatch the raven by the waist. *Dove*. This woman is no harbinger of peace. Her angel's wings don't fool me.

The tail of her hair whips behind one shoulder as she quickly spins to me, a gasp snatching up the air around us. Gripping her tighter, I bring her into my side, our lips almost touching. If I can just kiss her... Squirming, she cranes her neck so I can't reach.

"Let me taste you. Let me fuck you," I tell her, my mouth over her ear.

Darkness covers her eyes as she narrows them. "If we fuck, it'll be *me* fucking *you*."

She yanks from my grip and slips to the head of the bed without even a glance back at me. Once there, she slides her core over Janna's mouth and grips her silky blonde locks with one hand. Then she rides Janna's face, her milky thighs spread wide around the woman's head. Her defiant moans get me harder than I've been in a long time. Shoving myself back into Janna, she screams in between the pillows of Dove's legs.

While I pound into Janna's pussy, I'm pushing her forward onto Dove's cunt, like I'm the one fucking the feral feline through my partner. Duke opens his mouth wide and lets his tongue hang out just above his girlfriend's asshole. He tugs on his skinny dick furiously, watching my hips work his lover from behind.

"Yeah, she likes it hard like that. Fuck her, then put that thick cock in my mouth, man."

I've never done something with a dude, but what the

hell. Sliding out of Janna, I swivel my hips to put the head of my dick between his lips. He gobbles me up like a fat turkey. Ugh, it feels good. So, I try it again. Popping out of him, I plunge into Janna's pussy before sticking it back in his mouth. Holding Janna steady, my hand on one of her hips, I repeat the process over and over, feeding Duke a taste of his girlfriend on another man's dick.

The change in Dove's breaths and whimpers lets me know she's about to climax, and I'm desperate to help her. Leaning over Janna's back, I grasp her by the back of her head and force it to rub against Dove's clit harder, using my partner to make my bitch come. Looking to where she's writhing underneath Janna, our eyes meet again. Her face flushes pink and crinkles with pleasure, but she maintains contact with me. As she explodes into Janna's mouth, I feel Janna's pussy tighten around my cock, her cries eaten up by Dove's thighs. I'm making both women come at the same time.

Watching Dove orgasm makes me lose it. My balls tingle, needing their release, and I almost explode inside Janna's cushiony interior, pushing her up into Dove's center. I don't want to come like this. I want to use Dove instead.

It's too late, though, so I pull out and rip off my condom. Before I can react, Duke shoves his waiting mouth onto my cock. His soft, wet tongue swirls the tip, the sensation causing ecstasy to ripple down my spine until I drop my head back, shooting my load down his throat. It's a powerful feeling coming inside this cuck right in front of his woman. My hips push into him violently with each spurt while gripping his light brown hair in one hand.

After swallowing all my cum, Duke smiles and lies back on the bed as if inviting me for a taste of his cock. No, thank you. Fortunately, Janna takes the opportunity to straddle him and the two re-connect with each other. Dove slides off the bed and slyly starts to pull on her pants and top. Wandering to the corner, I wash up in the sink. By the time I'm done, Dove's already dressed and nearing the door.

There's no way I'm letting my temptress escape. Even if I have to run her down and trap her, I'm taking something of hers before the night is over. Quickly, I tug on my boxer briefs and pants, leaving them undone as I rush into the hallway where Dove's almost at the end. Her perfect ass sways temptingly as she hurries to the door.

"Hey!" I yell.

She stops and spins around to face me. "Yeah?"

"You done?"

"They'll be fucking each other the rest of the night. *We're* done." A tall heel of her boot pivots to face the exit once more, but I stop her.

"You got a number?"

Her billowy laugh echoes off the chambered walls, haunting me. Taunting me. Some familiar feeling hits me in the gut. My eyelids twitch. I recognize that laugh. Spinning back around, she greets me with a tiny smirk and lifted brow, reminding me of something oddly familiar...

"Max, Max, Max." Slinking down the hall toward me, her full tits almost bounce out of her top while she flips the long black tail of her hair over one shoulder, the gesture so memorable. "Don't you recognize me...lion?"

Fuck, it's... "Livia."

Three

LIVIA

My belly tightens with an even bigger laugh once Max realizes who I am.

"You look different," he says, narrowing his eyes to take me in as if seeing me for the first time. After a leisurely scan of my frame, his gaze lands on my chest, and my skin hums under his lurid inspection.

"You don't. Same overly confident little boy." I'm gambling with my poker face. He's wearing the same expression as our youth, still staring at me with wonder and fear. But his body has changed... Who knew my little lion would grow up to have such huge muscles with an equally massive cock?

His brow is heavy, eyes darkening beneath its protection. Safety or danger lay in their chocolate brown color, depending wholly on how cavernous the furrow sets. Subtle waves of thick black hair crown his head, which is thicker on top than the sides. Despite the rugged appearance of the stubble coating his sharp jaw, it's very well-manicured along on the edges. Just like him.

"You knew it was me."

A quick breath puffs from my nostrils. "Max, the entire town's aware of your return," I say, pointing to the cameras along the halls. "You don't think Strauss saw you coming here tonight? Who do you think that couple we just fucked works for? People can't just waltz into this sex club without a membership, without a medical test. You were led here."

"Then what the hell are *you* doing here?"

Sealing my lips into a purse, I change the subject. "Max, you've been gone too long and gotten soft."

Crossing the little distance between us with two long strides, his rock-hard body almost collides into me, sweat droplets from his recent escapades steaming up my cleavage. When he leans over toward me, his lips graze the skin of my ear as his deep voice vibrates my pulse. "Nothing about me is soft."

When he straightens up, the intensity of his stare makes it hard to breathe. I steady my chest rise so he won't notice. Taking one hand, I slide it up his firm pectoral muscles, lingering over a set of intricate tattoos winding up to the sides of his throat as he presses his waist into mine. He's right; he's not soft. Already ready to go again. "You have no idea how things work around here anymore."

"Then you're gonna teach me." As the breath of his words moistens my flesh, my neck erupts with goosebumps. Maybe scared little Max has changed. Thinks he's going to catch me with his rod. I won't let that happen.

"No, I'm not." Turning around, I head out the door, my leather pants rustling with every step.

Avoiding the corner camera in the lounge, I slide a silver key out of my pocket and palm it. Before I take my hand out of my pants, I rub my index finger three times over the other little metal object still in its secure hiding place. "One, two, three," I whisper to myself for luck.

It has taken me *weeks* of flirting with Janna and Duke to get this far. All it took was a fourth member to join us for me to steal the key from Duke's trousers. I suppose Max was good for something. The couple were likely too busy trying to distract Max so he wouldn't go exploring... Like I'm about to do.

"Night, Dove," Gerald says from behind the bar as I pass.

"Goodnight," I say, not smiling. If I do, it'll be a dead giveaway something is amiss. I never smile. It's for the weak unless you're about to kill your prey.

Pulling out my phone from my back pocket, I tap "send" on the ready text. When I approach the hall, the lights in the bar shut off. The darkness muffles not only my eyes, but my ears temporarily, until murmurs float through the heavy wooden doors from patrons yelling in confusion.

Go time.

Feeling my way to the entrance of the back hall beneath the stairs, I slip inside. I've memorized the way, not wanting to use any light to draw attention to myself.

Letting my fingers graze along the cold stone walls, I count the steps as I walk, careful of my footfalls. Once I reach the third door on the right, I feel for the smooth metal knob. I stick the key in with some fumbling, but the door opens with a jolt.

Before I can enter on my own, firm hands grip my biceps, pulling me inside. The door slams. I'm pushed against a hard metal shelf by arms with formidable strength. Hot breath caresses my face as the resonating tenor of a man's voice reverberates over my ear. "Livia…"

A slick, wet tongue outlines my mouth before pain surges through my body as he takes my bottom lip between his and bites down, spurting metallic liquid on my taste buds. Tiny whimpers escape past my clenched teeth, but I try to contain anything further than that, not daring to give him the pleasure of hearing my agony. Fucker would only get off on it.

Light floods the room, and I squint away the brightness. When my eyes adjust, I'm met with Vladimir Strauss's sunken cheeks and sculpted jaw. A red droplet lingers on his pale bottom lip. The upper one curls into a sneer as soundless chuckles escape with his quick breaths.

His tongue goes on a tour and licks up the splash of my life on his mouth. "You taste feisty."

"Hello. Fancy seeing you here," I say with confidence I don't feel.

Strauss shoves his body fully into mine, his raging hard cock thrusting into my belly. With a shift, I put a little room between our waists, but his leather pants prominently display his large package. "You've gone where you're not supposed to... Maybe I should do the same." Reaching between us, he unbuttons the top of my pants. I know about Vlad; know what he likes to do to his conquests. And I'm not interested.

Racks of the weapons I need line the room, but everything is locked behind metal mesh cabinet doors. This is the farthest I've gotten on my information gathering quest. AKs, ARs, shotguns, handguns, fully automatics... I even spot a flame thrower ripe for stealing. Taking inventory for later, I focus on trying to get him to stop unzipping my pants. Raising my hands, I thrust my thumbs in his eye sockets, but he grabs both, forcing them to my sides, then twists me around to face the wall.

My chest huffs out an involuntary "oomph" as it's pressed into the unforgiving stones. There's just enough time to turn my head, so my nose isn't scrunched. Biding my time, I wait for the opportunity to strike.

"Now, now, little girl. If you wanted it in your ass so bad, you could have just begged me." Reaching around, he continues his assault on my leathers, tugging them down to expose my bare cheeks. I push back into him, shoving my butt in his crotch. He laughs. "I know you like it rough. I've studied your security footage. I just didn't know you wanted to be torn." Peeking up at the corner, the blinking red light of the camera mocks me. I should have known my plan had been too brash.

He's likely been sitting in his castle at the top of the city, watching me every time I visited. Echoes told me she had taken care of his eyes... at least for tonight. But it seems as if my safety window is closing faster than I'd like. All his cameras are operational, which means that his spies are as well.

"Oh! Look at what a treat we have here. You came prepared, like my own personal piñata." Strauss's hot breath pulses over my neck as he speaks. "If I beat it, do you think candy will fall out?" Clenching my teeth, I shudder as Strauss pulls the butt plug from my ass swiftly, my exposed hole feeling quite vulnerable. "Don't worry, I'll be happy to stuff it with my cum."

Years of jiu jitsu training kick in. I'm not useless. I just need to get him in the right position to gain my advantage. If he gives me a finger, I'll take an arm.

Bending over, I wiggle my hips to entice him. Vlad's large hand slides around my pelvic bone until he starts to dry hump me, loosens his zipper, then peels the crotch open to take out his cock. While he's distracted, I subtly slide my fingers down to my calf boot.

Before he can react, I whip around with my fixed blade at the ready, nicking his throat with a quick stab. I miss the carotid but am fast enough that he stumbles back, clutching his throat without a sound. As he backs away, my hands yank up my pants, and I make a dash for the door. His heavy footfalls alert me to his presence just behind my left shoulder.

Pumping my legs, I don't stop sprinting, leaping up the large stone stairs two at a time. When I reach the heavy wooden church doors, I shove with my full strength until they burst open, the cold night air hitting my skin like I've been doused by a bucket of ice water. It's silent behind me. Strauss has either relented... or has set a trap.

Avoiding the obvious route, I dart to my left, toward town. Groups of people stumble out of bars or restaurants as I run down the sidewalk, pushing through the shoulders of annoyed patrons on the edge of South Side. Pulling out my phone, I practically scream into it. "Nine-one-one!"

"I saw, babe. It's dark out there." Echoes gives me the code that she has been shut out. I'm fucked. The call goes dead. Flicking my arm, I toss the phone into the thicket near the road in case it's traced.

I keep my legs churning, pumping as fast as I can go. If I can make it past the Strauss buildings on the south end of North Side, I should be in the clear. It's getting by his men that will be my biggest problem.

As headlights of cars drive by, I'm illuminated with revealing light. I monitor each passing window, seeing if it's lowering enough to stick a barrel out of. Roadways are too dangerous, especially with the streetlamps and business signs showcasing my every move. North Side is filled with clean, tall skyscrapers, everything too new and bright to give me much cover. Once I hit the South, it will be easier, the neon lights of the casinos and strip joints casting shadows over the drunken patrons who loiter the streets. More people to mix in with for disguise.

The alleys of the short brick buildings of Ace's territory edge closer and closer, the landscape changing from overbearing glass brutalist to modest mid-century. If I get between two, I can hide or climb onto a roof to make it to the southwest end of Main Street. Once I'm immersed in Donovan's area, I'll slip into the woods. And then home.

A sharp *zing* whizzes past my ear. *Fuck.*

The screech of tires over my right shoulder tells me the car is only a few feet behind and revving the engine. I'm a sitting duck. Especially if they try to run me over on the pavement.

Racing in a zigzag, a few more *pings* of bullets ring out around me. A coffee shop's large glass front window explodes when I sprint past it, the people inside screaming in terror. I rush inside the shop as patrons try to escape chaotically, likely used to the violent threats that erupt every so often. Someone not falling in line with the consort's demands, so everyone has to pay.

Shoving bodies out of my way, I make it to the back of the sleek, white-tiled store and push open the swinging black kitchen door. A barista dodges behind a counter, her eyes wide with fear. I stop and lean over, putting a hand on the cold stainless-steel surface, trying to hold my tired body up, heaving breaths of nourishing air.

I have to keep moving. I can't stop. They won't.

"Back... back exit," I huff out.

The barista lifts a shaky finger and points to a doorway near the rear of the store.

Oh! I know where I am! If I can just get to the roof...

Once I enter the darkened alley, the condensation puddles from old air conditioning units echo my steps between the red brick walls. It's cleared of men here, but screams filter in from the street. Car horns are honking erratically, but none travel past my alley. A fire escape ladder looks like my hope for rescue, its bottom steps almost down to the ground. Grabbing on, I use the full weight of my body to yank at it until it gives way, landing on the pavement with a loud crash. Like in my days of youth mounting a tree, I shimmy up quickly, heaving it back into position behind me so whoever was sent after me doesn't see.

After seven stories, my body almost collapses onto the gravel roof. A rusted ventilation fan sits in the middle, its side still spray painted with a blue "V." I drop to my knees and slide over to it, pebbles bruising my hip as I do. Reaching between the metal grate, I tug on the small door, revealing an alcove big enough for... my crossbow. It's loaded and ready, the bolt a little worn, but it will do.

Before revealing my location, I stick my hand in my pocket, rub the hard metal object and whisper, "One, two, three."

Shimmying on my stomach, I peer over the ledge to the street below. The black Mercedes is still parked at an angle near the front of the café, blocking any traffic from moving along the street. Two men look around with their guns pointed at the ground, speaking to each other words I can't hear. One shrugs, and the other, with a tattoo on his hand, appears to point around the area. They haven't spotted me. The tattooed hand guy pulls out his phone and yells something unintelligible into it, then shoves it back in his pocket. As the men get back into their car and drive away, a deep exhale eases the tension in my chest.

Rolling to my back, I let my skull rest against the sharp edge of the bricks. The chill of the night air restores some strength, and the night sky opens like a blank theater screen before me. My body rests as if I'd planned to be in this place at this very moment. But Strauss's people could still find me, so I need to get out of this area and head farther south.

Fortunately, I know just how to jump across buildings from this height and the pattern to get to where I want to go. Alpha, our top spy, taught me when I was sixteen. Everyone knows she's one of the best escape artists in the city, even besting Strauss's men a few times, though they caught her once. She knows every crevice and hole as if she forged the city plan herself.

Eventually, I make my way over to Ace's side of town and drop to the ground. Gnarled Pine Park is just a few hundred yards behind the wall of dirty buildings, gentleman's clubs, small-time gambling centers, and even a mock gambler's anonymous storefront, probably instilled when the government still pretended it wasn't owned by our consort. The rolling hills behind it condense into the deeper woodlands. And my safety.

Once I reach the trees, I let my shoulders hang for a moment. I know these woods better than anyone, except for Ace. And he's likely holed up in a poker game somewhere, too distracted, or drunk, to see his enemy waltzing through his backyard. Maybe he just doesn't give a shit anymore.

Though I'm jogging slower, I don't stop moving until I'm almost to the hidden lake. Slumping down in a coppice of ash, I catch my breath and listen for any followers. My skin inherits the iciness of the wind, but it's not cold enough to fog my exhales.

I'm alone.

For a fleeting second, I consider staying overnight, but Cal will put out a search party for me and just cause more problems I don't want. Shoving off the bark, I meander out of the woods, down the worn paths out of the trees, marking a "V" into some with my blade. The ground is cold and solid, at least, so I won't leave many prints to trace.

It's almost dawn when I stumble to the gates of Von Dovish Estate, clutching my side that's been in a constant cramp for the last four miles. I'm so tired, all I want to do is bathe and sleep, but the adrenaline keeps one foot in front of the other.

Nothing like almost dying to make you want to live.

Where the Freidenberg manor is a tortured Gothic Tudor and the Donovan monstrosity is all modern, our home is cozy French Country. The high white plaster walls surrounding our property greet me before I reach the wisteria covered gatehouse.

Our old gatekeeper shakes his head with disappointment at my approach, then sneaks a pointed look at his watch. Hopping into his golf cart, I stumble forward and let my body slump into the passenger seat. The whir of the little engine leads us down the winding lane in no time. "Thanks," I say as he heads back to his station with a small wave.

Opening the double glass entry doors, my lungs finally fill fully with air as I relax to the scent of roses and wood polish. I'm home. A housekeeper has already taken up the flowers that normally sit in the entryway vase and vacuumed the blue Persian Souf rug covering the black and white marbled floors. It's late, but I know I need to check in with my brother.

Climbing the wide stairs, I turn right and trail my fingers over the white wainscoted walls all the way down the hall. Cal lives in his room, but I don't bother knocking. He wouldn't be fucking anyone, the hermit. He covers up his mousy brown hair with his dirty black hoodie, and despite my dramatic flop on his Louis XIV bed, he doesn't swivel in his chair to look at me. Which means he already knows what I've been up to. Even though his body frame doesn't move an inch, I can tell he's disappointed.

In front of him is a wall of monitors, where he studies the replays of tonight's excursion at the Crimson Angel. His shoulders are slumped as if he has been at this for a while, possibly since I arrived at the lounge.

The side of my face scrunches. "Echoes told you?"

Flatly, he responds, "She didn't have to."

"Alpha said—"

Swiftly, he spins in his chair, his green eyes bloodshot from the blue lights of the screens. If his eyebrows got any closer together, they'd become one. Both hands come up and lower the hood of his sweatshirt as he runs his fingers through his waves. It needs a trim. Despite being twins, only our defined cheeks, big eyes, and cupid's bow lips are similar. I take after our mother. Cal always looks afraid.

"Alpha has nothing to do with this. Alpha, Delta, hell, Foxtrot are none of your concern. *Please*, Livia. I'm begging you to let this go."

He never says my name, at least never my full name. "*Calum*, I've told you before. We've been sitting ducks without weapons. If not Strauss, then Donovan, or now, maybe even *Freidenberg* could take us all out at some point. We'll be no better than Max's family, and then what? No more Von Dovish clan!" Sure, the skirmishes between clan crews have been raging for years, but now that Max is back... this could cause us all problems. Strauss won't like it and he may just decide to end us all.

Spreading his long fingers out to his sides, he explains, "Our business is enough. We're comfortable. We provide for everyone's families on the west side. We're safe." Cal stands as I sit up on the edge of the bed, rubbing the blue velvet of his comforter idly to soothe my irritation. He slowly eases next to me, wrapping his arm around my shoulders. "I've got us. We don't need to resort to violence, weapons, or an *armory* to protect ourselves. Look at tonight, you almost got raped... or killed."

"I didn't." My mind races elsewhere, calculating which informant snitched on me.

"But you could have."

A heavy sigh escapes my chest, directed at my brother. We have had the same conversation for years. He's never going to get past his pacifism, and I know what we must do to survive. Shrugging off his arm, I stand. "Did you watch everything?" My eyebrow raises, embarrassment flushing my cheeks at the reminder of tonight's activities.

His wide lips curve into a frown. "Did I watch you have sex with Mr. and Mrs. Dean? Hell no. I think I would gouge out my eyes out after seeing something like that." Relieved, I grin as I head toward the door, but he stops me. "So... Max is back."

"Yeah, he'll make good cannon fodder," I snap back.

Softening his voice into that trance-like tone he tries to use, he pleads, "Liv, that's not what I'm saying."

I stretch my neck from side to side. "I don't want to even think about it."

"You'll have to, eventually."

Twisting the cool doorknob in hand, I say, "No, I won't."

"Liv, *please* don't let our father's indecencies stop you from your future. From *our* future. For the future of West Side."

Without looking back at him, I head out of his door and slam it with a loud bang behind me.

I'm not going to think about Maximillian Freidenberg. I'm the one who needs to focus on our safety. Danger is at an all-time high right now with the lion's return, and that makes us an involuntary target.

Cal always has his head in the clouds, living in some carefree world that doesn't exist. He's my brother, my twin, and I love him, but he's not strong enough to do what needs to be done. We need to invade the arsenal and get those weapons. It doesn't even have to be *that* arsenal and *those* weapons. It could be any of the ones Strauss took over... If only I knew where they were.

Citizens of Gnarled Pine Hollow have been prey for at least two decades, ever since the Freidenbergs left. Everything I've been through to take over the industry they abandoned has made my resolve solidify like the diamonds sitting in our family safe. I'm not giving up, no matter how much my brother protests. I thought my biggest hurdle was Strauss, but now I'm wondering if it's my own flesh and blood.

Cal is too passive. He sits behind his computers and thinks he has a handle on everything. He says he can see what's coming by reading those black and white digits floating down the monitor like water droplets. *"The future is in those zeros and ones."* I don't know anything about computers. I haven't had to. I had him. And our spies, tanks, and hackers.

Echoes, one of our hackers, has lasted the longest out of all of them and I don't think she would tell on me. It *must* have been Alpha, one of our spies. Well, *Cal's* spy. Ever since she developed her little crush, she seems to be less of a lookout and more of a mole.

I'll devise a plan to deal with her after I get some food and sleep.

Sneaking to the kitchen, I grab leftover eggplant parmesan. Vegan, of course, at Cal's insistence. At least our chef prepared it well. Aside from disrupting Alpha's life, I'll order a steak tomorrow to make up for it. I sigh when I spot my brother's dirty dinner dish lying *next* to the dishwasher, then put it inside with my own. Do men never learn?

Walking up the stairs, my body feels the weight of the activities from the evening. My bathroom is generous in size and just what I need before bedtime. The steam rolls off the large clawfoot tub as I slide in, deeply inhaling the eucalyptus scented salts while I dim the lights with the remote control. Another button allows me to select gentle rain sounds on the ceiling speakers. Hopefully, I can fall asleep without bother tonight.

Unfortunately, the television in my brain only shows re-runs of Max. Max's muscles flexing as he plowed into Janna. Max's neck twitching as he watched me lick Duke. Max's thick, perfect cock. Max's deep brown eyes penetrating mine as I came.

Diving a hand into the bubbly water, two fingers slide onto my clit as my thoughts focus on my lion's stare, his jawline, his desire for me. Not enough pressure. The attached spray handle has always worked wonders with the water on full blast. Holding it over my sensitive flesh, I hump it while inserting two fingers inside. Max fucked me tonight with Janna's mouth. It was obvious whose tongue he wanted on my pussy. Thinking about him licking his lip, gazing at me while fucking Janna, my inner muscles clench around my fingers. My back arches against the porcelain while I cry out, "*Maaax.*"

No. No. No. I do not want him. He's just another stipulation I don't need. I can do this on my own. Besides, he is from the enemy clan and Strauss forbids intermingling. If three families vote against him on the senate floor, he's done for, but he'd probably destroy the city before he let that happen. So, we war against each other. It's always been this way.

After drying off with a soft, white towel, my naked skin slips under my silky sheets. Before I fall asleep, I reach into my pants pocket on the floor and dig out my good luck charm, rub it three times, and whisper to myself. As exhaustion takes me under, I remember bright summer days playing tag with friends and my lion. Back when our parents made things seem safe for us. Not this apocalyptic nightmare we now know.

As children, it was difficult to understand what was actually happening when our mother and father would lug us over to someone's basement. Whether it be the Freidenberg's cold stone or Donovan's white-walled tomb, us kids were never allowed to talk about the adults' clandestine gatherings. They were just fun play dates, with us safe behind the high walls of whatever manor we were visiting for the day.

Now, with a better knowledge of the history of Gnarled Pine Hollow, I know these meetings were extreme rarities for the clans. Ones that would have gotten our families into a lot of trouble with the consort if he ever knew the three heads were together outside of the senate boardroom.

The next morning, I dress and grab a banana from the kitchen counter before heading to the entry. Our butler, Giles, wanders through the main hall. His stiff tuxedo makes my eyes roll involuntarily. "Heading out, Miss Von Dovish?"

Trying to keep the annoyance out of my voice, I say, "Yes, but I don't need help. Just going to take the Victor out."

"I'll have the chauffer pull it around now, Miss." I could just walk over to the garage, but our chauffeur needs to feel important. He also loves to drive my cars, no matter how much it irritates me.

My blacked-out Aston Martin pulls up, and I hurry out the door to slide into the driver's seat as the chauffer jumps out. The engine purrs when I dart down our lane and onto the main streets, heading toward downtown. A few of our people wave as I pass downtown's squared green glass tech district, but I'm going too fast to acknowledge them.

Throwing it into a quick parallel park, I get out and lock up, hurrying in the direction of an old storefront underneath worn brick apartments just on the outskirts of West Side's center city. Some trash rolls over my feet before I can make it to the entry, and I try to snatch an old newspaper blowing in a gust of late autumn air, but miss. Feeling in my back pocket, I stuff two hundred dollars into Jim's paper cup.

"Thank you, Miss Livy."

"No problem, Jim." Things are becoming worse

around town. There used to be a middle class that afforded homes. Now, there's just us, some people likely paid off by Strauss, the workers who can get into small apartments within the city limits, and hordes of people like Jim. I know what needs to be done and seem to be the only one willing to do it. We have to be able to protect ourselves from the tyrant running the city before he decides to simply end us all.

The glass door chimes when I push on its metal bar. Dust flares up with the wind, causing my lungs to ache and produce a dry cough. Our new employee, Jane, looks up from behind the counter, her green eyes wide and bright.

"Oh, hi, Livia!"

"Hey, Jane." Glancing around, I don't spot Cal.

"Your brother is at the other location. He gave me full rein here today... solo." She smiles shyly. She is nice, but a little vanilla and wholesome, like I may break her if I tell her she left a decimal out of place. The only thing that makes me question her veracity is the flame of red hair that rests atop her head. Maybe that's prejudiced, but it makes me think she's zestier than she lets on.

"Actually, I'm not looking for him. Just here to check the inventory." Pointing a finger to the back, I pass the rows of computers and accessories, heading to the black velvet curtain leading to the warehouse. I call it ours, but, really, I've never worked on a computer for a day in my life. Nor would I know the first thing about how to.

What I *do* know about is shipping tech parts and putting the mushrooms or other hallucinogens in with the supplies. It's how our family makes money from other families outside Gnarled Pine Hollow, as well as within. It also keeps the populace happy. If they can't have nice things, at least they can get high.

Wandering to the third row of metal shelves, my fingers dance over the switch at the same time my thumb pushes in a button. The structure turns, and a room opens in the wall. Concrete crumbles in the path where the doorway leads. I guess she hasn't left in a while.

Shuffling inside, I am greeted with a small apartment that I haven't visited in some time. It's still messy and too dark, only lit by one yellowed lamp and the blue lights from the bank of screens. A curvy figure sits in front of them, her black hair in knots on top of her head. She pushes up her thick cat-eyed glasses and sits back slightly, grabbing a chip from a crinkly bag on the desk.

"What do you want, Liv? I'm busy."

"Hello, Echoes. I want to know if *you* know why Alpha told on me."

She rotates her chair toward me, shoving at the bridge of her fallen glasses. "Alpha did not."

Raking my tongue over my teeth, I consider. If Alpha didn't, then who did? Before I can ask, she responds, "I did." My mouth opens to argue, but she continues. "I mean, I didn't *mean* to. Cal got in... as usual. He saw me in there, in the Crimson Angel's security and lights system. He's the one who turned them back on."

My head hangs. After tossing a foul-smelling Northview University sweater onto the unmade bed, I throw myself across the orange plaid futon. The trash can is overflowing with takeout boxes, some piled on the mini fridge it sits next to. There's a sink full of dirty dishes near the hidden door. I don't even *want* to look at the toilet in the corner of the room. She really needs to get out more.

Once I scan the room, I allow my eyes to meet her piercing black ones. "Did you tell him anything?"

Shoving the last chip into her mouth, she shrugs. "I had to, Liv. He's my boss."

"*I'm* your boss, too!"

She pauses for a moment, and I bristle, knowing exactly what she's going to say. "Not like him, Liv. You know that." Swallowing, she gives me a stern school-teacher look. Quietly, she adds, "You know how things work in this city."

Lying back, I stare at the acoustic ceiling tile and murmur, "Yes, yes. He carries our name. I'm here to be courted and married and bear the next generation for some sadistic mobster." A sigh escapes my chest. It's the way it's always been for daughters of the clans. People like Echoes don't have to follow the rules, but if you're in a family, it's heresy not to.

"Speaking of, I saw the video feed last night. Um..."

"Don't even say it. You shouldn't be watching. It's weird."

"I wasn't watching *you*. Ew. I was mainly watching Janna. *Yum.* I mean, for your safety, of course. But I happened to notice a certain enemy has returned to Gnarled Pine and seems smitten." She wiggles her eyebrows up and down rapidly.

Sitting up, I rake a hand through the back of my hair, fluffing my mohawk, then flip the tail over my shoulder. My elbows meet my thighs and, as casually as I can, I say, "Yeah, he does seem to be. I'll use it to my advantage when I need it."

"Maybe you don't have to *use* it. Maybe you can *work* with it."

I shake my head.

"You can't do everything alone, Liv. You need other people to assist you with this mission. You need help."

A snort leaves my nose. "Look what your *help* got me. Almost raped by Satan himself." My legs carry me toward the exit without hesitation. This conversation will go nowhere. Max is from an enemy clan and us being seen together would draw the attention of Strauss and not in a good way. But, perhaps I can use his fascination with me to get the location of the armories.

Before I leave, I tell her, "You need to get outside more."

"I'm fine where I am. Alpha visits from time to time. And I have all *these* people." Her hand waves in front of the wall of monitors.

"Oh? Are you and Alpha—"

"She's just keeping me company. Don't start." One of her index fingers wags up and down at my face accusingly. "I gotta get back to work." The desk chair groans as she pivots back to her work.

Echoes is completely in love with Alpha. Who seems to be in love with my brother. If I can encourage Alpha away from my twin and into Echoes's voluptuous arms, I could kill two overly involved birds with one stone. They would be so busily in love with each other, Cal wouldn't keep all his eyes and spies on me.

Before I step through the door, Echoes remarks, "Say hi to Max for me."

Four

MAXIMILLIAN

Livia... I would say she ruined my night at the Crimson Angel, but her informing me about Duke and Janna's loyalties allowed me to escape before I got trapped in the church whorehouse. Once the lights went off in the building, I knew it was a shit time for me to play saboteur. Despite the disappointment in not being able to ruin something of Strauss's, I was happy to be alive and sleep in my own bed that night.

Our rendezvous was a week ago, but I have jerked to her every night since. Ever since I saw her last when I was a teenager, I wondered what she looked like grown and did the same. Now that I'd seen her, I can't get her off my mind. I have to, though. She's the enemy and, even though they have a fox on their family crest, the Von Dovishes are snakes, Franklin Von Dovish being a prime example of that. Can't even be loyal to their own spouses. On East Side, loyalty reigns supreme.

"Here, take a look at these. Says your grandfather and

great-grandfather paid the Strausses ten percent for *protection*." Markus shoves another set of yellowed papers in front of me on the desk in my office. Rolling up the sleeves of his flannel shirt, he rifles through another pile with his stubby fingers.

With a loud squeak, I situate myself in the wingback leather rolling chair, propping my worn black boots up on the mahogany desk. Our new housekeeper must have lit the fireplace along the far wall, making it cozy in here. The smell reminds me of when Papa and I would play chess on Sunday afternoons, and an involuntary smile jerks at the edges of my lips.

For once, I feel at home being man of the manor. Like this was meant to be my place all along. Papa never wanted this gig. It's the reason he took us far away. I took more after my grandfather, who I was named after: Maximillian Leon. I always hated my middle name. It's why Livia called me her lion once she found out what it meant.

She would chase me around the yard, roaring at me, her hands raised as if they were feral claws. My frame was small for my age, and she was tough as nails, but I would never admit how much she scared me. Any time she didn't get her way, she made damn sure someone paid for it. I both loathed and loved when she would come over to play with Cal, Ace, and I. I was the one who told them she could join our "boys only" tree fort in the woods. Of course, she made me regret it by burning it down after I beat her in a foot race.

It just made me revere her even more.

"But there's nothing about any deeds or titles?"

"No. I haven't seen them." Markus shakes his head and continues his organization efforts.

Tonight's mission is to inquire about the business licenses I need to get our family shops back up and running. Unfortunately, Strauss is the only one who grants permission for any commerce in Gnarled Pine Hollow. If you want your business to operate in peace, you need that certificate with his signature. Not having the weapons for the threat of constant war if we open unlawfully, I'm choosing the legal route. Otherwise, history tells me it will just be a string of "mishappenings" in the form of raided theft, dead employees, or burned down buildings.

Filing through the pile of paperwork I've needed to go through for a week, I spot nothing of use. These documents have been in the family for decades and are important for the estate, found in the attic trunk by a worker. Some contain our land deeds, but none held the titles to the car washes and body repair shops that we used to own, fronts for our gun running from the armories.

"I have to get them back. The people of Gnarled Pine Hollow, *my* people of East Side have been sitting ducks ever since Strauss stole all our armories."

"Well... not *all*." Markus points to the oiled portrait of my father above the mantle. Behind it sits our family safe. Inside is the location of the rest of the armories that has been a Freidenberg family secret for decades. This past week, I spent time studying it carefully.

Sadness strikes me peering at Papa's smiling face in

the picture, wondering if I'm disappointing him by coming back.

When I was fourteen, trying to exert my independence, I threw in Papa's face that I was an heir to the Freidenberg throne, could hold a place on the senate when I became of age after his death. The look in his eyes was of utter pain, forbidding me from ever coming back to Gnarled Pine Hollow, saying that it was too dangerous, but he didn't understand the true threat lay in leaving. Anyone who had tried ended up dead.

You can't just *leave* a family name, no matter how many fake government documents you have. Secrets and history run as deep as the river flowing through the center of town, probably masking blood and a flurry of murder weapons. There are too many wrongs that the four families have done to each other over the centuries to just let things go. He didn't know then what I came to learn over the last eight years.

No one gets out of Gnarled Pine Hollow alive.

Rebelling, wanting to see *my* homeland, I sneaked out of our suburban house one night. I was angry at him for denying me such an auspicious title and grabbed a Greyhound all the way into town after stealing their credit card. I didn't really have a plan, but when I stepped off the bus, I ambled into West Tech, where Cal was squatting at an old computer behind the counter. The city already looked so much different in the six years since we'd left, the whole of East Side appearing like a deserted war zone.

The heir of the foxes didn't recognize me at first, but

after a scan, he grabbed my shoulders, half in a warm embrace and the other with terror as he shuffled me to the back of their store.

"Max, you shouldn't be here. If Franklin finds us... If *Strauss* finds us... you'll be in danger."

Swallowing down my questions, I let my old friend move us toward the warehouse. "I know, but I wanted to come back to see my house. Thought I would take over when I got to be eighteen."

Cal's worried brow scanned my face. "I try to hang out with Ace, but he's taken up with some guys on South Side. I bet he'd want to hang out with us if he knew you were back, though. Maybe we could head to the park where there aren't any cameras. Make it like old times."

Livia waltzed in, then through the open garage bay in the back, looking like my wet dreams come true. Her long black hair and hazel eyes beheld me with that ferocity she always had, a small, smug smile on her face. I was stunned. No longer a kid, I was completely mesmerized by what the vision of her did to my body. Unfortunately, the sight of her gave me an instant erection that poked dramatically out of my jeans. To add to my embarrassment, she glanced down at it and smirked.

Just as I opened my mouth to tell her some stupid line, some of Strauss's men entered the store, their hand tattoos flashing as they reached for their weapons when they spotted me. Wasting no time, the three of us took off.

During the long chase through the city streets, Cal ended up getting split off from us while Livia and I were cornered into an alley with one of Strauss's tanks. He crept straight for her, probably thinking she was just another asset for their trade. I threw myself on him and beat in his face until he stumbled enough that I could grab his gun. Apologizing and backing up all the way, the guy took off with his hands in the air, but I was ready to shoot him dead even at that young of an age, all to protect my little fox.

"Lion... don't. He's gone. We're safe now." My arm shook from the adrenaline coursing through my veins, but steadied when Livia placed a hand on my bicep. When I turned to meet her eyes, we held each other's gazes seriously for a long moment.

"Are you okay, foxy?"

She swallowed audibly, the motion causing her plush lips to purse. A little nod answered my question, but like a homing beacon, my focus was on her mouth.

"H-how have you been?"

Livia's breath came out in a snort. "We aren't friends, Max. You're the enemy. I just got chased around town because of you."

"I came back to see you."

Rolling her eyes dramatically, she crossed her arms. "Yeah, right." But briefly, I saw a moment's hesitation. A vulnerability like she *wanted* it to be real. That fleeting face solidified it for me. Even at fourteen, I knew... I wanted her. Strauss's rules and family lines be damned.

Brushing some hair back from her shoulder, I leaned forward to take my reward after a hard-fought battle. "Can I kiss you?"

With a slight gasp, her eyes widened before dropping

to my waiting lips. "We aren't supposed to be together. Y-you're a Freidenberg, a bear—"

"Yeah, and you're supposed to marry some mafia asshat. I don't care. Please?" Like a poison, she'd infected me. If I drank her, I may die, but she was worth it. Still staring at my jawline, she barely blinked. "Just one kiss, little fox."

Shoving her bottom lip underneath her front teeth, she shook her head. And just when I was about to block her in with my body, she kneed me right in the crotch.

My last vision of her was running down the alley, granting me a pitiful look back while I doubled over in sheer agony.

Markus found me wandering on the street nearby and brought me back to Papa, who was so disappointed in me, he cried. I'd never seen my mother so upset, and I felt so guilty about what I'd done; I spent the next year just trying to make them trust that I wouldn't run off again, rarely leaving the house.

Papa's idea to join with the other two families to produce a majority senate vote got people killed. Strauss somehow received word of the clandestine unions and, because of that, carnage rained down upon us. My parents were likely betrayed by one of the other families. Or, perhaps, Strauss found out himself. I wasn't sure which.

"They all had it wrong... my father and mother, Asa Donovan's parents, and Calum and Livia's. Thinking they could combine and make peace. Look where it got us. Fleeing from the Day of the Raging Bull." I snarl with irritation. *Day of the Raging Bull*... like it was some fucking holiday. "Why did the war between the families first start all those centuries ago, Markus?"

My right-hand man sighs and slumps into the club chair across from the dark wood desk. "No one is certain. There're only legends. Maybe your ancestor killed a Donovan or a Donovan a Von Dovish. Who knows? There's just been skirmish battles ever since."

"Tell me about that day."

"Why do you want to go over that again, Max?"

"I just need to." It's like an accident I can't look away from, the story I've been over time and time again. Each recitation makes me ache for my childhood memories safe behind some manor's comforting walls, playing with my friends, yearning to make that a reality for my people's children.

Markus knots his fingers together and looks at his lap. "Vladimir Strauss killed his father on his eighteenth birthday. We always said it was a blessing, not sure which Strauss was most vile. For Vlad's birthday party, he sent his men to slaughter your family. Your cousins, your mother's and father's siblings." He shakes his head, remembering, his eyes growing distant. "We put you all in someone's old station wagon. Hid you and Ari under some blankets in the back. I told your father and mother goodbye and stayed. They raided the house after you left, but I got away." Tears form on his bottom lids until they fall over onto his cheeks. He takes off his glasses and cleans them with his soft, white cloth. "Maybe I shouldn't have."

That night, my mama awakened me in a state of rare panic. She was trying to hide it with calm instructions, but told me to leave everything I had. All I wanted was my little Barracuda matchbox car. That's it. But I had to leave it all behind. It wasn't here when I checked the toy box in my room the day after we arrived.

"And you're *sure* it was Strauss's men."

He sniffs. "The men had nothing visible. Everyone wore black, covered their faces and skin. I didn't see tattoos. I still feel like it *could* have been Donovan's men. They always wanted inside the armories. Plus, like the wolves they are, they always travel in packs."

"Yeah, but the day Vlad took over was the day all our businesses were razed, right? That was the day the armories were commandeered by Strauss."

Markus nods slowly. He seems unconvinced.

"Strauss is powerful; I know that, Markus. But I have to get our businesses and armories back, sire a son, and then kill him." It will be the last thing I do. I just need to stay alive long enough to see my plan succeed or have a son who would do it for me.

Markus darts his eyes to mine, pleadingly. "Maybe it isn't too late to leave again. It'll keep you and Ari safe, Max."

One doesn't just *leave* Gnarled Pine Hollow. There's too much violent history in our DNA to allow anyone solace, to leave without retribution. My parents were found eight years after they left. Someone burned them alive.

My entire world changed that night when Markus

walked into my buddy's place where we were just hanging out, doing everyday stupid stuff, probably. I knew it wasn't good if he'd traveled so far to find me at a friend's house. Barely a word was said as he drove me up to the site of horror. When I saw their blackened bodies being zipped up in bags and carried away, I knew right then my life was about to change dramatically. That was the moment I set my goal: Return to Gnarled Pine Hollow and take back the senate seat for the East, rebuild, and become the leader of the powerhouse our family once was.

For years, I considered that Donovan's people did it. An emblem of a white wolf was emblazoned on the hood of the scorched car. Before I arrived, their charred bodies had been trapped inside and were only identifiable by dental records. Ace was already head of his family then, at the young age of twenty, but he was too busy gambling and whoring to be distracted by the Freidenbergs. If he killed my parents in retaliation for his sister's murder, he had the wrong family.

Calum and Livia's parents were sneaky fucks. Rumor is, Franklin Von Dovish had their mother poisoned and ran away with his mistress, leaving Calum in charge of the clan for the last several years. But outright murder? That wasn't their style. Not even if they were trying to frame someone else. Plus, they had no motive. My parents had taken us away years before; we were no threat to them.

That only leaves Strauss... Probably out to prove that no one can escape him and get away with it, especially after my Papa's secret meetings with the other clans. You can't leave and you cannot disobey.

The butler interrupts my thoughts and alerts us that the new security guard has arrived. Jakob and Markus have been hard at work, setting up a full team. Stretching to a stand, I get up with Markus to greet him in the kitchen.

"Max, this is Derichs." Markus points to a tall guy probably a few years younger than me. He's built like one of the men I'd fight with in the cage, covered from head to toe in tattoos, including a black bear underneath his right eye, the Freidenberg house sigil. His caramel brown curls fall over his forehead, giving him a boyish look, but the deep set of his eyes tells me he's dependable. "Adal Derichs, this is Maximillian Freidenberg, your new master. Max, Derichs is Jakob's right-hand, and since you won't allow Jakob to leave Arianna's side, Derichs will go with you."

Extending a hand across the newly remodeled marble island, I greet him with a firm handshake. He grips mine just as strongly. "Sir, it's an honor to meet you."

"You can call me Max, not sir."

He smirks and nods. "I won't get in your way."

So, he understands my concern.

"I have to tell you, I've watched every fight you were in," he says as he glances at Markus, who is now raiding my fridge for lunch. "The ones that were tele-vised here, anyway. Picked up some good tactics for myself."

"You fought?"

"Not as good as you, but yeah. MMA and some boxing, too."

Sleeves of faded tattoos tell me he's spent time as well. "You got put away?"

"Uh, I got caught by Strauss's men for about six months when I was nineteen." His lips curl into a nefarious smile. "You actually start to like the waterboarding when they don't give you anything to drink otherwise." Catching a hint of his old-world German accent, my shoulders relax. He's my kind. Maybe a distant relative I had lost.

"Your father—"

"And mine were second cousins, yes."

A sad smile crosses my lips, remembering the day of slaughter Markus and I had just been discussing. "Do you have anyone left?"

The corners of his mouth and eyes tighten. "No. Just me."

Taking a deep breath, I clap my arm around his shoulder. "And me. And Ari." He nods quickly at my reassurance.

The older woman hired as our chef bustles in from the cellar, carrying a sack of potatoes. "Mr. Freidenberg! I didn't expect the master of the house in the *kitchen*. Lunch will be served promptly in ten minutes. Would you prefer it in the breakfast area or the dining room?" It's not a question; it's a choice given to me like I'm a toddler. She clearly wants us out of her area, just as she has screamed all week at the construction workers trying to do their jobs around the manor.

"Sorry, Mrs. Kroft. We'll get out of your hair. If you want to set a table in the breakfast area, we'll pick at it before we head out." Motioning to Markus and Derichs, we amble toward the living room.

Hanging dark wooden beams are now in their rightful place on the boxed ceiling, and the room is clean, but empty. Rich brown wainscotting covers two stories leading up to plastered white walls. A tinge of fresh paint hits my nose as I study the worker balancing on a tall metal scaffolding, repairing the centuries-old portraits of my ancestors displayed along the upper-level picture rail. Unfortunately, the skilled craftsmen Jakob hired were also insistent on fixing the old pipe organ, too, but no one had played it on my order.

Skirting around the sheet-covered furniture parked along one wall, we amble back to my study and connected library, neither of which had been touched, other than with a duster.

"So, tonight?" I address my advisor and new guard. Markus is right; I don't trust anyone to be near my little sister other than Jakob, whom I met with (and threatened to within an inch of his life). He was my mother's third cousin, our fourth. It made me feel better that he, hopefully, was not into familial relations. Now that I know Derichs and I are also cousins, I feel safer to have the two near Arianna.

Markus looks toward the young Derichs, raising his scruffy eyebrows.

"Oh, right. Um..." I can tell Derichs feels put on the spot, taking charge of security for the boss. He clears his throat and the bear tattoo under his eye folds into the skin with his concentration. "So, we'll enter the side doors of the warehouse. Aries and Gemini are your two spies, sir— Max. I've been informed we have three exits. Here." Pointing to the ledger on the desk, he grips the edge as I slide it over. He produces an ink pen from a small case on his belt and flips the large calendar paper. On the back, he draws a rudimentary layout of the building the meeting will be located in.

As the ink flows over the paper, he discusses the strategy. "We enter through this door. And here are escape routes if things go poorly. We meet here if we get separated and here for rendezvous or retreat. Holland has point position here if they don't see him, and Aries will be playing sniper tonight from here."

Holland, another of Jakob's security team. I hadn't met any of my tanks yet, nor any of my spies. Derichs's face meets mine for approval, and I study his sober brown eyes. He's young, but he's not reckless. He's me about four years ago. And he, too, has a bone to pick with Strauss.

Derichs's nature appears more serious than my own. That's a good thing. Where I am brash, he can be more calculated. We'll work well together, and I believe he knows what he's doing. I won't fully trust him; that would be unwise, but Markus's words come back to me. The ones about having to rely on others. Adal Derichs seems like the place to start.

"Alright. This sounds like a solid plan. What're you carrying?"

"Just my Smith and Wesson. Aries has the sniper rifle. The tanks and spies have handguns. We have a few rifles and one machine gun leftover in storage. There's also a box of grenades in the dungeons below us, but I'm not sure if they even work." He snorts. "We could try tonight."

"Ha. Yeah, actually. Let's take two. Just in case."

Pulling out his phone, he instructs his lackey, Holland, to pick two up for us. I hear some argument, but Derichs handles it as a good manager would. Like a commander, he ends the call saying, "I expect them here in ten." Slipping his phone in his back pocket, he sees me looking at him. "Taken care of."

"Okay, I'll talk with Strauss—"

"Oh, it won't be him. He never shows for meetings. It'll be Sergei Antonov, his right-hand."

I huff at the slight. "I'm Maximillian fucking Freidenberg. He's not going to meet with *me?*"

Derichs and Markus cast their eyes down.

Taking a deep breath in, I calm myself. "Tell me about Antonov, then."

"He's a big brute. Ugly, too," Markus says. "About my age now, I'd say."

"Still got a good right hook," Derichs says, rubbing his jaw as if recalling a run-in with him. He runs a hand through his dark brown waves and points to the shoddy map. "We enter here. Antonov will probably be here. His men will likely be here and here." As he points his finger, I memorize the locations. "Antonov will say no to your business license request. Be prepared."

"And then offer him something in return." Markus stands and wanders toward the dark green marble fireplace along the far wall, gold veins glistening in the light of the flames.

"Like…" My mind scrambles to find something I could offer before doom strikes me. *Fuck.* "Like the armory locations," I say, almost to myself. "The ones he doesn't know about."

Markus nods and Derichs appears unconvinced, but says, "I suppose so."

"I can't give him that. They can't know that *I* know where they all are. It would be a sure way to get captured and tortured. Perhaps I could offer him 10% of the profits, like my grandfather and his father did." Gripping a fragile document from the table, I hold it up for them to see. It was extortion, but that plan worked for hundreds of years before me. At least it left our businesses standing.

Markus's jaw flexes. "Yeah… it did keep some semblance of peace for a while. See what Antonov says."

"You want a drink?" Standing, I amble to the mirrored bar cart in the corner of the room. It has freshly cleaned decanters refilled with liquors. Hopefully, one is an old scotch.

Markus's eyes sparkle behind the thick frames of his glasses. I remember Papa telling me he had a drinking problem back in the day. "None for me, thanks." Licking his bottom lip, he looks like he wants to say anything, except no.

"Yeah, I'll take whatever you're having." Derichs

checks his gun and magazine before sliding it back in its hip holster.

Pouring two neat scotches, I hand him the crystal double. With a look of victory, I raise my glass to toast. "Should we drink to the old saying? *The den of the beast lies in the east?*"

Derichs nods, but with a small grin, his dimples fold into his cheeks when he says, "How about, good men die young... so, let's go be badass motherfuckers!"

With a chuckle, I clink my glass to his. "I'll drink to that."

Five

MAXIMILLIAN

It's 8 p.m. My hand perched behind the passenger seat, I wait in my Barracuda, narrowing my eyes through the darkness at the metal building blocking the view of the river. Derichs studies the area with me, dragging his palms down the front of his jeans. A light shines inside the warehouse, streams of yellow filtering through small gaps in the walls and doorway, interrupted at times by shadows waltzing through.

"Okay. Let's go," I say, breaking the tense silence. Derichs meets my gaze and nods. He's ready.

As we approach the side door we planned to enter, it slides open with some effort. The man holding it open is wearing a black suit and a smug expression, like he's got the upper hand. Marching in front, I keep my focus straight ahead. I approach the man in the middle of the room, standing with another just behind his left shoulder. My eyes dare a quick peek out the barred skinny windows above us, but I don't see Aries in his position. Hopefully, he's there.

Drumming in my neck, my pulse races as I stand in front of Antonov. His small eyes are just a hair too close together, which gives him an even more menacing look than the way he's holding his muscular body. He's younger than Markus alluded to, probably in his mid-thirties. Stroking his shaved chin in contemplation, his large red bull tattoo flexes across his hand as he eyes me suspiciously.

"S'not Antonov," Derichs whispers near my ear. My brow furrows as the deep and forceful rhythm of my heart flares from a bass drum to a rapid snare beat. If it's not Antonov, then who is it?

"Maximillian. Leon. Freidenberg. Son of Gerald Leon, who was a complete cuck. Did you know he liked to watch your mother take some big dicks? Well, before she was flame grilled, that is." A heady Eastern European accent comes through the end of each word. I will the sweat to stop pouring from my forehead and steady my breathing. This is bait, and I'm not taking it. "I'd still have fucked her holes after, honestly. She was a beautiful woman."

"And whom do I have the pleasure of speaking with? I'm told you're not Sergei Antonov."

The man's shoulders relax. Which means something has put him at ease. It was either me not succumbing to his taunt, or he feels confident in his safety. I sneak glances around the perimeter, monitoring the positions of his men. Derichs was right. They are exactly where he said they would be. His head is on a constant swivel just behind me.

"Morozov."

"Morozov. I was told I would be meeting with someone who could get me the business licenses. Someone worth a shit."

He snorts. "Antonov didn't think it was worth his time to meet with you." Holding out a palm, he adds, "I just came to collect the hundred it will cost you."

My mouth opens slightly, but I try to school my face as much as I can. "Hundred? Hundred k?"

He laughs and pulls his hand back. Turning, he walks a few steps away from me. Everything in me screams that I'm suddenly in danger. "Oh. You don't have the money? Hmm. That could be a problem." With a swift spin on his heel, he turns back to me. "For you."

"I can offer ten percent of the profits. Just like my grandfather and his father did. And I believe the father before that one." The skin on my right hand itches to reach for my Glock in its holster. An energy travels from Derichs's body, and I sense he's getting the same vibe. My jaw tightens.

Opening his long arms to his sides, he asks, "How about a trade? You tell me where the rest of the armories are, and I allow you to run your business." As he drops his arms, my eyes rest on their movement. He could reach quickly for his gun at any time. The man behind his shoulder already has a hand on his belt as I spy Derichs slowly moves his to his holster out of the corner of my eye.

"I don't know where the armories are."

Morozov's head dips back for a moment before he stares me down. "I was really hoping you wouldn't feign ignorance. It's so overplayed."

My muscles twitch, ready to escape. "How would I know? I've been gone from Gnarled Pine my entire life. My family never told me. I just want to run my car wash and body shop. That's it."

The air in the room condenses.

Morozov's eyebrows raise, and he smiles broadly, flashing a wide gap between his front teeth. "Oh, well, if you don't know... what good are you?"

His hand reaches for his gun at the same time as mine. The man behind his shoulder gets a sharp hole through his forehead as he slumps forward to his knees, then flat on his face. A red beam of light swivels through the upper window, Aries scanning to take more out. Morozov aims behind my shoulder and fires while both me and my man shift to our right, making our way to escape route one behind a set of thick concrete pillars.

Derichs groans loudly, but his legs keep running with mine. He's been hit, I know it, but we need to move. A thunderstorm of bullets rains down on us from the second story platforms, each pelt causing a cacophony of discordant sounds. The metal walls of the building ring echoes of each whirr as they pass my head. I'm focused on getting to cover by shooting my way around the room despite the chaos and confusion.

Just before I dive behind the wall of the pillar, I lift my gun toward Morozov. He's at a forty-five-degree angle, so my bullet only clips his shoulder. As his body jolts from the first shot, I put another in his chest, and down he goes.

Derichs creeps up beside me in a crouched position. He pushes his back against the wall and slides down it on weakened knees. His left hand presses against his shoulder, but he still clutches his handgun. Blood weeps through his T-shirt around where he's keeping pressure.

"Hang on," I say through gritted teeth.

His eyes frost over, but he nods.

We have to get out of here. Now. Footfalls from the rest of Strauss's men bellow from around the corner. Quickly, I shove against the exit door nearest us, but it's bolted shut. "Fuck!" In desperation, I heave with my shoulder against it with everything my strong frame gives me, but it won't budge. As I scan the small area behind the pillar, I come to the horrible conclusion that there's no way out. Our only escape route is across the open warehouse floor.

Snatching my phone from my pocket, I hit the number I was given for communications with Holland, our tank on the outside.

Heavy breaths answer me. "I'm on the move. Aries had to switch positions. You've got about six left standing —" A ping, then a loud groan interrupts him.

"Holland?" There's no answer. Ending the call, I stuff the phone back in my pocket, placing my back against the wall next to my man.

Strauss's men are moving in closer. Sliding out my magazine, I count three left, one in the chamber.

"I've got a few left," Derichs manages to say as sweat drips from his forehead, now paling to the color of ash.

"Slide behind that pillar." I point to one farther in the corner. "Hunker down over there." Concrete explodes near my head as someone picks off my location. Dipping into my pocket, my fingers grasp the heavy grenade. This could backfire, but I pull the ring with my teeth anyway.

If I don't die from the explosion, I'll die from a heart attack. My chest thuds from the panic desperate to escape from within as I grip the body and lever together as tightly as my fist will allow. I rear back my arm and launch it across the room to the other door and drop to my knees, covering my head with my arms.

The impact shudders the room until the floor tilts as if we're in an earthquake. Instead of bullets, crusts of plaster and dust plummet around us, splattering to the floor. When I look up, Derichs is still in position and the men moving in on us are down and rolling around, their moans of agony piercing through my almost deaf-ened ears. The wall has opened for us enough to get through.

Rushing to my partner, I heave him up underneath his good shoulder. "I'm okay. I got this. I'm fine, Max," he grunts. His feet kick repeatedly until he stumbles with me across the warehouse and out into the safety of the night.

"Rendezvous," my voice commands steadily, so he knows where we're heading. Darting through the alley next to the buildings, my body begins to relax as we approach my untouched Barracuda. Once I unlock the doors, Derichs collapses into the passenger seat and immediately slumps down, passing out.

The engine roars to life as I turn the key. With a squeal of the tires, I press on the accelerator fully, steering in the direction of the old car wash. Our safe harbor, one of the old armories. Holland should meet us there in a retreat.

Before I get out of the city streets, headlights blaze in my rearview mirror, blinding me for a moment. We've been spotted by a black Mercedes. Fortunately, I have a better car. Darting through some side streets, my enemy keeps up easily, even when I skip past red lights. Pedestrians dart out of the way, diving for the sidewalks as we speed past. The Mercedes keeps up close with a gun sticking out of the passenger window.

"Oh, hell no!" They better not hit my Barracuda. Switching pedals, I rapidly slam on the brakes and yank the steering wheel to the left. The Mercedes keeps moving forward as I pull a sharp turn, heading for the highway. I need an open road.

Once I reach it, the black car can't keep up with the amount of muscle I've put into the engine. Flooring the gas, I leave it behind as we head almost beyond the city limits before I turn sharply right onto an exit ramp.

Eventually, I make it to the car wash on the east side. It's well into Freidenberg land, but mainly abandoned now. The earth has reclaimed a lot of the buildings in the area, the asphalt cracked so deeply, I have to stop before easing over the bumps. Pulling through the old bay, I park in the middle of the ragged, dirty wash brushes.

Solid concrete walls refuse a peek inside, and the door to the office hangs sideways on its hinges. It's completely dark.

"Derichs!" I yell to wake him.

With a snort, he raises his head with some effort. "I'm okay. I'm okay." He's mainly talking to himself.

"Come on. Get out."

I jump out of my side and slide to his, pulling open the passenger door as he struggles to set himself upright. Throwing a shoulder under his uninjured one, I help him stagger into the office.

"I got a girl," he grits out. "Her name's Hannah. *Fuck!* Don't tell her I got shot." He groans again. "She'll just do something stupid." I toss him on an old waiting room bench.

"You're not fucking dying. Stop that. First time shot in the shoulder?"

He nods, his eyes trying to search me out in his dazed confusion.

"You'll be okay. I just need to get in touch with a healer." Other cities have their hospitals and doctors; I had never learned about such things until after we moved away. Gnarled Pine Hollow has always relied on alternatives; at least, the clans have their own. Those outside the families have their medicine people as well, but the coveted position of healer is to serve the head of a prominent family.

My finger shakes violently as I pull up Markus's number with some effort. After telling him about the situation, he says he's sending one to meet us in a worried tone. I haven't met any of my healers. Guess now is as good a time as any.

While I wait, I search the shop for any supplies. It'll take a lot of work to get the place back in shape, just like everything on the east side of Gnarled Pine. A creaking sound comes from my right, and I immediately draw my weapon. I didn't see any headlights approaching, but someone could have followed us.

Holding up my gun, I creep down the hallway. All the doors are closed, except for one to the old men's bathroom, which is cracked ajar. I flip on my pistol light and flash it over the open door until two shiny eyes peek out from behind it.

"Get the fuck out here or I shoot."

There's no movement. Aiming for the ceiling above the door, I waste a bullet as the plaster crumbles around us. Immediately, the face disappears, replaced with quick shuffling sounds. A shadow of a figure slowly emerges with arms up in a sign of surrender.

My gaze wanders up black leather pants and a tight black tank top, taking in the curvy figure of a woman topped with a tall mohawk of black hair.

"Livia?"

Six

LIVIA

"Oh, hey, Max." It's like any other Friday, the way my voice rings out so casually. "What are you doing here?"

He had lowered his gun from my head, but raises it again. "Cute. What are *you* doing here?"

"I thought I'd get my car washed, but this place has terrible customer service. No one's waited on me for *hours*." Slowly, I let my hands fall to my sides. "My arms are getting tired. Do you mind lowering your gun?" Blinking my lashes heavily, I lift a corner of my lips.

I can't see him with the flashlight boring in my face, but the silhouette of his body stiffens behind his weapon. "Yeah, I do mind. What the fuck are you doing here? I'll give you one more chance to answer before I—"

"Before you what? *Shoot* me?" There's no way my lion will kill me. My finger tingles with the feel of the metal charm I rubbed just before I emerged from behind the door.

He sighs. "Livia. Please don't make me."

"I was looking for the armory." May as well tell him. "And since you're here, I'm assuming I was right. One *is* here."

As he lowers his gun and flashlight, my eyes quickly adjust to the darkness, but spots flare wherever I look behind my lids. His face holds a worried expression, like he has lived days in just a moment.

Max opens his mouth, but before he can speak, I interrupt. "What's wrong?"

A muffled moan wafts down the narrow hallway coming from the office area. Our eyebrows raise at each other, and we hurry to the sound. One of his men has crumpled on a bench with a dark stain seeping through his white T-shirt near his right shoulder.

"Fuck," I say, taking him in.

"Fuck! Livia Von Dovish?" The man tries to sit up but doesn't have the strength, but he reaches for his gun.

"Oh, you're not going to do a damn thing. Just lay back down, champ."

Max's forehead crinkles as he squats next to his tank, helping him pull off his shirt as I grab my new phone. "Marianna, I need you. I'll ping my location."

"What the fuck are you doing?" Max stands and strides toward me in two steps, reaching for my phone, but I hold it behind my back.

"I'm saving your friend here."

His nostrils flare as he walks my body back until I hit the wall with a thud. Max doesn't stop moving and thrusts his palms on either side of my head, one still clutching his gun. "Give me your fucking phone." The growl of his voice causes my nipples to harden.

Slipping it into my back pocket, I jut out my bottom lip. "No." I try not to look into his eyes, but his head leans in until there's barely room to breathe without inhaling him. The smell of his sweat fills my nose, and my thighs clench together.

"Livy... Little fox..." He warns me with his deep bass crackling next to my ear. His head lowers, his lips hovering close to mine almost involuntarily. I turn my face, and his eyes widen as if no one has ever pulled away from him. Smoothly, he recovers by dipping his nose to meet my exposed neck. He slowly sniffs up the course of my artery, the tiny inhales tickling my skin. My pulse pounds until I'm worried he'll see it. The warmth of his lips taps on the corner of my jaw before he sucks with barely enough pressure to lift my skin between them. He straightens up to gaze into my eyes.

My hands move to his hips to push him back or pull him closer. I'm not sure which. I decide to push, but realize he has already pocketed my phone in his lowered arm. Flashing it in his hand, he smirks. He spins toward his friend, dropping to a squat beside him, putting pressure on the wound.

"*Fucker*. That's mine." Shoving off the wall, my body buzzes from the spell he just put on me.

"You'll get it back once we're safe." Glancing at it once more, he slides it into his pocket. "You got a tracer on it?"

"Yes. You know I would. Not that it matters. My

spies know where I am and why I'm here. What they don't know is that *you* are here with me." I shake my head. "Stop, you're doing that wrong." I slap his hand out of the way, grab the T-shirt from his friend, and put pressure on his wound the proper way. "Take off your shirt and put it under his head. Poor guy is dying here and you're making him lay on a metal bench."

"I'm not dying."

"He's not dying."

They say it at the same time. But Max obeys. Standing, he grabs the back of his black T-shirt and pulls it over his head, exposing those pecs that make my pussy water. *Damn*, he's even got those V muscles on the sides of his cut abs. The black bear tattoo on his chest makes me look away before he sees me blush. "Who did you call?" he asks.

"Just my healer. She's quick." He grimaces and quirks one eyebrow. "And quiet," I assure him. "Look, lion, your healer is probably some newbie who studied under mine anyway. They don't take part in these games we play."

"I'll try to find you something to drink," Max says to his invalid.

"What's your name, sport?" I ask the wounded man.

He snorts. "Derichs." He glances to where Max walked off to. "Taking your opportunity to finish me off?"

"No. I'm trying to keep you alive."

"Why?"

"Because you two have information I want. And once I save your ass, you're going to give it to me."

The corners of his eyes lift as he attempts a smile. "It's not my information to give. May as well kill me."

"You're loyal."

"Yes, I am. Not like you foxes."

My lips pinch at the insult, but he's got a point. My father is a piece of shit. Pretty sure every man in my lineage has lied, cheated, or stolen. Especially on their wives. Everyone, with Cal being the exception, but he's still got time.

"Touché," I say.

"Is this her?" Max comes barreling back into the waiting room, pointing at a gleam of light illuminating the back of the store through the bathroom window.

"I'll go check. Hold him." I let Max take over as I shimmy out into the car wash area.

A familiar Volkswagen pulls up and parks as the headlights click off. "Mari, this way!" The shadow of her large head and helmet of blonde hair turns toward me.

"Liv, what's wrong?" Her voice holds no panic. She's been doing this work for us for too many years to let anything rattle her.

"Man's been shot. Inside here."

She shoulders past me into the office, carrying her black leather physician's bag. Kneeling next to Derichs, she gets right to work. With a nod, she orders Max, "Help me lay him on that counter there." The two settle the man on the old sales surface, the open cash register shoved aside. An inappropriate giggle almost escapes me, thinking about him paying with his life.

"Livy, quit being useless and hold this flashlight," Mari commands.

I hurry to her and do as she instructs. While she cleans the tank and drapes him for surgery, I eye Max above the light. His handsome face contorts in concentration and worry for his man. Just like when Cal broke his leg falling from the tree house when we were little.

Mari gives Derichs some pills to take the edge off the pain and tells Max to pin him down while I hold the light. The tank is like stone. Despite her cutting into his flesh (which she has numbed), and then digging through tendons and muscle with tweezers, he grits his teeth and doesn't move. Max's hands press on his arms to ensure he doesn't. When she finds the fragment of the bullet and digs it out, it *plinks* when she drops it into a metal tray resting on his belly.

Derichs's head falls back in relaxation while she sutures him up.

"You did well, soldier," she says as she gives him a couple more pills to take later and gathers her equipment. I clean up the area, and Max helps Derichs to a seated position.

"Mari, thanks," I say before she reaches the door.

"What do I owe you?" Max asks her.

"Nothing. Just doing my duty. Make sure he drinks lots of water." She heads out the door.

Derichs clears his throat. The wistful smile on his face lets me know he's high as a fucking kite. His pupils are the size of pinheads. "Livia... despite being a fox, you came through. Thank you."

"Sure, bud. You wanna tell me where the armories are now?"

A hoarse chuckle leaves his chest, and Max rolls his eyes.

"I thought I would try while he's in the clouds." Meeting my lion's gaze, I ask, "Can I talk to you before you go?" My finger points Max in the direction of the back hallway toward the bathrooms.

Max lifts his eyebrows at Derichs, who nods in response. "Let me just put him in the car first."

Once he helps his hobbling friend get situated, he returns. Mindlessly, I rub my pocket charm three times and butterflies flap their wings like a strong breeze swooped by as he walks into the room. "Max, I need to know where the weapons are." His face sets like flint. "And you need to get business licenses."

"Yes?"

Taking a step toward him, I lift my lips into a small grin. "I can help you secure a meeting with Strauss for your licenses. He meets with me or Cal when we've needed them. And if you've pissed him off like you said... it would be safer to take me with you. I don't *think* he'd do anything with me there."

He gazes down at me with some heat in his eyes. "And what if he still says no? I just killed a few of his men tonight."

Moving another step closer, I stand just underneath his chin, tilting my face to his. "I can be persuasive."

His face leans into mine. "And what do you want?"

"Weapons."

Max considers for a moment. With a hint of reverence, he says, "Little fox." The side of his mouth curls upwards as he raises an eyebrow. "You want some of my guns?" Biting my lip, I nod. "Fully loaded? 'Cause you know I won't be halfcocked around you."

I inhale sharply, not able to monitor my chest rise. "Yes," I whisper.

Noticing his lips are only a breath away, I back away. His mouth huffs a humorless laugh onto mine. Too quickly, his arms wrap around me, and I instinctively clutch his thick biceps, but he's slid my phone into my back pocket and stepped back from me before I can blink.

"I hate to break it to you, Livia, but the armories are all empty."

My jaw drops. "Wh-what? Are you lying to me, lion?"

"No. We scavenged what was left and hoarded them for our team. I don't just need business licenses. I need to get our weapons, our other armories back."

"That means war."

"Not if I kill Strauss and his men."

The tail of my hair tickles my neck as I toss my head back with laughter. "Max, you can't do that alone. You haven't been here. You don't know how things work."

He crosses his arms. "I asked you to teach me."

Placing my hands on my hips, I even out my stance. "What's your plan? Did you even have one?"

"Go in there and fuck shit up."

I roll my eyes. "Like the fucking bear you are. You've hibernated all these years and now you're hungry and not thinking straight." He needs weapons. We need weapons. Strauss could pick us all off one by one if he has them all.

Holy shit. It dawns on me… Maybe our parents were right. Ugh! I hate that. My despicable father may have done something good. I can't think about that now; it makes my head fuzzy. Or maybe Max is making me confused. I need to focus.

Max glances over his shoulder to check on Derichs sitting in the car before leaning his back against the door. "Tell me your plan, foxy."

Inhaling deeply, I formulate one as I speak. "Well, you need your business licenses. I'll still get you the meeting and go with."

"And I'll demand he give me back my rightful properties."

Shaking my head at him, I say, "Max, he won't respond to that, and you know it." He closes his mouth and waits. "If he won't give them back, I've heard of a few contacts from Ace's people that may be able to get us the weapons we need to start up a trade again."

"*We?* Your family has been sitting behind keyboards for years doing fuck all. Mine was helping the community by running the guns for protection."

"*The community?* No, you guys hoarded them just like Strauss is doing."

"No, we didn't. We gave them out—"

"For the right price."

Freezing, he stays silent, because he knows I'm right. Eventually, he gives in and speaks. "So, what are you saying?"

"I'm saying we work together. I'll help you get your licenses, some gun contacts from outside the city... and you give me a third of the ones you run."

Spit flies from his mouth as he snaps out, "A fucking *third*?"

"I'm being generous. I should ask for fifty percent."

One of his dark eyes narrows at me. "You're ridiculous. Von Dovish, through and through."

"Don't fucking say that." I go to shove him out of the way, but he grabs my wrists, his touch smoldering my skin. If he feels any more of me, I'll ignite into flames.

"I'm a big boy now. You can't kick my shins in anymore, little fox. I'm a lion, remember?"

I swallow. "I changed my mind. I don't want to work with you."

Lowering my arms, but still holding my wrists, he leans forward as if to match his lips to mine. I draw back a boot, then wail on his leg. "Fucking hell, Livia!" He drops his grasp on me and bends forward to soothe his bones as I rush out the door and sneak off into the night without being seen.

Seven

MAXIMILLIAN

"F ucking bitch!" My rumbling yell meets a shield of silence as she's already escaped. That fucking hurt. Just like when we were kids.

Jumping in my Barracuda, I head toward the manor with the headlights off the whole way. Once we arrive at the gates, Derichs stirs in the seat next to me and eyes the gatekeeper, who's strapped with a rifle. Leaning into the driver's window, John's eyes dart around the area before landing on me. He's on high alert, as he should be, given that I just killed several of Strauss's men.

"Hey, John. Any trouble?"

John shakes his head and waves me inside, shutting the gates behind us.

"I should get home," Derichs says with a strained voice, trying to sit up.

"Nonsense. You're staying here for a while. That girl of yours, would she want to stay with us, too?"

His body slumps back into the leather seat, an arm

splayed across the ridge of the window. "N-no. She's from out of town. I don't want her here."

It's completely understandable. Moving to Gnarled Pines is a death wish. One I was willing to make when I came back, but I certainly don't wish it on Arianna, which is why I plan to keep her locked in the house with Jakob until I can get our properties back. And kill Strauss.

Markus and Jakob come out of the front door when I turn off the engine. Jakob's huge body lumbers at a speed I wouldn't think possible, his bald head gleaming in the moonlight.

"What did you do?" Markus looks as if he hasn't slept in days, and he probably hasn't. He rubs his hands through his white hair, then stuffs one in his pants, attempting to tuck in his flannel shirt underneath his pooch.

Jakob, ever the stoic soldier, calmly pulls Derichs from the car with an arm under his good shoulder. As he nears the front door, he spots me and nods once before heading inside with his man.

"What had to be done. It was us or them, Markus." Adrenaline still pumps through my veins. There's no way I could sleep now. I should clean our guns and reload, prepare for the next fight, which may be sooner than I anticipate. My muscles start to feel every tear in their fibers from the evening's activities now that I'm on my home territory. From experience, I know it won't be long before I'll crash. Markus follows me inside, a few paces behind.

Mrs. Kroft bustles out of her bedroom down the first-floor hall, a flowery robe flowing behind her with spongy pink curlers all over her grayed head of hair. "Mr. Freidenberg, I heated up dinner for you, but it's gone cold now. There's warm milk and cookies set out by your bed. But if you want cold cuts, I can place them on the buffet in the dining room."

"Thank you, Mrs. Kroft. I think the cookies will be fine."

Trailing me close behind, Markus clears his throat, waiting until we enter the study until he says what he's obviously desperate to unleash on me.

"Well?" he asks as I empty my pockets onto the desk, then pull out my gun cleaning kit from the bottom drawer. The leather seat creaks loudly as I relax into it, scooting it close to the forest green suede pad laid across the surface.

"Well, what? Things went south. I had to shoot, or... explode our way out. We're alive."

Jakob enters the room with a serious expression. But he never has anything different. "Derichs will be fine," he says in a deep bass. His habitus is such that I'd hate to meet him as an opponent in the ring. The tattoos weaving up his neck to the sides of his head make him even more foreboding than his large shoulders. All the hair on top of his head has migrated to his thick, black eyebrows, which furrow with some concern. "We lost Holland, though. He was a good man."

"I'm sorry about Holland. We barely made it out, but Von Dovish's healer helped us. Where was ours, *Markus?*"

Markus sighs and falls into the faded striped fabric club chair across from me. "She's new. She hadn't arrived from out of town in time and got lost on the way."

Clenching my jaw, I release the irritation with a deep breath through my nose. "Well, she could have cost us a tank." I eye Jakob. "She could have cost us a cousin."

Markus leans forward. "I'll make sure she's trained up properly. But Max... how do you ever expect to get a meeting with Strauss now?"

Avoiding any skin pinches, I take apart my gun, setting the pieces on the desk pad. Grabbing a cloth, my fingers polish the guide rod mindlessly. "I have to think."

"There's not much time to think. We all need to get paid. The workers here will stop or burn the house down if they don't get their money. Strauss will be looking to slaughter us all after tonight, and we don't have the weapons to fight back." Markus shakes his head and pulls off his glasses to clean them. "It wasn't smart."

"Oh? Wasn't smart to keep us *alive*? What would you have had me do, Markus? Die?"

"No, I just..." Almost stabbing his eye with the arm of his glasses, he swiftly replaces them on his nose and squints his eyes behind me at the picture of my grandfather and father. Papa is holding a baby me in his arms. Our foreboding manor is in the background. In the dimness of the light in the room, Markus's eyes glisten. "I'm sorry. You're right. I'm just worried."

Deciding to broach the topic that I know will cause a controversy, I clear my throat, then assume my role as master of the manor. "Livia Von Dovish had a proposition."

"Livia? When did she—"

"It's no matter. She can get me a meeting with Strauss."

"Even after tonight?"

I raise my eyebrows. "She says she can."

"And you believe her."

Gripping the little nylon tool, I plunge inside the barrel with a little twist at the end. "Yes."

"You know those Von Dovish are foxes, right? She could be playing you." Markus pauses, preparing me for an insult. "Are you just thinking with your dick?"

"No. And what other option do I have now?"

Markus stands and paces in the back of the room while Jakob's dark brown eyes study his movements, his neck twisting the ink there into distorted images. "I don't like it... But you're right. I think you need her," Markus says.

"I don't *need* her. I can *use* her." And my dick agrees, picturing plunging into her as the wire brush thrusts into the little hole I hold in my hands. And, if I'm being honest, I kind of like having her nearby. Keep your enemies close and all that.

Jakob moves from the wall near the door and sits down in the other club chair, his massive quads spread out as he puts his elbows on his legs. "What does she want in return?" he asks.

I swallow, preparing for an argument. "A third."

Markus whips around. "A *third*? Max, come on.

Think. A *third* of the guns to the Von Dovish clan could get nasty. Next, you'll give a third to Donovan!"

Looking down at my gun pieces, I respond, "I have a suspicion that I can work with Livia. Get her to lessen her percentage."

Jakob smirks, then nods in understanding. One black eyebrow raises with amusement.

"So, you're going to give her your massive cock and get her to fall in love with you?" Markus sits down and shakes his head. "You arrogant boy. She's too independent for that. She'd probably lop it off before she fucked it."

"I think he can do it," Jakob says.

"I know I can," I tell them. Getting Livia to catch feelings wouldn't be the worst thing in the world.

Markus sighs heavily before asking, "How are you going to contact her?"

"I'm going to visit an old friend." I smile.

Markus and Jakob eye each other in confusion.

"Welp," I say, putting my clean Glock back together and sliding in a loaded magazine. "I'm heading to bed. Make sure that new healer stays with Derichs. Kid's my new favorite. He did good tonight. You trained him well." On my way out the door, I pat Jakob on the shoulder, and he grins. "Goodnight."

The next morning, after a hot shower, I stop in on Derichs in the guest wing.

"Hey, man. I'm feeling better." Derichs wakes from his nap as the new mousy looking healer rises from the chaise lounge in the corner, a thick book sliding off her lap, hitting the floor. Large brown eyes widen as she takes me in. She looks terrified of me.

"No, no. Don't try to sit up for me," I tell Derichs when I step inside. "I just wanted to make sure you have everything you need."

"Max, I feel like I can get up today. I can go with you. Whatever you're planning, I'm ready." His arm attempts to hold his body up and scoot toward the edge of the mattress.

A grin spreads across my face. I like that he's eager to protect me, eager to help our family. "Today's task is a solo event. It'll be better if I go alone. And I highly doubt I'll be in danger, unless Strauss sends out some followers."

With a dazed smile and glassy eyes, he rests back against his pillows. "Alright. But if you need me, just come get me."

"No, I want you to rest up. We'll get a meeting with Strauss soon, and I'll want you there."

He nods. "Of course."

Turning to the healer, I ask, "Your name is Maggie?"

She nods. "Yes, Mr. Freidenberg. I apologize for last night—"

"Just don't let it happen again. Make sure my boy here is one hundred percent by the end of the week."

"Yes, sir." She looks at the ground, her long, brown ponytail falling forward over her tiny shoulder.

The upper hallways have been cleaned, but the wood floors are still warped as the carpenters continue to work on them. When I reach the dining room downstairs, breakfast has been laid on the tall, gilded sideboard. Arianna, Jakob, and Markus sit at the table, already eating. After preparing myself a plate of fresh hen eggs and thick bacon, I take my seat at the head of the table. Everyone is quiet with a tensity in the room coming from some unknown source. Studying the faces surrounding me, I quickly find out where the issue lies.

"Maxi, I'm planning to go out today." Arianna places her fork on her plate with a loud scrape.

Taking a big bite of my breakfast, I dismissively say, "No, you're not."

"Yes, I am. I can't just *stay* here all day and night. I've got cabin fever." She sniffs dramatically. "I need the outdoors."

"You can walk the grounds," I say, eyeing Jakob, who nods at me as if he's already told her this.

From the look on her face, I know she isn't done trying to convince me yet. "I thought I would get Dad's old motorcycle fixed up."

My mouth hangs open, a bit of bacon falling to my plate. "What? Since when do you like motorcycles?"

Looking at her plate and, as casually as she can muster, she shrugs. "I've been riding since I was sixteen."

"Huh." There were years I had been away from her. Times I didn't know her well because she was in boarding school while I was fighting, working for various organizations, and doing stupid shit to make ends. Maybe I didn't know my little sister as well as I thought. "You ever own one?"

She shakes her head, her espresso hair shining in the morning light streaming through the windows. "No, but I know how to ride."

Turning to Jakob, his eyebrows raise, mimicking the surprised look on my face.

"Who taught you?" As far as I know, Arianna is a virgin. She'd never had a boyfriend, and I intend to keep it that way. Was there a boy in her life who showed her how to ride? Is there some guy I don't know about hanging around her? As if claws are just underneath their surface, my fingers tingle with anticipation of a good fight.

"A friend from school had an older brother who rode. He taught us both."

"Which friend? Which brother?"

Her eyes roll. "Her name was Scarlett, my roommate from second year. Her brother's name was TJ. He was much older than us."

"What's their last name?" My spies can easily look them up and check into TJ, making sure he didn't put his *much older* penis anywhere near my sister.

"Max! Come on!"

Markus pipes in, "Our old motorcycle shop is still standing. We can take your father's bike there. Jakob and I will go with her, Max. I believe there're a couple of boys who do repairs in the garage for cash. They aren't affili-ated with any family. We could tell them we'll be starting it back up, check into if their talents are worth keeping or if we need to run them off."

Arianna perks up so much that I want to please her. I sigh and ask, "It's on the east side?"

"*Deep* into our side of town, yes," Markus assures me.

"Alright. You can go. Is there an extra tank you can take?" I ask Jakob.

"Yes, sir. I've replaced Holland already."

"Sounds good."

"So I can go?" Arianna smiles and her entire face lights up as bright as the candelabras in the room.

"Yes, you can go." Shoving her heavy chair back, she stands quickly and hugs me. "Don't do anything stupid and obey our men."

"I will! I will!"

"And Ari? When you get a motorcycle, I expect you to wear a helmet. And you won't be riding anywhere but around our grounds until things settle down. Do you understand me?"

"Yes, yes. I hear you." She sits back in her seat with a broad smile still in place. "Thank you, Max."

"Understand that I will *kill* any motherfucker who touches you."

Ignoring me, she picks up a piece of toast and wiggles in her seat in a happy little dance.

Tossing the cloth napkin on my finished plate, the chair legs give some resistance against the thickly tufted rug as I push back from the table and announce my departure. "I gotta go see a man about a meeting."

Markus speaks up. "You want backup?"

"Nope. I need to do this alone."

After sliding into my Barracuda, I head directly west across town. Once I hit the technology district, I ease off the gas. Pulling up to an old computer store, I get out, glancing up and down the street. I know eyes are already on me, but my spies should be here as well. The Glock in my holster brings me some comfort.

When I push it open, the door's electronic chime rings out into the empty store, rows of dusty laptops sitting on metal shelves, waiting for purchase from people who have no money. I haven't been here since I was a kid, but it hasn't changed much. Before I can take a step all the way in, a familiar figure greets me from behind the counter.

"Max..." Calum's face hasn't changed. His brow still looks eternally worried, the small freckles on his nose reflecting those of his twin's as it crinkles with his beaming smile. Waves of mousy brown hair pile like a wafted mess on top of his head, and the buzzing fluorescent lights catch a gleam in his green eyes holding back specks of tears. Unlike his sister, he missed me.

Rushing over, he grabs me in a tight embrace, and I hug him back with just as much regard, relaxing in his hold. I didn't realize I needed it. Maybe I was unsure how I would be greeted by the enemy clan's leader, but I should have known that Cal would want peace; he always has, trying to settle every fight Ace and I had when we were kids. He's shorter than me by only a few inches now, his muscles taut and lean, whereas I'm bulky like a bear.

Pushing me back to study my face with his grin, he says, "Brother, it's good to see you. I wish you'd come earlier, but I'll take now. Come to my office with me." Turning, he heads toward the back of the store. He called me *brother*. Warm childhood memories fill my mind, and I swallow a lump in my throat.

"It's good to see you, man," I manage to say once I can.

"I would ask how you've been, but given everything, I figure it's better not to."

Behind a black curtain is a large open warehouse filled with tall metal shelves. We enter a small cinderblock office with a wall of computer monitors in an alcove off the main floor. Cal sits in a dilapidated desk chair, and I take place on a cushy couch along the wall. Leaning forward, I fill him in a bit on my life.

"Well, after Strauss killed my parents, I started fighting. MMA mainly. Got arrested for deadly assault a couple times until I had to go to prison for twenty-four months. Was working for a small-time mobster in another town, trying to get the funds to get back here."

Cal nods and sighs. "And Arianna?"

"She's always been at boarding school. You know my parents were too worried about her being in danger, about Strauss's men finding her, so they sent her away. After she graduated, she went to a finishing school for a while, but once our parents... She ran away from there to live with me. Worked as an assistant until, well, I had to get her out of there, back to our home." He doesn't need to know about her old boss touching her once, then me putting a bullet in his head when she finally confessed what happened. That was the day we packed up for Gnarled Pine Hollow.

"I'm glad you're home, Max." The long strands of his hair fall across his creased forehead as he looks down at his lap. When he peers at me again, his bright green eyes glimmer. "But you being back here may cause issues. I know it has already. Last night—"

"Last night was Strauss's doing. He's out to end my lineage. You know this." And I know that despite trying to annihilate my parents for their disobedience and secret meetings, he'll pretend to be the perfect consort in front of the people by giving me those licenses. Just to try to get me under his control. It won't work, though.

Quietly, carefully, Cal speaks with narrowed eyes. "How sure are you that it was Strauss who killed your parents?"

A small gasp leaves my mouth. "What do you mean? Who else would it have been? Your father? Donovan?"

Cal shakes his head. "There're other players than our three families vying for his power, Max."

"What are you talking about?"

His expression grows wild, as if he's been sampling the product line he peddles. The irises in his eyes are large, like holes leading to an unknown universe. "Who controls Strauss?"

I scratch my head, then rub a hand over my stubble. Had Cal lost it since I'd been gone? He was always soft. Now he's talking like some conspiracy theorist. "I-I guess I never thought about that."

A sudden change comes over him as he settles back in his seat. Maybe the look on my face let him know how crazy I thought he was, but the change in his demeanor into this King of the West is strange. "What brings you over today? I'm glad you're here, but after last night's action, I would have thought you'd be in hiding?"

"I can't afford to hibernate any longer. I need a meeting with Strauss himself. Not one of his lackies. I need to get my businesses back... And my guns."

Cal's mouth flattens into a line. "I was afraid you were going to say that. You know I don't condone weapons usage. I think if we each stay on our sides, he'll leave us alone."

"Cal, come on! You *know* that's not true! He found my fucking parents, man! He had them killed! People are *dying* out there. They need protection!"

His eyes soften as he responds, "As I said, I'm not convinced Strauss did it. And I think spreading the guns around will only lead to more death."

"Be reasonable. *He's* the one who has them all now. He can pick us off any time he chooses. We won't be able to protect the people from him. We won't be able to *protect our families*."

Cal bends over in front of a mini-fridge and digs out a bottle of water. Holding one up, he offers it to me, and I take it from his grasp. Grabbing one for himself, he cracks it open, gulping a large swig. The action gives me pause to lower my temper.

Gently, he pleads with me. "I want you back here, Max. I do. I want you to get your businesses back and to give jobs to these starving people. They need the work. Your family always had a great thing going with the motor industries. But I can't help you get a meeting to get weapons. I just can't, Max. I'm sorry."

This was exactly what I expected he would say. But I wasn't here to convince Cal to get me a meeting with Strauss. I was here to *ask* Cal for a meeting with Strauss, knowing he would refuse... The rest of the ruse was already set into place just by me being here. Foxes are easy to snare once you set the right trap.

"I understand. Thanks for hearing me out."

"Will you come over for dinner sometime? You and Arianna?"

"Yes, definitely. And we'll have you two, um, *both*, over once our household is up and running."

A corner of his lip twitches into a smirk. "She's not changed much, has she?"

Did I dare tell him his sister's body has definitely changed? That I want to fuck her whenever I was around her? No. I'd kill him if he said that about Ari. "Her kicks feel the same, I can assure you."

The laugh that escapes his chest reminds me of all the times we played tag out on the lawn. "Can you hang out?"

"No, I've got a lot to do."

Cal smiles and nods. "Let me walk you out." Clapping a hand on my back, he leads me to the front of the store. I chug the water, the bottle perspiring in my hand, which I wipe off on my jeans. When it's emptied, he takes it from me. "Don't be a stranger. I'm serious."

"You ever speak with Ace?"

Cal's face falls. "No. He's busy with, well, being Ace now."

I nod. "Surprised he hasn't lost *everything* in some gamble."

"Not yet, anyway." Cal walks backward from where we came from. "See ya, Max."

"See ya."

Inside the car, I gun the engine, heading back toward East Side. Just as I start to wonder how long it will be before my brilliant plan takes hold, a blacked-out Aston Martin Victor pulls up close behind me. There's my girl. A sexy car for a sexy gal.

Livia weaves her front end around the sides of my car as I pretend not to notice. We race along the road, cars honking and flipping us off as she tries to gain on me by pulling into the opposite lane. Of course, her car is more powerful, but she has to swerve around the other drivers. Eventually, we make it onto a deserted side route, and I gun it to ninety miles per hour, the muscle in my car rumbling loudly. She follows close behind, then overtakes me and slides her beauty sideways as I slam on my brakes to avoid a collision.

The firecracker pops out of her car, wearing black jeans so tight they could be painted on. A low-cut tank top hugs her breasts snugly, the nipple bars poking through. Shit kicker boots ride her feet. She sure knows how to make my dick hard.

Climbing out of my seat slowly, I close the door and lean against my window. "Hello, foxy. Nice whip."

Livia doesn't stop and storms straight to me, huge tits bouncing with each step. I really hope she doesn't wallop my legs again. Maybe I should have worn shin guards. Shoving a finger in my face, she yells, "What the fuck, Max? What the fuck are you doing talking to Cal? You don't talk with him. You don't talk to *anyone* in my family, except for me."

Showing off my white veneers, I cross my arms. "You seem upset."

"Go fuck yourself."

"Only if you're there watching me."

She huffs and stands back, speechless, thrusting her hands on her hips. Her lips scrunch up into a cute pucker before she explodes. "Explain yourself!"

Dropping my arms to my sides, I shrug. "I was just asking Cal, you know, the head of the Von Dovish clan, for a meeting with Strauss." God, I almost laugh at the fury my words cause.

Nostrils flaring wide, she steams with rage. "I. Told. You. *I* can get you a meeting with Strauss. My brother wants nothing to do with it."

"You said you changed your mind and didn't want to work with me."

"Well, I just changed it back. I'm allowed." She lowers her hands from her hips. "Only if I'm still given the thirty-three percent I'm owed."

"I want some other things in there, too."

Her golden eyes narrow as she considers me with a toss of her mohawk tail behind her shoulder. "Like what?"

"I want you to write down your contacts for me... And I want to kiss you."

Her jaw drops open. "What? No. *To both.*"

A car passes and honks the entire way, frustrated with us taking up the road. All my mind can think about is that time in the alley when I saved her... Been wanting that fucking kiss ever since.

Opening my palms, I tell her, "That's my requirements. The contacts. And a kiss."

"I will *go with* you *if* I give you the contacts." She eyes me suspiciously, her top lip raised in a snarl before her gaze drops to my mouth. "And absolutely no kiss."

"You let that random fucker at the club kiss you, but you won't let me?"

"You're *special*," she says mockingly.

Before she can react, my hands snag her little waist and tug her into my body so we're both leaning against the hot metal of my car. Closing in toward her face, her breath catches. My lips rest just a hair away from hers. "I can take it if I want."

She turns her head slightly. "No," she whispers. My balls tingle, worried she may try to knee me again, but I take a chance.

Slowly, I lick my bottom lip, wishing it was hers. My tongue almost grazes the pink of her mouth as her body trembles in my arms. She's so delicate when she's like this. "Little fox... Please, let me kiss you." When I speak, some of my saliva mixes into her open mouth.

"No, Max."

Frustrated, I release her until she stumbles back a

step. "It's back to 'Max' now, is it? What happened to 'lion'?"

She chuckles. "I thought you didn't like 'lion'?"

"Maybe I do." Running a hand through my black hair, I will my dick to calm down. "Okay, Livia. If we need the other guys, you go with me. You can have your third." Just as she relaxes, I warn her, "And I'll keep asking for that fucking kiss."

She tamps down her victorious smile. Huh. I've never seen her look so happy. "Okay," she says like she's suddenly a shy girl, dancing on her tiptoes.

Sticking her hand out to shake mine, I grab it, then lace our fingers together and pull her in, so her body is pressed against mine. Nuzzling my mouth over her exposed ear, I say, "But pretty soon... I'm going to stop *asking* for it."

Eight

LIVIA

Shuffling away, I leave his firm body and his intoxicating woody scent. His eyes are so deep, I almost drown. From his resounding voice, my bones vibrate. My pussy feels so empty at this moment, thinking about how thick he could fill me up.

Raising one of his eyebrows, he smirks, knowing he's got me. Max's lips spread wider into a beautiful smile that makes me want to run back into his arms, but I don't. I clear my throat and narrow my eyes.

"I'll set up the meeting. Give me your phone." My palm opens impatiently, waving in the air for him to hand it over.

"No way. Just tell me your number, and I'll text you."

A thick sigh leaves my lungs, and I relent. My phone vibrates in my back pocket with his text. "Got it. I'll let you know the date and time. Just be available."

"Oh, I'm available. You want to go somewhere right now?"

Rolling my eyes, I sashay back to the car, knowing I'm showcasing my ass. "Bye, lion." I can practically *hear* the blood rushing to his cock.

The rage I had earlier dissipates as I spin out in my Victor, heading to the west side. My tires throw up road dust, causing Max to cough as I pass, and through the rearview mirror, I see him jump in his car to head in the other direction.

A third! We could get a third of the weapons! I just need to snag that meeting with Vlad Strauss. If Max can keep his bear temper under control and leave the speeches to me, we could possibly avoid having to use the other mob contacts to get the guns we need.

Nick Jordan is my brother's right-hand man, and he owes me a favor... Well, a lifetime of favors. I only call on his help when it's absolutely needed and now is one of those times.

As I approach our land, my thumb presses the button on the steering wheel to dial him. He picks up on the first ring. "What's good, Livy?"

"Nick. I need you."

There's a pause, and he asks with some restraint, "What do you need me for?"

"Set up a meeting with Strauss. This is for Max Frei-denberg and I to discuss business licenses. I'll take a lackey with me. *Not* Armel, because I don't want Cal to know anything."

Another long pause, and I check to see if the phone is still connected. It is. "Nick?"

"Livy, you're really going to make me do this?"

"Do you *want* me to tell Cal about you fucking our mother when she was alive?"

At least Nick had been in love with her. Had given her everything she desired those years they had their sordid affair. When I was eighteen, I walked up on them in the throes of passion on a workbench in the rose garden. Keeping silent, I asked my mother casually about it months later when I wanted out of an arranged date with some stiff's son.

My father was never faithful to her. After he killed her, he ran off to the South of France with who used to be our third nanny. Cal hadn't heard from him in years and had seemingly given up on trying to locate him. If he did, he wouldn't tell me. I'd be happy to tell Strauss's men right where they could find him if I knew.

"Okay, Livy. I'll do it. I'll send a lackey to accompany you. But Liv, what do you get out of this meeting?"

"A *third* of the weapons from the Freidenberg's business," I say, proud of my negotiation skills.

"You know there's a way we can get a hundred percent..."

"Don't," I warn him, my triumphant mood suddenly spoiled.

"Your parents wanted—"

"I don't give a *fuck* what my father wanted."

"Livy, think about it, at least. Not for you, for the *people*. For those who have nothing out there, left to—"

"Goodbye. Text me about that meeting."

Making it back to my castle, I leave the engine running for the chauffer, then march inside. My body is still buzzing from the busy morning. Tradition here in Gnarled Pine Hollow has never allowed a woman to run things. Max thought he could get by with speaking to Cal about his meeting, but I showed him who the *real* boss of the Von Dovish clan is.

In my room, my clothes are tossed into the corner pile as I don a leotard with leg warmers found in the top drawer of my dresser. Once I head down to the studio, the old ballroom, I turn on Wagner. Pulling out my pointe shoes from the cabinet, I flex them a few times while warming up my feet, then I slip them on and tie them up. Draping over my barre, I begin my stretch routine. A quick warmup of plies, tendus, rond de jambes doesn't last long before I feel the music rising and the urge to move tingles every nerve within me. My turns feel sharp while my body remains lithe as the crescendo hits.

After some time, I enter the *zone* where the rest of the world has ceased existing. My head snaps up to the sound of applause as I lose my footing. Cal leans on the doorframe with a big smile on his face. Shaking my head, I come back to the present from the trance I'd locked myself into.

"I haven't seen you dance in a minute. You still got it."

"I never lost it."

"Lately, you seem busy practicing archery or working on those cars out back. It's just been a while since I've seen you look so happy and relaxed."

Easing myself down to a crossed leg position, I start the process of taking off my shoes and comforting my feet. I'm wondering if he knows about the meeting. Is this why he showed up to watch me?

"I *feel* happy and relaxed."

With his sure steps, he walks to the record player and pulls the needle off, then closes the lid. "Would a certain neighbor have anything to do with this change in demeanor?"

I mean, did Max have something to do with it? Yes, I may get us the weapons we need. "Sort of."

My twin's smooth palms help pull me up to a stand. "Hey, that's great! I like you two spending time together."

Now, he's another man to ruin my mood today. "Cal, it's not like that—"

"I know. I know. But I did tell him I'd invite him over for dinner. Him and Arianna."

"A dinner is fine. You guys are childhood friends. Just don't expect more from me." Swinging the long ribbons around my neck, I carry my shoes upstairs and drop them off before heading into my bathtub for a soak. As I sit on the rounded edge of the clawfoot tub, steam rising up from the bottom, I get a text.

NICK

Tomorrow 10pm.

Just you two, tho. No one else.

Said he's looking forward to it.

Alpha will secure the perimeter, but that's all. U will be on your own.

It's on. After I text Max to let him know, he sends

back a kissing face emoji, and I smile. Oh no... I smiled. Like a fucking teenager in love. This is not good.

Instead of hot, I switch the tap to cool down before dipping my body in the water, trying to focus my mind on anyone but Max. Of course, that doesn't work. Frustrated, I scrub up quickly and get out of the tub.

Once I dress in my robe, I take a seat at my writing desk near the window to scribble up a game plan for the meeting. When I open the drawer to take out a notepad, I see it. My mother's will. Pulling it out, my fingers dance across the worn and faded ink on the yellowed page. She didn't know what she was doing. Married to a man who treated her so poorly, she lost all sense of self, staying with him until he killed her. She didn't make good decisions. I slide the paper back inside and take out a fountain pen and blank notepad. In two hours, I've got responses written down for anything Strauss may throw at us. I'm prepared.

The following day, I glide down our broad marble staircase to get a car for the meeting, but when my toes tap the fourth step, a tall man standing in the entryway, looking fresh as fuck, causes me pause. Max dons a sharp gray tailored suit, and a white dress shirt with no tie. The top two buttons are open, exposing his patterned black tattoos. When he sees me, his deep brown eyes trail longingly up my body, ingesting me with a hungry gaze. An involuntary smile brightens his face, showcasing perfect white teeth as he runs a hand through his thick black hair. He spent years fighting in the ring; his teeth are probably fake, but it doesn't matter. He looks good. And the smirk that jerks up his lips lets me know it.

Butterflies rapidly winging it in my belly make me consider turning around and beckoning him to follow me with just a finger, all the way to my bed. An image of riding his girthy, hard cock, squeezing him with my thighs as he comes inside me, infiltrates my brain until I realize I've been stuck on the step for probably a whole minute.

"*Hot damn*, foxy. You look good," he says, as if he's appreciating me as much as I him. My lips threaten to grin, but I contain it as I continue my descent.

"Cleaned off the road dust and blood, I see." When I get to the bottom of the stairs, he takes a few steps toward me and raises the back of his hand to brush my mohawk off my shoulder. I turn my head to see what he's doing, then step back from him. "Hands to yourself, lion."

Instead of his anger this time, I get another flash of a broad smile. "I think you like me." Before I can argue, he slides his hand into mine and tugs me through the foyer. "Come on. I'm taking you in the Barracuda."

"Max, my cars are faster—"

"Nope. I've done work on mine. If we get into trouble, we hit the highway, and I can beat them on the open road." I acquiesce and go with him out the front door. "Besides," he says as he gets into the driver's side door, "I'm a better driver than you."

Slipping inside, I slam the passenger door. "I'm not fighting with you before we do this. We need to be on the same page."

A wanton grin never leaves his face as he attempts to snare my hand again, but I pull it back. "Okay, I agree."

"Stop trying to touch me!" I huff, and he lets out a boisterous chuckle as he motors toward the end of our lane. My thighs clench together as I take in the interior of the car. The scent of his cologne raises my pulse until I can feel my heart pounding through my back into the leather seat. I run a hand over the smooth dash. "So, you finally got one after dreaming about it all those years."

Max twists his head, as if surprised, while keeping his eyes on the road. "Y-you remember I wanted a Barracuda?"

"Yeah." I roll my eyes. "Some days it's all you would talk about."

His face appears caught in a nostalgic smile. "I've had it for about ten years now. You remember that time I got so mad that you stole my replica matchbox car?"

"Do I remember that one day when you actually fought back? Yes."

"Livia, you scared the shit out of me. I'd had it with you by then." His eyes dart to the side as a corner of his mouth lifts, but there's a sadness in his expression. "That was my favorite toy."

I run my tongue over my teeth, behind my lips. Then, I do something I've never done with anyone. Reaching across the car, my fingers pry his right hand from the steering wheel before resting our hands on the wood paneled center console. His eyes glance to where we are joined and the grief that was in his expression is replaced with happiness once again. As he takes a deep breath in, his gray suit jacket pooches open.

"We could die in there today, you know."

"We could," I respond.

"So, if I pull over to this motel up here off sixty-seven, will you let me fuck you?" His eyebrows jump up and down.

"Max!" Attempting to snatch my hand back from his, he grips tighter. I allow him to lace our fingers together. He's right. We could die. Secretly, I consider his proposal, but it's not on the agenda. We need to focus. "I need you to let me do the talking. Will you?"

With my change of subject, his face clouds with seriousness. "Yes."

"No bear tactics. Strauss is a bull. He won't respond well trying to push him over. I'll handle him."

"How will you handle him, little fox?"

"My foxy ways."

He gives a curt nod and lets silence fill the air for a moment. "I don't want him to touch you."

"I'm not yours, Freidenberg." The muscle in his jaw pops as he clenches his teeth. He lets go of my hand. "But I don't want him to touch me, either." Looking out the side window at the shadows of autumn trees dying in the cold air, I add softly, "Who knows what kind of diseases his dick has."

Silence fills the car until we pull up to the iron gates. A uniformed guard waves us through after opening it. It's been a few years since I've been to these lands.

As we crawl around a bend, the old mansion appears

before us. If Max's manor is Gothic, Strauss's is the dark Romanesque haunted house from children's nightmares. Onyx brick and stone cover every surface. Except for a few narrowly arched windows breaking up the brutal masonry surfaces, there isn't much light coming from the foreboding structure. Even the glass only shows flickering candles burning within each. Turrets jut into the black sky, so high they almost puncture the clouds. I'm sure if we listen closely, we'll hear the screams of his sex slaves from the dungeons. I shiver.

Max stops the car for a moment and peers up through the windshield, shaking his head. "This is exactly the type of place I'd picture him living in." He pulls around to the front and parks. Stepping out, I pull my leather jacket tighter around me. Max walks around the Barracuda and shuffles me to the door with a hand placed protectively on my lower back, his action spreading warmth throughout my limbs. I wish he didn't have such an effect on me.

Two large men in black suits approach us. The wind catches the jacket of one, flipping open to reveal two guns housed in holsters on either side of his belt. They are wearing small clear wires that reach into their ears.

"Stand still," one commands. Max and I halt. The skinnier of the two, if you can even call him that, stands in front of me and the large man in front of Max. Each takes their time patting us down thoroughly. Max is eyeing the man touching my breasts, my thighs, and my ass.

"Alright. That's enough," he says, pulling the guy's hands off my backside.

The man smirks at him, but steps back. The larger of the two holds his arm out to us, showing the way to the front door. We walk up the darkened wood steps carefully while they file behind us.

"They're here," the large man says in his earpiece.

Before one of us can use the bull head doorknocker, it opens, and a beautiful woman wearing a leather collar, girdle, wrist cuffs, and stilettos answers the door. She keeps her eyes cast down at the floor and the sight of her makes my stomach knot. Hopefully, Strauss doesn't keep me here and force me to wear that, to perform who knows what kind of debased activities. Max stammers, but the woman uses her arm to wave us inside. The two stoic security guards wait at the door.

Black damask wallpaper covers the long entry hall. There are double doors every few feet and a dark wood staircase to our left. Lit candles in wall sconces light the low ceiling, which reflects the dancing flames ominously.

The butleress shuts the door behind us, then sways in front as we follow down the plush patterned red carpet. At the end of the hall is a full-size portrait of Vladimir Strauss standing in a regal posture in front of the cemetery located on his grounds. Like he's pompously showcasing his work. We turn left and enter through a set of intricately carved wooden doors.

A two-story ceiling is the first thing I notice about the large space, then the massive stone fireplace along the back wall. Sounds from an eerie piano song fill the room, and I recognize the composer as Mussorgsky. Though I don't see him, I know Vlad has prepared the piece for our arrival. After a few moments, the notes stop. The quietness seems more terrifying than the discordant chords playing before it.

"Ah, so glad you two could make it. Welcome to my humble home." Vladimir Strauss strolls in from a far room where the grand piano sits in the middle of a rounded turret. His bleached white hair is slicked back, emphasizing the granite like features of his face. Lines of numerous tattoos are visible just above the V-neck of his tight black shirt with long sleeves. Leather patches cover his shoulders as well as his signature pants. He claps his hands twice and smiles. "Drinks?"

"No, thank you," Max immediately says, and I touch his hand to remind him not to speak.

"And you, Miss Von Dovish?"

"No."

He seems offended but opens his palm toward the sofa and chairs surrounding the fireplace. "That'll be all, slave." My body cringes as he addresses the woman who showed us in, and she turns to leave the way we came. But Strauss tuts his tongue. "No, I think I'll have you practice tonight. Upstairs with you now. Bring slave three with you." The woman nods, always looking down, and walks to the stairs along the far wall. "Now, shall we? Unless... Mr. Freidenberg would like a taste of my slave for an appetizer?"

Every time he says the word, my insides jostle, and I can tell Max's ire is building as well. Yes, the rest of us in the city are used to illegal trade. The Von Dovishes have dealt in hallucinogens for years. The computer stores make good fronts for us. Freidenbergs always had their weapons. Donovans, their gambling. But dealing people... it makes me sick. Part of me understands Strauss set up this scene to infuriate the bear, put him on tilt. The other part knows he's just a monster.

"Sit, sit. Please, make yourselves comfortable." I don't want to, but we sit. Max and I glance at each other. "It's good to see young lovers back together again after so long."

"We're not lovers," I say.

"Oh? How odd. Well, nonetheless, young *friends* back together then." Vlad smiles at Max, his hollow cheeks becoming bonier as he does so. "So you've not tasted her?"

Yes, he's definitely goading Max. Lion does well, though, and says only, "I'm here for my business licenses. For the car wash, car shop, and motorcycle repair. Just those three will do. I understand there's a price, and I'm willing to pay ten percent, like my ancestors have done."

He did well. I'm impressed.

"Oh. Yes, that makes good sense. I like that arrangement. Fine, fine. Yes, you should have your family businesses back. Now that all your family is dead, I mean." Max gristles, and I put my hand next to his thigh. It doesn't go unnoticed by Vlad. "Her blood is the best thing I've had in my mouth in quite some time." Max turns to look at my face. My eyes dart to his to tell him to maintain his composure.

"The business licenses?" I ask, keeping the subject on track.

Vlad stands. "So eager to talk about paperwork." He sighs dramatically. "How boring. I'm dying just as much as he is, Miss Von Dovish, to get a taste of your cunt." Max grips my thigh protectively. Vlad turns his eyes to him and smirks. "I'm sure it's more potent when she doesn't want it sampled. Wanna see?"

Max stands and places his body somewhat in front of me. "I want to talk about getting those licenses. You said you agree to ten percent. *That* is the reason I'm here."

"Yes, Mr. Freidenberg. I hear you... Let's shake on it, shall we?" Strauss stands in front of the fireplace and holds out his slender hand to Max. The lion stalks toward him carefully and takes his hand. Before they can shake, however, Strauss lowers his arm. "Only... there's just one thing I want before I agree." He turns in a circle, then back to us. "Actually!" He laughs. "Forgive me, there're *two* things I want before I agree."

Max glances at me. "Yes?"

"Yes. I want *her*"—he points at me with a long finger —"to suck my cock."

My mouth falls open at the same time Max almost yells, "No. Not going to happen."

Vlad smiles, as if he's got us. *Fuck.* "Relax, relax. You look tense." He puts a hand on Max's shoulder and squeezes. Max takes a fighting stance, his fists at the ready. "If *she* won't, then you can."

"What?" I ask before I can keep my composure.

Max is frozen, except for his eyes, which narrow.

"If you're not going to suck it, he can. Sadly, it doesn't suck itself." Vlad smiles broadly at first me, then Max. "I mean, if you want those business licenses. I'd *love* to have a Freidenberg on his knees in front of me."

There's a thick silence in the room for at least two minutes. "I'll suck you off," I say eventually.

"No!" Max's face is red.

"Hmm... we seem to have a problem. Okay! I've got it! I have a solution." Vlad wanders over to a large plush red chair, then sits, crossing one ankle over his knee. "I want to see the fox blow the bear."

Max's eyes dart to mine at the same time I look at him. "Okay, I'll do it," I say, watching his face. It softens from fear into concern.

Max walks the two steps to me and threads his fingers through my hair, putting his face in front of mine. "You don't have to do this."

"Yes, I do."

"This should be fun!" Vlad says and claps loudly. He leans forward, placing his elbows on his knees. Max studies my face. "Well? Get started. On your knees, girl. Show a man what a woman's mouth was made for."

Max's eyebrows raise, as if asking a question. I nod slowly. He dips his chin to seek out my lips, but I turn from him. This is a job. I don't have to enjoy it. And I don't want to make it a connection. Just like Duke and Janna. Or anyone else I've slept with. For information. For safety. For some tangible good I couldn't get. That's what this is and nothing more. At least, that's what I keep repeating in my head.

I run a hand down Max's chest and push him back slightly. He's still got that reverent look on his face, but it seems more fearful than anything. His hands make grabbing motions as if he's reaching for me, but knows I'll just push him away. Because I will.

"On your knees, Miss Von Dovish. Kneel in front of the bear."

Strauss momentarily thwarts my attention. I do as he says and hit the floor in front of Max, who bends over me protectively. Almost trying to hide me from the creature sitting in the chair, watching intently. Max takes a finger and puts it under my chin, lifting my face to meet his gaze. "You don't have to do this. I'm serious."

"Yes, she does." Strauss laughs like it was the best joke he's heard in a long time.

I nod at him again, then start to rub his massive cock in his dress pants. Max lets out an involuntary sigh, and his head drops back. He's getting hard already.

"That's a girl. Now take out his cock." I wish I didn't have Strauss's commentary, but I follow it. Max helps me undo his belt and trousers. Pulling down his black boxer briefs, his thick mass flops out at me. It's not fully erect, but it's aroused. And it's a thing of beauty.

When I stick out my tongue and lick the girthy and perfectly shaped tip, Strauss moves forward in his seat and moans. Max's fingers thread through my mohawk ends gently. I swirl my tongue more, getting the head wet, but Strauss grunts and says, "He needs sucked, little girl.

Can't you see that? He needs your mouth. Show him your worth."

I glance up at Max's face and the gentle look has changed into desperate neediness. He holds my jaw and strokes my cheek with his thumb. Parting my lips, I suck the end of his large cock into my mouth and the grip on my hair tightens.

"Yes, good girl," Strauss says.

Letting him move farther down my throat, I work Max's shaft. Taking my hand, I grip the base and twist while using the other to fondle his balls. With my index finger, I gently drag it over his taint, then press up. Max chokes on his spit. "Fuck, little fox," he whispers to me.

My pussy begins to pulsate and dampen, so I move my thighs closer together to get some friction. As slowly as I can, I writhe against the seam of my pants. I'm enjoying Max's cock in my mouth way more than I should. Slurping on his shaft, swirling his head, using my hand in coordination, I'm into this job like it's my calling.

Strauss rises from his staring chair and creeps up behind me. "Here, let me help." He puts his hand over Max's on the back of my head and shoves me down the length of my lion. I gag, tears filling my eyes. Strauss holds me there. Max tries to take a step back, but Strauss commands, "Don't you dare move."

It's difficult to breathe. Strauss makes it more difficult by pinching my nose until I can't get any air. My pulse runs rapidly, and I panic, trying to push Max off my face with a shove on his thighs. As Max pulls back, Strauss releases my nose. I gasp for air around the muscle still in my mouth.

"Again," Strauss commands. Max grips my head from Strauss and pushes. I think he's trying to control things, so Strauss doesn't. I can get a sip of air, but then Strauss pinches my nose. My vision darkens and my head goes fuzzy until the world fades out. Once I'm aware again, I find my body gasping for air around his cock.

"This is what women were *made* for, Livia. You should feel proud to be doing your duty, fulfilling your role. Worshipping a man like this was why you were created." He pushes my head again, and before I pass out, he says, "Know your role. Idolize this dick."

This is how he trains them. His slaves. He repeats this process as I pass out, then come to sipping air. Strauss is telling me that I shouldn't be trying to lead. "Just follow. That's what women are good for. Just an orifice. Let yourself be used. It's your purpose."

My mind slips in and out of consciousness. Like a nightmare, I hear the words even when the world goes black before I'm back to the light again.

Barely breathing, Max pumps wildly in and out of my mouth as if trying to rush and finish. His balls tighten in my hand before I almost fall over. My limbs go loose at my sides. Strauss pinches, then releases my nose, and I breathe enough to taste some cum spurt down my throat. Max's cock vibrates in my mouth as he yells, "Oh fuck!" He holds my neck at an angle that I taste every drop while staring into his deep brown eyes. I hate that I love it. Swallowing all of him down, I use the back of my hand to wipe my chin of the saliva that's dribbled out.

Max stares at me with guilt behind his eyes. I can use that. I can't let him know how drenched my cunt had become. Max grips me under my arms, lifting me to a stand before wiping some wetness from my bottom lip with his thumb.

"Are you okay?" He holds my limp body up with his firm arms.

I nod and swallow, my throat raw and sore. "Yeah."

With a hand on the nape of my neck, he squeezes gently. "Stay with me." His lips breeze across my forehead. "You're okay. I got you."

"Oh, Mr. Freidenberg..." Strauss wanders off to the corner of the room and pours himself a drink before returning to the glowing lights of the fireplace. "She enjoyed that much more than you realize."

Fuck. Strauss is going to blow my cover. Max's head snaps to me, and I look at the ground as if I'm ashamed, as if I'm upset with him. Hopefully, he buys it. I need him to owe me.

Max releases me, checking to make sure I can stand, and stuffs himself back in his trousers. "I did what you asked. Do I get those business licenses?"

"Yes." Strauss takes a sip, the ice clinking in the glass irritatingly. "I enjoyed the show. Good job, young lady." He says it as if he's not just ten years older than us. "She just needs more training, Mr. Freidenberg. I'd be happy to lend a hand, break her in for you."

"How about you lend a hand to shake on those

licenses instead?" Max thrusts his arm out at Strauss, who eyes it.

"Well, now I did say I wanted two things."

My heart stops beating, and Max slowly lowers his arm.

"What is that?"

"I'll give you your business licenses. And, as proof, I'll make the call now." Strauss picks up his phone and hits a button. Eyeing us both, he says to the person on the other end, "Approve Mr. Freidenberg's business licenses. Yes, *all* of them. Yes." He ends the call and smiles. When Strauss smiles, it's terrifying. "You can run your businesses. It's good for the community."

"And is that it?" Neither Max nor I relax.

"There's just... You know I have so many weapons. Well, Livia here knows." He nods his head at me. "It's tough because I have so many more than I know what to do with."

Max's jaw clenches. "Go on."

"I'm sure you would like to restart your family trade."

"Yes, that is the plan."

"Well, I'd be happy to part with fifty percent."

Quickly, I start doing math of how much thirty percent of his fifty percent would be.

"Okay... and what is the catch?"

"Oh, there's no *catch*. I just want something in return."

My multiplication stops as nausea creeps into my belly.

"What do you want?" Max asks quietly.

Strauss retreats a step and turns his back to us. Downing his liquor, he sets the glass on a marble top end table. When he spins around, there's a flash of sadness in his eyes, a squint in his brow, before it's gone just as quickly as it appeared. "Arianna."

Max gristles next to me, his entire body going rigid as if that was the key word needed to poke the bear. Before he can move, though, I say, "It's a deal."

Nine

MAXIMILLIAN

"What the fuck, Livia?" My rage turns on my supposed partner.

"It's a deal, Strauss. He'll do it."

"Like hell I will."

Strauss's face lights up like a kid as he laughs. "I don't want her for *trade*, Freidenberg. I need to produce an heir. It's time I settled down before I reach forty. And what a better one to marry than the beautiful, *young* Freidenberg princess."

"He'll allow it."

"No, I won't." Snapping my head at her, I ask through clenched teeth, "What the fuck are you saying?"

"Can we have a minute?"

Despite keeping my eyes steady on Livia's face, I see Strauss stand and walk into the adjoined conservatory out of my periphery. Once he shuts the doors, the notes of the song he was belting when we stepped in the room haunt the air again. I want to fucking kill him. I could, very easily.

"What. The. Fuck. I am *not* giving up my sister to a monster."

"Hush. Max, please, please listen and trust me. Strauss loves her—"

"Strauss loves nothing. You're crazy." Giving her my back, I face the fireplace, but she latches a hand on my shoulder, and I let her turn me around.

"Listen! Strauss *truly wants* her. I read it on his face. It's our in with him—" I try to interrupt, but she continues. "Stop. It's our leverage, but there is *no way in hell* I will let him touch her. I wouldn't do that to anyone, let alone your sister, Max."

My eyes narrow. She's being clever. I don't know what her aim is, but I don't trust her. The Von Dovishes are snakes, and I would be stupid to trust anyone here. She's talking as if she cares about me, about my family, but she could just be playing me. Holding my hand in the car like she wanted me. After a careful moment, I say, "You sound like you have a plan."

"I do. We need the weapons. He wants Arianna. We'll get what we need and promise his marriage to your sister." An involuntary growl almost erupts from my chest, but she continues. "Shh, stop. We will *promise* it, but she won't be able to marry him."

"Why is that?"

"Because..." She bites her lip, then swallows. "Because Max? She will be already married to someone else."

"What?! No way!" My baby sister married already? I know she's twenty-four, but she's much younger than that emotionally. There's no one I can even consider who would be good enough for her. No one I wouldn't want to kill for touching her.

"*Shh!* He'll hear us arguing. Not that I mind much, so he thinks he's getting what he wants."

"Who is she supposed to marry?"

She has someone in mind. The thought is practically written on her forehead. She pauses for a long while, then tells me, "Ace."

"No, no. No way. Nuh-uh. Nope. Not happening." Ace Donovan? Serial womanizer, gambler, all around asshole? No.

"Would you rather he *take* her?" She points to the door of the conservatory.

She's right. Strauss wasn't *asking* for my sister's hand; he's just going to claim it. He steals women; it's what he does. He may at least want to *marry* Arianna, but he'd torture her all the same. I can't let that happen. Arianna must marry into a family. Ace Donovan would protect her better than Calum Von Dovish would. Maybe I could work something out with Ace, some type of arrangement. He could use a turkey baster, and she could give him an heir without him ever having to touch her.

But it's fucking Ace Donovan. The boy used to eat caterpillars. He owns casinos and strip clubs. And probably fucks his workers.

"No."

Her face falls. "Max, for the good of everyone. You

know that would mean at least some level of senate control... You're not willing to play this game?"

"Not with my sister. No." *And I don't trust you.* But I don't tell her that. She just sucked me off when she really didn't have to. *Fuck*, my cock twitches just thinking about it again.

Livia's shoulders slump. "So, no weapons?"

"We'll try to garner some with your contacts before I go down the route of promising my flesh and blood to Strauss. I'll increase her protection."

"What good will protection be if the man has flamethrowers?"

"We use your contacts," I say, jutting out my chin. I'm not backing down.

She looks at the carpet, disappointed her plan didn't work. I still don't trust her. Does she truly care for us? Unlikely. She's a fox and Von Dovish blood runs through her veins. "Okay, Max. We'll try with my contacts first, but if—"

"If it doesn't work, we'll resort to your plan." Pinching under her chin, I lift her face to mine. "And, hey. I'm sorry about..." I nod my head to her knees. Strauss was trying to suffocate her with my cock, and I don't like that I loved it as much as I did. I'd just rather have used my own hands, though.

"So sorry that you'll try my plan now?"

"No. Not that sorry."

She shrugs. "Thought I'd try one last time. I don't know what kind of trouble we'll get into in the other cities."

My eyes lift as we meet gazes, holding them in some unspoken, serious exchange. "I'd say a lot."

The lilting melody ends and the piano bench scrapes against the floor before the double doors are thrown open. Strauss's solid frame is lit from behind by the candles in the rounded room, casting a long shadow. The blackness crawls across the carpet as he strolls toward us.

"All finished? It got quiet in here. I was thoroughly enjoying the bear fox fight."

"I'm not doing it, Strauss. It's a no," I say with hardness in my voice. He may have a gun, but my weapons are always with me. Instinctively, my fingers curl into fists.

Strauss looks bored. "Oh. I'm sorry to hear you say that." I see it then, what Livia was talking about. It's not boredom; he's sad and trying not to show it. This fucker wants my sister. If I *were* a bear, my haunches would be prickly right now. "If you change your mind..."

"I understand the deal. My sister for your weapons." His light blue eyes dance in the firelight as he raises them to my face. "But Strauss? She's worth more than that. She's worth more than *you*."

He turns into a statue. I believe him to be dead, with his gaunt cheeks, pale skin, and vacant gray eyes, but the despair that radiates off him is palpable. After a small eternity, he breathes, then smiles, flashing his bright white teeth. "Alright then. One last thing, Mr. Freidenberg. I expect your businesses to stay clean. Gnarled Pine Hollow does not condone an underground weapons trade, and if you're rejecting *my* weapons, then I don't see any reason for East Side to carry them. It seems your clan has forgotten those rules in the past, but I have a feeling you'll obey." Despite his eyes remaining flat, his lips curl upwards into a cat-like smile. His face is unholy.

Vlad claps his hands twice, and another woman appears. This one is tall, brunette, beautiful, and wearing an expensive dress. She's not wearing a collar, nor an air of defeat, but there's a thick layer of pearls surrounding her neck.

"Dilan, show my guests to the door, then come back and take care of me."

"Yes, darling."

She lifts a slender arm, and bracelets that look like emeralds sparkle on her wrist. "This way, please."

Livia turns, and I protectively place a hand to her back as she walks in front of me. Once we reach the door, Dilan bids us well, then leaves as we depart. The guards are still on the porch and only give us a cursory glance, as they continue to gossip in another language and puff out cigarette smoke in our direction. My car sits ready for us on the drive, and I open the passenger door for Livia, but before she gets in, I put my hand over hers to stop her.

"We need to talk strategy."

She pauses after looking at our hands and stares up at me. "Okay, Max."

The overwhelming urge to kiss her returns, but I know she'll just shirk me off again. Letting her smooth hand slide out from under mine, I release her and she gets inside. Once I'm behind the wheel, I point us toward the Von Dovish estate.

"I have a contact, but I'll call tomorrow. It may be

hard to get a meeting with him, but it's all I know to start with."

I nod.

"But Max? He'll want something from us. I don't know what."

"As long as it's not Arianna, I'm okay."

"How is she, by the way? I haven't seen her since she was just a tiny child."

"You should come over. Meet her again."

Livia gets quiet and looks out her window. It makes me rage. If I can't kiss her, the burning violence is going to escape. I have to know why before I destroy something. "Why can't I kiss you?"

Her neck twists as she snaps her eyes to mine. "What?"

"You won't let me kiss you." I eye her soberly. "I want to know why."

She opens her mouth to reply, then shakes her head, rethinking things as she looks out the window again.

With my eyes back on the road, I mumble, "I'll take it sometime."

She doesn't respond, so we ride in silence.

When I reach the Von Dovish gatehouse, her man opens it with a smile and a wave. As I approach her front door, I let my back tires drift on the small stones, throwing up dust. It clouds her side of the car. Livia whips her face to me and scrunches her brow, letting a disgusted sneer tug at her upper lip. "Ugh!"

She gets out, and before she can slam the door, I yell, "Call me!" Her shoulders rise to her ears for a moment, then drop as she spins and runs inside. I chuckle to myself.

I don't hear from her for a few days.

Derichs is feeling well enough to start his own physical therapy, utilizing my gym I've set up in the old dungeons beneath the house. It's makeshift and doesn't have all the equipment I want just yet, but it will do for now.

The workers have been less restless since my meeting with Strauss. Most have moved from the manor to fixing up the old car wash, motorcycle shop, and body shops on the east side of Gnarled Pines. No one has hinted that there's no money. Only Markus and I are very aware of that fact. I need those guns.

"Hit me."

"I'm not hitting you," I say, circling Derichs. "I'll tap."

"Fuck you, hit me. I can take it."

I punch his bad shoulder lightly, and he groans, taking a step back, doubling over at the waist.

"You told me to hit you."

He laughs. "I did. *Fuck*. Okay, maybe I'm not ready."

"You will be. Here." I grab a paper cup of water from the cooler in the corner and hand it to him. He wipes his face with a towel and sits on the rickety wooden bench, his normally curly brown hair flattened with sweat.

"I just need some cardio, I think."

"Mr. Freidenberg? There's a lady here to see you." Quieter, the butler adds, "A Miss Von Dovish, sir."

I smile. So maybe she did come through. Still didn't call, though.

"Send her down."

Derichs chuckles under his breath.

"What?"

"You. You've got it bad for this bitch. I don't blame you. She's definitely... Well, she's not hard on the eyes." He finishes his cup of water, and I watch the stairs to see if she's coming down. "But Max?" He waits until my eyes turn to meet his cocked eyebrow. "She's a Von Dovish, a sly fox. Just keep that in mind."

I nod. I know. I don't trust her. I can't. I just want to get inside her. To kiss her, fuck her until she's addicted. Until she's such a fiend for my dick, she'll do anything I tell her. Until she submits. My cock twitches at the thought.

And the stupid part of my brain wants her for more. But that's the part I try not to pay any attention to.

Her footsteps resound on the stone steps. As she enters, my dick thickens. There she is again, showcasing her perfect ass in tight leggings. Our eyes meet, and I stop breathing for a moment, but notice her chest doesn't move, either.

"Hey," she says.

"Hey." Derichs starts to stand, but I stop him. "No, you relax. Drink your water."

"How's the invalid?"

143

"I'm doing okay. Thanks to your healer." He smiles shyly. "And you. Thanks to you, too."

"Of course." She nods, turning her face back to mine. "Um, I have the meeting info." She darts her eyes to Derichs.

"Yeah? Tell me." I want my tank to know what's going on.

"Friday. In Appleton City. He obviously wants us to come alone. Just you and me."

"And *he* is?"

"Lavinio Merli. They call him '*The Ear.*' I think he likes to take them as souvenirs."

"Well, that's promising." I inhale deeply, not liking the sound of this at all. "Okay. Just you and me. My man's not in top shape yet anyway. What do you think The Ear wants in return?"

"I don't know. But I know he likes handguns. And supposedly has a lot."

"Would we be running them for *him* or for ourselves?"

"I guess that's what the meeting will determine." She looks around the room. "You sparring?"

"Yeah. You wanna have a go?"

A corner of her thick lips lift, and her cheeks flush. It's probably the closest to a genuine smile that I've seen from her. "You think you can take me?"

I snort. "Foxy, I've been doing this for a long time. Went to prison for it, too."

"I know."

"You know?"

"I saw you fight."

My mouth hangs open. "You *saw* me?"

"Let's go, lion."

"No wait. I want to hear more about you watching me fight."

"Are you going to spar or talk?"

"Both." I go to grab her, but she shirks and darts to the side. That has her lips curling up into a grin. There's a sparkle in her eyes, and I know my expression matches hers. "So, tell me, little fox. When did you see me?"

I squat into my stance, then go for her wrist, but she slides away again and giggles.

"Oh, a few years back."

"Were you in the audience?" We circle each other, waiting for the other to make a move. She slips between my legs and wraps an ankle between her thighs to flip me down on the mat. I catch myself, gripping her waist as I do, then roll us until she's in guard.

Panting, she says, "Maybe." Her black mohawk hangs over a shoulder.

"And did you like what you saw?" I buck my hips into her with my rigid cock.

She narrows her eyes and smirks, then grinds *hard* against me. *Fuck.* I want to rip off her leggings. Peeling my fingers from her waist, she pins my arms above my head. Her lips are so close to mine, the warmth of her lavender-scented breaths hit my mouth.

"Maybe," she whispers. We're frozen there for a moment until the tiny muscles in her fingers begin to relax, but I can't let her go. With my superior training, I flip her hands around until they are held in mine. Gripping her middle with my thighs, I flip us until I'm on top. Holding her arms in one hand, I use the other to feel her neck, letting her know she's done. She should tap out. She squirms a little, which only makes my erection throb with anticipation.

Leaning closer, I almost let my lips nibble on hers. Prepared to tell her I warned her that I was going to take it, she strains her neck up and tries to slide out from under me, but she doesn't have the strength. She's overpowered completely. Just like I want her.

"Please," she whispers, the air of her words coating my skin, causing me to become desperate for her.

"Please, what?" I ask.

"Please, don't, Max." Her eyes are suddenly watery. Like the fox may cry.

I hesitate. Beneath me is everything my blood is telling me to take. I haven't felt this way since that time in the alley. It's at my mercy. I could steal it. But then I'd be no better than Strauss.

Sitting back on my haunches, I let her sit up. I offer her a hand and pull her to a stand as I do.

"That was the worst porn I've ever seen," Derichs says from the bench. I had forgotten he was there, and Livia must have because she jumps at the intrusion. "Didn't even get a money shot." He laughs when I turn to look at him with ire. Livia's cheeks flame maroon, and my dick grows to full capacity.

I clear my throat, reaching down without any

decency to tuck my erection into the waistband of my sweats. "So, Friday?"

"Well, Appleton City is hours away, so I thought..." Her eyes move quickly to Derichs's and back. "I thought we should go on Thursday. Spend the night and scope out the place."

"Very smart. I agree."

I *feel* Derichs smile.

"Okay, well. Um. See ya." Livia starts toward the alcove entrance, but I stop her.

"Wait, Livia." Walking to my sweatshirt lying on the ground next to the water cooler, I dig out my Glock. "Here. Do you know how to use this?"

One sarcastic chuckle erupts from her mouth. "Do *I* know how to shoot? Yes, Max. Despite not being able to get hold of many guns, I *do* know how to use it."

"Effectively?"

Her nostrils flare. "Yes. Should I demonstrate now?"

"Ha, no. But here, take mine. I'll use a different one."

She takes the firearm but has nowhere to put it other than her hand. She points it at the ground. Giving me a nod, she starts up the stairs.

"Oh. And, little fox? I'm driving!"

"No, you're not!" She sprints up the rest of the stairs before I can argue with her, and I laugh, like full on belly laugh.

When I turn around, Derichs has his eyebrows raised. "What?"

"Man, you're in so much fucking trouble."

Ten

LIVIA

Thursday arrives. Each day that led up to it, I awoke with panic, but today, I didn't think my heart could race any faster. Despite a shower, my skin feels sticky with sweat again. As sneakily as my fingers could type an encoded message, I told Echoes about our meeting so she could help me out with the logistics. No one from my team would be coming with me, and it made me leery to know I'd be alone with a bear. But I refrained from letting Alpha know.

My fingers brush over the rough carbon fiber of the Glock in my waistband holster. Touching it lightly for the hundredth time since I got dressed quiets some of the panic building in my throat. Out of habit, I reach in my front pocket and stroke my lucky charm three times and breathe a count in a worshipful whisper.

Setting my overnight bag on the checkered marble floor in the grand foyer, I make my way to the kitchen for lunch. Our chef has prepared vegan egg salad sandwiches and placed them on a tray in the refrigerator. Grabbing one, I take a big bite, but before I can even taste it, there's a commotion clamoring from the front of the house. And, once again, there goes my pulse rising as high as a skyscraper.

Giles dashes from the servant's hall into the kitchen, then from the dining room through the foyer, and out the front door with me following like a Chihuahua at his heels. A black Plymouth Barracuda sits at the bottom of the steps, exhaust smoking out of the back pipes. Max is laying on the horn, peeping his smiling face beneath the frame of the passenger window. My jaw falls open in outrage. I slam the door closed, almost losing a piece of lettuce. *Fucker.*

Back inside, I snatch my overnight bag and scurry out to the car. Giles is politely tapping on the driver's window and requesting "Mr. Freidenberg" to "refrain" from honking, but Max's mouth is open in a wild guffaw as he ignores the old man. Near the trunk, I use a fist to bang on the metal. It unlatches for me, and I toss my bag in the wide space along with two other black bags. Who knew Max would pack so much?

Walking around to the front of the car, I notice the back seat stuffed with pillows and a blanket covering a puffy figure. When I open the door, Derichs is lying in the back bench seat, looking cozy but squished.

"Hey, foxy!" Max grins, letting off the horn. Derichs nods at me with a big smile. Despite there being a second bear inside, my nerves seem to squelch with the tank's easy nature. Also, having a buffer between me and

Max is probably a great idea for reasons I don't even want to think about. But, if I had known he was coming, I would have brought someone from my side to keep things even.

Before I get in, I lean with my arm hanging on the open door. "Hey. I thought we said no one was coming with us."

"Derichs is our backup. He won't attend the meeting. Jump in."

Sliding into the comfortable passenger seat, I slip on the seatbelt. As I turn to ask Derichs a question, his face pops between the seats, still holding that excited grin. "Are you sure you don't want to sit up here? It looks cramped back there."

"No, I'm good. Max insists on treating me like an invalid, so I'm lounging back here."

"Road trip!" Max's eyebrows wave up and down at me before he guns off down the cobbled lane. The thrust of the engine throws me back into the seat, and I grip the door handle and hang on. Spotting my reaction, Max's smirk transforms into a wide smile.

Once on the road, I take another bite of my sandwich. Derichs leans forward between the seats and snakes his head around to stare at it with envy. "Did you bring us one?"

Not even bothering to chew, I answer, "No."

"Oh." He punches Max in the arm. "Told you we should have brought food."

"We'll stop halfway. Six hours total, right?" Max asks me.

"Yeah, about six hours," I say after swallowing the last of my unfulfilling lunch.

Derichs settles back underneath his puffy blanket as Max's large hands grip the steering wheel, staring out onto the interstate.

"My spies tell me this guy has a grudge with every family in Appleton City. Says he has the goods, but no heir to give it to. Doesn't want his enemies to end up with any of it," he says, gliding his chocolate brown eyes across the cabin to crawl up my body to my face. Even the hint of his gaze heats my insides. I hate it.

"Hmm, that would definitely work in our favor... I doubt a man with the title *The Ear* would just give us something for free, though. Even if he wants rid of it." The fact we don't know what he wants is eroding the lining of my stomach, along with the fake eggs in that sandwich. Money would be easy. But these men usually have enough of that.

"Yeah. I don't have much to offer him, other than taking the guns off his hands." Max passes a few cars by pushing the gas to the floor. The rumble of the engine makes my thighs tingle, causing me to shift in my seat. Max's eyes dart to my lap for a moment. "Aren't you glad I drove?"

A corner of my lips jumps into a smirk. "Well, I do have an SUV. Your tank would have been more comfortable. We could have made him a large bed in the back."

Muffled, Derichs's voice rings through the interior of the car. "Hey! Max, you didn't tell me that! It's overcrowded back here."

Max narrows his eyes at him in the rearview. "Go back to sleep."

Derichs shrugs and turns on his side to get back into his napping position.

A large palm slides onto my thigh as Max grips my two folded hands in his large one. We ride in silence for a few moments, and I think he's going to turn the radio back on, but he says in a low voice, "If shit goes down, you get out."

My mouth opens, scrambling to find an argument against him. I can take care of myself. I know these men better than him, since he's been out of the game. Before I can use my voice, he asks, "Do you hear me, Livia?" He squeezes my hands, the ridges of his dry palms scratching my skin. My heart flutters.

Bobbing my head in a small nod, I respond, "Yeah, I hear you." My tongue finds its way to my cheek as I refrain from snipping.

"I want you out of there if anything goes wrong. I mean it." The commanding nature of his voice makes my skin tingle all over. He's protective. Always has been. And I'll let him protect me.

For now.

Turning my face to look out the side window, we continue a quiet ride for quite some time until Max turns on the radio again, then slips his hand back under mine. It's warm and cozy. His palms are rough from years of fighting, and I try to focus on that sensation. If I let myself think about surviving without Max... I wouldn't like it. Now that he's back in Gnarled Pine Hollow, things are complicated. If he left, if he were *killed*, I'm not sure I could live with the guilt. That's what it is—guilt. I'd have to look at poor Arianna and tell her that her brother died. That would be horrible.

It's nothing more. Nothing I want to entertain anyway.

Breaking my hands free of his hold, I slide one into my jeans pocket to rub a finger over the little metal object quickly three times and murmur, "One, two, three."

"What's that?" Max lowers the volume of the radio with an accusatory look at his empty palm.

"Oh, nothing."

Derichs's cute face pops in between the seats again, and he yawns before stretching as much as his large body will allow in such a tiny space. "Is it time to stop for food yet?"

As if it weighs a hundred pounds, Max pulls his arm back from my lap and places it on the steering wheel. "Yeah, man, we'll pull over up here. I gotta fill up, too."

In a few miles, he takes the exit, but only tall grass fields greet us on either side of the ramp. Traveling a few miles off the highway, he finds an unnamed gas station with a gray cedar general store next door.

"Ugh, do they even have anything edible in there?" Derichs watches as we pull up to one of only two rusted gas pumps.

"Beggars can't be choosers. We're running on empty."

Clamoring out of the car, my legs ache, needing to be stretched as Derichs stumbles out and gains his balance before jogging lightly toward the store. I follow to look for a restroom. There're two on the outside of the building. When I go to the women's room, it's locked with a sign that says to ask for the key from the cashier. Once the old man behind the counter hands me the oversized plastic keychain, I eye it suspiciously. It's grimy, the yellow covered in dark brown stains. I'll wash my hands twice.

Before heading back out, my eye catches Derichs struggling with a shopping basket, attempting to hold it with one arm awkwardly. With a little sigh, I sidle up to him and grab the basket out of his arm. He lets me, with a small smile of appreciation. Helping him out, we venture down each aisle, and I load it up with things he points out.

"And Twinkies."

Tossing the package in, I ask, "Do you have a girl-friend, Derichs?"

"Yeah, why?" Bending toward the Oreos, he picks up a bag and throws it in. When he stands, some of his brown curls have fallen back across his forehead, which he pushes back with his good arm.

"Does she know you eat shit like this?" I ask, waving a palm at the junk in my arms.

With a devilish smirk, he raises his dark brown eyebrows. "Only when she's not around."

I shrug and place his basket on the checkout counter, then head to the restrooms. Once in the bathroom stall, a quick movement catches in my periphery before I squat on the toilet. There's a hole in the wall opening to the men's room on the other side. The light coming through is blocked, as if someone just covered it. I hear a zipper being lowered and some shuffling before a girthy, long, and perfect cock comes through the hole.

Max. I spent enough time getting to know his dick during Strauss's meeting that I'd know it anywhere. He must wiggle his hips because it jumps up and down a little, as if enticing me to touch it. The smirk on my face drops when I bite my lip, my pulse pounding heavy in my chest, then down lower. He must think I won't take him up on the offer, but staring at it makes me hungry and definitely wet between my thighs. Maybe Vlad's conditioning worked on me.

With the anonymity of the wall between us, I could get off on it and never have to mention it again. It would be like it wasn't even Max. My clit pulses, thinking about him offering his cock to me as a personal dildo. At least it's probably warm and flush with life instead of the cold, hard plastic thing sitting in my bag.

I don't know what Max has stuck it into, but I'd imagine his cock has been on several world tours. He's not wearing a condom. It jerks at me again, like the anticipation and my hesitation is only making it more aroused, a tiny dribble of liquid escaping the tip. My chest rises rapidly as my breathing escalates.

Smooth, straight, rounded tip... Thick.

It's just a dick. A toy...

I walk over to the wall and bend my head over to gather the oozing tip with a curl of my tongue.

"Oh, fuck!" A muffled yell rings through the tiles on the wall.

When I stand back up, a string of moisture leaves my

mouth and snaps off when I roll my lips together. Undoing my jeans, I lower them to my mid thighs, along with my black thong. Backing up, I rub my hole just on the tip of his dick to dampen it. Max exhales a deep groan of satisfaction, the sound causing my inner muscles to flutter with anticipation. Instead of putting it inside me, I straddle him, letting his hot skin nestle between my pussy lips. I'm so very wet and he feels amazing between my legs.

Crossing one leg over the other, I make a tight seal around his dick. Undulating my hips, the tip of his long cock claps the diamond of my clit ring when I push my ass back. The sensation makes my entire core tingle, but I force down my own moans of approval. Like he's my personal dildo pole, I work him back and forth.

"Fuck! Goddamn!" Max tries to help by pushing himself through the hole more whenever I bring my ass back. Tensing my thighs, though, I halt his movements and control my own pleasure. "That's it, baby. Use it. Use me." The deepness of his voice makes me feel a bit hollow. Like I want those vibrations close to my ear, his hands on my body like they were at the Crimson Angel.

But I use him. Riding it like a horse, I hump his thickness, dousing the length with my arousal. I'm panting like a dog, and his equally rapid breaths echo off the mint green tiles between us. Reaching across the stall, I lean forward and press my hands against the opposite side so I can writhe harder.

Just as I get my rhythm down, Max pulls back from the hole while I'm on a backstroke. He then tries to jam inside me, but I jolt forward before he can. His low, mischievous chuckle filters through the tiny gap, and I narrow my eyes at his play, despite him not being able to see me.

Resuming my position, I strangle his cock with my legs even tighter. But now, he tries to dip his tip in my opening every time I push back. The fear that he may enter me at any moment adds a new level of excitement. Part of me wants him to succeed, but the other knows it would only lead to trouble. A war of frenzied passion and fury erupts in my mind as much as the one firing off between my folds.

On one backstroke, I slow the pace down to allow the head of his dick to almost push inside me, toying with the possibility of connecting with him fully. His breath catches. I wiggle my hips with it just resting at the entrance... Right there. He doesn't force himself inside, only holds himself steady before I move forward and resume writhing on his muscle.

As if he can't hold his breath any longer, he forces out a loud, "Fuck! Foxy! You're gonna make me come." His hips thrust faster between my thighs, and my stomach swoops. He must have watched me come into the bathroom to know it was me. Hopefully, he won't bring this up later and embarrass me. I was enjoying the anonymity, but some part deep within me is enjoying this moment knowing it's him, too. "Let me come inside you, please. Please, foxy. Let me come inside you." The desperation of his pleas and rapid grunts makes me crazy, my orgasm rising just as fast as his. Max, my lion, wants to come inside me... Just the possibility that he would has me losing it.

One flick of the tip of his head against my ring and I let my reservations go, coming all over his cock. Unable to refrain myself any longer, I arch my back against the wall between us and scream, the muscles of my throat clenching as much as my inner muscles. As the pulses within me dissipate, my legs go numb. I feel like collapsing, but his cock works itself rapidly in the cradle of my pussy lips until he lets out a loud grunt of release. He throbs between my folds, spurts of white cum leaping in ropes out of the tip of his cock and spewing down my thighs.

Neither of us moves. We catch our breaths in silence, minus the heaving air moving through our lungs separated by that tiled wall. I dismount and clean myself up with bath tissue, then use the toilet once I see the light shine through the hole again. Taking my time, I wash up (twice) before returning the key and grabbing some food and water. Anxiety surges through my chest, fearing Max may make a crude joke about what just happened in front of his tank. Ready to snap with embarrassment, I saunter back to the loaded car, wiping the rest of my damp palms on my black jeans.

When I get inside, Derichs is happily munching away on a bag of Cheetos Puffs in the back seat, an open bag of Oreos on his lap. He nods at me in acknowledgement, orange dust coating his lips. Max stares straight out the front windshield, his face as solid as stone. "You ready to go?"

"Yes." It seems like he isn't going to say anything, and I find some comfort in ignoring it myself. Relief floods my frazzled nerves, glad Derichs came to play an unknowing chaperone. Otherwise, I may make some stupid decisions. Like continuing what we started in the gas station bathroom tonight at the hotel. That can't happen.

Eventually, I fall asleep to the radio. When I feel the car slowing to a stop, I open my eyes to the busy lights of Appleton City. It's a shitty town, but a hell of a lot bigger than Gnarled Pine Hollow. The mafia here runs as deep as the Apple River through it, so it's no surprise Nick's contact is here.

Max drives us straight downtown and pulls into a shitty motel that makes the Bates's place look like a five-star resort. Glancing up into the smoky black sky, I think part of the roof has caved in, but it's hard to tell in the dark. The neon sign flashes randomly, a few of the letters not bothering to light up. People puff on cigarettes in groups outside along the outer corridors. Oh. One man just fell over from intoxication.

"I think there's a Waldorf downtown, Max," I say.

He shrugs a strapping shoulder under his tight black T-shirt. "Figured we should stay where no one can find us."

Pursing my lips with disgust, I scan the building again, nausea rolling in my stomach at what may lie in one of the bedrooms. Derichs leans forward. "Nicest place I've stayed in a while, if you don't count the manor."

It dawns on me... Max isn't doing this to be sneaky.

He doesn't have money; his legacy is focused on reconstruction. The Freidenberg income has been dried up for years since they've been gone.

I've never once had to think about money. My brow furrows as I consider if he feels too ashamed to tell me he can't afford a decent place. How am I supposed to pay for us if he's too proud to take it from me?

"Well, I do happen to know a manager at that location on Main Street, if you want me to use my contact to get us a couple of rooms." My eyes scan the side of Max's face as he pulls up to the front office. He still won't look at me as his jaw muscles tense. My contact? That's my credit card, but he doesn't need to know that.

"Do they have room service?" Derichs asks like a kid expecting to go to Disney World.

"Yep! And a bar and restaurant, too." Scrambling for more ways to upsell my idea, I add, "And no bedbugs."

Max holds his bottom lip under his front teeth and looks at his lap. Collapsing through his frame, he relents. "Okay, foxy. Let's try your contact."

The tension in my tight neck muscles eases as I smile broadly. "Okay."

"Yes!" Derichs sits back in his seat as we head toward the city's skyline.

When my lips relax, I realize my face was in a smile. Like a genuine one. Who knew the relief of not having to stay with roaches would make me grin so much? A creeping thought in the back of my mind tells me it's more than that, but I shove that down.

Once we approach the front of the hotel, a valet steps

out from behind the glass doors to help. Max hesitates before getting out, and I place a hand on his tattooed arm. "Let them. I got us; it's fine." Pushing his chin forward, he nods, then hurries out of the car. Maybe he's embarrassed. Or maybe he doesn't want anyone to touch his car. Perhaps he doesn't trust anyone to help. I can understand that.

Folding my seat forward, I stand aside so Derichs can squeeze his tall body out of the back. Max snatches all our bags, ignoring the bellhop with a brusque shift of his shoulders, his eyes reaching over the kid's head. At least he allowed us to stay here.

At the front desk, I get two junior suites while Max paces with the bags hanging from his shoulders behind me, his black boots scuffing the shiny tiles. Derichs looks around like his head is a Ferris wheel. Once we're checked in, we enter the gleaming elevator.

"I'm gonna order room service." Derichs buzzes with excitement. "Do you think they deliver alcohol?"

A small chuckle escapes my mouth as I hit the button for our floor. "I'm sure they do. Get what you want. My contact is covering it all." Shit. I could buy the hotel with cash tonight just to see his satisfied grin as he leans against the back wall of the metal cage and crosses his arms and legs. Next to a very grumpy looking Max.

I like Derichs. If he wants a buffet of overpriced food brought to his hotel room, I am happy to pay for it. Being from East Side, or, hell, Gnarled Pine Hollow in general, he's probably never been in a place like this, and I want to treat him. It's not often our citizens get to make it out of the hellhole.

Max stoically stands with the bags over his shoulders, watching the numbers on the lighted panel escalate. Once we reach our floor, we find our adjoined suites. Max unlocks and enters his door without a glance at me. Derichs meets my eyes with his serious rich brown ones, then shrugs and walks in behind him. Part of me had been worried Max would try to put up a fight about staying in my room, so I let my shoulders hang before going into the room next door to the boys. It's not disappointment I'm feeling.

It's not.

Opening my door, I take two grands jetés and flop onto the king bed, then sit up to take off my sweaty boots and socks. Stretching out over the cozy comforter, my body relaxes. Maybe I'll also order room service and get some wine.

A tapping sound through the connector door interrupts my peace. Easing off the bed, I glide over to it and slide open the lock. Max's beefy shoulder leans against the door frame as his fingers dangle my bag in front of him, swinging enticingly. "Mind if I come in?" With his other hand, he jiggles a little bottle of whiskey at me, as if that's enough to seduce me.

Grabbing my bag, I throw it onto the bed. "You stay over there, mister. I'm not catching cubs from you tonight."

Max huffs a laugh and unscrews the bottle, then downs it in one pull. He tosses it into the small trash can near the dresser, then curls a hand above the door frame as if he can't go past the line to my room. His lips glisten from his drink. While scouring me with his espresso eyes, his tongue escapes his mouth to slowly lick them clean. "What do you mean, foxy?"

"You know what I mean."

His face falls, his brow scrunching with sudden seriousness. Derichs is loudly ordering room service in the other room. Max peeks at him for a moment, then turns back to me and lowers his voice. "You mean... you're not on birth control?" Instead of horror or fear there, he seems like he's found a thrilling challenge, like my womb is the location of his next cage match. A sparkle hits the whites of his eyes while the corners of his lips dance upward.

"What? That's—that's none of your business!" I snap my fingers at him as he crosses the threshold. "Get back to your corner, lion."

He ignores me. Three long strides and he's on me, snatching me around the waist with a taut arm and holding me firm against him with a flex of his generous bicep. My clit pulses as he squeezes the air from my lungs with his tight embrace. His breath reeks of weak malt rye, but his body smells of sweat and fortitude. "Is that why you wouldn't let me put it in you today?"

Looking into his eyes, I melt like butter. Any thoughts I had flatline. My lips tingle as he exhales so close to my skin, I have to suppress a shiver. Trying to muster some sort of coherence, I ring out, "I have no idea what you're talking about."

Like the dark villain of a horror movie, a smirk rides up his face, the thick black stubble gleaming in the lamplight of the room. His bottom lip is bigger than his top, which has a firm Cupid's bow. A wild mess of hair tops his head from today's long journey. Once he's ten years older, there'll probably be a permanent crease between his eyebrows from the amount of furrowing.

"Oh? You didn't just hump my cock like a rabid coyote in the women's bathroom?"

I shake my head slightly, the only thing I can control of my body at this moment. Involuntarily, I'm sweating, and my pussy is dying to do more than just hump it. His deep voice makes my belly vibrate with each word. My gaze catches on the slow bob of his Adam's apple.

"It's cool if you're not on birth control. This lion needs a cub before I die." Lowering his face beside my ear, his voice drops another octave. "If you're up for being my lioness." Max's waist thrusts into my belly, and his hardness rubs through his jeans. Placing his lips at the juncture of my neck and shoulder, I feel the muscles pull into a wide grin as he toys with me. I shove hard against his chest and slide from his hold.

"What do you want, Von Dovish?" Derichs calls from the other room, shaking my daze of arousal.

"Uh... rare steak and potato. With a bottle of red. Cabernet. Best one they got." Dropping to a murmur across the rooms, Derichs continues his order.

"You should have told me. I got a rare steak right here, extra juicy." Max grabs his crotch, jerking twice, and I roll my eyes, though the vision of him playing with himself entices me more than it should.

Placing my hands on my hips, I tilt my head up. "I'm eating my dinner. Drinking my wine. Enjoying a bath—" His eyebrows raise. "Alone. And then going to bed early. *Also,* alone."

"It's on its way, Miss Von Dovish!" Derichs yells.

I squeeze past Max, who has his mouth open, obviously still trying to come up with some witty reason to stay in my room. "Thanks, Derichs. Call me Livia, please."

Derichs already has some mini-fridge items spread across his double bed. "Okay! Thanks, Livia. I'm gonna call my girl and tell her about this place."

My heart aches, saddened that he and others like him haven't experienced something as mundane as room service. Now that I think about it, it's not just West Side that's been affected by everything. It never occurred to me, but East Side, Freidenberg territory, is the most derelict from years of neglect.

The people who either survived the Day of the Raging Bull or ones who moved into the territory have been destitute ever since. And not poor like Jim in front of the computer store. Jim has his own place. He begs because he receives a lot from panhandling all day. More money than a job would pay. He has food and friends. The people on the east side, people like Adal Derichs, they have nothing. Their homes are made from the remains of fallen structures and technology is primitive. People grow their own food on small plots of grass that have sprouted between the cement, and I've seen the little makeshift stores people throw up to sell their home-made wares to each other. It's like a different world in that part of town.

Before he can call his "girl," I stop him. "Derichs. Did you also order dessert?"

His jaw drops, but then he grins widely. "No, but I can. What do you want?"

"Tell them to send one of everything."

"Really? Sure! Fuck, wait till Hannah hears about this." Snatching the phone, he calls room service again, punching the buttons with zest.

Max's hard body presses into my back. Leaning over, his stubble caresses the skin exposed by the neck of my top above my collarbone, rippling fire through my veins with each tiny scratch. In a murmur, he says, "You didn't have to do that. You didn't have to do any of this. 'Cause I know you did. Not some *contact*."

Shoving a shoulder into his chest, I turn to face him. "I don't know what you're talking about. My friend—"

Raising a long finger, he strokes the end of my nose. "Please, little fox. Quit being clever." I press my lips together. He found me out. "Thank you, but *why*?"

Shirking a brow at him, I ask, "Huh?"

"Why are you doing this?" His lids narrow at me suspiciously.

Confidently, I tell him, "For the guns."

"And that's it?" he asks, as if expecting more from me.

"Yep. I wanna help my clan. Same as you." The people of West Side need the weapons just like those in the East. My ears drift to hear Derichs excitedly talking with his girlfriend about all the things he's witnessed today, and there's some small desire that plants its seed deep within me to help those in Freidenberg territory, too. I mean, they have nothing, so it wouldn't be terrible for them to eat. But Max waits, as if he expects me to bow to him as King Consort of the East Side and agree to sacrifice my blood kin for his people. Unlikely.

Thrusting his wide jaw forward, he nods at me once, the line between his brows deeply embedded into his skin. Brushing past me with a shove, his voice is firm when he says, "Go on. Go back to your room. I'll tell them to drop off your food over there. Goodnight."

Practically forcing me into my side, he closes the adjoining door. Then, throws the lock, the metal screeching into the silent room. I scoff with irritation and do the same.

Eleven

LIVIA

The next morning, I sleep in as long as possible. Every time I roll over in the night, I know I'm going to be battling a hangover as soon as I become aware. My raging headache argues with me when I attempt to open my eyes. Okay, so I overdid it.

After my lonely dinner, considering knocking on Max's door the entire time, I plunged into a hot bath and a full bottle of red. I may have dabbled with my vibrator a few times before falling asleep. All the while feeling terribly ashamed about replaying the day's glory hole experience every time I orgasmed.

Had I wanted to go beg the lion to come keep me company? No. Absolutely not. Nope. Ugh... yes. It was only so long I could lie to myself about fantasizing about the enemy.

My mind wandered to the last time he made me feel safe and cared for, in that alleyway south of West Tech. Even at fourteen, I knew kissing him would only lead to heartbreak, despite my overwhelming desire for it. Every nerve ending had screamed at me to grab his jacket and kiss him; it would have been my first, but possibly my last, if Strauss and his men knew we were fraternizing. And even if I were killed for it by the consort, if Franklin found out, he would have murdered Max himself.

Still... part of me didn't care.

I'm sure the concierge would send up some aspirin and water to help wipe away some of the throbbing and shame. Maybe Derichs would get me some from the hotel store if I asked politely. Max would probably just make the pain worse.

Sure enough, loud pounds vibrate the adjoining door before I can get vertical.

"Go away!" I yell, but the incessant knocking continues. He's so annoying.

"Open up, little fox. Let me in." Max's muffled bass rolls through the thin wood divider like he's the big bad wolf, and I know he'll turn into a bear if I don't answer him.

Sighing, I slip out of bed and stumble across the room, unlatching the bolt and opening the door widely. Max looks chipper and clean with a perfect style to his black waves, his stubble replaced by a smooth face. My body feels the urge to fold itself into his.

"You okay?" Max's eyes scan my bare legs up to my breasts. I'm only wearing a thong and a tank top. My nipples harden under his gaze, and I cross my arms over my chest.

"Yes, I'm fine now, thanks."

With a tiny smile, he says, "I was worried you drowned in your tub."

A little snort escapes my nose. "What have you guys been up to?" I peek around the corner of the door. Their room smells like boy, some mixture of dirty socks and cologne. Derichs has his back to me at the dresser, loading a handgun magazine.

"Heading to a shooting range. You up for it?" Derichs asks over his shoulder.

"Ugh, I'm sure that will do wonders for my headache, but okay. We should be prepared for tonight." Max is still leering at me, his eyes roaming freely up and down my body. "I'll just go change."

"You don't have to," Max says, fluttering his long lashes.

"I'll be ready in ten." I say, rolling my eyes and slamming the door in his face, muffling his hearty chuckle that seeps underneath the gap in the threshold.

In a few minutes, I'm ready to check out of the hotel. Before we leave, I observe Derichs staring longingly at the restaurant, his tattooed fingers mindlessly fiddling with the strap of his backpack.

"I'm hungry," I announce.

"Me too!" Derichs says, a big smile crossing his serious face.

Pointing with my head, I ask them, "Do you want to eat in there?"

Derichs darts his eyes to Max, who rolls his and sighs. "Fine." Max throws my bag and his over his shoulders and shoves off the front desk to lumber over to the hostess stand. Like he's an unruly teenager.

Once we get a table and place our orders, Max seems to have softened in his resolve to not allow me to pay as his hand grips his growling stomach. Making sure other patrons are out of ear's reach, he goes over our game plan.

"Derichs will sit in the car, in case we need to get away."

"Yes, but what do you think he'll *want*?" It's all I could think about last night in the tub before the wine took away negative thoughts. Now that we're getting ready for the evening, my throat feels tighter again. I'm a fox. My type is *used* to planning things well in advance and *The Ear* will be a complete unknown to me. I hate surprises.

Could I have asked for my brother's help? Yes. And he would know everything about the man in seconds. But... he wouldn't help me, I know. I didn't need another pacification lecture.

"Markus called this morning. No updates from our intelligence. We know everything you do, unless you've learned something—" Max tilts his head at me and pauses while the waiter sets our food down and asks if we have everything we need.

"How's Hannah, Derichs?" I ask him, changing the subject while we get situated.

Derichs's deep-set brown eyes become glassy, dreamy, a man in love. "She's good. She was jealous of our picnic last night. I took pictures for her."

That's sweet. He's a good man, I know. How do I

know? Because all I've known is pieces of shit and Derichs is not one. "Is she in Gnarled Pine?"

"No. She teaches pre-school in Drussville." That's about an hour away from us.

"Oh, that must be hard. Is she planning to move closer?"

Chewing slowly, he swallows his club sandwich partially. With a bite still in his open mouth, he says, "I-I don't want her in Gnarled Pine." Wiping the corner of his mouth with a finger, he takes another bite, stifling his conversation.

Max and I lock eyes, understanding passing between us both. It's smart. If I had a choice, I wouldn't want to live in our town or have any of my loved ones anywhere near it. Derichs is noble for staying and trying to help his clan. Maybe all of us are. Or maybe we're just insane. The constant threat of death if we leave helps keep us in line, I suppose.

"Well, we should meet her sometime," I say politely, breaking Max's entrancing stare.

"Sure," Derichs says just as graciously. He doesn't mean it and neither do I. If he loves her, he'll keep her far away from the Hollow and our kind. We don't play well with others and their children may end up in one of Strauss's trafficking rings, or worse.

"Maybe we could meet her there sometime," Max says to him, giving me a glance. He means him and I. Like a double date. I sigh heavily, staring at the remnants of my thick burger.

"Hey, that would be fun. They have this bar arcade

there that's pretty cool. We like to go. Friendly competition with the Skee-Ball?"

Shifting my hips in my seat, I suddenly wish I'd never brought up the subject. Both seem to feel as though I'm part of their crew, a Freidenberg... a bear. Strangely, it makes me feel very isolated. Sure, I was used to being alone, even in my own household. What with Cal running everything as ruler of West Side while dipping his eyes into every camera around town. I was only expected to marry someone with a name and have babies, get cheated on with a governess or two, and perhaps get murdered. Rubbing my hands on my napkin, I look at my lap and swallow.

Max slides his eyes to me and notices my sulk. "I don't think foxes are skilled like that," he goads me, tapping an elbow into my ribs, but I flinch before he makes too much contact.

Snarling, I tell him, "Better than bears. You probably just jam the ball in the hole without any finesse."

Max snorts. "Foxy, I'd jam your fine ass with my balls, and you'd still love it."

"Aw, does the big bear have some blue balls? Not getting what you want, hungry lion?"

Derichs clears his throat and throws his napkin on the table. "Uh... Gun range?"

I nod, and Max laughs loudly but agrees it's time to go.

Once we arrive, we pay our fees and gear up. Max asks for an AK, and one for me as well. I've never shot a rifle, but before I can protest, Max says, "I'll teach you."

The rumbling in his voice makes me want him to teach me a lot of things as it vibrates all the way down my body and to my core.

"Try your best, fox!" Derichs smirks and heads to the outside range door. Max and I put on our earmuffs and eye protection, then head out behind him.

Placing his chest to my back, Max cozies up behind me in my booth to show me how to load the rifle and hold it properly. One thick muscular arm wraps around me, and a large hand grips my hip bone, which makes concentrating on my target much harder than it should be. I try to steady my breathing, but any time I inhale, my nose tangles with some of that steely scent from him, and I want to moan.

"Just like that, foxy," he says next to my electronic earpiece. I take aim through the sights and fire with steady pressure. Recoil isn't as bad as I thought, with him there holding me. The paper target has a hole through the center of the chest. "That's it. Good girl." My clit throbs. I lean into him more. Max's chuckled breath hits my exposed neck, the cool breeze a needed retreat from how hot he makes me inside. "Be good. Focus." He gently pats my ass a few times with an open palm. Then moves to his own booth. Immediately, my body misses where he isn't.

Derichs pops away at his target, filling it with bullet after bullet straight through the head. Max aims and does the same. Sensing the need to show off some skills to the men, I set my sights and put a bullet through the neck, but was aiming for the head. A few more rounds, and I feel ready to flip to semi-auto. After firing, I realize I am not. Nope. Too much for me. I take some deep breaths and try again.

Derichs puts his rifle down and comes to my booth. "Want me to give you some tips?"

"Sure!" He seems to have a good grasp on how to do this properly, and Max showing me is too much of a distraction.

Derichs guides me on how to better grip and hold, folding into the gun. Using my breath, I take more precise aim. The next steady pull of the trigger lands a spray of bullets into the head, and I steal a glance at the bear, who nods at me with a smile.

Putting the rifle down, my tiny palm meets Derichs's large one in a high five. "Thank you!"

"No problem. You just need a bear to show you how to fight. We don't do that stealthy shit." Pursing my lips, I give him a wry grin. He's right, though. Von Dovishes are not known for using weapons of these kinds. Ours are much more sinister.

We check out of the range, but Max stops off at their locker rooms to change his outfit for the meeting. Derichs and I wait while leaning against the Barracuda's trunk. The autumn wind billows in gusts, and the air smells like rain, but it's not so cold we want to miss out on the golden sunset.

Kicking a small stone on the ground, Derichs crosses his arms over his chest. I'm about to ask him how his shoulder is feeling, when he interrupts me.

"Don't hurt him, okay?" His serious eyes stare me down with such a flat look, my pulse thumps in my belly.

Swallowing a sudden dryness in my throat, I answer him, "I don't know what you mean—"

"Don't hurt Max. I don't know what game you're playing, but stop. He's a very good man. The absolute best one I know."

Under his gaze, I feel like I've just been asked to make a public speech. "I'm not playing a game." At least... I'm not trying to. When he's given me advances, I try to shake them off, despite his ruggedly handsome looks and bravado attitude that makes me want to ride his face. I can't and I won't. Alone is the best way for me to go. Safety in solo, that's my motto.

"Good." His face lightens, and he ruffles the top of my mohawk. My shoulders relax with his sudden change in demeanor, and I pretend punch him in the gut as he mocks a loud groan. Before he can grip me into a full headlock, I twist his good arm behind him carefully. We're laughing when Max approaches.

He's changed into the suit he wore when I first saw him at the Crimson Angel. Derichs slides out of my arms and gets in the back of the car, and I sidestep so Max can throw his bag in the trunk. As nonchalantly as possible, I try to sniff his cologne, which makes the nerves already wrestling within my stomach escalate into a full battle.

"What?" Deep brown eyes scan my face suspiciously. I guess I wasn't as casual as I thought.

Shrugging, I reply, "Nothing."

He smirks with his pussy pulsating grin. "Get in, foxy."

Driving down to the bay area, we locate the address

of the meeting place Nick texted me. A narrow alley sits between two nondescript brick buildings. It's night now and only darkness escapes from the hole, but the sidewalks are still filled with people bustling about. Despite the lateness of the hour, everyone seems to be dining in nearby restaurants and glass fronted cafés. Outside of the black hole, life exists with zest, but within... who knows what awaits us. My teeth clench to keep from chattering.

"Derichs, keep the car running," Max eyes him like a father telling a naughty child to behave. "I'm assuming they'll take our weapons, so—"

"They won't find mine." Max's head tilts to me with curiosity. I reach down into my boot for my hidden blade, showing him the spot. "I keep it here. Always."

"I'm sure they'll find mine, so I'm leaving it with you." He hands his blade to Derichs, who tucks it in his waistband. We stow our guns in the console.

A blast of cold air makes me grip my leather jacket tighter around my middle when I get out of the car. Traffic is heavy, so we wait before crossing the road. Max slips my hand into his as if I need help, pulling me with him into the alley and never letting go. His palm is sweating as much as mine, but he doesn't feel like he's shaking like my muscles are, anticipating that danger could lurk around any corner. Like the bear he is, he charges full speed ahead into the ebony void.

Eventually, my eyes adjust until I can spot a large man with a rotund gut hanging over his dress pants standing halfway down the alley. He waves us forward as if we're wasting his time. Once we reach him, he pats both of us down halfheartedly before opening the solid metal door. Maybe I could have sneaked in my gun. A narrow wooden staircase leads to a lower level and creaks with ominous tones with every step. Only one lone light-bulb hangs from the ceiling, swinging as the door closes behind us. It feels as if we're being led into a trap.

At the bottom, Max guides us along a dark, narrow hallway until we reach another metal door with his big paw surrounding mine. He turns to me, asking what we should do, but I shrug. With his free fist, he knocks, the sounds resounding through a large room on the other side. The vibrations mimic the pounds of my heart wildly beating in my chest.

Another big guy, this one older, opens the door and turns to walk away without a word. We follow him into a small, dark alcove filled with curls of smoke. The area is set up as an office without windows, just dark masonry walls. White puffs from a cigar billow off fluorescent lights as they waft near them, bouncing around the low-beamed ceilings and back to us, the sweet smell reminding me briefly of Franklin, my father.

A portly man with a shiny bald head and thick gray mustache sits behind a large wooden desk, leaning on his elbows with his hands clasped together. Holding up his double chin with both index fingers, he gives us a small grin as we enter. A crystal ashtray with pointed ends sits near the edge of his desk. Maybe it could be a weapon if things get hairy; otherwise, I see no escape and no other choices. Max could definitely take the man behind us, and I can outrun this one.

"Come in, come in. Mr. Freidenberg, Miss Von Dovish. I've heard a lot about you." He lowers his hands to wave them at the two wooden chairs across from the desk. The entire place looks like it was just set up for tonight's encounter, temporary, not a usual meeting place for them. "Please. Have a seat."

We sit, me on the edge, and Max casually all the way back with his legs spread wide as he asks, "How do you know a lot about me?"

With a look of surprise, as if Max should already know the answer, he responds, "Oh, from the fights and Tony Two Fingers."

Max's chest expands with a deep inhale. "Ah. Yeah..." He clears his throat. "Are you friends?"

"Nope." He leans back in his chair, and it groans loudly under the weight of his body. "I'm glad to hear you're not working for him anymore."

My lion leans forward casually, relaxed now. "No, no. Gave that up to go back home. And you're, um, *The Ear?*"

The man's neck rolls bounce with a chuckle. "Call me Lavinio, please. But yes. That's the nickname for me. I understand you've come to me to talk about some weapons." Lavinio's open nature seems to be putting my partner at ease, but I'm still waiting for the other shoe to drop. My pulse is less hurried, but still steadily keeping me aware of any extra noises that may indicate he's brought more backup.

"Yes, sir. I have. I understand you've got some *stocks* you want rid of. We can take those off your hands." Max has probably done this before, during those years after his parents died. I know Cal has been keeping an eye on him, and sometimes I'd glean some intel from my twin, but not as often as I would've chosen, never wanting to seem too eager. A few times I had sneaked into his fights to watch him, just to see his body move, reminiscing about the time he fought off that man in the alleyway and saved my life. And I figured he was part of local mafias, but I didn't allow him to ever get a glimpse of me to find out.

"Yep, that's true; I've got a lot of stocks to unload." Lavinio picks up the cigar and puffs on it a few times. "I have a proposition for you."

Max's throat bobs, and I try not to lean forward in my chair, showing how anxious I am about his request. Mindlessly, my fingernails scratch at the leather of my jacket as I cross my arms. The man could ask for anything and we'd probably agree. We need those guns, and my tongue is on the verge of just saying yes before he's even asked what he wants from us.

"What's that?" Max's deep bass rings out in the dead air.

"Well, I know you've spent time before. You're obviously a good fighter and probably did some other, ah, *work* for Tony. I think you'll be up for my little task." Does he want Max back in the ring? Eyeing Max, I wait for his reaction, but he's as still as a statue, waiting for the next words out of our contact.

Lavinio stands and goes to the edge of his desk, leaning a hip against it while adjusting his brown leather belt, which holds no weapons. The desk almost shifts under his weight. "You need my supply and I have plenty for you. Glocks, Smith & Wesson, Rugers... Any handgun you want, I got it. I run this town's supply, and I don't want these fuckers anywhere near it when I die... And I'm dying." Quickly pulling a fist up to his mouth, he coughs, then he hacks as if he can't stop himself from the ruckus expelling from his chest. Through a strained voice, he says, "Lung cancer," as his guard approaches with a glass of fresh water. He sits again and drinks, his voice wet as it comes out in a burst once he collects himself. "Ha! Who woulda thought Lavinio Merli would be taken out with cancer!"

"Um. Sorry to hear that." Max eyes the guard briefly, sizing him up, but he walks back to his position near the doorway. "So, yeah, I would like to get back into my family's business of trading. Things are being arranged, and I can move those guns quickly. What do you need from me?"

Lavinio's gray eyes look back and forth between Max and me. "I figure this could be a win-win situation. You get my supplies of the handguns if you get me my ear."

Max blinks heavily, and I hold my breath, my pounding heart clouding my hearing. "I'm sorry, your *ear*?"

"Yes. You see, there's a cleaner, a fixer, if you will. I think you people in Gnarled Pine Hollow call them 'necros.' Anyway, this necro is from your parts. He stole my collection of trophies, and I'm not letting him get away with it. I want to see them one last time."

Max's brow furrows. "And you want the, um, ears back?"

"Yep. And *his* ear." Max licks his bottom lip as Lavinio continues. "After you kill him, of course. But I want *all* my ears. The necro goes by the name Ken Doyle. That's not his real name, of course. His real name is Anthony Renzo, and he's Tony's nephew. Did you ever meet him on your adventures?"

Max shakes his head. It could be trouble if we take out a mafia leader's nephew... But Max seems to know Tony, so I'll have to defer to his judgment on that.

"Oh, that's good for you, then. He tried to get out of the business and hide underground. I want him gone for stealing from me. I want his ear and my collection back once you've completed that job." He taps the desk with a thick index finger three times. "Then, you get your guns."

Max quickly glances at me, and I nod. This *sounds* like a simple enough task for him, and I believe we can do it. But we'll have to be stealthy to avoid rumors of who took care of this necro. My mind races with ways to sneak in and out on a kill mission.

"Yeah, okay. No problem. Where is he?" Max asks with more confidence.

"Ace Donovan's casino. In the basement, probably."

The blood stops moving in my body. This is not good.

I hear Max's breath catch, and he sputters a cough. "Uh, why would he be there?"

"Oh, he's Donovan's necro, didn't I say?" Lavinio's eyes widen as he looks between us. "Is there a problem?"

Max's shoulders tense, and he stops himself from glancing at me before he speaks. "Well... if I dispose of one of Donovan's people... I mean, that's-that's declaring war against him."

We shouldn't get into war with Ace. That would cause a chain reaction of chaos I don't want to see. His people, *our* people, east siders. All three in battles that would delight Strauss to no end. Max's hesitation pours out of the sweat glistening on his forehead.

Lavinio chuckles. "Maybe you can ask your fox here for some tips on how to be sly, then. No ears, no guns." Before I can ask how he knows my family's crest, he responds, "I knew your father. He would've found a way to do this." Yes, he would have. And not given a fuck who he hurt in the process. Was he loyal to the West and caring for the people? If it suited him.

I place my hand on Max's thigh, but he must take it for reassurance instead of my reluctance. Before answering Lavinio, Max is already nodding. "Yeah. Okay. I'll take care of him for you. And get the collection. Happen to know where he keeps it?"

The boss shrugs. "No idea."

"Alright, I-I'll figure it out." When Max finally looks at me, I raise my eyebrows, not wanting to disagree with him in front of Lavinio. This all seems like a bad idea. If Ace ever finds out...

Lavinio offers us some drinks, but we decline. Sensing a need to discuss this in private, Max makes an excuse for us to leave quickly and snags my hand in his again. My mouth is ready to burst with concern over our agreement.

Once we get back to the car, Max's large hand

pushing into my lower back the entire way, I relax some. Rubbing my shoulder gently, he opens my door. Before I slide in, I turn to meet his darkened gaze, my lips pursed.

"We could be starting a war, Max."

He looks up and down the street and lowers his voice. "I have to have those guns. It's our only protection."

Taking a deep breath, I tell him, "I know." And I do understand the urgency. It's only a matter of time before Strauss takes us all out.

Brushing a warm thumb over my cheek, the touch sending sparks through my face, Max pleads with a soft gaze, "You can help us do this sneaky like. Come up with a plan, okay? I'm relying on you, foxy."

I nod.

His throat tightens on a swallow as fear radiates off his skin. Staring intensely into my eyes for a long moment, he presses his lips to my forehead lightly before I can pull back. "Looks like we're heading into Ace's territory."

Twelve

MAXIMILLIAN

"Where do you think he is?" Brushing off my suit arms, I sneak a glance at my pants to make sure the creases are straight. It's the only one I own. Dry cleaning bill was a bitch in between leaving Appleton and coming here, the White Wolf Lodge back in Gnarled Pine Hollow. Livia looks as hot as the sun in her tight black leather dress. Probably would burn me just the same. Her curves are certainly baking up my boner.

"Lavinio said the basement, *probably*. I have a map my hacker gave me." Pulling it up on her phone, she studies the directions we've been over forty times already. We had to go through the metal detectors, so couldn't bring weapons, but I managed to sneak in a thin wire disguised as a bracelet to wrap around the necro's neck. *If we find him.* My hackers were somewhat helpful. At least they said the building was correct. If I rely on Livia's intel, then Ken should be in the basement of this stuffy casino. She wants these guns as much as I do, so I have to trust that the information is honest.

Transported back to a minimalist 80s decade, we stand in the entrance of the posh casino where everything on the floor of the club is white, puffy, and round. Like a bad art deco replication. The place is packed with gamblers and old ladies at the slots, but we wanted that for our plan to work. Well... my little fox's plan.

Livia nods in the direction of the nearest bar. Before we arrive, a group of expensively suited men, all looking like the fighters I've been around over the last eight years, comes strolling out of the bank of elevators. Outfitted in creams and grays, they look every bit the seething pack blasted on every sigil in this place.

"Right on cue," Livia says quietly, flipping the tail of her hair over her shoulder. I move closer to her body protectively.

The one in front, built like a boxer and looking like he's ready to swing, is aiming straight for us. Crystal blue eyes penetrate my skin like daggers. His short, blonde mohawk stands straight up, perfectly styled. There's not an inch of exposed skin without a tattoo, other than his face and head. He's grown a short beard and mustache to look like he's rugged, but it, too, is perfectly manicured, as are his suit, nails, and shoes. The only thing rough about him is his attitude. I'd recognize him anywhere.

"Ace. Good to see you again." Bracing myself for a hit from any direction, I steady my stance.

"What the fuck are you doing here, Freidenberg?"

His entire posse surrounds us, shoulders bulked up, ready to spar. One huge guy even pounds a fist into his other hand, his wolf tattoo looking more like a walrus, given the thickness of his neck.

Disappointment. That's what I'm feeling. If there was any hope he would've welcomed me home like an old friend, it's dashed immediately with the scene in front of us. "Come on, man. I haven't seen you since we were eight."

As Ace nears my face, wafts of beer stench roll off him like he's bathed in the suds. Lowering his voice, he snarls at me. "You killed my sister. You're dead to me. You can leave."

My body stills. He's looking for a fight. To start one, I could accuse him of killing my parents, but I don't think he did it. "Did you kill my parents, Asa?" I call him by his given name.

His brow furrows with confusion. "No."

"We didn't kill Ashley," I say flatly, hopeful he'll actually believe me.

"Don't fucking say her name." Clutching the edge of my pressed black dress shirt tightly, he pulls me into his body. There's only about two inches I have on him. I'm bulkier, but I know Ace fights just like he plays. Dirty.

"We didn't. I didn't. No one from our clan did." My collar vibrates in Ace's grasp as his hands twitch with fury. The whites of his eyes are latticed with broken veins like he hasn't slept in days. Probably hasn't. Softly, I say, "We didn't do it, Ace. But I'll kill the man who did. I'll kill him with you."

The grip loosens on my clothes before his palm gives my chest a warning shove. "You're not welcome here."

"I come here to keep the peace. I just got into town, man. Wanted to catch up with you, my old friend." Opening my palms at my sides, I show him I've got nothing to hide. His wolves retreat as he does with a calculated step backwards.

"You want peace? Bring me back my father! Bring me back my mother! Bring me back my sister... Fuck the world, Maxi! There's *no such thing as peace*." Snatching a pint of Guinness the bartender set on the counter for him, he chugs while narrowing his gaze at me. "And I'll make damn sure no one keeps it."

He waves his hand at the bartender for another. Instead of downing this glass, Ace takes a sip and shrugs, then turns to me and throws the full beer in my face.

Dry cleaning bill. That's all that goes through my mind as my fist flies, darkness covering my vision as rage takes over. Turns out, he is a boxer. Ace is ready for my hook with an elbow block, but I grapple him and take him down in a choke hold. Before I can squeeze too hard, his men descend on me, tearing me off his body, their claws gripping my throat. Ace chokes and gasps, but stands, then kicks me in the groin. The sheer pain doubles me over in agony, and if I yelp, I can't hear it with the amount of blood rushing through my ears. My knees can't hit the ground because my arms are being held back in a tight squeeze by a few of the guys. Spluttering a few breaths, I swallow back my vomit.

Once my hearing stops its ringing, vicious echoes of laughter call out like howls on a moonlit night.

"Take him downstairs," Ace says, then narrows his gaze at Livia. "And her, too."

I don't think they'd hurt her. Cal would already be here if that were the case. He's probably watching this whole scene now from one of his trusty monitors. Hopefully, it looks like we were just here for a friendly welcome visit that went sour, leaving the Von Dovish clan leader none the wiser. Tomorrow, I'll be sore... if I even live to see another day.

Livia's strategy better work.

Once we exit the elevator in the basement, the wolf pack continues to force my shuffles to a windowless room filled with cinderblocks. It looks like any interrogation room I've been in. And I've been inside plenty of police stations. A lone wooden table with two chairs on either side squats in the middle as I scan the area for any weapons.

I know what comes next. My only regret is that I spent my money on veneers thinking I was done fighting. Looks like I may have to pay for them all over again as I take the first hit to the jaw. Walrus boy behind me locks my arms up until they almost snap. Another guy with electric blue hair circles the man punching me, waiting for his turn. Blue hair gets one in my stomach as the first man busts me in the nose.

My eyes are bleary from the flurry of hits, tears involuntarily dripping from my sockets. Blood seeps into my mouth from my broken septum. To keep from choking on it, I spit on the floor. The beating doesn't hurt, yet. Adrenaline is pumping through all my arteries, so the only thing I feel is numb.

Hit after hit lands on my body with rank precision, and I take it, hoping to get knocked out quickly. Blinking rapidly, I scan the tiny room as Walrus turns me for another pelting, and my already quickened pulse rate skyrockets. I wasn't planning on fighting back, until I don't see my little fox anywhere. She's supposed to be here with me. If they've done something to her...

Shaking the cobwebs from my head, I try to scan the room, but another hit makes my vision double. The lids over my eyes are so thick with swelling, I struggle to keep them open, but I still don't see her, terror replacing the rage within my soul.

"Foxy!" I manage to yell, but my tongue is fat in my mouth, my lips distorted in size. My heart beats faster than I thought possible as I struggle against the man holding me back.

The guy hitting me laughs. "Oh, we'll be taking turns with her, too. Right, fellas?" Like a pack of hyenas, they all cackle, probably not understanding their sheer demise were they to try such a thing with the Von Dovish sister.

That's it. With what's left of my strength, I flip the guy holding my arms over my back, throwing him into the man trying to punch me. The two of them barrel over and tangle up together on the floor. I box blue hair with three quick jabs before he knows what hit him, the last landing on his windpipe. Grabbing him around the waist, I thrust his body into the other two, and the three almost fall over as I make a run for the exit.

Snagging the doorknob, I twist, but it's locked. My vulnerable backside is open, and someone gets a lick at the back of my skull. Everything fades to black as I yell, "Livia!"

"I told you. He needs a necro. Not just a fucking healer. Your pack did this to him. Get your necro here. Now."

Livia's voice is commanding, and it soothes the sheer shock of pain erupting throughout my body. She's operating the plan. If I can just keep it together and see straight, I'll be able to focus on the next step.

Blinking rapidly, I rub my face. Fuck! My nose is broken again. Popping it back as straight as I can, I hock out some blood from the back of my throat as I sit up. Strings of mucus cling to my bottom lip, but I cut them off with a brush of the back of my tremulous hand. The cold concrete floor of the interrogation room offers no cushion for my aching bones. Putting my head between my knees, I take inventory of my body. I'm good. I've had worse.

"You okay, lion? Can you do this?" Livia squats next to me and grabs my fingers with both her little hands.

"Yeah, baby. I can do it." I swallow, then poke around my mouth with my tongue. My teeth seem to be intact. "I yelled for you. I couldn't see you. I was worried..."

"Oh, they stuck me in another room. Ace knows who

I am. He knows there would've been war if they'd hurt me. Cal's likely watching every move." She eyes the door at approaching footsteps. "He's in here!"

A lanky guy with some outdated dyed navy emo haircut billows inside the room, his long black lab coat giving away his profession. Pretty sure he's never seen the sun. It must be our boy.

"This guy's alive," he says with a bass voice that rattles the doorknob, one lanky finger pointing at me sitting on the floor. Man's a genius.

"Who are you?" Livia asks as if she didn't call him in here.

"Ken. You asked for a necro. I'm not a fucking healer." He looks like he's about to leave, but Livia jumps up and shuts the door before he can escape.

My voice sounds dry and cracked, but I manage to get out, "It's the strangest thing. I was dead, but I just came back to life. Does that make me some kind of god?"

"Where are the ears, Ken?" Livia asks from behind him, pressing her lithe body against the door.

Ken looks from me to her. "Huh?"

"The ears? Lavinio's ears. Where do you keep them?"

His face darkens as his black eyebrows pull closer together. "The fuck? You workin' for him or something? That'll be a problem with Donovan."

With some effort, I get myself to a standing position, narrowing my gaze as he casually glances at me over his shoulder. "She asked you a question, my man. Where are the ears? That's all we need from you." It isn't, but I'll put him at ease before I lay him to rest.

The guy makes a motion to run, but I grab him from behind in a bear hug. Before I realize, he pulls out a blade from his wrist and repeatedly jabs at my chest. I let go of him, not even sensing the small cuts. Fear and rage rush through my veins like opiates. When he twists, though, he gets in deeper jabs with the sharp instrument.

Stumbling back, I look down... he's stabbed me. A few times. I clutch at the wounds, which start to ooze like ink through the black shirt covering it. Ken continues to move with my body, striking out with his blade while I ward off his attacks by holding up my cut arms. Reaching around his neck, I squeeze, but one of my tendons is loose, unable to assist. As my legs go weak, he falls with me, that fucking knife pointing straight at the center of my chest.

As he raises it above his head for a final blow to my heart, a thunderous pop shatters the silence through the room. My ears deafen, filling with cotton. The necro's body falls on top of mine as we collapse to the floor together. I'm tired. Just want to go back to that blackness and get some rest.

Before I do, Livia's peeling the dead guy off me. "Get the fuck up, lion. Get the fuck up." Everything is so heavy, but she tugs on my arm, then by my dress shirt. Squatting low, she tries to get me to sit up.

"Where'd you get the gun?" My voice sounds far away. Even speaking is a chore I'd rather not do.

"From that room they put me in. Now come on before they get down here. We need to find the ears.

They have to be in his room or something. Move your ass, lion. Go!"

Pulling me to my knees, she leans her body under my shoulder, helping me stumble to a standing position. "You could have shot me."

She smirks, and I want to kiss her fucking lips right off her face. "Yeah, but I changed my mind and shot him instead." Livia leans me against the wall and walks back to the bloody body oozing all over the stone floor.

"No, let me do it." I'm starting to slump, my knees shaking like they're made of jelly. She doesn't need to see this.

"I got it." She picks up the knife from the necro and starts sawing off his ear like it's just another Tuesday. "Shit!"

"What?"

Glancing up at me with her golden eyes, she hesitates, then says, "This is harder than I thought."

Heaving my body off the cinderblocks, I snag the blade from her hand. "As I said." With a quick flick and thrust, I rip the ear from his head, a string of skin snagging as if not letting go without a fight. Eventually, I tear it enough so I can pull it loose and shove the whole thing in my pocket. With the necro's lab coat, I clean up what blood I can from my hands, then use my belt to hold the blade in case I need it later. "Let's go."

Hobbling behind her, we make our way through the wide concrete tunnels of the lower floor beneath the casino. Red lights flash from cameras in every corner. It's only a matter of time before we get caught. I'm sure Ace will finish the job himself if he sees me.

"Here." Livia shoves her shoulder against a gray metal door almost the entire way down the dark corridor. It's unlocked. "Echoes says this is the necro area."

Walking into the white-tiled room feels like stepping into a refrigerator. One wall has a bank of gleaming body coolers, but to cozy up the place, there's a human incinerator near the back. In the middle is a stainless-steel slab. Fortunately, it's empty.

"He'd keep them frozen, right?" Livia darts around the room like a squirrel, diving into every locker and crevice she can find. Involuntarily, my knees give, so I lean against the wall, gripping my wounds to slow some of the bleeding. The world is fading in front of my eyes, with every blink getting slower and longer to recover from. "Wait! Here!" Her excitement wakes me from a short slumber, a snort arousing me further.

Livia points to a small white door underneath a large vent. Using the table in the middle of the room, I lumber toward her and enter a small apartment. With a shoulder resting against the door frame, I watch as she overthrows the mattress, bedding, dresser, and kitchen supplies, silverware clanking against the floor as it scatters.

"Foxy." Snapping my fingers, I point to the mini fridge covered by a tapestry and microwave.

Scrunching her adorable face, she looks at me with disgust. "Ew, don't you think he kept food in there?"

I shrug as she bends over to look inside. The sight of her

tight ass protruding through her jeans makes me feel healed already. Maybe I will live another day. If I want inside of it, to mark it, to deposit my cum in it, I'll have to push on.

"Gross. Let's go." She tosses a large plastic baggie at me. Catching it, I peek at its contents. Yep. We got the goods: a clear bag filled with ears of varying skin colors and sizes. I really don't want to see a tiny one. Reaching into my pocket, I pull out the fresh part and add it to the others.

Before we can leave, both of us halt. Loud shouting echoes down the hall as footsteps sprint toward us. As if it's done pumping all the blood out, my pulse doesn't even escalate. Scanning the room, I don't see any cameras, but security had to have seen us come in. "Shit," I curse.

Livia hurries to a body cooler and opens it. A white sheeted stiff lies on the metal tray. "Get in."

"No way."

She grimaces, and her eyes get so big, I can see the whites surrounding the entire honey iris. I've seen this look before when she would threaten me not to make a sound while playing hide-and-seek after finding her hiding spots. Foxy would pull me down with her and tell me to stay quiet or she'd kick my shins in. "Get the fuck in! Or we're dead."

Squeezing my eyes closed, I hurdle myself onto the cold, hard body, laying on top of it. My aching fingers grip the edges of the cloth, attempting to wrap myself until I do a decent job. Livia shoves my tomb closed with a clang of finality as darkness surrounds me and I feel like

I'm being raptured home. A chill permeates every pore of my skin, the person lying underneath me providing no comfort. Each wound I sustained slowly transforms from tender to numb. And despite the fact I'm cuddling with a cadaver, it's peaceful. Perhaps I should just stay here until my heart becomes one with the dead.

Nah, I gotta kill Strauss before I die. And give Arianna the home she deserves.

And put my dick inside Livia.

And kiss her lips.

The men enter and search the room. Some body trays are opened and shut repeatedly. Fuck, of course they would look around here. Terrible hiding spots. Clutching my friend closer, I snuggle under the sheet, hoping they don't open mine or Livia's coolers.

"No, I don't see them," one of them says. "Maybe they went to the vault."

"Then get the fuck back here! Call the healer!" someone else barks through a radio.

Lots of pounding steps, then the room is silent once again.

Some unknown time has passed, and I feel like I must have traveled to the netherworld because the light hurts when it hits my eyes. As I become aware, Livia is staring at my face with a look of terror. The sight warms my heart, thinking she may have caught some feelings for me, and that half dead part comes back to life, realizing I've done the same. "Oh my god. You're okay."

"Yeah, foxy." Coughing, I press myself up, each wound aching again as the temperature rises in the room.

More blood lodges in the back of my throat, and I hock it into the sink along one wall. "You worried?"

Ignoring me, she grabs my hand and tugs. "Come on. I think there's an exit through a garage on the northwest wall. Echoes showed me. Let's go."

After my nap, I feel stronger and even more so knowing my foxy girl feared for my life. With Livia under my shoulder to help support me, we make it to the garage bay. The warehouse is empty this time of night or early morning. Limping the entire way to her car, I'm grateful she drove.

As soon as the door opens, my body collapses into the passenger seat. It's the last thing I remember.

Gentle strokes graze my forehead, brushing back tickling locks of hair. My nose senses I'm back in my own room, a scent of rustic wood mixed with my cologne. A shadow crosses my closed lids with every tender touch, which causes tingles from my scalp down to my neck with every caress.

It's been years since I've felt so safe and loved, comfortable and cared for. If there's such a paradise, perhaps my spirit has moved on from the horrors of the world to the heavens.

"Mama?" My question fills the air with a hoarse dryness.

The movements cease. Lifting my eyelids slowly, I meet Livia's amber eyes, both glistening in the dim light with wetness. I prop myself up on an elbow and cup her cheek. It's hot and flushed, as if she's been crying, and the sight rips me from my high into hell.

"Shh, shh. Little fox, what's wrong?"

She quickly shakes her head, preventing her tears from falling. Tiny hands push me back to a lying position as she straddles my waist. When she leans toward me, her black mohawk tail tickles my face before her thick lips press against my forehead, kissing me lightly. When she pulls away, her breath heats my skin, the sensation traveling down my abdomen and into my dick. Involuntarily, my hips gravitate toward her core, seeking its natural habitat while my balls quiver in anticipation.

"I'm sorry about your mother, Max." Puffy pink lips linger so close to mine as she snares my eyes with hers. I crane my neck to tap them with my own, but she backs up slowly. She's just out of reach.

"Please." Threading my fingers around her head, the shaved hairs along the sides graze my palms. "Please, Livia." We hold like that for a moment, reaching into each other's gazes, seeking what the other wants. She diverts from my lips to suction hers against my cheek a moment, then sits back on my lap as I let her go with frustration... and awe. "You saved me."

"Your healer came up here. She stitched you up." Livia's smooth, pale skin shines brightly next to my tanned and inked chest as she shows off my new bandages, fingers crawling over each one delicately. "You'll be fine."

Squeezing my abs, I sit, grabbing her by the back of

the neck. Her eyes widen and she pants with an open mouth, filled with fear. Instead of forcing that kiss just now, I suck on her exposed neck like a teenager. Using my teeth, I tear into her skin enough to draw a drop of blood. I need to taste her and leave a mark. Her moans ripple through her chest and into mine as she digs her nails into the bare skin of my back.

Yeah, she wants me. Just as much as I want her.

"Lie back," I command her. She does, and I climb on top of her body. As I loosen her jeans, she puts a hand on mine to stop me.

"Please. No, Max. I don't want to."

Narrowing my brow, I shake my head in confusion. "You don't want to what?"

"I-I-I don't want you to get inside me." Several blinks while reading her face, the truth settles within me. She's lying. I think I'm getting to know her well enough. This girl is lying to my face. Why, though? She doesn't seem to be the prudish kind. I watched her get down with a couple, for fuck's sake. I'll respect her wishes, but...

"Are you on your period or something? 'Cause I would love to soak my cock in your blood. I don't think you understand just how much." Rolling her bottom lip under her front teeth, she shakes her head, suddenly shy. "Can I at least repay you? For what happened at Strauss's meeting? For saving my life?" Hooking my fingers in her waistband, I slowly tug downwards as she gives me a slight bob of her head. "I need more than a nod."

"Yes."

That word is like a long-lost melody to a tune I've

been singing since we were kids. The beast within me just hears *go*, but I forcefully try to focus on her needs instead of myself, not wanting to scare her off. But a man can only wait so long. Once I get a taste of her, I *know* I'll want more.

Slipping her pants down, I toss them and her thong on the ground. Easing her knees apart with my hands, I lay between her legs and stare at her perfect pussy lips. The crown jewel piercing the top is begging for a polish with my tongue while her wetness shimmers by the light of the window. Scooping her waist with one forearm, I ignore the pain from my cuts and flip her over onto her stomach. Her head is near the bottom of the bed, and I scoot myself behind her. Pulling her hips up into the air with a firm grip, I raise her cunt to my mouth and get my first taste of my little fox.

Fuck. Her honey pot is just what this bear needed after a long hibernation. A low growl escapes my chest as I inhale her scent. She gasps when I dive in like I haven't eaten all winter. Because I haven't. Not like this.

Licking from her front to her back, I suck on her clit diamond, then her taint, then fuck her asshole with my tongue before doing it all over again. My teeth grip the ring and tug, and she squirms, a high-pitched keen fluttering from her mouth. Hmm, she likes it. I do it again while stroking her repeatedly in a pattern, making her body shiver in my arms. The fact I'm able to control her like this sends a rapid rush of blood to my dick.

Livia tries to push back into my nose, but I've got her hips in a tight grip. Shoving my entire face into her, I shake my head to tell her no. I'm in control here, and I want to bathe in her sweet nectar. Drown in it until I die.

Lying back, I pull down my sweatpants. My cock is a flagpole, erect and flying high. Grasping it with my right hand, I tug madly to relieve the pressure built up there. The tip is oozing with need.

"Get the fuck up here and mount my face, foxy."

Livia doesn't hesitate. She scooches up to sit on me. My nose rubs her hood ring, and my tongue circles her hole. Writhing her hips back and forth, my day's stubble grazes her inner thighs as she rides. We're both going to get rug burn.

It doesn't take long for my little minx to grip my head into a vice and squeeze while screaming, her wetness running into my mouth while I greedily lap it up. Hearing her wails of ecstasy makes me explode in my own hand. I'm drenched from head to toe with sweat, nut, and foxy's scent.

Livia slides back to sit on my chest. Gripping her thighs with my cum-covered hands, I suckle each of her legs in turn, making little red marks pop up along her creamy skin. "Want another ride? You don't need a ticket. Just hop back on." I smirk at her, letting my tongue gather up her residue around my mouth.

She looks at me with softness as her fingers brush back hair that's stuck to my forehead with perspiration. Groaning, I close my eyes to memorize the sensation. When I open, I'm greeted with another view of her perfect pink pussy lips lounging on my tattooed abdomen.

When my eyes meet hers again, she dismounts, and my hands fall to my side. Leaning up on my elbow, I ask, "Where you going?"

"I need to go home. I've been here too long. I'll call you if I hear anything." She scrambles off the bed and dresses, then throws on a jacket and darts out of my room. If I hadn't just orgasmed, I'd chase after her.

Flopping back on the mattress, I huff with irritation. Foxy's feline ways are getting tiresome quickly.

Thirteen

MAXIMILLIAN

It's been a couple of weeks since Livia walked out of my bedroom and holed up in her fox den over on the west side. Both Derichs and I made full recoveries. Nothing was badly damaged, and I didn't need surgery. We'd been sparring to keep up our strength, and occasionally the little fox would stop by for a tussle. Never the kind I wanted, though.

Things around Freidenberg Manor as well as the east side have been flourishing. The house is looking better every day, and its electrical and plumbing systems are finally modernized. Our motorcycle repair place, car wash, and body shop are all running smoothly. Strauss didn't cause any problems for us, and Arianna has stayed safe behind the walls of our property or with Jakob, still working on getting our papa's bike fixed.

The financial situation is looking good now that we're stocked with all the handguns one could ever use, courtesy of Lavinio. He was pleased when I stopped by to bring him the baggie of ears. So much so, he told me I was his son, since he never had one. His men run the guns to ours in batches, a third going out to the Von Dovish clan and a third are sold to Donovan's, despite his hatred of me. It's a good income and funds us being able to get more weapons.

I don't mind, as I want everyone armed. We all need to be if this is going to be a war. Strauss's men haven't interfered with the trade, so either they don't know yet, or are waiting to ambush.

Fortunately, I haven't had a run-in with the wolves since the casino. Hopefully, Ace won't retaliate for clocking his necro. Maybe he forgives me, since I'm supplying the entirety of South Side with the renewed armories. After our rendezvous, it looks like my backup plan of having Arianna marry Ace to save her from Strauss may be out of the question, though.

"And then you turn this like this," Wyatt Steele says, my eyes melded to his hands like he's my next prey. This man has apparently been getting close to Ari, Jakob informed me. Guy's been running the shop and is not part of any clan, but he's a good mechanic. I let him stay on, but I thought I should pay him a visit. Let him know where it's appropriate to keep his hands...and where it's not.

Arianna twists back and forth on the little stool next to him, studying his instructions like she's asked for a milkshake at a soda bar. She told me he's teaching her how to work on her bike. I don't like him. And she can't be with him. He's not in a family and doesn't carry a name.

A faded snake inked along the back of his neck twists into an impossible position as he turns his head to stare at Ari until my throat catches in a protective growl. When I pretend to clear it to mask the noise, Wyatt sits up straight. Dude is big, about my size, and covered in gang tattoos from his crew. A few of them lean on the walls in the garage, with their leather coats flouting the patches showcasing their own family of sorts. I've seen them ride together through East Side. All the unaffiliated motor-cycle gangs usually have their own hangouts away from the clans on the outskirts of town.

The only thing clean about Wyatt is the high and tight cut of his light brown hair. His affiliation and clothing aren't what make me mistrust the guy. It's his eyes. They're small, narrow, and very light blue. The two beads are also always scowling whenever he looks at anyone...except for my little sister.

"Hey, man. Didn't see you come in." He also calls me "man." Disrespectful. I hold back from telling him so as is my right.

"Yep." I suppress myself from popping the 'p'. "Ari, get in the car."

Arianna's golden face shines up at me, her big brown eyes pleading. "But Wyatt was just teaching me to—"

Gritting my teeth to keep myself from lashing out with claws, I command her, "In the car, Arianna. Now."

Huffing, she stands and gathers her stuff, muttering complaints under her breath the entire time. Both the mechanic and I watch her leave, but I'm making sure she's doing what she's told. Wyatt's checking out the view. Once she clears the area, I lower my voice. "I'd be real fucking careful with how close you're getting to her."

Without even looking at me, he returns to his task with a socket wrench, the grinding of it fraying my last nerve. "Yeah? Why's that?"

"'Cause it looks like you need to use your arms."

His bass voice laughs without any joy behind it as he turns his deep-set eyes on me. "Big brother protective vibe. I dig it." Standing, he starts tossing his tools in a box along a bench as his buddies continue to smoke and gossip nearby. Wyatt's back muscles twitch underneath his tight-ass T-shirt as he says, barely turning his head, "Need a new shipment, boss. Already sold out of what we had."

"Oh?" This half surprises me.

"Yeah, got my boys to run it all over the city. Seems to be working out that way." Finishing up his sorting, he turns back to face me, crossing his legs and arms as he leans against a workbench to light up a cigarette. Taking a big drag in, he says, "Strauss's guys can't keep up with our bikes."

Licking my bottom lip, I force myself to tell him the truth. "That's smart." And it is. I just hate that the idea and work ethic came from him.

Blowing out smoke, then following it with his eyes, he surmises, "Smart enough to earn a date with Arianna Freidenberg?"

This guy has steel balls. Part of me wants to whip out

my blade and cut him right here. Just one long trip across his fucking throat, but he's good. He just sold our entire inventory faster than anyone. I need him, and he knows it. "What's your interest in my little sister?"

"I've gotten to know her over the last few weeks." Squeezing his eyes to be almost non-existent, he nods his head to Jakob over my left shoulder and stamps out his cigarette on the ground. "He can attest. Never laid a fucking finger on her. I wouldn't. But we understand each other. I'm into her." He swallows, and it's the first time I see a hint of vulnerability, his clear blue eyes finally meeting mine solidly. "A lot."

"Hate to tell you, son, but you understand we live in Gnarled Pine, right? She's a Freidenberg, and you're...not someone she can be with. So, if you can't marry her and make her respectable, that means you only have vulgar intentions." My hands are on my hips like I'm the warden, but really, I'm ready to fucking hit him at the slightest provocation.

His large shoulders shrug. "No. I want to show her a different world. One where anyone can be with anyone they choose. That's what I want."

Shaking my head, a sarcastic chuckle escapes, letting him know what he's saying is a complete joke. "My answer is no." Walking toward the garage door, I turn to him one last time. "And keep your distance."

When I get in the car with Jakob, Arianna twists in the passenger seat and bounces with energy. "I don't understand why you're so rude to him. He's a good man."

Catching her childlike gaze, I tell her firmly. "Arianna, I don't want you coming over here again."

"But—"

"That's final." I eye Jakob in the rearview mirror and his bald head nods once, taking the words as his command.

As I gun the engine and head toward the manor, Arianna's little shoulders shake as she sobs. Jakob hands her a handkerchief, which she uses to blot at her eyes and blow her nose loudly. I can't stand her tears, and I know she's been through a lot, but she can't be with someone like Wyatt. "It's for the best, Ari. He's not good enough for you."

Long brunette hair flips around wildly as she glares at me across the car. "Who *is* good enough, Maxi?"

My hands grip the steering wheel tighter. If I could take away her pain, I would. "No one, but definitely not him."

Her jaw flops open in outrage. "Shouldn't I be the judge of that?"

"Arianna, you didn't have Papa and Mama telling you about these things. It's up to me to guide you, to look out for you." Calum Von Dovish pops into my mind. Perhaps he could...nah. The man's a pacifist, and I think he may be going mad. We should eat dinner with them, though. It would give me the opportunity to scope things out between the two. See if they hit it off.

Throwing hands up dramatically, she cries, "I'll die an old maid!"

"No, you won't. I will find someone suitable for you."

She settles back in her seat, crossing her arms and not daring to look in my direction again. Lavinio called me his son; it's too bad he doesn't have one for Arianna. Gnarled Pine Hollow is too small for us.

Before my young sister gets hitched, I need to get started on making "cubs," as Livia called them, continuing the legacy. Thinking about impregnating the little fox makes my dick thicken inside my jeans.

Speaking of, as we pull through the gates and to the house, a familiar Aston Martin Victor shines in the sunlight, parked near the fountain. Leaning against the driver's door is the dark seductress, looking like pure sin and pleasure. My heart rate picks up at the sight of her.

Arianna leaps out of the car and runs to her as soon as I park, throwing her arms around Livia in a tight embrace. Despite avoiding me, the two have been talking over the last few weeks and have become, dare I say, close friends. It irks me for some unknown reason.

No, I know the reason. It's because they gang up on me, and Ari doesn't seem to mind as well after she talks with the Von Dovish sister.

"Maxi says I can't date anyone!"

Livia's golden eyes sparkle at me over my sister's shoulder, little creases in the corners lifting in a smile. "He's a fucking brute. I'll kick his ass for you." She gives me a wink before I can ask her to roughhouse with me in the basement gym. Her presence here at the house makes me calm, yet excited at the same time. I'm growing dependent on her visits.

Arianna sniffs and wipes her nose. "Thank you. Are you here for me, or him?"

"Him, unfortunately, but I'll come have dinner with you after." She tucks a piece of hair behind Ari's ear.

Arianna heads off into the house, but I stop her. "Ari, we're going to have dinner with the Von Dovishes tonight. Clean up." With a sigh, she nods, then goes inside.

Taking a drink of poison, I let my eyes scope out Livia's body. Her teases over the last few weeks have left me sick with blue balls. I'm about to head to the Crimson Angel to bust my nut if she doesn't show any sort of green light. Walking over to her, I pin her against her car with my body. Leaning my full weight on her, chest to breast, I plant my arms on either side of her head.

Lowering my voice to its deepest, I ask, "What's good, foxy?"

"I came about another meeting." Blinking heavily, her hazel eyes don't dare to meet my face.

"You can come for something else, if you want."

She snorts and presses her palms on my pecs, but doesn't push hard. "Don't be lewd, Max. This is business."

Diving into her neck, I sniff a long column up to her ear, gathering up her amber and vanilla scent. A sharp inhale into her mouth swishes by my ear as she holds her breath. "Your body *is* my business. Let me eat your cunt again. I'm fucking starving for a little fox tail. Give me that flower."

With a full exhaled laugh, she finally shoves me away. "Behave. This is serious."

As I take a step back, I grab her hand and tug her with me toward the pond at a slight jog.

"What are you doing?" she squeals, like when she would get mad during a water balloon fight in the summers.

My face broadens into a large smile as I yearn to relive those memories, or maybe just that carefree, safe feeling. I miss it and it seems to be one I have the most whenever she's around. "Remember the old swing? I made them fix it."

"No, Max. I don't-I don't want to." Digging her heels into the grass, she tries to slow our progress, but I tug on her harder until she has to follow.

"Come on!"

When we reach the old oak, I swing her around to the round wooden bench seat and Livia reluctantly gets on, straddling the rope. It's new and sturdy. Last week, I sneaked and tried it when no one was looking, almost going for a dive in the pond, but it's too cold for that now. With my hand pressed into her back, I give her a big shove, and she goes flying over the water with a shrieking laugh, a beaming smile lighting up her face. It's exactly the one she made when we were young. And suddenly I know why she was resistant to trying this again.

Bittersweet. That's what this is. My chest tightens, remembering those golden days, and a lump forms in the back of my throat until it's hard to swallow. I miss my mama and papa, my friends, a time that was so simple and carefree.

Our parents never let us know the battles that were waged outside of our high walls, but now I see it. Things aren't safe. Maybe they never were, but I want to create that for future generations. Gripping the rope, I pull her to a stop.

"I want to go again!" The giggles continue until she sees my face. Dismounting, she crashes her full body into mine, wrapping her arms around my waist in a tight squeeze. "It's okay. It's okay, lion." And like she can read my mind, she chimes in, "There'll be new memories. We can *make* new ones." With a wave of her arm, she showcases the land in front of us, but it's hard to see with heavy eyes. "Look, this place is turning out beautiful. Better than it was before."

Nestling my face into her mohawk tail, I nuzzle her neck and embrace her, using her body for comfort. Seeking solace, I move to press my lips to hers, but she bends her forehead so they are out of reach. We hold there. Both our heads held together, mind to mind, exchanging air into each other's mouths.

Quietly, my voice drops as I breathe the words between her parted lips. "Come on, Livia. It makes sense for us to be together. Who you gonna get with? Ace? Strauss? Some asshole mafia prince?" Desperation erupts in my whisper as I plead, "Be with me."

Still attached, she squeezes her eyes shut and shakes her head. *Fuck*, I hate that I want her so badly. Her presence in my life is becoming a need. I don't even want to think about how much. I'm getting tired of this. I drop my hold on her and take two steps back, cracking my jaw.

"Fine." I sigh. "What's this business you came about?" I ask, folding my arms over my chest, trying to hide the annoyance in my tone.

Swiping at her eyes with her thumbs, she gathers up some wet substance. It couldn't be tears. This raven obviously doesn't have emotions, that's for sure. Swallowing deeply, she sniffs, her voice cracking. "Um, we have another meeting. This one in Cliff Harbor with Tony 'Nickle Eye.' I think he's Russian. Echoes says he has a penchant for jewels. He has rifles, fully automatics. We need those."

I give her a small nod as I roll a rock under my shoe, then kick it. "Yeah, okay, when?"

"Tomorrow night, which is why I motored over here so quickly when I found out. We need to get on the road early if we're going to make it by then. He wants to see us at his lake house. Alone, of course. He specifically requested me."

I don't like the sound of that. "Why?"

"Not sure." Her eyebrows raise as she tries to catch my eyes, her bottom lip rolling under her teeth. At least she's smart to be nervous.

"Okay, let me inform my people and we'll get set up." We turn toward the house.

"Max."

I get the sense she's going to apologize for being such a fucking ice freeze on my balls. I don't want to hear her excuses. She's not a lesbian; it's apparent she likes the D.

Maybe she has someone on the outside of the city. If so, I'll kill him. Simple, easy, clean.

"I'm inviting your brother and you to dinner. Stay. We'll have some wine, steaks. Despite how mean she is, Mrs. Kroft makes amazing spätzle."

"Yeah, okay." She threads a hand through mine to slow my steps. "Max." I stop and turn to her, meeting her gaze. Those honey eyes could have me falling to my knees. "You really are doing amazing things here. It's all coming together."

"Thanks." Looking at her hand in mine, I reluctantly fling it off, then walk inside, pulling out my phone to call Cal. He agrees to come over and I busy myself in my office with the doors locked while Livia heads upstairs to Arianna's room.

The paperwork pile is slowly dissipating after weeks of working on it. Still feeling low from my reveries, I sit at my desk, staring at the various piles without even really seeing them. The crackling fire soothes some of my dejection, as does the sound of Markus in the corner, shuffling through old books. Texts of the Freidenberg history, I'm told.

Moving toward me while cleaning his glasses, he points to a smaller pile of papers on my desk with the earpiece of his horn rims. "You may want to look at those."

Blinking, my vision clears as I look to where he's aiming. "What are they?"

"Your mother and father's will."

My jaw tightens just thinking about that. Between

the swing with Livia, fond memories of childhood, and this...I don't feel like revisiting that pain again today. The pile stares back at me like it wants to stab me with paper cuts of the past.

"There's something important in there." Marcus slides his glasses on and nods with encouragement toward the folder.

Taking a big inhale, I pull out the first document: The Last Will and Testament of Gerald Leon and Mari Lynn Freidenberg. Even the ink on the page hurts to look at, but there it is in black and white.

"I thought the will from the estate reading was final. Why do I need to go over it again?" Eight years ago, listening to the lawyer read off the words was excruciating enough. Even though I knew I had been gifted a large property, all I wanted was my parents. I'd had given anything to have them back. I don't give a fuck about wealth or this estate. The only reason I care now is because I feel closer to them by taking part in the legacy. And I want to provide a life for Arianna and the people here of East Side, my people. Carrying on the legacy of Freidenbergs is also in those cards so they have someone to look out for them when I'm gone.

Markus runs his hands through his white frazzled hair. As he does, his flannel shirt lifts, revealing his gut hanging above his belt. "Uh, well, we, uh, had the lawyers look at this one. It was found by the workers in the attic, hidden in a trunk. It's more recent than what was read after the funeral."

My brow furrows. "Is that legal?"

"Well...there's only one change. One paragraph difference. And the lawyer says, yes. This one is the correct one."

No. I've already lived through the trauma of my parents' deaths, and this piece of paper is just a reminder of that day. Thinking of them, kind, loving, and warm, talking with their lawyer about what to leave me and Arianna in case they died? It makes that dull ache in my heart a full-blown piercing stab. Getting rejected by Livia was a pain on its own, but this is just overkill.

"I can't deal with this today, Markus. I thought I could, but...I'll try later."

Markus nods slowly. "Okay, Max. I wouldn't let it sit too long, though."

"I have dinner to eat. The Von Dovishes are joining us and...honestly, I'm curious to see what kind of a match Arianna and Cal would make."

A dramatic cough cuts through the dull air as Markus throws his head back with surprise. "I don't think-I don't think they would make a good pair, Max. Arianna's, um, very spirited. I'm not sure their tempers would mesh. And I don't think your parents would have wanted that, either."

Oh. Hmm. I hadn't considered what Papa would want for Arianna... "Yeah, you're right, I suppose. I did think of Ace, but he's probably going to kill her now instead of marrying her." Pushing the rolling chair back from the desk, I stand. "Make sure the rest of security sticks with her. Between Strauss, Ace, and that fucking kid at the motorcycle shop, *Wyatt*, I just don't have a good feeling about her safety."

"Absolutely. Jakob is already on high alert."

We head into the living room as our butler, Fritz, escorts Cal from the foyer. When he does, Fritz stumbles and almost falls over the step up to the dining room. He's elderly, so it seems I end up caring for him more than him for the house, but I don't mind it. Hopefully, he can spend his last days fixing up the indoor garden he loves so much. Catching his arm, Cal reaches for him to help steady his back. "Excuse me, sir. So sorry."

"It's alright, Fritz. Tell Mrs. Kroft we're ready." Grasping Cal's hand, we pull each other in for a half hug. "Hey, glad you made it."

"Yeah, Max, but I said we should eat at our place. Figured yours was still worse for wear, but everything is tip top!" With a weird grin on his face, his pupils are blown out into black circles. Maybe he's been sampling too much of his product. Motioning to the table, we sit in the high-backed velvety cushioned chairs as Arianna and Livia enter, Arianna's face now fresh, without a trace of puffy redness.

Cal stands and goes over to Arianna, and they hug, greeting each other for the first time in twenty years. "It's lovely to see you again, Arianna."

"Thank you. You as well." She's doing her polite smile, and Cal barely looks at her, his eyes scanning the tall candelabras standing around the edges of the gold room. Maybe he's gay. I never thought to ask. My sister's an incredibly beautiful woman, and most men can't keep their eyes off her. Not Cal. Taking a seat across from Arianna, he sits next to his twin sister while I command the head of the table.

"Well, thanks for coming." Mrs. Kroft enters and announces the first dish, a cucumber and tomato salad.

"I appreciate the invitation, Max, I do. But..." Livia places her hand on Cal's arm to stop him. Giving her a subtle glance, he meets my gaze with his hazel eyes that match hers. "But I don't appreciate the trade you've started back in the city. Nor my sister's involvement. I think it's only going to cause strife and bring more attention from Strauss."

"I disagree," I say, and Livia nods.

"I'm sure you do. But look at what happened with Ace. We've had a somewhat amicable peace between us for several years, but now that's gone. One of his lackies attacked one of ours earlier this week. Things are going to get hot, and I don't like it. I'm begging you..." He pauses and looks at Livia, then me. "*Both* of you, to stop."

"Strauss could kill us all at any time he chooses. I won't stop. I'm sorry, Cal, and I hope this doesn't mean we have a problem."

Cal sighs heavily and shakes his head. "Not at all. I just wanted to say what I had to say, and that's it. I've said the same to my sister for years, but she won't listen, either. You never have, Max. I understand that. I know you. We're brothers. There won't be any bad blood between us. I just wish it were different." He takes a sip of water, and I let relief wash over me. At least I have the Von Dovishes on my side. "Now, I've said everything, and I'm done. You know where I stand. That's not going to change." Taking a small bite, he says quickly, "This salad is amazing."

"It is," says Livia without even tasting it, clearly wanting to change the subject as much as her brother.

Arianna looks bored, staring into her lap. Is she— "Arianna, do you have a phone at the table?"

She looks up from the table, her eyes wide. "Um, sorry. I was just looking stuff up."

Snapping my fingers, I open a palm toward her. "Let me see."

A sharp breath exhales through her nose. "Max, no. I'm a grown adult. No."

"Let me see it, Arianna. Now." The entire room quiets when I slam my fist on the table. Since when did she start disobeying me? If she's choosing *now* of all times to do so, she has another thing coming... I'll lock her up if I must just to keep her safe.

"Max, don't," Livia pleads with a quiet tone. Meeting her bright golden eyes, she shakes her head, the tail of her hair falling behind her shoulder. "Don't, Max. Let's enjoy our dinner."

Ugh, these two are now thick as thieves. "Do you know what she's looking up?"

Sticking her chin out, Livia answers boldly, "Yes."

I gasp. "She could be in danger." And the fox doesn't even seem to give a shit.

"Max, we're always in danger. All the time. It's fine. It's girl stuff, and you don't need to worry about it. Leave it alone."

Mrs. Kroft enters with our main course, and the smell of the steaks almost has me forgetting my anger. "Fine, just put away the phone at the table." Girl stuff. Maybe it's about tampons or something. Better not be about birth control or babies or some shit like that. She's too young.

The rest of the meal is peaceful as Cal and I catch up on some funny stories from our youth, brightening the earlier doom I felt with Livia. He's still mad that Ace and I hid behind the coffins to scare him.

When we wish the Von Dovish clan a good night, Livia tells me she'll be by early the next day. By then, I've forgotten about Arianna's phone and whoever she may be communicating with.

Fourteen

LIVIA

Cliff Harbor is a beautiful town. Clean. Its streets are well kept, and people are out late at night when we arrive, mulling about with their families. Passing the docks, I spot kids with cake cones filled with swirly white ice cream and couples holding hands. The toxin that is Gnarled Pine hasn't infected the air here, which is thick with salt and sugar.

"Should we stop and grab a drink before? We have time." Max points to a bar that looks like an old, boarded wharf with gray cedar shingles and a lit-up red crab for a sign. It's been remodeled to attract tourists like us and the large parking lot off the main street is almost full, so their marketing must be working. Turning the wheel of the Victor, I pull into the last spot.

When we get out, both of us take a moment to stretch. I didn't stop as much as I wanted on our trip because every time I dared to pull over at a gas station, Max would exclaim, "You have to pee *again*?" If I never hear those words coming out of his mouth, it would be too soon. Now, I was bursting at the seams. Holding it would prevent his annoying expressions of consternation, though.

Taking a few steps toward the boardwalk, Max strides next to me and grabs my hand. When we reach the pier, I notice other twosomes leaning against the rails, taking selfies, and talking or laughing. Max tucks me into his side and puts his cut arm around my shoulders. Like I'm his.

We must look like one of those couples. One of the ones where things appear normal just before they aren't. Happy. Until we're eating dinner at a restaurant, not talking to each other and wishing we could look at our phones instead. Before Max gets more interested in younger pussy and decides to off me.

Nothing lasts. Certainly not healthy marriages in Gnarled Pine.

My parents' marriage was a testament to the state of matrimony in the Hollow. I loved my mother dearly, but she made poor decisions. The worst of which was letting her guard down around my father. It's hard enough for me to trust anyone, but especially men, seeing that it's the ones closest to you who can do the greatest harm.

Despite my overwhelming nihilism, my fingers feel for the little metallic object in my pocket. As if wishing will make reality any different. As if I don't *want* to accept the truth that I should. As if true love exists. The tiny hope that things could be different for me... That glimmer of my dream needs to die. Because if it doesn't,

I'll get deeply hurt. Possibly killed. Just like Franklin did to my mother.

Divorce was not an option for clan leaders. In the history of Gnarled Pine Hollow, no senator had left his wife, except through death. So, whenever the men were done with them, had their heirs and simple affairs with the mistresses weren't enough anymore, a sneaky sudden death would occur. I guess it was always a threat to the womenfolk on how to act right. A woman of stature in Gnarled Pine Hollow should learn to be obedient, bear heirs, and be a good helpmeet... or else.

All I learned was that it's safer to be solo.

Twisting out from under Max's embrace, I turn to the restaurant.

"Uh, okay. Apparently, you don't like to be touched." Max huffs.

"No, it's fine. It's just a little, um, couple-y for me. Let's go." Using my head, I point to the boarded door of the place, hoping he'll just drop it and not get offended.

Max stops and glares at me with his hands on his hips, his wide chest puffing up. He shakes his head, then moves toward the entrance. "I don't get you." His body brushes past me to open the door, and with a quick flick of his hand, he motions for me to enter, holding it open like I'm wasting his time. Clicking his jaw, he says with annoyance, "Go pee. I'm sure you have to. I'll grab us some beer and food."

After using, then cleaning up in the restroom, I rub a hand along the sides of my head where the hairs tickle my palms. I need a fresh shave. Dreading returning to the dining area, I stall and primp my mohawk, apply some lip balm, wash my hands for a second time... Max is going to treat this like a date. And I don't want that. Not if I want to live.

When I do go back, his broad body fills out a small wooden chair near the front window that leads onto a covered patio. There are a few locals around, but mainly the place is filled with out-of-towners wearing novelty T-shirts or pastel-colored hats purchased from the gift shops along the pier. The chair creaks as I drag it along the stone floor to take a seat, the intoxicating aroma of the large, juicy hamburger in front of me causing my belly to squeeze with hunger. Max is chomping down on his burger with gusto. Two large pints of a blonde ale sweat on the table.

"Figured you like meat," Max says with his mouth full. He smirks and winks at me.

"I do. Thanks." After a healthy bite, my taste buds feel impressed with the quality of the local dive before washing it down with the hoppy beer.

"Kind of a strange place for a mob boss, right?" Max wipes his face with a napkin and narrows his eyes out the window, staring off into the water where colorful boats bob with every wave of the wind. This city is like a farce of perfection, and I realize some of the hunger pangs in my stomach must also be from nerves. I'm not used to such a sparkling city.

"Yeah. Makes me more worried about what he wants. And what we'll be able to offer."

Turning to me, his piercing gaze always makes me

feel like I'm under a heat lamp. "Your people have no idea?"

Chewing slowly, savoring my tasty food, I shake my head. Swallowing, I say, "No. Only that he's known as the 'Nickle Eye.' I don't know what that means."

Max takes a big swig of his pint, a little of the foam settling in the corners of his generous lips, which his tongue gathers as his eyes grow wide. "Fuck. What if we have to collect eyes next?"

I almost choke on a bite. "I really hope not." Ears were gross, but eyes... That would be too much for me. Shoving the pictures in my mind out of my head, I focus on consuming a French fry.

"I can do it," Max says. My eyebrows raise in surprise. Lifting a hand from the table, he gives a shrug of nonchalance. "I mean, if we *have* to. Not that I want to."

Max sits back in his chair, done with his food. He pushes his plate away and rubs his stomach. Finishing his beer, he blinks his long lashes into the setting sun. "This is a really nice place. Not like home."

Monitoring where he's looking, I watch some of the children laughing and running along the pier, parents yelling behind them with smiling faces. Kids in Gnarled Pine grow up fast in the skin trade or by numbing their minds with drugs. Many have to go to work for their families at young ages and schools are barren because of it. "No, not like home."

His espresso eyes dart to mine. "What's the deal, little fox? Why are you so slippery, huh?"

I take my last bite and look at my near empty plate as

if it's the most interesting thing in the world. "I don't know what you mean."

Max nods and scans the bar, leaving me to relax out from under his interrogation. "Sure, you don't. Livia, I don't get you. We should be together. You're not a lesbian, right?"

Ugh, he's so disgusting. "Because I don't want you that way, you think I'm a lesbian?" I roll my eyes. "Sorry, lion, but I'm just not into you like that."

The tightness of his black T-shirt stretches as he lets out a soundless snicker. "*Riiiight.* I don't fucking buy that for a second."

"We're working together, Max. Let's just keep it that way. You're a Freidenberg. I'm a Von Dovish." Plain and simple. Enemies who need each other for the time being. That's it.

Brushing a hand through his dark waves, his mouth develops a wan grin. "Yeah, you're right. Maybe Nikolai has a daughter."

My lips involuntarily purse as my belly fills with lead along with the big meal. Picturing Max with someone else makes me rage inside. To hide my face, I wipe it with my napkin and pretend to be distracted by tourists outside the window. Max sits back in his chair and folds his arms behind his head with a sly smirk flickering over his face. He knows he got me with that comment.

Throwing my napkin on the table with aggravation, I ask, "Are you ready to go?".

"Sure, foxy. But I need to change. Car first, then gas station?" Nodding, I agree with his plan.

When we reach the car, Max gets his suit out of the back. I really need to buy him another. He's got money now, I know. Maybe he's just too cheap to buy a new one. After dropping him off at a gas station restroom, he reemerges, looking even more appetizing than my burger.

"Why do you keep wearing that same suit?"

"You don't like it?" He looks down at his clothes as if they're new, fluffing the sleeves with a dusting of his large hand.

Flipping my hair behind my shoulder, I try not to stare at his gloriousness. "It's just the same thing you always wear. I need to take you shopping."

"It brought me luck whenever I'd fight. Wore it to the press conferences. Never lost." Showcasing the jacket with jazzy fingers, he says, "It's my lucky suit."

I sigh and roll my eyes.

"What? Don't tell me you don't believe in luck." Max reaches over and touches my pocket charm, but before he can get to it, I slap his hand with a loud *smack*.

"Don't," I warn him.

"What is that thing?"

With my upper lip curled in a snarl, I tell him, "None of your business. Keep your hands to yourself, lion."

"How about you keep my hands for me?" Narrowing my eyes at him, his face brightens until he releases a hearty chuckle. "Okay, foxy. Let's go." His cologne, his minty breath, his amazingly sculpted muscles filling out his stretched suit... it's all annoying the shit out of me.

Throughout the silent car ride, Max fiddles with his suit buttons, his hands, looking at the view, checks his hair out in the mirror, constantly moving. That irritates me, too. Around some beautiful winding roads that lead us along the water's edge, we almost drive into a mountain tunnel, but just before the entrance is a cobblestone gated drive. Lanterned house numbers dangle from the glass gates, glowing with the address Nick gave me.

"This the place?" Max asks as I drive up to a black metal box on the side, and I press a large silver button, announcing our arrival. The walls slide open for us, and I pull in around an ornate triple tiered fountain.

The house is something out of a seaside magazine. It's as large as the Von Dovish estate, and bright white, even in the evening's dying sun. Each window glows with a landscape spotlight and seems outfitted with its own porch. Gables and shingles spawn from every eave of the roof. Guest houses surround an Olympic-size pool behind a hedge wall on our right and the house opens to an L-shape on our left. Despite its vast size, the estate is beautiful and homey.

Four men in cream linen suits exit the front and approach the Victor, opening the car doors for us and immediately pat us down as we alight. My guard takes his time around my ass after removing my Glock and sliding the full magazine out before he slips it into his pocket. He checks the empty chamber, then hands the gun back to me. Fortunately, he didn't spot my knife as I notice Max's deep eyes drift to my boot, making sure it's still there. Slyly, I nod to him once.

A squirrely looking man with a bowtie and round wire-rimmed glasses approaches from behind the wall of suited guards. "Mr. Freidenberg. Miss Von Dovish. I'm Ovid, Mr. Nikolai's secretary. Please, come with me. This way." On a heel of his Italian loafer, he spins quickly toward the house while we follow.

Ovid leads us through the massive white halls to an office located in one of the rounded corners of the house. A lit fire keeps out the draft of the cool autumn air, creating a cozy room along with several overstuffed wing-backed chairs. Floor-to-ceiling bookcases cover the walls, filled with thick leather tomes of varying heights.

Behind a massive, whitewashed desk sits a muscular guy, probably in his late 40s, with a sprinkling of gray at the temples of his onyx hair and mustache. The broad smile betrays where his black eyes stare at my tits, and I feel the need to cross my arms over my chest. Max's shoulders drop as he scans the room with his mouth slightly opened.

"Please, please. Have a seat. I am Tony Nikolai. It's wonderful to meet you." As he indicates the two chairs in front of him, his gaze focuses like lasers on my face. Max lounges in his seat, kicking one ankle over his opposite knee, while I teeter on the edge. Something about Tony's stare is unnerving, along with his sharply handsome appearance.

"Can I offer either of you a drink?"

"No, thank you," I say.

At the same time, Max says, "Do you have bourbon?"

Mr. Nikolai smiles and rises from his chair, then pours a double for the two of them before handing Max a glass without ever really seeing him. A waft from expensive oak greets my nose as my partner swirls his before taking a sip and my dry mouth regrets declining.

With a creak, Mr. Nikolai sits back in his maroon leather seat and addresses me. "Miss Von Dovish, I don't know if you know me, but I knew your mother. I knew her family well. Very well, actually. Did she ever mention me?"

Wracking my mind, I try to recall anything about my mother's childhood. His confession shocks me because, as a young girl from France, my mother never mentioned knowing a Russian *family* member. "Um... no. I'm sorry."

"We were engaged to be married."

My breath catches, and if I thought I couldn't get more surprised by his previous words, now I'm stunned. Falling open, my mouth makes some type of noise like, "Oh?" He knew her that well? Did she love him? Could he have saved her?

Out of the corner of my eye, I catch Max watching our conversation like a tennis match. Tony folds his hands in front of him as if he'd prepared very well for our meeting.

"Yes. I was quite smitten with her." His smile falters. "Unfortunately, she ran away with that piece of shit. Excuse me, your father."

Taking a deep breath in, my throat relaxes. "No, no. You had it right the first time."

Mr. Nikolai chuckles. "It's a good thing he disap-peared. It's not only Strauss looking for him." His eyebrows come closer together, casting a shadow over his pitch-colored eyes, giving him the look of someone possessed.

"Uh, Nikolai?"

"Please, call me Tony. Did anyone ever tell you that you look just like your mother?" Barely noticeable, the tip of his tongue juts out to snag a drop of bourbon from his bottom lip.

I find that my head is slowly nodding as I answer him. "Yes. We were very close." But not close enough that I knew about Tony. Why wouldn't she mention him? Would my father have beaten her for talking about it?

Tony's not wearing a wedding band. What if he wants a night with me? What if he wants to marry me? Suddenly, Max seems to sense my tension and leans forward in his chair, his smile vanishing as Tony's stare heats up my body.

"I want something from you, Miss Von Dovish."

"Livia," I correct him with some fluttering of my eyelashes. Maybe it's the fact that I can sense Max's jealousy from one foot away, but I decide to use my feminine whiles to their fullest. If Tony wants me and we want his guns, may as well. The only kink in the chain would be if the bear loses his temper.

"Livia." With a flick of his tongue against his teeth, he sounds out my name like it's a love song. Max opens his mouth but shuts it again as I tilt my head to catch his awareness. "I want something from you, Livia. I understand you"—he looks at Max for the first time—"and Mr. Freidenberg need rifles. I have plenty for your arsenal, as many as you desire. I've always felt an urge to spoil Yvette's daughter."

Sitting back, I casually cross my legs and lay my arms on the sides of the chair, placing my chest on full display. Tony's eyelids lower, as if he likes what he's looking at.

"And what would you desire from me?"

The man grins like the Cheshire Cat, and I know without a doubt that Max is ready to jump across the desk at him. *Please* hold it together, lion.

"My father was a jewel man. It's how we made our money. We were in possession of two exceedingly rare gems. They were perfect in quality, cut from the same stone. Legend has it that each half was made for two lovers, each taking a piece with the other. I always had a penchant for them; must run in my blood. Your mother liked them, too. I gave her one of those rings when I proposed, while I kept the other. They are the only two in the world. I want it back. It was—"

Closing my eyes tightly, I try to stop the words from coming out of his mouth, not wanting to hear any more. "I know which ring it was. The purple sapphire?"

"Yes. Did she mention it?"

As if I died and am just returning to life, my pulse thuds back after a pause with a strong, forceful pace. "She willed it to me." There's no way. She willed that ring to me. It was the only thing she loved, and now I understand why. She was pining for Tony. That ring was her mental escape from my father, dreams she must have lost. Sometimes I would catch her staring at it in her room with tears in her eyes, seemingly in a faraway trance. She once told me it was a family heirloom, and I hadn't pressed her more about it, figuring she missed her childhood in the countryside. Tony gave the ring to her with love. It was hers, the only thing that wasn't tainted with Von Dovish blood.

"Wait, all you want is a ring?" Max relaxes fully, as if he's found an easy solution to a problem. My ire raises at his callousness, not even bothering to discuss things with me before speaking.

Tony peers at him. "Yes. I mean, I wouldn't say no to an evening with Yvette's daughter..." Tony gives me a wink, and I cross my arms. Darting his eyes back to Max, Tony smiles at him smugly. "But I have a feeling *you* would have something to say about that." He chuckles. "Besides, Yvette wouldn't have liked it."

"Do you know where it is?" Max's black waves fall in his face as he turns to me, and I want to slap his cheek. Getting that ring is out of the question. It is *mine*. It was hers. It's the only thing my mother had that was her own, and now it's the only thing I have of her.

Both men stare at me, awaiting my reaction, and all I can do is nod my response.

"Oh, well! That's easy! Done. When do you want it by?" Max asks Tony.

My mouth falls open in outrage, heat rising to my cheeks and out of my mouth. "We will *not* be giving it away! You *gave* it to her!"

Tony's long fingers spread before he drums them on his desk. "Yes, but I collect jewels. I gave it to *her*, not the Von Dovish clan."

"She gave it to *me*. It was the only thing—" Snapping my lips closed, I stop myself. It feels like I'm going to lose this battle. Memories of my mother caring for me tenderly as a child flood my mind while picturing her with that ring in her jewelry box... Finally, my voice squeaks out, speaking only to Max. "I'm so sorry, lion. I can't."

He looks perturbed, his brows lowering as he purses his lips. As if strategizing a plan, he asks Tony, "You said there are two rings. Where's the other one?"

Placing an arm on either side of his chair, Tony rocks back. "It was stolen years ago by a very crafty jewel thief. I heard one of my acquaintances from Appleton City may have bought it from him. But I don't think the new owner would give it up for anything. Not even for a turn with Miss Von Dovish, despite her overwhelming beauty."

"Appleton City. Who?" Max asks. Maybe he'll let it go. I stay still, as if moving will cause this quest to get even worse than it already is. Can I trust that Max won't try to steal it from our estate?

"A collector. I only know him as Zayne. He owns a museum, but we supply his guns. I'd be happy to divert that flow to *you*, Mr. Freidenberg, if you bring me Yvette's purple sapphire. Perhaps you can convince your lover here to give it up."

Downing his bourbon, Max clears his throat and responds confidently. "Yep. I'll get you the ring."

"What?! I didn't agree to that." My spine snaps into a straight line as I sit up.

"I'll get you that ring." Max nods at Tony, the two ignoring me completely.

Speaking over me, they continue their conversation. "Thank you, Mr. Freidenberg."

"Call me Max. I'll bring it back to you."

"No, you won't!" My voice is almost a scream.

Max's firm hand grabs me by the bicep, pulling me to a stand. While he's dragging me out of the office, I yell at Tony over my shoulder. "No, he won't!" But the man's handsome face just darkens as he gives me a sly half smile.

"Shut the fuck up," Max growls low in my ear, the sound causing ripples in my system of hating and tingling at his tenor. Shoving me out onto the front porch, the guards open the car doors for us. Max continues to push me into the driver's seat forcefully and jostles me inside. Leaning into the car, his large body hovers over me as he places his face inches from mine. "Shut the fuck up, Livia. I got this one. You stay out of it."

I *knew* I couldn't trust him. This is the entire reason I hadn't let him inside me. Emotionally or physically. "You will *not* steal my mother's ring," I say, venom spewing from my lips. When he doesn't move, my eyes look past him and out the windshield. Quietly, I say, "It's the only thing I have from her that's mine, and I'm keeping it." Sneaking my fingers in my front pocket, I rub my charm three times. It doesn't feel so lucky anymore.

Max snorts. "Who knew Livia Von Dovish, mistress of pain, would be so sentimental over a fucking ring." He reaches to grasp the hand in my pocket, but I pull it out quickly and snatch his. His fingers stroke the object. "Is that it? Is that the ring?"

Speaking through my clenched teeth, I tell him, "No. And take your fucking hand off me."

"You've got a hold of *me*, foxy." He shakes his hand. "Let go." I drop it like his skin just burned me.

He chuckles and walks around the car to get inside. I should just take off and leave him here with his best friend, Tony, but as soon as he gets in, I punch the start button for the ignition. One final warning leaves my lips as I jolt off toward the seaside road. "You're *not* stealing that ring."

If he does, I'll kill him.

Fifteen

MAXIMILLIAN

In the next few days, I don't hear from Livia, as to be expected. It really is better that way because Derichs and I have been on a reconnaissance mission to find the collector in Appleton. The fox made her point loud and clear about her mother's ring, so I knew immediately I'd go on the quest to find the alternative. Sans Livia. It would be my gift to her for her connections. Maybe, secretly, I was hoping it would finally get her to open up to me.

Cruising down the main strip, I look for a decent hotel that's somewhere between the Waldorf and the roach motel we almost stayed at during the last visit. Derichs's long legs are bent wide in the passenger seat next to me while his voice rings out in the cabin, talking to his girl, Hannah, on the phone. "I told you she was jealous of you, baby. Don't pay any attention to her."

Using a loose fist, I punch his upper arm and point to a respectable-looking establishment. He nods in agreement with my decision and continues to chat up his girl. Pulling into the parking lot, I find a spot in the back, away from everyone else. It's dark, but at least no one will hit my car.

"Baby, I love you so much. I miss you. I'll see you soon, okay? Yeah, Max wants to meet you, too. We'll all go to play pool or bowling or something. Love you. No, I love you more... Bye." He hangs up and sighs heavily, happily. "Hannah says hi and to take care of me."

"How exactly does she want me to take care of you? 'Cause I'm not really into dudes. Sorry." I grab our bags from the trunk and shove his into his arms. Part of me is annoyed at missing something I've never had. Something I can't even put my finger on. Safety? Security? Love...

A short chuckle interrupts my jealousy. "Me either, but a beer tonight before we scope out the joint would be nice."

"You want me to get you liquored up first? No problem, I can do that." Once inside, I get us a room with two doubles, and after dropping our bags in the room, we head back to the bar area for some grub. Before I exit the elevator, though, a familiar voice calls out, causing my heart to stop beating.

"Million-dollar Maximillian. How is my Maximum East?"

Fuck. Slowly, I turn around to face the man who ran my life for most of my early 20s. "Hey, Buddy." Buddy Dapper. My handler from my fighting days, known associate of Tony "Two Fingers." And he's using my old stage names. This cannot be good.

"*The* Buddy Dapper?" Derichs's jaw drops as he whispers the name in reverence.

"Hey, Max. Good to see you! It's been a long while. What are you up to?" Buddy grabs me into a half hug, his pudgy middle poking me more than it did in years past. The scraggles of his thin gray comb-over tickle my nose before he pulls away.

Clearing my throat, I attempt to sound resolved. "Went back home and am working on setting everything up."

"Like you always said you'd do. Good for you, kid." His fat fingers pat me on the back as he eyes Derichs.

Shoving a finger toward him, I say, "Oh, this is my friend Derichs."

"Hello. Looks like you know your way around a ring, too."

Derichs nods, but keeps his mouth shut and eyes wide, staring at Buddy like he's a god.

"What're you doing around Appleton tonight, Bud?" I ask with some trepidation.

"I'm glad I ran into you. We have a fight going on in a bit, and I need that money you owe me."

Damn. I thought I'd never run into Buddy again. At least I was planning on it. There was one fight I was supposed to throw back in the day that lost him twenty grand when I just couldn't. Pride costs a lot. "Sorry, man. Can I get it to you soon?"

"Ha. No can do, Max-a-million. If not me, then you know Greedy, or Kinks, or Falsies will pay you a visit. I said I would be the one to tell you. As a friend, you know." So, they've been watching me since I got back into town... Can't say I blame them. Maybe recognized the Barracuda. I know the other guys won't hesitate to start breaking bones or taking off body parts, so at least it was Buddy who found me first.

The money I had earned from our gun trade was going into renovations and East Side's hands. Rebuilding the community was expensive. Our earnings belonged to the workers, the ones risking their lives to sell those weapons daily, the ones on the front lines of facing Strauss's men. I didn't want to pay off this debt. I also didn't want Tony Two Fingers to send his goons after me. If I owed Buddy for a fight, that meant I owed my old boss. And he always got paid either with a pound of cash or a pound of flesh.

Buddy's shoulders slump. "Ah, son. You don't have it, do you?"

Swallowing the tight lump in my throat, I tell him flatly, "Not right now, but I can get it."

"How about you *earn* it? Tonight." Above his heavily sunken sockets, his light brown eyes sparkle with his proposition.

Pinching the bridge of my nose between my finger and thumb, I allow a heavy breath to escape my lungs. "I'm not fighting anymore. I'm done with that. In the ring anyway." It's not that I *couldn't* throw a fight for them, it's that I was master of the east side. If anything happened to me, what would happen to Arianna? To my employees?

"We're gonna need something, Max."

"I know—" Just as I think about giving in and taking a few hits, my right-hand jumps in.

"I'll do it," Derichs says quietly behind me. My body snaps to his, almost protectively.

Tightening my lips, my voice grits out, "No, Derichs —" He doesn't need to take this fight for me.

"Oh? Sure, kid. Can you throw a fight?" Buddy ignores my protests.

"Yes. I can." Derichs stares me down with his serious eyes.

Turning my body to face him, I grab both his shoulders in a firm grip. He winces, but quickly schools his face. "Your shoulder," I say quietly, pointing out his weakness with a dig of my thumb.

"Max, I got this. For you. For East Side." It's quick, but I catch a flick of his jaw muscle as he tenses.

"You'll get hurt, and I need you."

"I can do this." His face is resolved.

"Kid says he can do it, Million. Let him."

Shaking my head, I say, "He's got a hurt shoulder. Can your guy—"

"No worries. We'll tell him to back off. Which one is it, kid?" Buddy asks Derichs.

Derichs shrugs off my hold and tells him, "The right, sir."

Buddy nods, then leads us to the parking lot. I silently try to argue with my tank the entire time. Derichs keeps his face sternly locked and ignores me completely the entire walk two blocks over to the hidden location where the match will take place. The cool winter wind whips around the corners of the brick buildings, slapping me in the face with loud whines, making my arguments even less heard.

When we all arrive at the warehouse where the ring is set up, Buddy leads us to the back entrance. I'm familiar with the joint, having fought here in several matches eight years ago. This time, however, I'm less angry than my young twenties self was having just lost his parents, but the same drive to succeed drifts over me when we enter the stands. My hands involuntarily twitch from rote memory, and I stretch my fingers at my sides to ease some tension building there.

Derichs doesn't appear nervous at all. We discussed his previous fight history while sparring in the manor basement, and I know he's good. His technique is on point, and if I were in a lower weight class, I'd be nervous. But it takes an exceptional fighter to throw the match without getting caught. As I stand with Buddy ring side, my eyes size up the other fighter who's somewhat familiar to me. Briefly, I recall that he works for a different family based in Appleton.

My tank is set to drop in the second and Buddy informed the rival to avoid Derichs's right shoulder. I'm not letting my eyes leave the match to make sure the guy follows the rules. We came to get Zayne, not have Derichs wounded in a cage match.

When the round starts, Derichs hits him with some fantastic hooks right off the bat, proving he knows exactly what he's doing. The guy wastes no time trying to wrestle him to the ground, which is a smart play since Derichs was beating him with the punches. Derichs doesn't fall for the move and gets the opponent in a leg lock right away. The two are evenly matched until the end of the first round, but my man proved himself well. If it went for three rounds, he may be declared the winner.

"Atta boy. You gave it to him straight away, no punches held back. Great job." Shoving a water bottle in front of his face, I spray some water down his throat, droplets splashing everywhere, as he wipes down with a towel. "He thought he'd lock you on the floor, but you did good. Proved yourself out there."

Derichs nods once, huffing out breaths. "I got this." Given everything we've already been through, I know I can add Derichs to the small pool of people I trust. He knows what he has to do to end things, and as soon as the break is over, he heads back inside the cage, dancing on his feet. The referee signals for the start of the round.

Right away, the opponent grips Derichs's bad shoulder in a lock and twists his arm behind him. The scream that comes from his chest spikes my adrenaline until I feel my body moving inside the cage at a predator's pace before Buddy can stop me. The crowd noises fade as my entire focus narrows to destroying the thug that has Derichs's arm in a hold.

The referee doesn't notice when I sprint up behind them, Derichs now pinned to the ground in agony. His legs flail, trying to get any footing he can while he taps repeatedly on the mat with his free hand, gasping wails breaking my concentration. Once the ref calls the match, I shove the opponent off Derichs and grab my boy up into a bear hug. Dragging him over to the sidelines, he falls into Buddy's arms with a few stumbles.

Swinging around, I charge across the ring and hit the fighter in the back of the head with a full fist while he's watching his coach. Spinning, he spots me with an evil eye, but I grip his arms and almost pick him up to throw his body. He starts to laugh, blood spewing from his nose.

"The fuck! You knew to avoid the shoulder," I yell at him, standing over his body now on the ground.

With a taped hand, he rubs the back of his head, before checking his palm for blood, still chuckling. "That was for working with The Ear. Boss's orders." His men surround him and shove me back with a hand to my chest. When the referee points to the other side of the cage, instructing me to leave, I'm already returning to Derichs. Buddy has him up and my tank holds his own elbow delicately.

Shaking my head, guilt fills my belly. "Fuck! He shouldn't have—"

"Max, it's okay. Thank you. I'll be fine. It's okay. No permanent damage." We head toward the back hall, Buddy beside us.

"I thought he was going to rip your arm off." I swallow. "It looked like he was going to kill you." I don't think I could forgive myself if he'd gotten seriously injured, especially since all he was doing was for me.

"It felt like it." Derichs rotates his arm a few times with a slight grimace on his wide lips. "I got you, man. I can still back you up anytime. I'm not going anywhere. Even if I only have one arm, I'm there for you."

As we walk, I grab a clean towel and toss it over his shoulders, then hand him an ice-cold bottle of water. Everything better be copacetic. I never want to hear of Two Fingers again. "We square now, Buddy?"

"Yeah, Million. We're square." Before we make our way to the hotel, Bud grabs my arm, turning me to face him, his comb-over flopping in the freezing winter breeze, only blocked by the closeness of the buildings nearby. "I don't think the boss will like hearing about you taking up with Lavinio, though. I miss you, son, but please avoid this city." He sneaks a glance at Derichs. "For your own safety."

Nodding, I let him know the plan. "I have one more job that I came for. Then we'll be out of here."

"Better make it quick. If word gets around town, especially after tonight's antics..."

"We'll be gone shortly." Just another reason I wished no one had known I had come back. Now that word had gotten around I was working with Lavinio and had caused a problem in the ring tonight, it could be bad for me. Somehow, Gnarled Pine Hollow is safer for me now more than ever, and that's a strange feeling. Comfort in the uncomfortable.

Once we get changed back in the hotel room and Derichs takes some anti-inflammatories, we ride over to the building we need in the Barracuda. Zayne lives in a penthouse at the top of a ritzy glass building in the middle of downtown. After circling the block a few times, scoping out escape routes, I park down the street, but make sure there's a clear way out if we need to leave in a hurry.

Fortunately, Zayne's housekeeper is broke. She's also an unwilling sex slave at times. The guy likes whips, chains, and cigarette lighters and she doesn't seem to appreciate the burns.

It was easy to give her cash, promise her safety, and get her to locate the purple sapphire for us. Zayne keeps most of his jewels locked in a bedroom safe; she told my spy Gemini over the dinner date he wooed her with. My hackers located the plans for the building and the codes to get inside. Wearing all black with ski masks stuffed in our pockets, Derichs and I enter through the glass doors of the building, prepared for our midnight trek.

We're able to waltz right past the sleepy security guard and into the gleaming silver elevators without any issues. The trick is to always appear like you're supposed to be where you are, or maybe having Derichs look as busted as he does is enough to scare off any questions. We don't look friendly.

Riding up to the top floor, I tap a quick message on my phone to Skipper, my lead hacker. Before the doors open, he's already disabled the security cameras and says he's working on Zayne's electronic lock on the penthouse. Derichs and I tug on our masks, then head out onto the top floor. The solid white hallway holds only a single plain door, modern and sleek, where we wait for only a minute before a loud click, then a buzz echoes through the barren hall. I enter the apartment with Derichs close behind my back.

Derichs nods at me when I point to the entryway. He'll take the six and monitor for anyone trying to come in without warning. Sneaking toward the hall, I find the main bedroom from the floorplan I was given. Everything is laid out just as Gemini drew for me.

Placing my hand on the cold handle, I ease it down as slowly as my muscles will allow to open the door without a sound. Curtains block all light inside the room, but as my eyes adjust to the blackness, I can make out a heap of a figure lying under puffy blankets on the large bed near the center. Gently placing one foot in front of the other, my boots curl up in a creep to the open door of the closet on my left.

Edging inside while steadying my breathing, my hands grab a handful of his freshly dry-cleaned shirts to slide them aside, but as I do, their plastic covers rustle louder than I anticipate. I freeze, but don't hear any movement after waiting for at least one full minute. A green glow of digital zeros lights up a metal box sitting on the wall, the safe right where the housekeeper said it would be. She gave up the code willingly, and I press the buttons one at a time, pausing between each loud beep to monitor for any sound coming from the bedroom. Everything is still.

A creak interrupts the calm as the metal door finally clicks and swings open, causing my heart rate to spike. I ruffle through the contents using my phone as a flashlight, but there're only papers and file folders and a book. No jewels. *Fuck!* It's not here. Maybe I missed it or maybe there's another safe. I go through it again, but there's no purple sapphire. Blood rushes in my ears, making hearing anything behind me difficult. Did the housekeeper lie?

"Zayne?" A high-pitched female voice breaks my panic, my arteries rioting as all the blood rushes into my extremities, ready for a fight. Fumbling with my phone, I turn off the flashlight and quiet my breathing, but my heart is pounding so hard, I fear whoever it is may hear it. "Zayne? Is that you?"

Holding my breath, I glance around the closet. There's nowhere for me to hide without making noise. Footsteps slap the ground assuredly in my direction before a shadowy figure of a woman peers around the corner. She flips on the closet light, momentarily blinding both of us. When our eyes adjust, she gasps, but my body is already in motion from years of experience.

My arms surround her, wrapping one hand around her neck and the other over her mouth. She kicks in the air with her feet, but given she's so much smaller, I lift her body until her flails meet open space. Squeezing my hold, I feel the breath collapse from her lungs as a cough escapes around my palm. Her body calms in my grasp. Some of her long, blonde hair catches on my tongue, and I spit it out as her bony, cold fingers grip the hand on her mouth, trying to pull me off. The metal of her rings cuts into my skin.

"Don't make a fucking sound. Nod if you under-stand." Rapidly, she nods while moaning a whimper.

Placing her feet back on the ground, I forcefully march her body back into the bedroom, but I can't make out anyone else in the dark space. Releasing the palm over her lips, she inhales deeply with a gasping breath.

"Let me see your hands," I command. Dropping the arm around her neck, I maintain a hold on her waist. Now that she can move, her body shakes violently with desperate sobs.

"Please, please, don't hurt me. Just take anything."

"Let me see your fucking hands." I give her waist a squeeze with my bicep to let her know how serious I am, and she holds them up in front of us. There it is, sparkling in the light of the closet on her perfectly polished ring finger. Dropping her, I pull out my phone, and flash the light on it to be sure. "Give me that ring."

She hesitates, staring at her outstretched hands. The dumb bitch actually hesitates. Snatching her wrist, I almost crush it, attempting to rip the ring off along with a finger. Wails of pain rip from her mouth, but I twist it off, then shove it deep in the pocket of my jeans. Just as quickly, I gather her back into my arms and reach for my Glock sitting in its holster on my belt. Holding the barrel to her temple, I shove it into the skin as she cries in frantic, muffled pleas.

"Where's Zayne?" I ask, my voice gruff, my finger with steady pressure on the trigger. She only whines and shakes her head in reply. "Where the fuck is Zayne? Is he here?"

Arms wrap around my biceps, and the sudden jarring causes me to drop my gun. Tight hands grip my throat in a chokehold from behind. My mask works its way off my face as I kick with my legs to try to gain a hold, but the guy is just as talented as me. He's got training. With a small torque of my waist, I'm able to bend over and flip his heavy body off me, but he maintains a hold on my head until we end up on the ground in a wrestling match.

Eventually, I gain a lock with my legs on his while those large hands maintain their grasp around me. I'm losing air and can't yell for Derichs, the world fading in and out from black to deadly. Leveraging him with my thighs, I flip us and finally get in guard, despite his continued squeeze on my neck. Using my elbows, I beat in his face, then dig my thumbs into his eye sockets, building up the pressure there and not letting go.

His fingers loosen their clutch on my life, and my breath comes back in small pants as he relaxes. The blood rushing through my ears slows, replaced in pulsating sonic waves by shrill screams of terror from the lady standing over us. Derichs busts in with his gun raised. Grasping the guy's brown hair with one hand, and his jaw with the other, I push up quickly until I feel each bone in his neck pop in a neck crank. His tongue lolls out of his mouth as he groans, giving up resistance, paralyzed. Fingers threading around his windpipe, I squeeze until his eyes gouge out of their sockets, and his last breath exits his chest with a haunting, rattling gurgle.

Haven't had to do that in a long time, but I've still got it. And my shoulders relax some as I realize I at least got out of that match alive.

Derichs quickly runs to the woman and clasps a hand over her mouth. "Shut the fuck up, lady."

Standing, I look around the area for my gun. "I've got the ring."

"What do we do about her?" Derichs tries to contain her floundering body, the silk negligee she wore working its way up to her waist, exposing her lacy thong.

Scanning her up and down, I take a deep breath to try to gather some brain cells back. I need to think. I've never had to kill a woman before. Not that I am opposed, but something doesn't sit right with me about it. "Can you keep quiet?" I ask her.

Derichs lowers his palm enough so she can talk. "Yes, yes, I'll be quiet." What little light the hallway afforded makes the tears on her cheeks glisten like a road on a rainy night.

From behind her, Derichs shakes his head at me. "I don't think that's a good idea, boss."

"Please, no. Just let me go. You can have the ring. I won't tell anyone."

I consider my options. A gun will be heard at this hour, and I have no silencer. Perhaps a pillow could work... But I don't want to strangle a lady to death unless it's Livia.

"Let's go." Making up my mind, I give the command. Derichs reluctantly releases her body from his arms as he cocks one eyebrow at me, as if he is still unsure, but willing to follow anything I say. We shove our guns back in their holsters and dart toward the front door. Now that my adrenaline is wearing off, dull pain invades every muscle. My vision is cloudy from the lack of oxygen I sustained in the dead man's vice grip.

I reach for my mask but shove it in my pocket instead of wearing it. It was too late to put it back on once the woman saw me. Hopefully, she didn't get a good look at my face in the dim lights.

My voice comes out hoarse when I tell Derichs, "You gotta drive. I don't know if I can even see right now. Go straight to Tony's place. I don't want this ring on me any longer than it has to be."

We jump inside, and Derichs revs the engine before darting out into the city streets. He's a good driver. If anyone is allowed to drive my baby, it's him. My eyes slowly regain their focus as I wipe up blood from my nose and take some deep breaths, each swallow of air into my lungs restoring my sight. Resting my head back on the seat, I try to relax my body. The drive will be several hours, but Derichs doesn't let off the gas.

He pulls over at a few rest areas for us along the journey, but we never stop for long. We pause twice for gas, switching out drivers, but motor toward Cliff Harbor as fast as possible, one of us trying to catch some naps in the passenger seat while the other finds their way to Nikolai. The jewel feels like a homing beacon in my pocket, and the less time I have it on me, the better.

Mid-morning, a guard opens the gate for us once we reach the mansion. Ovid greets us at the door and shuffles us to the office. The silk dressing robe Tony wears rides up his arm as he waves us inside with a rotating motion of his hand. Before he can lounge back in his leather desk chair, I take two long strides and drop the ring in his open palm. "Will that do?"

As if I just created new matter from nothing, he gawks at the object, his intense eyes never leaving it as he says, "Please, please sit."

"Excuse me, sir, but we've been driving a long way." I glance at my tank, who's shifting from foot to foot behind my left shoulder. "I don't think either of us wants to sit right now." My back aches. I'm only twenty-eight, but between the years of fighting and now driving for hours, there's no way I'm going to ease back in one of his awkward puffy chairs. Not only that, but the guy is creepy. The way he looked at my foxy was enough for me to itch to see his blood pouring from some orifice. Best not to trust myself to stay around him for very long.

Nikolai rummages in the drawers behind his desk before he produces a jeweler's loupe. Prominent white teeth crawl out from behind his wide lips as he mutters to himself, "Yes. This is perfect." He takes a deep breath and sighs longingly. "How did you ever convince the little fox?"

I grab my crotch pointedly. "You know how women are."

With an opening smack of his lips, Tony busts out a loud laugh as Derichs's jaw drops. Poor guy looks appalled.

"Whatever works, my man. I dig it. Good luck to you. You'll be hearing from Tiny Jim out there to set things up in Gnarled Pine Hollow. He'll take good care of you. Enjoy." Standing, he sticks out his hand, and I shake it briefly. Business done, I turn to head out the door,

Derichs's deep eyes scanning my face, still stunned by my confession.

Tiny Jim is anything but small. Ovid has us wait in the foyer when the big guy ambles out from a back hallway. His T-shirt clad arms can barely bend to hold his phone when we exchange numbers, veiny biceps twitching as he does.

Ovid opens the front door for us and leads us back to my car. Derichs follows closely behind with his stare still palpable on my back. Once inside, I start the engine for the long drive home, fully recovered from the night's activities. Derichs's head turns, as if he's waiting patiently for me to speak.

Amused, I take off out of the drive and ask, "What?"

"*'You know how women are?'*"

"Yeah, sometimes I can read people well. It'll keep him from trying to get with Livia and stealing her family's heirloom. Hopefully, he nor anyone else knows what went down with Zayne and we never hear about that ring again."

Derichs snorts dramatically as we head onto the main road. "Since when do you care about a Von Dovish heirloom?" His face smirks so hard, I want to smack the expression off. Instead, I reach over and slap the back of the head while his mouth broadens into a wide grin as he laughs, the sound so joyfully contagious, I join in.

～

A few days later, I'm training in the basement alone. Derichs got time off to see his woman while Jakob has been busy keeping an eye on my sister, making sure that kid Wyatt doesn't even breathe near her. So far, I'm told it's working.

Fritz pops his head downstairs and announces formally, "A Miss Livia Von Dovish to see you, sir."

Snagging a rough white towel from the bench, I rake it over my neck and face. "Okay, send her down." Despite just working out, my pulse spikes higher as the excitement of seeing her washes over me, and I chug a bottle of water to cleanse my dry mouth.

Long, sculpted legs are the first thing I notice, covered with some type of leather thigh-high boots. Hips, covered with a barely-there skirt, gently curve up to her taut abs. As my eyes drink up her body, all I see is smooth tattooed skin, ripe for cutting with my blade. She's only wearing a tiny sports bra looking top, causing the blood that was pounding in my ears to rush into my groin when I get to her full, round tits, which try to jump out of her shirt and into my mouth. Hmm, this raven is certainly dressed for an occasion, but what kind?

"Hey," she says, and the sound is like auditory porn for my dick.

"Hey," I respond as casually as I can, but I'm unable to stop from roving over her body like I'm looking for water on Mars. "What's up?"

She stands about five feet away from me, cautiously fidgeting with her fingers as if she doesn't know what to do with herself. Swallowing, she ever-so slowly takes a step in my direction, her hips swaying with each one until she is directly in front of me. "I-I heard about the ring."

My breathing slows to almost non-existent. Some hair falls in my face as I nod my reply, unable to form words. That signature amber scent fills my nostrils, and desire overtakes me, filling me with primal need. If I inhale, I'll taste her, and I won't be stopping this time. My cock jumps in my shorts.

Batting her lashes, she says softly, "Thank you, Max. You didn't have to do that."

The urge to touch her face makes my fingertips tingle, but I hold back. "I did. I didn't want—I wouldn't let him take your memories from you."

Her long fingers reach out and smooth over my bare chest. Everywhere she touches feels like wildfire spreading along the skin. My heart stops beating. Crawling up my neck until her hands thread through my hair, her voluptuous breasts mold into me, soft against my hardness. Dare I use my arms to circle her back?

Livia's face rests inches from my own once I lean down to her, maybe to embrace her fully or just the hope that I could. She tugs on the back of my head and lightly brushes her pert pink lips to mine, and I savor her flavor with a swallow. All the traumas that have been locked deep inside me begin to feel like they happened someone else as she deepens her connection with my mouth, the taste of her intoxicating me until I can't hold back any longer.

Snatching her by the waist, I thrust my tongue inside

her, desperate to have her saliva mix with mine. I need our mouths to blend into one. It's vital that we collide. I can't live without this, the unadulterated hunger for her causing a frenzied panic in my lungs. One hand runs through her silky dark hair, the other gripping her firm ass as she pulls me closer. When my tongue meets hers again, a whimper sounds in her throat, divulging how much she needs me.

Lifting her by her thighs, I push her against the nearest wall as those long legs surround my waist with a tight grip. Only thin athletic shorts shield my cock, and it's dying to escape deep inside her cave, to fucking maul her. Nails embed in each other's skin. Our tongues slow from their raging battle and begin soothing each other's wounds with gentle caresses.

Pulling back from me, she places her forehead against mine as we pant heavy breaths onto the other's lips. "I want you," she whispers in between huffs.

"I want you," I repeat back to her. Removing one hand from her leg, I start to tug down my shorts and expose myself.

Her little hand touches mine to stop its movement. "But you shouldn't, Max. I can't—" She bites her lip and her voice cracks with strain. Those golden eyes fill with tears until they sparkle like rain on a sunny day. "I can't. You shouldn't want me."

Straightening up, my burning skin turns ice cold. All the heat I built up morphs into rage. As I take a step back, I drop her to the ground, and she stills, leaning against the wall, barely able to look me in the eye. "What in the actual fuck, Livia? Do you enjoy torturing me? Torturing my dick?" Grasping my full erection, I give it a shake. Those bleary champagne eyes glance at it, then flinch away as her cheeks flame pink.

"No, I wanted to thank you for what you did for me," she cries out, tears now freely streaming down her face. "Nothing more." Wiping her nose with the back of her hand, she tries to hide her face by looking down, but I tip her chin up, so she has to meet my fierce gaze.

"*Nothing?*"

She shakes her head rapidly, but keeps her lips tightly sealed. Her reluctance to open up to me after everything pisses me off more than anything.

"Why in the fuck are you *crying?* Why shouldn't I want you, Livia? Answer me."

Swiping her wet cheeks with her thumbs, she sticks her chin up and glares at me. "You'd just get attached to my pussy, and I don't have time for your clinginess, Freidenberg." The weepy damsel in distress tone is gone from her voice, replaced by bratty bitchiness.

With my hands on my hips, I stare her down for a full minute, contemplating any sort of reply. God, it fucking *hurts*, whatever kind of game she's playing with me. I can't take this rejection anymore. My chest is tight from the pain as I manage to squeeze out, "Get the fuck out of my house." Snapping my thumb and finger together forcefully, I point to the stairs, my hand shaking with fury. "I'll just go to the Crimson Angel. They don't have cockteasers there."

She gasps with an audible click in the back of her

throat, the harpy having the audacity to look hurt. Then she spins on her heel and leaves.

Sixteen

LIVIA

Try to show a little affection to a man and all he wants is to take it all the way. I only wanted to thank Max for what he did for me. That's it. Really. Instead, he tried to turn that into something more.

It doesn't matter that I *want* his cock. I know that if I use it, there'll be no going back. That kiss was enough. Despite him doing a noble thing for me, I still cannot trust him. Not completely. Not in the way royalty from Gnarled Pine should trust a mate. He's a man... My mother put her faith in my father, and it got her killed. And she was even able to play the perfect wife. She wasn't damaged like me.

Goes to show you can't trust anyone to protect you, to not hurt you. Everyone is out for themselves. It's better to be alone; it's safer. And I wouldn't be if I kept kissing Max. At least my heart wouldn't be. I'd want more.

Maybe I should give in to him and just fuck him

once, then be done with it. Could I do that? No, there's no way. I need to be honest with myself. I can't let us be together. It would break us both.

We still have to work together to get the rest of the weapons, and I can't be getting distracted by his perfect dick. Oh, and what a perfect cock it is. Smooth, thick, long, straight, round head... I have no right to be as jealous as I am, but if he heads to the Crimson Angel, I should get with someone else, too. Maybe it'll help me get over him.

Only a week after the run-in with the grouchy bear in his home gym, winter has set in our city. The biting air mauls my skin, causing my fingers to stiffen when I grip my leather jacket tightly as I maneuver myself out of the Barracuda. Max insisted on driving again. We rode in silence during the entire three-hour journey to our latest meeting spot. Just the two of us, because Derichs is still babysitting Arianna while Jakob recovers.

Poor guy apparently got clipped in the leg during a firefight with Ace's guys. Ari said it happened while he was trying to sneak something to her from Wyatt under the guise of delivering her bike parts. Their relationship was already causing issues, but our rendezvous at the casino seemed to have some dire consequences. It's getting more dangerous to walk on the streets.

Stretching my neck with a sigh, I remember my promise to the younger Freidenberg that I would speak with her brother about letting her go to the motorcycle shop. However, now is most definitely not the time. Max and I haven't spoken in complete sentences to each other since our kiss. Well, "kiss" implies something simple, like mouths combining, but that was something far beyond anything I'd ever experienced. Transformative... and dangerous.

Echoes informed me he went to the Crimson Angel a couple of times. Then snapped her mouth shut, saying she was instructed not to tell me anything further. Just thinking about him with someone else makes me want to vomit. Or kick his shins in.

"You loaded?" Max pops a bullet in his chamber before putting his handgun in his holster. Irritation rings underneath his husky voice, shaking me from my inner thoughts. It's the first words he's spoken other than "gas" and "let's go." I do the same with my weapon, dramatically jerking the slide with a loud clang.

"Yes," I say with just as much flatness as he mustered. Without looking at me, he lifts his finger toward an alley of the brick building we pulled up to.

"Move." I pop my jaw at his brusqueness, but head across the street with him, trying to keep up with his long strides.

Owned by a Mr. Gabriel Sosa, the head of some ring of trafficking, the building is supposed to be an underground sex club. Briefly, I wonder if he's great friends with Strauss... and what trouble that could cause us.

Lecherton is a grimy metropolis filled with corruption much like home. But they have weapons. Lots of weapons. If we broker a good deal with Sosa, we'll be set.

No more of these day trips to seedy joints. No more quests. Max and I can part ways and our men can do the exchanges without us ever having to interact again.

When we arrive at the solid metal door on the side of the building, it doesn't matter that we have our handguns. Once again, our weapons are confiscated before we can walk down the stairs. At least I have my trusty blade tucked into my boot. After one large security guy pats down Max, I notice he skips his knife tucked in his waistband.

Another city, another sordid boss. This one, however, is lounging on a purple velvet sofa with three women's heads knelt before his open pants when we're shown into a playroom. It's filled with a large bed, several sofas, and black lava lamps. Not too unlike the Crimson Angel, so Max should feel right at home.

Gabriel is attractive. From what I can tell under his black dress shirt, his body is cut, and he doesn't look terribly old, probably in his late thirties. His dick must be big because the three girls each have a piece in their mouths. Leaning my head to the side, I make out that one has one ball, one has the other, and one has the shaft. It's economical, the way they have it divided up, and I nod my approval as Max stares at the situation with an unamused expression.

"Come in, come in, baby." Gabriel motions us inside with just his fingers, each filled with gold and black rings. With the top of his black-haired head, he points to a sofa next to his as he brings a palm up to stroke his goatee, his dark eyes continuing to watch the show between his knees. We sit, Max with his legs wide apart, leaning forward with his elbows resting on his thighs, his eyes never leaving the girls at their work. But instead of lust or longing on his face, he seems disgusted. I drop to the seat beside him, feeling Gabriel's gaze scan my chest, my waist, my hips, my thighs. As my eyes meet his, his long, black lashes flutter at me longingly while petting two of the women's heads as if they are dogs.

"You want?" Gabriel asks with a glance at Max. He pulls one girl off his sack, snatching her head by the hair and holding it back so Max can get a look at her gaping mouth. Like she's property. Max shakes his head, a slight frown meeting the corners of his lips. Gabriel settles her back to her job.

Thrusting his hips up, he obviously finishes down the middle woman's throat while the other two moan in pleasure, suckling his testicles. Gabriel's head is thrown back for a moment in ecstasy before he slides back into his seat to relax. "Fuck. Clean me up, dear. Share some with the others." The girls swap the semen between one another's mouths dramatically, allowing strands of white jizz to string between their chins and lips while seemingly eyeing him for approval. My stomach rolls at the sight of it.

Gabriel tucks himself back into his pants and zips up. When the women stand, he swats two on their asses and smiles. "That's my good girls." Stretching his arms across the back of the sofa, he asks, "Now, what can I do for you?"

Gabriel's post-ecstasy face and dark brown eyes stare

right at me, so I take the lead. "We're here for weapons. I think Nick spoke with you—"

"Yes, sweetheart. I understand. I can get you all the weapons you need." His head rests lazily against the sofa as he lulls in a monotone voice. Like it's a Tuesday. "Grenades? Flamethrowers? Shotguns? Automatics? A tank? What do you want?"

He's oozing with confidence and seems laid back. With his boldness, it makes me feel more at ease until I let out a small chuckle. "Um, all of it."

Gabriel smiles broadly, causing his face to change from attractive to quite handsome. Max's shoulders stiffen beside me as I answer, but I'm not sure why. He just got a good show. As a frequenter of sex clubs, I'm sure this is nothing new for him.

"I'd be thrilled to give them to you." His smile falters as his black eyes turn to onyx with some level of foreboding, causing me to feel like I forgot to study for a test I didn't know we were having. "You really are beautiful."

"Thank you." I glance at Max, who's staring down Gabriel, like he's ready to pounce at any moment. The guy is a bit smarmy, but he seems like he will work with us. "So, what do you want in exchange?"

"I want to fuck you."

My breath catches with my open-mouthed gasp. I didn't expect that. "Uh—"

"Absolutely not," Max interrupts, his voice ringing out with finality while his paws clench so tightly the knuckles turn his olive skin white.

Gabriel relaxes back farther and sighs, as if he has

won a game. "Oh? One little fuck and you can have everything you want. Does she belong to you?" He looks at Max. Max turns his eyes down briefly to glance at me, then slowly shakes his head like when he would lose a match in the ring. "Okay, then."

"I'll do it," I say with assuredness. Fake it till I make it, right?

"No, you won't." Max's eyes flare when he whips his head to me. I've never seen him look so tense. His piercing stare gashes my self-control, and all the irritation I've had over the last week spews up and out at him.

"You went to the Crimson Angel. I'm going to fuck Gabriel for weapons. No big deal." The words snap out of my mouth like a whip, hoping they cut into his icy exterior.

"The *fuck*? Try me, foxy. Try me and see what happens." If he were a bear, his haunches would be all the way up. I'm sure Max has had his recent fill of women. Why is he so concerned? This could give us both the distance we need from each other. If I have sex with Sosa, maybe I won't be so attached, and Max could get over trying to own me.

Snubbing him, I turn to Sosa and ask, "Just one fuck, and then we can have the weapons?"

Gabriel chortles, a loud, boisterous sound, as if we were just put on a comedy show for him. "Yes, just one time where I get inside you. That's all I want, beautiful. Well, all I *wanted*. Now, I really want *him* to watch us." He points at Max, who glares at him, his nostrils puffing out with his exhales. This only makes Sosa roar with laughter.

Max grips my thigh with his large palm. "I'm telling you, Livia. Do not do this."

Lowering my voice, I speak through gritted teeth. "And I'm telling *you*, I'm fucking this guy. We *need* those weapons."

"No, we don't, little fox. We have plenty now. We'll make do. Let's go." Pulling on my leg, he attempts to make me move, but I hold firm.

"All this arguing between you lovers is getting me hard again." Gabriel chuckles and grabs his dick that is firming against his thigh. "I think I'm going to last a while with you, sweetheart." He holds out a hand to me. Watching Max's rage rise in his flaming cheeks, I gracefully stand from my seat and stroll over to take the man's outstretched palm. It's soft and warm.

There's comfort in fucking someone you don't care about. Intoxicating power. Like I can get away with something bad without feeling guilt or shame. It feels safe in a way. Sex with Max could cause a pain I'd never be rid of.

Sure, yes, most of me wants to get back at Max for going to the Crimson Angel. For giving up on me so quickly when I wouldn't give it up to him. Making me feel like a cheap plastic toy he would throw away once he played with it. Now, he's just trying to claim what isn't his. It's not like he really cares about *me*, just the idea of me or what he can't have. His legacy, his heirs... all that Gnarled Pine Hollow poison ingrained in him.

Max jumps up and snatches my loose hand before I

sit. There's a desperation in his eyes I've never seen before, a vulnerability there I didn't know was possible. "Foxy." His voice is soothing. "Please, don't. *Please.*"

My tug breaks our contact. If my right hand wasn't still in Gabriel's, I'd rub my lucky charm. Instead, I sit on the boss's lap. "It's just one fuck, Max," I say, fluttering my lashes as if I'm trying a new style of fries at a fast-food restaurant.

Gabriel nuzzles my neck. Into my hair, he commands Max, "You can sit there and observe, or the chair in the corner. Whichever you prefer."

I slide off his legs as he stands, then guides me by the waist to the bed at the back of the room. Max's figure looks like a gargoyle in front of the sofa, his shoulders still tensed up to his ears, still and foreboding.

Gabriel pulls me into his taut body, wrapping his hands around my head while he kisses me with his large, plush lips. A taste of stale cigars blows into my mouth, so I lean back, breaking his grasp to get away from it. When I open my eyes, Max is staring down Gabriel's back from his guarded position, fire flaming from his countenance.

Ignoring the bear, I undo Gabriel's buttons as he helps me undress. His hands immediately grasp my breasts and twist my nipple bars like he's never seen them, while he huffs an excited bitter smelling breath in my face. When Gabriel's tongue moves to lick my rings, Max stalks to the corner chair for a closer inspection. His gaze remains dark and intense, the rage radiating off his body causing the temperature to rise within the room.

Moaning loudly, I let my head fall back and stroke

Gabriel's dark, short hair. With a scoff, Max removes his dress coat, then unbuttons his shirt, letting it gape open at the top. Gabriel lifts me up and tosses me onto the bed, the pillows greeting my head when I land. He crawls between my knees and slaps them apart with an open palm, the sting causing me to jolt with shock. Giving a cursory smirk at Max, he dips his head between my thighs and laps his tongue straight up my center. He's not skilled, but it's getting the job done.

Even from this distance, I sense how antsy Max is fidgeting next to the bed. I wish I didn't. Can't I just fuck someone else and forget the spell he's put me under? Just like he did to me?

Gabriel's careless mouth works me sloppily until I'm wet with his saliva alone. Yet here I am... All I can think of is the man sitting next to me.

Shoving two fingers inside me, he does that thing guys think gets girls hot, but really, it's just annoying. Grinding his fingers roughly inside, punching my cervix repeatedly. I pull my hips back to show him where it feels good, but he misinterprets my movements. "Yeah, baby. You like that?"

No, I don't. I want to say it, but now I just want him to finish. Grasping his wrist, I show him where to touch me. Crooking a thick, dark eyebrow, he seems confused that someone would be so forward with him. His dick juts out starkly between his legs when he sits back on his knees. "Be a sport and grab me a condom there, would you?" he asks Max with a snarky smirk.

Max seems to have softened in his expression. Or is it

resolve? The eerie calmness replacing his ire is making me even more nervous than before and, for the first time, I reconsider jumping in and agreeing to do this. Casually, Max grabs a condom from a nearby table, then hands it to Gabriel, tucked between two large fingers.

Gabriel rips it open and suits up, then leans over my body. Hopefully, he's better with his dick than his fingers. "You ready, sweetheart?"

Wrapping my legs around him, I nod. He lines up and shoves in. His hips thrust erratically, without much rhythm. Despite his obvious sexual proclivities, he likely has never had to think about pleasing anyone *else*. His gyrations make it painfully obvious he's only here for his own gratification. I could be anyone. Like a pocket pussy. Settling back on the mattress, I will it to be over as soon as possible. At least we'll get the weapons. And Max will be pissed that I slept with someone else, just like he did.

Gabriel grips my hips and sits up so he's kneeling while jackhammering into me, and I arch my back, my eyes meeting his squinted ones. He's not really looking at *me*, perhaps just imagining a scene in his head. Maybe it's better if I close my eyes, so I don't have to remember this. Squeezing my lids tightly shut, I try to think about anything else. Like the mantra of "rifles, flamethrowers, and grenades, oh my" over and over with every annoyingly painful stab of his dick inside me.

After only two more awkward thrusts, the bed dips, and Gabriel lets out a choked grunt. His thumbs dig into the apex of my hips with such force, it feels as if he's tearing me in two. The biting pain screams through me like two red-hot pokers until a spasm jerks him free. A warm spray hits my face, chest, stomach, and thighs. Who knew he would have so much cum and so quickly, too?

My eyes snap open at a gurgling sound just in time to see Max kneeling behind Gabriel on the bed. A wide, crimson grin erupts from his neck, like a gaping maw that grows deeper as Max draws his knife across the divide. Gabriel's eyes and mouth are wide with horror, his throat open in a savage smile matching his silent scream while his head flips back at an awkward angle.

Red gushes in spurts, landing in my open mouth, my eyes, my hair... It's all over me, coating and soaking into every surface. There's no escape from the scalding tidal wave of life leaving his body. Max shoves the body, and it slumps forward, Gabriel's forever frozen stare leaning ever closer to my face, but before the dead falls on me, Max pushes it to the side. Gabriel hits the floor with a loud thud.

A panicked shriek rises deep within my belly, clawing its way through my windpipe, but Max lays his naked body on top of mine, causing the air to be knocked from my lungs. His bloodied hand slaps across my mouth, dripping wet hot liquid over my face. Gripping my waist, he pulls me onto his lap until we sit together. As I open my mouth to let the sound escape, Max crashes his lips onto mine. My scream is sucked into his lungs as he plunges his hardness inside me, his thick cock filling me completely as his tongue entwines with mine, muffling my terror and transforming it into something else entirely. His hand clutches the back of my head, steadily holding mine to his, and on impulse, I hold on to his shoulders just as harshly.

The sheets of blood coating our bodies cause them to slicken against each other. Our thighs slap with each punch of his hips, spurts of droplets spraying out when we meet. The urge to yell subsides with every stroke of his dick, soothing and comforting me with inconceivable safety. Instead of a scream, a whimper erupts from my chest, oozing out pleasure and shock.

Max pulls his lips back just enough to growl in a commanding voice, "I told you not to fucking test me, Livia. Look at me. Look. At. Me." He gathers my hair and pulls my face back, our eyes locking with a searing gaze. "You're fucking *mine*. Do you hear me? *Mine. Mine. Mine.*" He accentuates his point with each stab of his cock. "No one else's. No one else. You and me. We're together."

Gripping him tightly, I grind my hips down every time he thrusts deeper. My fingers beg to grasp more surface of him, slippery with the blood of our enemy, the smell, the metallic taste of the liquid invading our lovemaking.

"You see this? This is us as one. You and me are one now. That's it. You hear me, little fox?" Gripping my chin between a finger and his large thumb, he asks as my vision blurs with the tears that gather there, which spill over to mix with the red smears, cooling the pink of my flaming cheeks.

I'm crying because I need him. Because I've wanted

him. Because I never allowed myself to indulge in this, and now, we're here. I cry because I fear I'll never feel this fulfilled again. That he'll love me and then leave. That he'll kill me... He may even kill me now.

Laying me back against the pillows, he remains inside me, but cups my face with his large hands. His thumbs stroke the tears from my cheeks as he pushes inside me slowly, repeatedly, arduously, like we have all the time in the world and he's going to take longer than that. He's now covered in all the blood that was on me. Our perspiration has combined, leaving us a sticky mess, glued together everywhere.

"Shh, shh, foxy. Don't cry. I told you, you're mine. Do you understand?" The soothing sounds he makes have me wrapping my fingers through his black waves, wet with sweat and serum.

Nodding my reply, he scoops my lips into his again. Tingles erupt from my core, twinkling around my spine, and shoot through my legs and into my arms. Wrapping myself fully around him like moss on a tree, his cock works deep within me until there's no inch to spare. He was made for me.

Moving my hips in rhythm with his, I hump him as much as he writhes against me. With one last shove, my being unravels, the elation trickling from my soul as the squeal I dampened earlier comes out like a raging beast. No thoughts stream through my mind; all I know is ecstasy.

Returning from the throes of pleasure, my fingers sense the thick strands on his head, his warm skin and my pussy clutched onto him, holding him down as if his cock is the flying buttress of support for the cathedral of my body. If he leaves, I'll collapse into rubble. "Fuck! You have a *grip* on me, foxy. I can't pull out. I'm going to come inside you."

His hot seed spews until I feel so full my womb could explode. My legs tremble around his waist, nails still stuck like pins into his back. Strong boulder biceps surround me, squeezing me, before he drops his head onto the pillow next to mine. Between gasps for air, a muffled moan breaks through his mouth, barely audible, covered by the layers of fabric.

A minute passes, and he lifts his head to give me a dazed look that returns to laser focus as his chest stops huffing breaths. "We need to get the fuck out of here," he says, as if suddenly realizing the danger we just put ourselves in.

I make some type of affirmative sound. Max leaps off the bed and tosses me my clothes while quickly dressing, and I do the same. Both of us look guilty as fuck, covered in Gabriel's blood from head to toe. At least our clothes only have a few spots. Max shoves his knife back in his waistband and grabs a pistol from Gabriel's pants lying on the floor. Gripping my hand, he leads us into the hall, putting his body in front of mine.

Wails of pleasure and pain echo throughout the building as we hasten to the exit. Before I know what's happening, Max pulls my body tight to his chest, his arm engulfing me as his sports coat surrounds my face. He turns us sideways while raising the gun, firing two shots into the guards on either side of the entrance, dead between their eyes. Burying my face into his corded chest, muffled screams greet my ears and resound off the walls in the reception area. As I peek up from his protective embrace, I watch several patrons scramble in panicked chaos around the room.

"Move, foxy." Reaching into my pocket, I rub my charm three times, counting while running out the door with Max, his warm hand still intertwined with mine.

Once we reach the Barracuda, Max throws me over his shoulder, and tosses me into the passenger seat before sliding across the car's hood on one hip like a vigilante. He swiftly jumps in and takes off with a full press on the gas, and as we motor away, he punches the ceiling of the car. "Fuck yeah! Woo!"

The intensity we just had breaks, and I smile with a small laugh at his exhilaration. "Great shots. Fantastic aim."

Grasping my hand under his, he uses our laced fingers to shift gears. "Yeah, glad I went to the range." His eyes scan the rearview mirror, checking for any followers. Turning, I watch behind us to keep an eye out for any danger. No one's there.

"We could be in real trouble, Max. They know us."

His Adam's apple bobs. "I know." Lifting our hands, he kisses my knuckles, then lowers them to the gear stick and shifts into fifth. "He wasn't going to take what was mine. And you are, Livia. You're mine. Tell me you understand that now."

"I do." And I do. I am his. Probably always have been,

and I know that. The problem is, being his doesn't mean I'm safe. It doesn't mean I can trust him. And once he finds out how damaged I am...he'll probably toss me away or kill me.

Lifting a corner of his lips, he smirks while monitoring the road. "I told you I'd take it."

I purse my lips at his arrogance, but still can't help the grin threatening to escape. "You did."

Max points us to the highway. "Uh, do you think..." His deep-set eyes glance toward my abdomen.

"What?"

"Is there a chance you could get pregnant?" There's that look again that he got in the hotel room. Almost as if he'd win a second round tonight if I answered him affirmatively.

"No."

His brow furrows as he turns to me with something like disappointment. "I thought you said you weren't on birth control!"

"No, I didn't answer, and you just assumed I wasn't."

"Oh." Max focuses on the road, going quiet.

I try to pull my hand back, but he won't loosen his grip. "Sooo sorry you won't get your precious *heir* from me." Letting the sarcasm fly heavily, I swivel my hips away from him in my seat.

"What the *fuck* did you just say?"

Jutting my chin out, I crack out the words I've wanted to say for a long time. "Is that what you thought? Thought you'd impregnate me for your legacy? I'm worth—"

"Let's get one thing straight, foxy. I want you. Let me rephrase. I want *you*. I have since we were kids. *Fuck!* How could you not see that? I mean, yeah, I'd love to knock you up, get an heir, but that's not why I want to be with you." Squeezing my fingers tighter, he shakes his head. "You're fucking ferocious, you know that? You're more a bear than me. No one else could... I think we make an amazing team, and I want you on my side. Not kicking my shins in."

Snorting, I huff a loud breath. "How was the Crimson Angel?" All the talk about being his. What a crock of shit.

Max drops his head against the back of the seat. "Echoes tell you I was there?"

"Does it matter?"

"I thought you weren't mine, huh? Isn't that what you said? Livia, you just fucked some rando to piss me off."

A deep sigh leaves my lungs as I purpose my gaze out the passenger window into the dark night. Max finally drops my hand, only to put a finger under my chin and force me to turn to him. "I didn't fuck anyone else. As much as I wanted to cut every inch of your infection out of my skin, I couldn't do it. You're my brand of poison. And I only drink what's bad for me."

That emotion of being together in the room returns and my throat clenches with relief. His confession fills me with that never-ending ache and longing for him all over again. Maybe, for once, my hope isn't a bad thing. What if we could actually work?

Gathering his hand off my face, I press my lips to his fingertips one at a time. "I'm your poison, huh?"

Max relaxes in his seat and smiles while looking back at the road. "Yeah."

"You're mine, too."

Lacing our fingers back together, he says, "Yep. I am. Always have been."

Seventeen

MAXIMILLIAN

Pulling off the highway, I choose a small town, not a major city to hunker down in. We're hours outside Lecherton, in case Sosa's men find us. It's the dead of night and we need to clean up and rest. Stealing a glance at my little fox, she doesn't object when I pull into a piece of shit motel a few miles away from the exit.

"Do I look presentable?" I ask, waving my hands down the front of my stained suit.

"Just tell them you had a bad shaving accident." One side of her deliciously plump lips curls up, and I want to suck them off her face. Thinking about the blood covering her body and my cum still inside her makes my dick twitch.

The car is still running when I get out in case foxy needs to split. A cloud of marijuana smoke billows out of the small motel office when I open the glass door, but looking around, I don't see anyone attending the small counter. After ringing a bell, a lanky kid with bloodshot eyes comes out and barely even looks at me. "Yeah?"

"Just a king-sized room if you have one." I pay for the room and grab the key without raising any suspicion. Once we park and I grab our bags, I shove Livia inside the door. My cock is requiring service again.

Snapping my fingers, I point to the bathroom door. "Shower. Now."

"You're so demanding." She trails fingers up my chest as she smiles.

"Not yet, but I will be. Move your ass, little fox." As she walks in front of me, I spank her firm cheeks while we both peel off our sticky clothes, dropping them on the crusty carpet.

As soon as we get inside the small tub, I pick up my fox by her thick bottom and shove her against the tiles. My teeth find the crook of her neck and sink in, sucking with my tongue as her cry of shocked pain deafens my ear. I wrap one hand around her tiny neck and hold it there. No pressure yet, just getting a feel for how easy it will be to crush it underneath my firm tendons and eager fingers.

Pink waves of blood sheets off under the pelts of hot water. With her legs spread wide for me, I don't hesitate and shove myself fully inside her sheath with a low moan reverberating past my lips. "I loved fucking you in his blood. Cutting him wide open and letting him spray all over you." My head relaxes back with a groan as I inject her with the first thrust of my hips. "Believe that I will kill any man who tries to touch what's mine, little fox." And I will. Anyone so much as looks at my girl from now on is getting his eyes removed. She needs to understand how serious I am. "Nod if you understand, foxy."

Each finger tightens its grip around her windpipe as her golden eyes widen, but her pussy clenches. Pressing my chest more firmly into hers, the air is squeezed from her lungs with a raspy gasp, as the look on her face dazes when she begins to lose consciousness. Before she's completely out, I demand, "Nod your head, foxy. Then come all over my cock."

Each sparkling fleck of her hazel eyes fades to a muted olive, but it's not time to let up. Her legs lock behind me as she rides my cock like a toy, using the wall as leverage. At the peak of her orgasm, a guttural sound tries to escape her open mouth, but I clamp down tighter until she croaks.

This is her punishment and my pleasure. I could kill her for allowing that dude inside her, but if I do, I'd be no better than Franklin Von Dovish, the boogeyman of her nightmares. Vile hatred gushes around in my gut thinking about that slimy fuck inside her tonight. It would be easy to just continue squeezing the life out of her like this.

Her entire body freezes against mine, clasping my cock in as tight of a grip as I have on her neck until I can barely move inside her. She's almost gone now, almost out of air. The whites of her eyes have lost moisture, are focused on what's she's seeing in an afterlife. If she dies here under my grasp, our time together would be too short.

But I realize... I can't live without her. And I don't want to.

Easing the grip on her throat, I observe each color come back into her eyes like a movie fading into a bright autumn scene. Olive to brown to gold... Her scream echoes around the ceramic pink tiles as she climaxes until every tiny fasciculation in her muscles relaxes with elation. She's given up any resistance to me. I don't even need to ask her anymore; her body has told me she has accepted me as her truth.

Every cell of blood in my body works its way to my cock, and I want to inject it all inside her, so we are mixed in every way. If I don't have her, I have nothing. She's the reason for my existence now. As my cum shoots into her, I whisper the prayer of her name over her ear. "Livia."

Gripping my wet hair, she claims me with her mouth. For several minutes, we stay like this, combined as one, while I continue pumping into her with a semi-hard dick. She washes each strand on my head with her fingers and bathes my lips with her tongue. Peeling back, I place my forehead to hers, the water dripping off our lashes onto each other's cheeks. Heaving breaths flow between our mouths.

"Fuck. Your pussy is my heaven." Letting her body slide down the wall, I kiss her temple. "Let me clean you up." We take turns washing each other's bodies with soap while our mouths find each other's in between strokes of the rough cloth. Using my hands for comfort, I massage her arms, the back of her neck, her ass cheeks, and her legs.

Once we're cleaned up and dried off, I pull her onto the hard mattress and throw the stiff white sheet over us. Tucking her into my arm, she lifts her face to mine for another deep kiss.

This. This right here is where I want to be. Despite the mildewy smell of the room and the loud hum of the old heating unit, I never want to leave. All the evils within Gnarled Pine evaporate with the heat of her curves spilling onto my hard chest. The steady thump of her heart beats through her bones that resonates into mine. It's enough to send shock waves through my ancient pains, break them up, and destroy them into tiny pieces. I've never felt like this with anyone before.

Both of us need each other. I think we always have. And now that she's here, now that she's mine and hidden under my protection, some strange hope fills my soul. Eight long years have passed since I ever considered living for anything other than for revenge.

Now I have her.

Livia's breathing evens out, and I touch the top of her head with my lips before I fall asleep.

Snapping awake, I check my phone on the night-stand. It's mid-morning. We need to get moving, but every strand of DNA within me craves to stay in this position with her leg thrown over my stomach. I'm rock hard, too.

Briefly, I consider just sticking it inside her sleeping body, but we really should get to safety. Sosa's associates could find us on the way to Gnarled Pine Hollow if they just stop along the highway. We could take our time getting back, though. Maybe stop off and fuck somewhere.

Cal needs to know about us once we get back. A small knot forms in my stomach, thinking about his reaction. Will Livia be upset? She better not be. It seems she understood what happened between us last night.

She stirs, lifting her head to look at me. Her heavy-lidded champagne eyes drink me in, a little smile forming on her bubbly lips.

"Morning, foxy. You ready to head out? I'm getting nervous not having my men near us." Pressing my lips to her forehead, I taste her amber-scented skin. "Want to get back behind our walls. We should also talk with Calum about us."

"Sounds like you've been thinking a lot this morning." Her voice is husky and sultry. Hmm, I may not be able to wait until a rest area.

"I have." Leaning over, I tap another kiss to her straight nose. I can't stop touching her. It's my new drug, and I get a little zing of a high every time I do it. "Come on. I have to keep you safe. It's what us bears do."

Once we freshen up, we jump in the car and head to a drive-through for coffees and breakfast. On the road, memories of being on vacation with my family come to my mind. Everything is as light on the inside of me as the sun shining outside. I'm as carefree as a kid playing tag with Ace and Cal. Pumping up the radio, I start belting out a song I recognize. Livia's warm hand is on my lap and her fingers squeeze my thighs. She giggles at my off notes. Like a girl. I reach across the car and brush my thumb over her flushed cheek as her bright eyes follow me.

"I fucking love when you smile. And I love that you only smile for me," I say.

Her lips spread wider, showing her white teeth. She's even got a dimple on the left side I haven't seen since we were little.

"How do you think Cal will respond when I tell him about us, foxy?"

She pauses for a moment, with her smile dropping slightly. "I think he'll be fine with it."

Just when I thought I couldn't feel any happier, that shit just made me want to shout into the air outside. So, I do. Once I roll up the window and fix my wind-blown hair, I look at my woman. "Yeah? Well, good! I'd hate to have to kill your twin to keep you."

She punches me in the arm, and I laugh. Grabbing her little fingers, I squeeze them in my palm, putting our hands together on my leg.

"Do you need to stop? Fuck in the rest area?" I bite my lip to keep from laughing harder at the look of irritation she sends my way. Especially when I take her hand from my leg and place it on my semi-hard cock. My hips jut up into her touch. "Or here, whichever."

"Max!" Her eyes widen with shock as she tries to tug her hand back, but fails, then giggles madly.

"What?"

"Eyes on the road, lion. I don't want to die in a car crash outside of... Where are we?" She gives up her fight and leaves her fingers dangling on my crotch.

"I don't know. Some small town." Checking the road signs, nothing has come up for a while, until I spot one that says there is food at the next exit. "Seriously, do you need to stop? Maybe we can grab some lunch. It's been hours. I'm *sure* you need to pee."

Her voice rings out in waves like a bell peeling with laughter. "Yeah. That's fine."

Once I pull into an old gas station and diner, I fill the Barracuda with premium and head inside where Livia has a booth seat ready for us. She sits with her eyes to the door like my clever little fox. Sliding in next to her, I toss my arm across the back, then tug on her hair on the opposite side of me.

"Ouch!" She smiles and slaps my thigh with the back of her hand.

"What do you want, little fox? Salad? Some lettuce? What do foxes eat?"

Rolling her eyes, she shakes her head, losing the grip my pinch had on her locks. "Pfft. You know I eat meat."

"Yeah, and you do a damn fine job of it, too." I lean over to kiss her, but she pulls back with a wide smile, her mouth open in fake shock.

"Max!"

The waitress comes over, and I order us two hamburgers and fries.

"We need to talk about the weapons. Sosa's weapons," she says, after taking a sip of her cola.

"I don't want to talk about Sosa ever again. We're good on weapons. I think we're set. The trade is going well, so we should hunker down now." I take a drink of my ice water. Rubbing the cold condensation from the plastic cup on my jeans, I clear my throat. "I do think we need to talk about moving forward. Uh..." Why am I so fucking nervous? My stomach feels twisted in on itself and one hand raises up to scratch the back of my head. I've only ever felt this way before a big match, but usually could deal with it. Now, my heart is racing, pounding out of my chest, and I don't know how to form the words I need to, the ones I'm so desperate to.

"Moving forward with the guns?" Livia's bright eyes are large as she investigates mine.

"Uh, with us. Moving forward." I swallow deeply. "This isn't a formal proposal, but we should make us official. For the legacy. Talk about heirs when the time is right. And, um, all that."

Livia turns her head away from me, and now I know why my shoulders are tensed around my neck. She's going to say no. The knots in my stomach and neck unravel as the bear comes out to play. My claws are itching to rip into her the moment she refuses.

"Here you go! Need anything else? Some ketchup?" Livia looks at me briefly, then shakes her head at the waitress. Neither of us move toward the food. After the waitress walks away, Livia leans forward to take a hearty bite of her burger. She chews slowly while I monitor every morsel roaming around in her mouth. Waiting.

"Livia," I say quietly, letting it fall into the open air as she half pretends like she didn't hear me.

"Hmm?"

"Livia, come on. What is it? I thought you understood last night. You—you're fucking *mine*, foxy." She takes another bite of her burger, then a long sip of her drink. Sitting forward, she stays still as can be, pulling away from my touch, not even looking at me. That's the part that does me in. "Answer me. Goddamn it, Livia, answer me!" Pounding a fist on the table, the saltshaker spills on its side, emphasizing my point further.

With a swift inhale, tears spring to her eyes before flooding cheeks, droplets splashing onto her pile of fries. A silent desperation focuses on her face as her shoulders shake with silent sobs, the movement causing my heart to shatter with every rise and fall. She seems to be crying a lot around me. The first time we kissed, the first time I entered her...

Reaching across the orange Formica table, I snatch a handful of thin paper napkins from the stainless-steel dispenser. She takes them from me, and I wrap an arm around my woman, pulling her back into my side, where she belongs. I only feel an ounce of relief when her wet face buries into my neck as she weeps, her back heaving as she pants for breaths, knowing she isn't totally closing me out. The sound of her whimpers drives me insane with agony. All the happiness I felt yelling out the car window now makes me ache with pain.

"Do we need to leave? What's wrong, Livia? Please, talk to me." My large fingers stroke through the back of her hair as I press my lips close to her ear and say in a low, calming voice, "Is it Franklin? He's a dick. I'll hunt him down and kill him myself if that will make you feel better. I won't hurt you, foxy. Please, just talk to me."

Her heaves settle, and her cries become sniffles against my shoulder. The moisture from her face has soaked into my shirt, but I don't mind. I need her back together, or I'm going to fucking break. She's my wild mustang, my badass bitch, and I'm not quite sure what to do with her like this.

"Max. I-I can't have children. I'm so sorry. I'm broken. You should be with someone else. Be with someone else to have your legacy."

Everything in me stills. My heart falters, its chambers closing. Lungs stop exchanging air. And for the first time since Markus found me to tell me about my parents dying, tears form in my eyes.

Is this what she has hidden from me? Why she's avoided me this whole time...

I can barely hear my own voice as it comes out. "I'm so sorry, Livia." My arm envelopes her body as I hold her closer, flush to me. "But if you even *think* for a moment that means I don't want you, or that I should be with someone else, you banish that thought from your brain right the fuck now. You're *mine*, foxy. Nothing changes that. Nothing." Gripping the tail of her hair, I pull her back to look at me, tears streaming down her pinkened cheeks. "If you can or cannot have children, I don't give a shit. If you want kids, we'll have some kids. Whatever it takes, adopt, surrogacy, I don't fucking care. I'll be happy to die alone with you, if you don't want any, but I *will* be with you. Fuck the legacy."

She swallows roughly and takes a moment to stare at me before she says, "Okay."

My lips find hers, wet and sloppy. I'm still surrounding her under the protection of my arms. When I pull back, I sit up and point to her dish. "Now, eat your meat. And let's get hitched."

Wiping her face, she remains quiet while I dig into my food and say with my mouth full, "I'm serious, foxy. No kids is fine. Eat up. We can get married whenever you want. But we're getting married."

She leans into my shoulder and picks up a fry. "Thank you, Max."

Taking a bite of my burger, I kiss the top of her head. "No need to thank me. This is what I want. This is what's happening now."

Seeming to shake off the doldrums, she sits up and begins to eat again.

"So, wedding at the Crimson Angel, then?" I ask with a smirk. She shoves her shoulder into mine and snorts. "I mean, we did meet there after twenty years. It's only fitting."

A piece of her meal sticks out of her mouth as she says, "I am *not* getting married in Strauss's corrupt cathedral."

Nodding slowly, a small smile crosses my face. "But you'll marry me."

Taking another few bites, she nods. "Yes, Max. I suppose I'll marry you."

"Jesus. Don't sound so excited, foxy." Shaking my head, I let a heavy sigh ring out.

"It's hard to break the conditioning that I was born to

produce an heir for you. And I'm worried you'll regret marrying me and kill me off."

I *knew* Franklin had something to do with her cold nature. Maybe I could ask Cal his whereabouts... String him up to a tree and let loose some Yellowjackets after covering him with honey. Is that enough for the pain he's caused my fox?

"Nah. You know me. Once I make up my mind... that's it. We're together. From now until forever." Grasping her hand sitting on the table, I rub my thumb over her left ring finger, imagining it filled with my band, the external symbol of what's mine. And what I feel inside for her.

She finishes her meal, but her lack of enthusiasm is killing mine. Once I finish up, I wipe my mouth and throw some cash on the table. We amble out to the car, but she sneaks in the passenger side before I can open her door. Pausing my steps at her slight, I continue to the driver's side.

Tossing my hands on the wheel, I turn to look at her while she busies her eyes, pulling lint off her jeans. "Do you want kids, Livia?"

"It doesn't matter." It's said almost as if she's used to saying this repeatedly, maybe to herself.

"It *does* matter. If you want them, I'll get kids for you." I pause for a moment. "That sounded wrong. I mean, we can get kids another way, like adopt or something."

Finally, she glances up at me. "I'm not sure, Max. I'm really not."

"Okay. No worries. I'll be happy with what you decide."

She quickly grasps my hand before I put the car into gear. "Max, I-I never told anyone that I couldn't have children."

"Who told you?"

"A specialist I saw outside of Gnarled Pine Hollow. I mean, I never tested it with anyone, and I always used condoms. But I was having trouble, and the doctor ran some tests, and I can't have children. That was that. So, I stopped wanting them, or never did, or... I don't know. I don't want to think about it right now."

Running a finger over her warm cheekbone, I try to assure her. "Hey, foxy. We can talk about it or not. As I said, I'm with you. Whatever you want to do, I'm good with it, but that better not stop you from marrying me. I can't be without you." I lift our hands and kiss hers as we finish the last leg of the trip to Gnarled Pine Hollow.

Gripping her hand, I stroke the back with my thumb as I pull out of the parking lot and onto the main drag toward the interstate. Once on the highway, she continues to sit quietly like a vast hole pulling all my attention, and I have an overwhelming urge to take away her pain, but I don't know how. "You said you were broken. You're not, Livia. You're my perfection."

Her eyes meet mine, and she smiles sweetly. "I feel as if I'm keeping you from something you want by being with me. Like you have to give up your future in order to marry me."

"You're all I've ever wanted, foxy. Ever since we were kids. I'd give up everything to be married to you."

She covers our clasped hands with her free one and squeezes. Livia dozes in the car for the rest of the trip while I focus on the road. Occasionally, she stirs and wraps her arms around her middle. Noticing, I shirk off my coat and toss it over her. Her eyes blink and find mine until she gives me my smile before wrapping up inside it while taking a whiff of the collar.

Pulling up to the Freidenberg manor in the late afternoon, my brow furrows. No one is monitoring the gate. Looking up through the windshield high above us, I notice there are no guards in the towers, either. As the car crawls to a halt, Livia wakes and sits up in her seat, stretching her back. A lazy grin greets me as she reaches over to grab one of my hands with her tiny ones.

"Where's John?" she asks as she also notices things seem off, head scoping out the scene with me.

It's not normal for him to be gone, unless he's changing shifts or doing some rounds. Before we drive in, I pull out my cell phone, but there're no messages or notifications.

"I don't know. Maybe he's on his rounds."

Jumping out of the Barracuda, the gate easily swings open, the lock unlatched. That's also unusual. John would never leave it like this. Sliding back in the car, I ease us down the lane, an unsettling feeling causing my belly to tighten with discomfort. Livia sits upright, scanning the grounds, the black tail of her mohawk twisting as her head turns back and forth from her window to mine.

Nearing the house, I lower my window as I spy several workers mulling about the front of the house, but instead of their usual business, all of them stare in the same direction, like ice sculptures. The wind gushes through the trees, picking up fallen leaves and swirling around the windows, some landing inside the car's cabin. If there's a temperature to it, I can't tell what it is, because all my body feels heavy, laden with numbness. Blood rushes into my ears while my heart races, making it impossible to hear over its pounding.

This isn't normal. Something's wrong. Slicking my palms over my jeans one at a time, I attempt to dry them from their sweat.

Almost as if she's in another room, Livia's voice reaches me in an echo. "What's going on?"

"I don't know. You stay right here and don't move." Parking the car far from the manor, I urge my legs to help me stand as I get out. Livia doesn't stay like I told her and follows me closely behind. My arm instinctively sticks out to the side like I'm stopping her forward momentum. The tightness in my chest makes me pull out my handgun and slide one into the chamber, though I keep the barrel pointed at the cobblestones. Swallowing, I fake bravado and yell into the crowd, "What happened?"

Craftsmen part like the Dead Sea, their heads bowed low as I pass. The only figure in front of me is the large collapsing body of Mrs. Kroft. Her wails ring out in an ocean of silence, a beacon of the horror that lay beyond. The thuds in my chest still until it feels as if my heart has stopped, and my mouth goes dry. As we approach the front of the manor, my eyes wander slowly across the threshold, but it's as if I can't comprehend the image before me. Almost like my brain protecting itself, confusion is the only thing I feel when I analyze the scene.

Black boots, sloppily tied with one lace broken. Dark jeans, ripped a little at the knees over firm legs. Taut and sculpted arms, hanging by the sides of a muscular torso. Hands, each holding a rusted, metallic spike through its center. Neck, crooked at an unnatural angle, with a rope tied three times around it, marking the skin blue and red underneath. Mouth, agog with a tongue lolling out of the side. Eyes, those serious brown eyes... popped from their sockets in their last search for any air.

Doom strikes my soul. The ground meets my knees when I crumple like the old cook, unable to hold myself upright any longer. Nothing could have prepared me for this.

Someone has nailed Adal Derichs to the front door of Freidenberg Manor.

Eighteen

LIVIA

"I'm sorry, Miss Von Dovish. Like I said, he isn't here."

"Let me by." Shoving past Fritz's large shoulder, I pummel into the Freidenberg's coffin-like foyer, terror causing my throat to constrict. "Where's Arianna?" Managing to choke out the question, my eyes dart around the large front hallway.

"Miss Arianna is out. If you would like for me to—"

Spinning on my heeled boot, I head toward the dark wood staircase before he can finish. After the scene at the front door yesterday, Max was surrounded by his team of men. All of them shoved me out of the way and carried his collapsed body inside. But not before one of them thrust a finger in my face and told me to return to my fox lair. Only to help my brother with Von Dovish security did I obey. Once things seemed calm, I tried to call my lion, but there was no answer.

Until ten minutes ago, when Arianna called in a panic about her brother. Too hysterical to tell me any details, I rushed over and almost had to cap one of his new gate security just to get inside. Now Fritz is trying to block me from getting to him.

Intending to inspect the residence myself, I push into Max's room. Empty glass whiskey bottles line the floor near his bed. Shattered glass shards lie underneath a picture frame along one wall and, as my eyes travel upwards, I notice a large, wet stain as if he'd thrown the bottle there in a fit of rage. The bed sheets appear to have been mauled. Most worrisome is a box of bullets spilled on the dresser. The entire area looks like a den of despair.

Markus stands in the center living room as I descend the stairs slowly, trying to contemplate my next move. His gray hairs spike out in every direction, as if he's been rubbing hands through it repeatedly. There's always a hint of exhaustion behind his eyes, but now he looks haggard and completely hopeless. His glasses have fallen down his nose, and he pushes them up as he waits for me. When I approach, his mouth remains closed, as if he's lost the will to speak.

"Just tell me where he is," I plead.

"Miss Von Dovish—"

"Stop it, Markus. You know me. Call me Livia. Where is Max? My spies haven't spotted him, or..." They won't tell me. Echoes refuses, saying it isn't part of her work mission and I'm crossing a "dangerous boundary." Aries is under Calum's thrall, and he's instructed them both to stop giving me intel.

Things around the Freidenberg manor are as still as the air before a devastating tornado, the halls feeling like a morbid tomb. Workers are nowhere to be seen, other than the groundskeeper digging a gravesite in the family's cemetery for our beloved tank. I don't know if anyone will return here after what happened.

Right after Max stood from his grieving at the front door, he pulled out his gun and shot his old gatekeeper square in the head, blaming him for not doing his duty. The agonizing look on my lion's face was torturous to see, but I was thrust away before I could reach out to him.

Markus is reluctant to tell me where he is. It's understandable the bears don't trust me fully, but I must find Max before he does something stupid like get himself killed while drunk. Arianna is forbidden from leaving the compound, which has me worried about where she headed, or worse, what has happened to her.

"Livia, he's stepped out."

Begging with my eyes, I try again. "Where's Ari?"

Markus's withered hand raises to pull his glasses off and clean them with a soft cloth from his shirt pocket. "We bears are trying to recover from our security breach. Given everything that's happened, I suggest you stick to your side of town right now. I'm not at liberty to discuss my master's whereabouts or his sister's. No matter how much you—"

Before he finishes saying it, my legs dash to the foyer. The heavy wood deafens me briefly when I slam the front door. So, I'm back to being a full-blown enemy. Do they think I had something to do with Derichs's death? Hopefully Master Freidenberg doesn't believe that.

If Max is gone, then Arianna must have taken the opportunity to sneak away. There's only one place I know she'd escape to. Well, one person...Wyatt. Her fascination with the mechanic is bordering on obsession, and I fear the feelings go both ways. Despite their attraction, these types of matches never end well in Gnarled Pine Hollow.

The commercial district on the east side appears livelier than the eerie calmness inside the estate fences. Clean and bright signs advertise new businesses while bars and restaurants showcase their goods on sandwich boards lining the swept sidewalks. Asphalt smoothly paves the roads along the main strip. Less zombie-like people roam about or stand on deserted street corners, filled with the drugs Strauss's men so willingly give out for the small price of a soul.

Before I reach the motorcycle shop, an ominous pillar of black smoke rises above a line of pines that has yet to die. Slowing as if it's afraid to behold what my eyes are seeing, my SUV creeps around the corner. Bright orange and red flames engulf the establishment. Heat waves make the scene difficult to assess, but clusters of men stand around in leather, motorcycles parked around in a circle. All faces peer up at the firestorm as if it's a hole to Hell opening before them.

Her long dark hair is visible before anything else as her face is hidden, tucked into the protective, corded arm of her secret lover. Gently, his hand caresses circles on her back as I approach.

Clearing my throat, I stand with the crowd, in awe of the destruction before me. "Ari."

Lifting her head, her chocolate brown eyes sparkle with tears, and despite me being an ally for the two of them, Wyatt instinctively turns his body into hers as if to shield her away. It's not going to work. Her lithe arm reaches toward me, and I embrace her. Sobs wail in my ears as I hold her shaking body against mine.

Pulling her back, I grasp her face in both of my hands. "Arianna, who did this?" Wyatt has not let go of her hand.

"We don't know," he answers for her. "But, if I had to guess, it was Strauss. Just like with Derichs and a few of our men."

"Not Ace? Or... anyone else?" We have so many enemies now. It could have been anyone.

"Nah. Rogue had some trouble with one of Strauss's guys here yesterday. He thinks he must have planted something and then detonated it this morning. We just got here to open up shop and were greeted with this." He nods at the roaring flames, narrow eyes becoming almost invisible as he squints in the heat.

"Wyatt, man, they're reviewing the footage." One of the workers calls him over, and he kisses Arianna's temple briefly. "I'll be right back, vix."

Arianna reluctantly lets go of his hand, their fingers extending toward each other by some invisible force, but her tiny hand still has mine in a tense grasp.

"Vix?"

"Vixen. The spies are looking into things, but Max is

convinced. I think..." She pauses. Swiping at her face, she shakes out her hair. "Livy, I think he left from here to do something really stupid. The look on his face—"

"Where did he go? What did he say?" Gripping her face, I jar her slightly, hoping the answers drop out of her mouth.

"I don't know. He's been drinking *heavily* all night. He was all paranoid. Once he was alerted to this earlier this morning"—she waves her hand at the fire—"he took off, drunk and mumbling. He said something about revenge. About going to—" Biting her generous bottom lip, she stops herself and glances toward Wyatt.

My fingers grasp her little shoulders and shake her back to my attention. "Where? Where did he go?"

Batting her lashes at me like I'm one of her simps, she says, "Uh, please don't get mad at him, Livy. He's just really messed up about Adal."

Her whiny tone only makes the ire in my neck rise. "*Where, Ari?*"

She sighs and peers into the flames, the reflection causing her olive skin to redden. "I think to the Crimson Angel."

Motherfucker. If he so much as put a hand on his zipper in front of one of the whores there, I'll burn down another of his establishments, too. Pining over me *hard*, only to, what, ditch me for something he had to pay for? Just like my father...

Checking for my knife in my boot, I get a vision of slicing off that perfect cock of his.

"Wait, Livy!" Arianna calls out.

I'm already gone. Jumping back into the driver's seat, I rocket toward the lounge. Each mile causes the blood to move from a pulsation to a gushing sound within my ears while sweat pours down my back despite the chill winter air. Driving over gives me a bit of time to think up some strategy, but the rage inside makes logical thought impossible.

Before I can enter the bar area of the brothel downstairs, Clive, the bouncer, stops me. Hungry for a feel, his rough palms explore my body for weapons in my robust cleavage. Impatiently, my foot taps as I heave a sigh into his face. I hope my breath stinks.

"This is ridiculous. I wouldn't walk in here with a gun."

Fingers dig into my breasts on either side as his thumbs brush over my nipple bars under my black T-shirt. It's a last-ditch effort to satisfy his need for domination before he steps aside. Small dick asshole. Using my full force, I shove the bar door open dramatically.

"Hey, Dove!" Gerald pipes up when he sees me enter, wiping a glass clean with a white towel.

"Save it, Gerald. You know I'm Livia. Where's the bear?"

His light eyes look at the cloth in his hands briefly before darting to the left. "I don't know who you mean, Livia."

"Bullshit. Where is Freidenberg?"

Several patrons glance up from their tables, some

nervously scattering from the room. A large hand grips my shoulder. "Careful, fox." Clive's deep bass rings in my ear. Twisting my torso quickly, I shrug off his warning hold, then slide to the right, dipping to the back hallway. Clive is big and slow, not able to keep up, but Strauss or another of his men will be here before too long, which has me dancing away as quickly as I can.

There are three halls with boudoir rooms, so many it could take a while to find him. And with the cameras humming as they follow me, I don't have much time. Picking randomly, I sprint down the hall to my left. None of the rooms have locks, so I just need to open the doors fast and move in a line.

In the first suite, I find three men together on the bed. One is riding a laying man reverse style, while sucking the standing man's cock. No Max.

Another door is filled with at least ten people in various stages of sex, but still no lion.

By the sixth door, I spot the curvy hostess, Jade, cleaning a flogger in her palms. She flips her head to the door as I fling it open, her eyes widening, then they narrow as she scans my body, sizing me up.

Jade turns fully toward me as if she's going to be able to take me in her stilettos and tiny strapped dress. "You're not allowed in here."

"Where's Freidenberg?"

A change comes over her face as her dark eyes sparkle, her generous maroon lips straining to contain a smirk. "Oh... Max left here not too long ago. *Great* dick, don't you think? It's so sexy when he growls like a bear as he comes."

Her words cut me through the chest. *Did they?* Closing my mouth, I swallow and raise my chin. "Where did he go?"

"Probably to my bed for a second round. I don't think he has use for you anymore. At least that's what he told me." With a few long strides, she saunters closer, leather straps in her hand gleaming in the dim light as she smacks it into an open palm. "So go on home. I'll take good care of him."

As she nears, each waddling step of hers causes my rage to grow from stunned pain to full out fury. Her hands reach out to grab my arm, but I bend, sliding my hand into my boot and flicking open my knife. When I jerk to a stand, my fingers grip her neck, pulling her body close to me.

Before she understands what has happened, I allow the wrath inside to take over and my fist stabs her in the chest rapidly, repeatedly. After each slice into her abdomen and ribs, I dip and spin with perfect piqué turns. Shocked, she stumbles, arms flailing without any coordination.

As she falls backwards onto the carpet, I lunge and sit atop her, gripping her torso with my thighs. With the tip of my blade, I puncture her carotids on either side until the red gushes from her open neck wounds, spurting like geysers onto my hands and exposed forearms. Her body jolts in frantic twitches until it settles, her eyes stiff and wide with horror. Her last sight was me hovering over, delivering her to death.

Catching my breath, I wipe off each side of the knife on my jeans, then shove it back into its home.

Well, I guess I've killed a person. Before I can think too deeply about that, my shock is interrupted as my phone buzzes in my pocket. Even before I slide it out, I know it *has* to be Echoes. She probably spied on the entire situation. Scrubbing my hands on the dead woman's dress, I answer the call.

"Yeah?"

"You look like you could use some help," she says in a voice that's way too calm and patronizing.

"Shut up and fucking do something. Now."

The lights in the place go out a second later. For months, I studied the cavernous hallways of the brothel to get the armory key, and I was the best at hide-and-seek down here when we were little. If Echoes can hold off on Strauss's security coming to find me, I'll have a chance to get back to my car... and hopefully find Max.

The feel of the cold stones cuts into my finger pads as I graze them along the walls, counting the doors until the seventeenth on the right. Pushing in, I enter my escape room, the old kitchen cellar with some stairs leading out to the back of the building. Shuffling along the floor, I edge toward the west, blindly reaching out for a doorknob.

Lights blare brightly as they turn back on. A brassy ornate knob sits in my hand, and I turn it until the winter air blasts me in the face, the threat of snow hovering in the purple sky.

I'm able to sneak through the back grounds toward my car, scanning the lot for Max's Barracuda, but I don't see it. As I dart out into the main street, I consider where he may be and come up with only one conclusion.

Strauss.

And certain death.

Flooring the gas, I speed through the south's streets, heading north as bile rises into my throat. Dusk spills over into the light quickly, filling the sky with darkness as I approach dangerous territory. My heart rate climbs as images of what I may find near the consort's land invade my mind.

Ravaging down the twisted lanes leading up a small incline to Strauss's mansion, I have to turn on the head-lights in order to see anything meaningful in front of me. When my phone jiggles in my pocket, I almost release a terrified scream, but I pull it out and toss it onto the passenger seat, knowing full well it's either my brother or Echoes, telling me not to do what I'm about to.

Each twisted pine and old oak hides something I may not want to see behind it, but I still strain my neck to peer around them as the car approaches the tall iron fence at the entrance.

Before I reach them, I slam on the brakes at the horror before me.

The gates have been blown off their hinges, guard towers leaning dangerously sideways with the stones from their base crumbled in rough piles like everything has been blown up.

On the largest pillar of rubble stands my lion, on top of a bloody battlefield, a heap of dead men surrounding his feet. In one of his hands hangs a machine gun, and in the other, a severed head. Tendons and clinging skin swing from the base of it in the crisp winter breeze as it drips with what was left of the man's life.

Other pieces of Max's stage are almost indistinguishable. Maybe a half of a leg here, some arms there... eyes and entrails. A guard has only a torso, but remains alive and attempts to crawl away on the only elbow he has left. Max raises his gun and sprays him with bullets in the back of his skull, brain matter shooting out from the large wound with each bullet.

If my vision could make out that what was before me was indeed real, I believe I'd vomit at the sight.

Turning slowly, Max's half naked body puffs up to the largest I've ever seen it. The T-shirt he was wearing has been shredded, almost blown off his top, leaving his exposed chest sliced with small cuts from debris, each oozing with blood. From all the carnage he's caused, ash and gore coat almost all his skin, blackened as much as the look he gives me through the dusty windshield.

When he sees it's me, something falters in his countenance, and he drops the gun and head, collapsing to his knees. Hurling myself out of the car, I dash over to him. Despite everything on him, the stench of liquor is still strong, pungent over the smell of burning destruction.

"Fox," he moans with a sluggish slur as my feet near his body.

"I'm here, lion. Come on, we have to move."

"No! Leave me." Every word he says is mumbled so heavily, they seem trapped, barely able to depart from his thick lips. Squeezing his eyes shut, he avoids my gaze. Quietly, he meditates, "Just fucking leave me here."

Grasping under his large arms, I try to pull him to a stand. "Up and at 'em, soldier. We've gotta move."

When he's able to, his eyelids open, the wide pupils finding mine after a moment of unfocused haze. "Help me," he says in a tiny voice I haven't heard since he was squatting over a hornet's nest one time during hide-and-seek. I'll deal with his dick later. Right now, I need to get us both out of here.

Shuffling to his feet, he leans on me as I walk him over to the Victor and shove him inside. As soon as I close the door, he slouches, resting his dark head of hair against the window.

"Where's your car?" I yell to keep him awake, but when I look at him, his eyes are focused, the orange lights of the dashboard lighting up his stoic face. Reversing quickly, I spin around and head back down the winding drive toward the main street.

Max moans and slumps farther in his seat. He rubs his chest with a hand, probably attempting to soothe his open sores. "Left it down the road... Gemini can get it."

I'm not even sure I want to ask the next question or want the answer to it, but I have to know. If he stuck his cock in someone else... I can't be with him. Men cheat, I know that. But I want someone different. Someone special, someone who *would never* even think of being with someone else. I want someone obsessed with me.

Max seemed that way. He always did, ever since we were kids, and I was so used to the way he would stare at me with wonder, fear, and reverence. Now, his eyes are glassy with a distance I've never seen before. He won't even look at me. Like he doesn't even care I'm here with him.

"Did you fuck her?"

Without a peek over or reaction, he only murmurs a question back, "Who?"

Attempting to shove some saliva down my constricted throat, I squeak out, "Jade, at the Crimson Angel. Did you fuck her?"

Max's head slumps back against the seat. "Livia." He says it as if he is about to scold me, then pauses. A quick snort of air leaves his nose while his jaw clenches. "Just fucking take me home." Not sure how to digest his irritated response, I decide to address it once he's sobered up some, despite everything in me wanting to pull the answer from his jowls with forceps. A sigh escapes my nose as he continues to fixate his gaze out his window.

When I approach the manor gates, three guards aim their rifles at me. Two are in the stone towers built above the high walls, while one sits in the guard station. Clearly, he's ex-military, with lots of tattoos on his forearms, showcasing his branch. The crewcut he wears only makes his thick neck look like a tree trunk.

He approaches my window with a look of disdain as I lower it. "Miss Von Dovish, you're not welcome—"

"Let her in," Max growls from the passenger seat.

"Oh, Mr. Freidenberg. So sorry, I didn't see you there. Hang on." The grunt moves to open the iron gate for us, and I proceed through slowly. For once.

"What happened?" Markus's harried face greets us when I pull up, tugging at the ends of his gray hair. Jakob skirts around him and gets right to work, opening Max's door, the two shuffling inside. Markus stares at me like I'm the one responsible for his master's condition.

Tossing the tail of my hair over my shoulder, I straighten up and stare him down. Right now, Markus is not my favorite person. "Your boy went to Strauss's for revenge and may have caused a war."

He closes his agog mouth and gives a slight nod, as if everything I said was just confirming his worst suspicions. "I'll get the healer." Markus strolls into the house quickly, and I follow before anyone can throw me out. Taking the steps two at a time, I brush up toward Max's bedroom, the door left open as Jakob walks out of the bathroom, the sound of the shower running.

Jakob eyes me suspiciously for a moment before sliding outside, closing the door behind him. I take the time to straighten Max's bed, fixing the sheets and moving some of the broken shards. Despite needing some answers and being unsure of what exactly transpired, I don't want him hurting himself even more. Before the water turns off, I ease out to the hall to use the other bathroom to clean myself up.

When I return, Max's head rests back on the cushioned headboard, propped on a sea of pillows, his eyes squeezed tightly shut. The skin of his exposed chest looks like a carver had his way with it, cuts and gashes oozing in the dim light of the lamp. Not sure quite what to do with myself, I stand near the door and shift my hips.

I open my mouth to ask an unknown question, but Max murmurs before I can. "Why are you here, Livia?"

Scoffing, I beeline for the bed and sit next to him. "Why wouldn't I be here?"

His eyelids twitch before lifting slightly. Dark eyes peer at me without moving his head. "Why do you fucking care, Livia? I chased you. You obviously won't trust me. Don't know if you ever will. Maybe you shouldn't..." Spoken with barely a whisper, his voice is strained and cracked. "What kind of leader lets his man get nailed to the front door?"

The stubble along his jaw tickles my palms as I grasp it, forcing him to look at me. "A good man." Maybe he was right. Max is loyal and honest, always saying exactly what he means. He goes after what he wants and never backs down from a challenge... The realization hits me, along with the flavor of guilt.

"You didn't have sex with her."

The thickness of his brow increases as his upper lip snarls. "How the *fuck* could you think I'd do something like that? I'm in love with you, Livia! You're pissing me the fuck off, not being on my side."

"I *am* on your side. I have *always* been on your side!" Digging into my pocket, I thrust my good luck charm into his big palm. "Here. You wanted to know what I carry around? I've had it since we were eight years old. I stole it before you left."

Peering into his hand, his eyes widen as he gasps. "My...my matchbox Barracuda? You've had it this entire time?"

"It meant something to you. So, it meant something to me. I wanted to be a part of your life. I wanted to be a part of your dreams. You've always brought me luck, even when we were apart. I could feel you whenever I'd look to the east. I love you, lion. I always have."

Now it was his turn to grab my head, pressing his forehead to mine in a tight lock. "Fuck, Livia. I love you. I've always felt you, too. Always. You were my compass home."

My eyes fill with tears as his lips seize mine, desperate to close the gap between us. Droplets fall down my cheeks as he engulfs me. As our air combines, his soul and mine irrevocably intertwined. The warmth of his mouth heats me to the core as he breathes truth into me. It's a realization. An epiphany.

"I trust you."

His fingers trickle down my chest, then to my tucked leg, and slide into my boot as he maintains his grip on my lips. The familiar flick of the knife pierces the air as he holds the blade up close to the sides of our faces.

"You trust me?" Molten brown eyes appear menacing as he flashes the steel back and forth in his hand.

"Yes, Max. I trust you." And I do. He isn't Franklin Von Dovish. He's my little lion. The boy who rescued me from the monster under my bed during sleepovers. The man who almost got killed stealing a ring so I could keep my mother's. Someone who has sacrificed his own happiness and safety for the good of his people on East Side.

Max presses his lips on my forehead, then grabs a whiskey bottle from the nightstand by the neck. Pulling out a tissue, he pours some of the liquid onto it, then rubs down the blade of the knife. Drying it off, he glances up at me.

"Take off your clothes." Sliding off the bed, I stand and peel off my tank top and bra. Unbuttoning my jeans, I shimmy out of them, tugging down my thong. His eyes hungrily observe every movement of my hips. Stepping out of my boots and pants, I bare myself completely in front of him. "My perfect fox." Max licks his bottom lip, then sucks it in underneath his front teeth. "Sit here." He pats the bed in front of him.

Moving closer, I cross my legs as his surround my hips on either side. Max places the sharp edge of the blade just above my left breast. Involuntarily, I snap an inhale, both from the coldness of the metal and in anticipation of his next movement. At the sound of my breath, the sides of his lips tug up in a smirk.

Slicing slowly across my skin, each line sends lightning shocks down my chest, vibrating the silver bars piercing through the tips of my tits. As he leans forward, his own cuts and wounds seeping with serum and blood. Gazing down at the sheet bunched at his hips, Max's very obvious erection pokes out like a tent pole.

"Those nipples make me fucking hungry..." he barely

murmurs above a whisper, as if it were a thought he accidentally said out loud. They are hard as rocks, and when I peek to where his eyes are staring, the blood has dripped down from the small cuts onto each.

The final cuts make me doused between my legs. Each slice causes my pulse to progress to a rapid pace until I let my neck fall back while closing my eyes.

"Mmm, foxy. I gotta..." The resonant tones of his voice have my skin tingling with anticipation.

Lifting my head, I get the sense Max is barely hanging on, his eyes telling me the bear is about to maul me.

A sharp flux of air brushes past my open mouth. Looking at my breast, I see his work complete. "Your initials." It's filled with dripping red droplets, but a clear *M* and *F* are sliced just above my heart.

"Mine." Max meets my face with the solemnity of gravity. Dragging a finger through his blood, I smear it carefully across his chest as he stares at the motion, a breath catching in his lungs as his ribs puff out. His dick surges between us, the sheet stretching as his cock tries to claw its way toward me.

"Mine," I say, making sure he meets my gaze when I do.

Putting the blade down, he grabs my hand and forces my bloodied finger into my mouth. "Suck."

A salty metallic liquid fills my taste buds. I lick over my teeth and around inside my cheeks to get more flavor everywhere. I need more.

Max can't contain himself any longer. "Fuck!" He

lurches forward and places his full open mouth over his carvings on my breast. His teeth gnash into my skin as his tongue sweeps over the wounds. If my clit wasn't pulsing before, it's now throbbing with desire, my hole empty and desperate to be filled by him.

His mouth moves lower until he latches onto a nipple bar with first his lips, then his pearly whites, in a rugged motion. As he tugs on it, I moan loudly. "Max, please."

Brown eyes squint up at me as he holds a nipple between his teeth. "Please, what?" he asks while biting down.

"Please, please give me... I need your..." I'm heaving breaths and reach to fondle him with my hand over the sheet.

A feral growl rises from his chest and reverberates into the metal bar of my nipple, the vibrations sending waves of pleasure down into my pussy until it soaks the cotton beneath me. Max leans back on his hands, exposing more of his tanned, broad chest lightly dusted with black hair, a trail leading to exactly where I want to go.

"Suck me." As he had done to my wounds, I suction my lips to one of his weeping cuts, lavishing in the flavor with my tongue. "Oh, fuck, foxy." His head drops back, and he leans farther into the pillows, unable to hold himself up. The iron tinge hits my mouth, and I move to another cut, licking it dry. Before I move to the next, Max lifts my thighs with his broad palms and settles me onto his hot, reddened cock head. "Sit, baby. Sit on my dick. I have to be inside you while I drink your blood."

Easing myself down, I place my arms around his neck as our foreheads connect. Both of us moan in ecstasy as I glide over his entire length, sheathing his fullness as deeply inside of me as he'll go. Once settled, I sit on his lap, just nestling him there, combined.

"*Fuuuck*, foxy." With a palm on my shoulder, he leans me back so he can savor my cuts, occasionally switching to a nipple as I writhe my hips up and down his long, thick shaft. Every inch of his cock fills some need I have within me. He belongs inside me, and I belong to him.

Raising his heavy-lidded eyes to mine, I see a smear of my blood on his full bottom lip. I know what he wants. Our mouths meld together, swapping our crimson souls as I taste myself on him. His arms wrap tightly around me, the dark hair on top of his head tickling my chin as he squishes his cheek against my thumping chest. "I hear your heart. It says you're mine. Say it."

"I'm yours."

"And I'm yours."

With one last downstroke on his cock, he holds me there, preventing me from moving while I wiggle until my clit brushes repeatedly against his pubic bone. Screaming in the throes of my pleasure, I reach the height of my ecstasy, and Max erupts within me with a loud roar. His cock and cum stretch me further than I thought I could go as he yells out my name. We hold each other, catching our breaths. Every throb of him inside me, emptying into my womb, every pulsation of my pussy, soaking it in... We ride out the waves together, taking our time and never parting.

He leans back, bringing me with him until I'm laying on his firm chest covered with tiny sweat beads. Through his bones, I feel his heart beating rapidly, making his cuts ooze more between us, coating our skin and causing us to stick together. He slowly dissipates within me, but I refuse to let him slip out by squeezing my inner muscles, embracing him, and keeping him inside where I want him.

"That was our ceremony." The tenor of his voice lulls my eardrum into a trance as I stare off into space without a thought in my mind other than pure satisfaction.

"Hmm?"

"That was our ceremony. We can sign fucking papers or whatever, but we're one now, foxy. You can take my name if you want, but if you don't, just know I'm carved on your heart, and in your blood."

Raising my head, I brush some of his black hair back, getting lost in the seriousness of his eyes. "Do you mean we're married?"

"Yep. We are. That was it. I'll put that purple sapphire on your hand, feed you some cake, take you to a beach somewhere sunny, but you're my wife now. You'll live here, at the manor. You go where I go. My people are your people. You're a bear now, even though you'll always be my little fox. Okay?"

If I didn't think I could form more tears, I was wrong. It takes me at least a minute before I can even choke out the words. "Yes, okay." He's my husband. Maybe he always was, because this was meant to be.

Leaning down, his lips tap the top of my head. "Mrs. Freidenberg."

Meeting his eyes, I feel the comfort with him now to confess something I should have all along. Something I've been holding back. But now he is mine and I am his. We are one. No more secrets or trying to tear us apart. I see that now.

"Max, our parents... I think they were right about something, no matter how screwed up they were."

His lips don't stop pattering over my skin, my hair, my ear, anywhere he can reach. "What's that, foxy?" he asks between kisses.

"Their wills. They wanted us to get married, wanted me to birth your heirs."

Black eyebrows raise with his shock. "Really? I mean, I never took the time to look at the latest one."

"Yes. They wanted something different from our ancestors. There's a section in my parents' will that talks about wanting our three families to combine to overthrow the tyrant. You know that with three families agreeing in the senate, then they can cast out the sitting consort." Shaking my head, I lean up on my elbows to take in his handsome face. "I just resisted it all this time because my father... Well, fuck Franklin Von Dovish and whatever he wanted, you know?"

A corner of his lips lifts as he nods. "Yeah, that makes sense." His large palm brushes my hair and plays with the short strands on either side of my head as the divot between his brows grows deeper. "So, Calum was to marry..."

"Ashley Donovan."

"Ah." He swallows. "Wait, that means... Arianna and—"

With a grimace, I let him know the truth. "Ace, yes." His forearm muscles twitch and tighten around me as he pulls me back to his chest, placing his hand on my head, stroking my hair.

"He'll just kill her to spite me."

"We won't let that happen." As his arms flex, he tugs me into him tighter. Those dark eyes turn almost black as his stare seems to find something far away.

"No, we won't."

Nineteen

MAXIMILLIAN

"So it's official, then?" Markus struts to the fireplace in my office, hands behind his back like he's won some victory.

"Yeah. We signed the certificate at the courthouse just now." I place my parents' wills back in their file and kick my feet up. Livia was right. The added section discussed their secret plans to overthrow Strauss by combining our families. Donovan, Freidenberg, and Von Dovish joining to dethrone him from power with a three-vote majority in the senate. Our families, despite their ingrained generational hatred, had become weary allies, then friends. Their secret meetings disguised as having us play together were part of their strategy for peace.

"Congratulations. I think the pairing is a good one. Arianna—"

"Is *not* going to marry Ace. I won't let that happen. He'd just torture her or some shit." Brushing a hand through my hair, I consider what would be most likely. "Maybe give her syphilis."

Widening his palms with a question, he shakes his head. "Max... if she doesn't, who will she marry? Strauss?"

"No! She can remain single until—"

"I'm an adult, and I will choose who I want to be with, Max," Arianna says as she strolls into my office unannounced. When she stops, she perches a hip on the front of the cherry wood desk, her little pink dress riding up, too short for my liking.

It's not even worth arguing about. She *will* marry someone, and it won't be some mechanic with a bad attitude. "That's not how things work around here, Ari, and you know that," I murmur, trying to pretend to busy myself with paperwork on the desk.

Jakob peeks his head inside the door my sister left open. "Sir, a Miss Hannah Smith is at the gate, asking for you." His face is slightly less grim from the dark grief he held there for the last few weeks.

"Hannah? Oh! Hannah. Derichs's girl." Oh no. Dread fills my heart as I have to face the person I least want to after losing my true friend. But it's necessary, and I invited her to come.

"Yes, sir. Should I—"

"Let her in. I'll meet her in the parlor. Where's my wife?" Scanning my crew's blank faces, no one answers me.

"I'm right here, lion." Livia enters from the basement door. Her little hand slides across my back, and I wrap an arm around her, kissing the top of her head. Her skin and hair are damp.

"You've been dancing?" She nods, then lifts onto her toes to suction her lips to mine.

"Good." We set up a studio area just for her practice. It's not finished yet, but it'll get there. Sometimes I sit in the corner and watch in awe at the way her body moves. But, of course, that doesn't last long before I take her against the barre.

"I'll meet her with you. Let me just clean up real quick. Ari, can I borrow your face wash?" She grabs my sister by the hand and leads her out of the office. I know she's using that as an excuse to gossip about strategy to get me to change my mind about that prick, Wyatt, and it's not going to work. I'll make sure of that. She's still very young and has plenty of time to marry someone appropriate.

Before I give that too much thought, I prepare myself for the pain of meeting Hannah. A small family room adjoins the study, which is more of a library with a large TV and games table. A second entrance from the foyer makes it a convenient place to meet guests. As I pour myself a scotch from the small wooden bar along the back wall, I try not to get emotional thinking about my toast with Derichs. Mrs. Kroft scuttles in and places a tray of cut sandwiches with a bowl of sliced fruit on the coffee table, then slips out of the door she entered from without a fuss.

"Miss Hannah Smith, sir." Fritz stands aside and allows a small blonde woman to enter. Her eyes are wide as she takes in the room filled with rich, tobacco-colored bookcases that line the walls. The furniture is soft red leather, tufted, and well-worn, sitting on rugs that have been restored, but still show their ancient age. I remember playing board games with my parents here. Listening to jazz on the record player while Papa poured a gentle glass for himself, and Mama would dance with me. It's my favorite room in the manor.

Does she know I caused his death being such a shit leader? Will she be disgusted with me? And who could blame her if she is?

"Welcome, Hannah. Can I pour you a drink?" I ask from the raised platform circling the back of the room. It leads to a small conservatory filled with plants, where Fritz spends most of his days.

"N-no, thank you, Mr. Freidenberg." She twists her fingers together, then fiddles with her purse. Her frame is petite, fragile. I can picture her and my cousin together well, and that makes my heart hurt even more.

"Oh, no. Call me Max. Derichs was more than a soldier. He was my friend." Motioning to the loveseat with a wave of my hand, she sits. "Food? Water? Anything."

Blonde curls vibrate as she shakes her head rapidly. "No, thank you. Beautiful place. He said it was."

Reclining back into the sofa, I consider my words carefully. I'm never one to shirk my responsibilities, and it's time I got this over with. "I'm sure you're angry with me—"

"What? No, not at all." Pink lips part on an audible gasp as she answers.

"But... I'm the one responsible—"

Hannah places a small hand on my knee. Her blue eyes are wet as she peers at me from across the space between us. "No, Mister... Max. You helped Adal so much. Before he met you, he was lost. His legacy was to serve the Freidenbergs. It's all he ever wanted. He loved you. He loved his home, his people. He *wanted* to help. Adal knew the risks. It's why he refused to let me move here. I came here to meet you, his friend. I know how much he admired and respected you."

Now I am the one with tears in my eyes. Livia slips in through the office doors, and I clear my throat, then shirk away a tear with the pad of my thumb.

"Hannah, it's so good to meet you." Livia walks to her and sticks out her hand, but Hannah stands and the two briefly embrace.

"I'm hugging a lot more people nowadays. It's impor-tant," Hannah says. The two women sit together on the loveseat.

"Adal meant a lot to me. He was a good friend," Livia says.

She smiles. "Yeah, he mentioned your adventures. He was so excited the night he got to order room service." Her hand moves to her stomach, and my eyes follow.

An uneasiness sets in my core at the motion, and I feel nauseated, but I have to know. "Um, forgive me. Are you, uh..."

Her smile broadens. "Yes. I'm carrying his child. He

knew. He was so happy, but I told him not to tell anyone until I made it to the second trimester."

My chest tightens. He had a child on the way... Fuck. The pain becomes unbearable once again. Livia's tears spill over her cheeks.

"Um..." I pause, trying to maintain some composure, but breathing is difficult. "I'm taking care of you and the baby. For the rest of your lives. Whatever Adal would make is yours."

"Oh, no, Max. That's not why I came—"

"I know it's not. But, *please*. I need to do this. For him. For his child and his legacy. You will always have a home here, as will your child. Whatever you need, you come to me first, okay?"

Her mouth tightens into a line as she nods slowly. "Thank you. That was unexpected and... Thank you."

"Do you have anyone to help?" Livia squeezes Hannah's hand in her lap.

"Oh, yes. My family is in Drussville with me. I moved back in with my parents. My younger sister is excited for her niece or nephew to arrive."

As if the walls are invisible, I spread out my hand to showcase the lands. "Well, as I said, if you want, we have plenty of cottages here on the grounds. I'll be happy to settle you into your own home anytime."

She shakes her head. "Thank you, but Adal wouldn't have wanted me here. I feel bad even visiting, but I did want to meet you. Both." Livia puts her arm around her shoulders.

After chatting about some of our favorite memories

with Derichs, I have Markus arrange to get her set up with a special account we can deposit funds into. When we bid her farewell, Livia stands with me in the foyer and wraps an arm around my waist.

"I love you, Max. You're a good man."

"Sometimes." Leaning down, I capture my wife's lips in a warm kiss. Hopefully, the construction of our new main bedroom is finished by the evening. We've been staying in my childhood bedroom for the last two weeks since we had our ceremony. It started off with a bunch of naughty teenage fantasies, but now it's kind of weird. We need a room that's just us. And Livia got over the cowboys on the walls days ago.

"Cal wants to meet for dinner to discuss the rebuilding plans."

A shiny plastic bandage peeks out of the deep arm of my wife's loose tank top. "What is that?" Grasping her shirt, I pull it up as she tries to stop me.

"Max! Stop!" She grabs my hand, then tugs me toward the hall bathroom. "Come here." Pressing my lower body into her, I gather the fabric and lift up to reveal her bare chest.

On her ribcage, where once was a lone fox, is now a bear tattoo, the two animals combined. She's truly mine. The sadness from the last few weeks seems to dissipate the longer I stare at it.

"You got a bear."

She nods with a slow smile creeping onto her face. "Yeah. To go with my fox."

Seeing that ink, those lines and marks on her skin... it

means she's made a choice. She trusts me enough to become a Freidenberg. To be part of my people. The west and the east are combining forces. It had been just me trying to take back what's mine, and now I have two-thirds of this city behind me to take over from Strauss. We can win.

"I love you, my foxy bear." Seizing her pert ass cheeks in my hands, I lift her onto the sink counter, pressing my body into hers, needing to touch her all over. Tilting her head to the side, I nibble down the column of her neck as she shivers.

"I love you, Max, but we need to go," she whispers.

"Nah... Cal can wait. And we didn't get our honeymoon yet."

"We should go..." The words she says don't match her fingers, which are unzipping my jeans and sliding them down my legs, along with my boxers. She hops off the counter and spins around. Her own pants drop while I chuckle a breath in her ear at her hurry. Her hands dance behind her and find my hard cock. As she lines herself up, I grab one of her soft breasts in each of my hands. "Oh, god!" she yells as I enter her.

"Fuck! Your cunt feels so good." Watching my wife in the mirror above the sink, her face flushes red as her pussy engulfs me. Without wasting any time, she starts springing off me, her ass bouncing against my abs, jiggling as if it's calling to me. I swat it, leaving a red handprint. "Are you using my dick, foxy? Using me like a toy?"

"Y-yes," she moans. "I told you I'd fuck you."

With each backstroke, her pussy clutches onto me like it won't let me leave. Standing still so she can grasp her pleasure, I reach a couple of fingers around her smooth hip to stroke her clit. My lips meet the crook of her neck and suck it in, her familiar amber scent filling my nose. She trembles in my arms and her legs shake, so I hold her tighter, taking over the work with a deep, steady rhythm. Just how she likes it.

Raising my mouth to her ear, I whisper, "Come for me, my little fox. Come for your lion, your husband. I want to watch you unravel in the mirror." Shifting my eyes to the glass, I see her face screw up as she howls at the peak of her orgasm. Giving her one long, hard thrust, I let her tense around me.

"Now, be a good girl and let me fuck that tight ass."

Livia's mouth opens as she inhales quickly, the sensation tightening on my dick. Reaching over her to the medicine cabinet, I find some baby oil and drizzle it on her backside. Taking first one finger and rubbing around the area, I add a second and push inside her as she jolts forward.

"Max..."

"You trust me?"

Livia bites her lip and nods. Fucking her ass with two fingers, I continue to slide in and out of her pussy. She moans and pushes back against me until I can add a third finger. Her back arches as she takes it.

"Baby, I love you... Let me show you how much by filling your ass. Claiming all your body with mine." Grabbing her hips, I slide out and then press the head of my cock against her tightly puckered hole. She groans as I thrust my hips forward, slowly entering her.

"Wait... wait." Pants come from her mouth as I continue to edge inside. It's hotter here than anywhere in her body. She fits my dick like a glove.

"My cock is meant to be inside you."

Curving her ass back into me, I'm able to fit all the way in. Her head drops forward with a whimper as I control her body. Rapidly shifting my hips, I fuck her while pulling her toward me so I can fit all the way in with every stroke.

"Damn, foxy. Your ass is something else. I'm gonna fill it with my cum. You ready?"

"Max... Not inside."

"Shit. Shit, Livia..." It's too late. My cock spurts cum inside her ass, pulsating waves of my pleasure deep inside her. As I try to pull back, her tight ring only forces more inside her until everything oozes out between her cheeks. "Fuck, baby, I'm sorry. I couldn't stop."

In the mirror, I see her lips raise into a smile. "It's fine, it just... feels weird."

Our lips find each other's in a tender caress. Panting breaths into her mouth, I tell her, "Fuck, I love being married to you." She reaches a hand to stroke my face and the scruff that's accumulated there along my jaw.

"I love being married to you."

Pulling up her panties and jeans, I help her get dressed. "The thought of you eating dinner with my cum up your ass is making me hard again, you dirty slut." She gasps, and I spank her ass hard. "Let's go before I fuck you again."

Over the last few days, we've made love so much, I barely have any supply left. A quickie was necessary, though. Better than spending an awkward dinner at her brother's with a painfully full erection. Now, I'm only about half-mast.

When we arrive at the Von Dovish estate, I'm greeted like a king now, instead of something the cat dragged in. Giles quietly resents me instead of overtly trying to annoy the shit out of me. My place is apparently near the head of the table, as he waves a suited arm toward the chair near Cal.

Before I can make a move, Cal grabs me in a giant hug. "Brothers. We're truly brothers now."

Involuntarily, my mouth curls into a smile. "Yeah, we are. Sit down, you sap. I'm starving."

He laughs, then calls for dinner. Livia sits next to me, and I pull her hand into my lap. There's not a moment I can live without touching her.

"How're the finances there on East Side?" Cal asks me.

"We're... okay. But we may need some help with the motorcycle shop rebuild."

"No question. I got you covered." He swipes on his phone and texts someone, his thumbs blazing over the keyboard on his screen. "It's done. I'll have the money wired to you in the morning when the banks open. Do you need workers?" The butler brings him a bottle of champagne, and he approves it with a nod. Giles pours us all a toasting flute.

"Uh, no. I think it would be best if the people of East Side rebuild it."

Cal nods. "That makes sense. This will be a weird transition for everyone in the west and east. We're family now." He clears his throat as we each raise a glass. "To my sister, Livia, and my new brother, Max. I wish you a long and happy marriage." Tapping glasses, we all take a sip.

His offers are generous, expected even, but I worry about owing him things. "I have to pay you back. Let me give you some guns—"

"No, absolutely not." Cal shakes his head.

"Cal, come *on*. Be reasonable," my wife interrupts, and I squeeze her hand resting on my thigh.

"I am being reasonable. I want to keep West Side as far away from the weapons and war as we can."

"Pretty soon, we may not have a choice," I tell him.

Cal takes a spoonful of his soup. Quietly, almost disturbingly, he says, "I'm focused on other things."

"Oh? Like what?" Livia snaps at him.

"I would like to celebrate my sister's marriage. Let's just enjoy a meal."

We all stare at our bowls for a moment. He's right. I don't think Cal will budge on this. But I'm not going to stop West Side from buying our weapons. The more armed the citizenry, the better our chances against Strauss if he decides to hold an anniversary of the Raging Bull. If Cal doesn't want to be involved, then he doesn't need to know.

Livia looks on the verge of an argument, but I thread my fingers through hers and give her a look. I'll back her play, but it's our brother. Peace and his alliance are more important than anything.

"Is it lonely here without me?" Livia changes the subject with a strained grimace.

Cal's face brightens a bit. "Well, you were never home anyway. But, yeah..." Grabbing a roll from the basket, he breaks it in half. "Feel free to use the dance studio whenever."

Livia's eyes crinkle as she smiles at me. "Max put one in for me at the manor... but I'll be back to visit. I can't stay away from my big brother."

"And we expect you anytime, Cal. Our home is yours," I say. Cal nods, but his thoughts seem faraway.

"Thanks. Appreciate it. I've been pretty busy with work lately, but yeah. We should make family dinners weekly or so."

The rest of the dinner is peaceful, focused on the meal and cake that the Von Dovish chef made for us. We relax in the living room together to watch a movie before Livia and I decide to head home. Hanging out, doing something so perfectly peaceful, under a blanket, no less, made my cock grow to its full capacity. Being that close to my wife, her head resting on my shoulder, leg thrown over my own, it was enough to just about make me fuck her in front of her brother. But alas, I restrained myself.

As we say goodbye to Cal, Livia slips her arm around my waist while I throw one over her shoulders. She leans into me as we stroll to the Barracuda together. "I'll convince him. He has to get on board, or we're all dead now that he doesn't have gates... or guards," she says with a careful look my way.

"Foxy, let's just leave it for now. He's our brother. If Wyatt and his club sells over here, I'm not going to stop them. Cal hasn't said anything about that so far. Hopefully, he won't."

Heading across town, I notice a Mercedes tailing a few cars back. I don't want to worry Livia, so I grab my phone and dial Skipper, my hacker.

"Hey. You got eyes right now?"

My wife sits up straight in her seat and glances behind us.

Skipper's melodic voice rings out, "Yes. Not sure who it is, though. They have a block on my feed, which means it's probably Strauss. I can guide you. Let me turn some of those lights green for you."

Immediately, the light I'm sitting at changes, and I press the gas pedal all the way down. "Get me to the highway. I can take them there."

"Left."

Tossing my phone at Livia, she catches it with one hand and puts it on speaker, grabbing onto the handle of the door as I spin the wheel. We make a sharp turn, but the Mercedes catches up easily.

"Two streets up and take a right."

Focusing on Skipper's steady voice, I will myself to calm down. He's not fazed by anything. Meanwhile, my heart rate climbs steadily as sweat pours from my forehead. Gripping the steering wheel tighter, I follow his instructions.

"They're still there," I say through gritted teeth.

"Quick right as soon as you can, then straight for three and a left."

"In this alley?" I almost panic yell.

"Yes. Go now."

Squeezing the front of the car between buildings, I gun the engine, pushing my girl as fast as she'll go. Flying through gears, my breath catches when I have to slam on the brakes at the end of the alley. Another Mercedes blocks the exit. Two men stand beside it with guns pointed at us. The other black car pulls in behind us, its bright headlights bathing the interior of the Barracuda in blinding white. Livia grips onto everything she can in the car with strained fingers.

"Max! We're trapped." Her voice is breathless, the sound of her fear tightening my chest.

"I'm getting Aries in position, Max. Hang on." Skipper comes through the phone as I swallow deeply, my constricted throat almost causing me to choke. The guy in front of us motions with his hand to raise ours, but I think about my gun sitting in my hip holster. How fast can I reach and shoot?

"I don't have time for that, Skip." Instead of waiting, I take off. Shots ring through the glass, fracturing it into a billion spectrums of light. The guys jump out of the way as I crash into the side of the Mercedes at the end of the alley. It moves sideways, but not enough for us to get through. Backing up, I ram into the one behind us, but when I turn to look at where I'm going, Livia slouches, clutching her arm.

"D-did you get hit?" My voice is fully panicked now. I can't lose her.

Her wet eyes meet mine, and everything in my world shatters. "Max... Keep going."

"No! Foxy! Keep your fucking eyes on me, baby." Tears blind my vision, and I blink rapidly to clear it. "Don't close your eyes. Do not close your eyes. You look at me." I snatch her face between my hands and force her attention on my face. Her tears spill over onto her cheeks.

"Lion..."

Another two bullets graze through the glass in the back and one in the front. The front of the Barracuda is smoking, smashed in. The tire is bent, I can feel it. My wife. My wife... My world.

Throwing my body across the seat, I shield her. "You're going to be okay, baby. Stay with me." Heat rises in my back as a sharp pain infiltrates my coat. "Fuck! I got hit!"

Before I can react, my door is thrown open and someone yanks me out by my ankles. My hands grasp at Livia, but the men toss me to the ground. One of my arms is useless, and I'm unable to protect my face as I hit the pavement. Livia slumps in her seat, utter shock and terror covering her face like a mask.

"I love you, Livia!" I yell before they drag me away. Each man has hold of an arm, the pain ripping through my torso in pulsating waves of agony. My gun is snatched from my holster and my knife ripped from my belt.

They aren't going after my wife. Our eyes never part from each other's, holding the tie that binds us together. I'm never letting go. Just before I'm pitched into the back of the damaged Mercedes like a sack of flour, her lids close slowly. "I-I can't see! Livia! I can't see!" I scream. The overwhelming terror that she's broken our bond by dying feels worse than any shot I could take. "Please, Livia! I can't see your eyes! I can't see!"

The two men in the car behind her advance toward the Barracuda, but I watch as each of their heads snaps backward, racked with a hole in the middle. Aries, my spy...

"Shit, move," one of my captors says to the other. I'm chucked inside the back seat, groaning in torment as my shoulder hits the other door. The bullet isn't too far in, if at all, but the hit burns. Doors slam and we jet off down the rain covered roads of Gnarled Pine.

If Livia lives... I'll be okay.

If she dies, I'll stay alive long enough to burn down this whole fucking city.

Lifting my arm makes the pain shoot down my nerves like fire, but I'm determined to throw myself from the moving car. Wherever these guys are taking me can't be good.

"He's moving back there," the driver says to the passenger. Before I can snag the door handle and pull, the gaunt man, who has two deep scars slashed across his face, reaches around, and punches me. His red tattooed hand pulls back enough times that I memorize it... a bull. Two more hits to the temple and the sear in my shoulder, the throbbing in my head fades away. The devastating agony of losing my wife is all that remains as I drift from consciousness.

～

"Where are the weapons, Mr. Freidenberg?"

Pain is all I know as I become aware of my own existence. Sheer, utter anguish lives everywhere. Have I been set on fire? There's a loud rumbling, some humming in my ears that's almost deafening.

"The weapons. Where are they?"

A momentary release from the burning allows me to wake up more, but the reverberating groans lull on... It's me. I'm making those sounds. Like a living, breathing entity embedded deep inside of me, the pain returns with a surging force. All I want to do is move into a more comfortable position, as if there is such a thing, but I'm bound.

"Mr. Freidenberg. You disappoint me." Sharp stabs lash my back. Blinking, I take in my surroundings. Stone walls, weeping with moisture. My head and arms are locked within a black wooden stockade. Straps cross my feet, holding me to the base. Involuntarily, my naked body shivers with cold and the shock of pain.

"What?" My voice halts its moans to edge out the question.

"What? I told you not to bind yourself to another family, and you went and did it anyway. I told you to keep your businesses clean. And yet, they're distributing weapons. And then you go and wreck those iron gates... I liked them. Oh, and my men, of course, too, I suppose. I'm disappointed in you for disobeying your master."

Strauss. I recognize the way he makes his 't' sounds like those of his old country.

"You're not my master," I say.

The rip in my skin that comes after takes my breath away. There's no air for me to cry out, so my mouth opens in soundless suffering.

"I'm everyone's master. Didn't you know?" I can't see him, but his voice resounds from behind me. Obviously, he's using a whip, perhaps with something attached, as I feel my back being shredded, muscles and sinew exposed without any protection.

"You killed Derichs. You will die," I somehow manage to grit out.

His laugh is as terrifying as the prospect of the next zing of the whip. When it hits, my knees buckle, and my bladder releases itself down my legs. The stings cause my stomach to lurch with nausea. Is it even possible to live with this much pain?

"It's either you or her." Strauss shows himself in front of me, grabbing me by the hair to lift my head in a tight grip. Leaning over, his gaunt cheeks poke sharply from his face as his lips lift into a broad smile. "You or Miss Von Dovish must die. That's my payment. I mean, she *will* return to a Von Dovish if you're gone. I'll make sure of it. And that there are no remnant cubs within her womb."

"Me. Take me." Gathering up what's in the back of

my throat, I launch blood into his face. His eyes crinkle into a smile as his tongue laps up some of my saliva that landed on his mouth.

"Unless..." He's so close I can see the twitch in the muscles of his face as his grin falters. "Unless Arianna will agree to marry me."

"Kill me." As soon as I let the words fly, I regret them. Because if I'm gone, who will protect my wife and sister? Jakob? Calum? Markus? No. There's no one. I have to get out of here.

But how?

Twenty

LIVIA

A man with a black outfit and ski mask lifts me into his arms gently. "Max. Get Max."

"We're on it already. I need to get you out first, Mrs. Freidenberg."

It must be his spy, Aries. There's such comfort in hearing my new name and title, but it's not enough. My other half is missing. "Help Max..." It's all I repeat like a mantra. I'm not dying; I just need to get my jacket off and the burning would stop. The blackness overtakes me again as I pass out, no longer wanting to feel the pain.

My shoulder wedges against Aries's broad chest. We sway together as he walks swiftly to a vehicle awaiting us down another alleyway nearby. "Help Max..." That's what I say before I faint again, feeling the car jet toward the manor.

Jakob grabs me from the passenger's side of the car when we get home. Aries murmurs something to him about Max as I grip Jakob's thick neck tighter. He smells of pine and peppermint, like my grandfather used to. Closing my eyes, I pretend I'm that little girl playing with him again, only to seek some comfort from the agony of losing my mate.

"Egon and Gemini are on it. We'll get him back, Mrs. Freidenberg." Realizing Aries is leaving, I suddenly spawn awake, pain be damned.

Before Aries takes off, I yell, "I'm coming with you!" Beating my fists against Jackob's tight chest, he wrestles me tighter against his body.

Aries shakes his head, still donning the black mask before jumping inside the vehicle and speeding off in a cloud of dust.

My husband... Max could be anywhere. Half my heart is missing. How does a person live without their heart inside? No. There's no way I'm leaving my partner alone. No matter how much Jakob tries to hold me back. Max needs me and I need him.

I'm going to get him back.

Acquiescing for the moment while Jakob brings me inside, Maggie waits in the small parlor for me with a medical kit.

"It's fine. I don't even think it penetrated. Just... hurry," I say, shucking off my coat and peeking at my shoulder. There's a lot of blood loss, but the bullet falls out of the sleeve as I rip off my clothes.

Maggie sets to work, quietly stitching where the bullet cut through my skin and some muscle. It hurts, but I was a wuss to lose it in the car. Especially when Max told me to keep my eyes on him. I held on to consciousness as long as I could until they threw him in the back of that car. The man who took him... he had a tattoo like Strauss's men did who chased me a few months ago.

Once the healer has completed her work, I run upstairs to change into slick leather pants and a fresh jacket before dialing Alpha. Despite her obsession with my brother, she's taught me everything I know about staying stealthy. Sneaking into and out of places undetected is what she is known for in Gnarled Pine Hollow's underground channels, and I need her skills now more than ever.

"Please, Alpha. I'm desperate. I *will* go alone if you don't go with me."

A small sigh breaks through the speaker. "Livia... I can't let you do that! Cal won't like it."

"So come with me."

"Echoes says Aries and Gemini are in the vicinity of Strauss's place. I think they have it covered. They'll bring him home."

"Alpha, you're in love with my brother. I know it. If he were in trouble..." I bite my lip to prevent a sob from escaping. The torment of even thinking of losing Max is too much for me to bear. I *won't* lose him. We have always been. We will always be.

After a moment's pause, she replies, "Okay, Livia. I'll take you. Be outside your gates in ten."

We hang up, but before I step downstairs, Arianna emerges from her room in a hurry, her normally perfectly managed espresso-colored locks disarranged.

"What's going on? Jakob said—"

Taking a few strides, I grab her hands in mine and squeeze. "Strauss has your brother."

Arianna's eyes fill with tears, her thick bottom lip quivering. "This is about me, isn't it?"

My head tilts in confusion. "What do you mean?" How much does she know?

"He wants me. Strauss wants me. Wyatt told me—he told me that Strauss burned down the building to get me. Said that Strauss sent his men to kill Derichs. Max never tells me anything."

Pulling her into my body, I tighten an arm around her waist in a hug. "Yes, he does want you, but there's no way we will let that happen, Ari."

She nods against my shoulder. "You two have always protected me. I love you both." Letting her go, I take a few steps away, our hands lingering as long as possible.

"Stay with Jakob." Turning toward the stairs, I pause. "I'm getting him back, Ari. I love you."

Within eight minutes, Alpha arrives in a blacked-out Maclaren. Sliding into the passenger side, I grip the seat as she takes off like lightning toward the Strauss mansion.

"There's a back entrance through the crypts. It's not pretty, and it's creepy, but you better follow and not make a fucking sound. Got your boots on?"

"Yes. Covert mission outfit engaged. It's been a while, but I remember everything you taught me. I'm ready. I have to be." She pulls the car under some trees down the street. Snagging her sleeve, I stop her before she bolts out of her door. "Alpha, he's *mine*. He's my lion, my husband, and I won't live without him."

"Desperation can force mistakes. Take your emotions out of this. Now, move."

Winter has settled in the valley, causing my skin to ache with the sharp cuts of the cold air, but I ignore it. This is the night all my training has led me to. We climb a steep incline, grabbing roots to lift us on the particularly slick parts, the path chosen because there are no cameras in this area.

Spiked iron fencing lines the property. There's a spot that has just enough space for us to slide under. My jacket gets caught on a rod, but I tug it free and scramble to my feet as Alpha motions with her finger to remain quiet. We're on Strauss land now. In my mind, I play a twisted game of would you rather. If I got caught, would it be worse to be a sex slave or be tortured for eternity?

Sliding along the edges of the property lines, we make it to the graveyard at the back of his large estate. In the middle is a Gothic mausoleum with thick stone columns in front of two intricately carved dark wood doors leading to the entrance. Once inside, Alpha motions to a back wall. There, she shuffles her foot on the ground and taps out the lines of a trapdoor in the floor with her toes.

She points with a finger for me to kneel, and as I do, I find a metal ring through the ancient dust and tug on it with my full strength. The cover is extremely heavy. But for Max, adrenaline pumps through me, and I give it another pull to get it lifted. Alpha gets underneath and pushes with her weight until the cover is off, revealing a set of stone steps leading down into nothingness.

Alpha grabs me in a hug. We've never touched before, but I quickly realize she is doing this in order to speak closely in my ear and not for any show of affection. "You're on your own from here. I cannot enter, or that's a declaration of war on West Side. Head down the hall, which will lead to a conservatory near the entrance of his dungeons. Gemini and Aries are here somewhere on the grounds, but I don't know where."

And before I can say a word, she deftly vanishes out of the mausoleum, leaving me standing in utter terror and determination in front of the hatch.

There's only one way to save my husband, and it's through the dark hole.

Using dancer's steps, I lithely slip through the crypts beneath Strauss's estate. My hand trails along the cold stone walls. No light seeps through, but occasionally, I use my phone's flashlight to see how much farther I have to go. It seems like miles. I can't rest, though.

On and on, each stone underfoot causes my brain to become confused. Without the light, I can't see where I'm going and feel like I may be headed in other directions. The sound of my footsteps is so monotonous, it matches the drumming of my pulse until they are one. A person could go crazy down here.

The air is dead, stale. And maybe I have died. Maybe that bullet took me, and this is my hell. Wandering, searching for my lion for all of eternity with half of my heart lying somewhere outside of its rightful place. Its chambers lying deep in the dungeons of this purgatory. Will it ever be able to beat again?

Finally, the atmosphere changes. It's less dense. Particles are looser and I can breathe easier. Purple light creeps toward my feet as I approach the tunnel's end. It's another set of stairs leading to whatever level of damnation awaits above.

Pressing myself against the curving wall of stone, I slide soundlessly up the steps. Loud echoes of water dripping greet me as I alight. Reaching the top, I peer over the edge of a short rail, finding myself in an underground conservatory of sorts.

Rows and rows of tall, hazy green plants are lined under blacklights. I thought West Side had a grip on the marijuana industry, but Strauss seems to have his own, even growing different strains Cal raises for sale. Instead of focusing on my ire at his thievery, my eyes quickly scan the area to find an exit.

Shuffling to the metal door, I peek out of the glass window. Three halls branch out from a main area outside the door. One to the left leads up another staircase. The one straight appears to dead end with one dark wood door. And the one to the right has several doors, all closed.

Small red lights blink in two corners of the hall. Cameras. Those are a definite problem since I don't know where I'm going. Sneaking won't help if Strauss can see my every move.

Frustrated, I turn around and study the room I'm in. It's dark enough that I'm hopefully unnoticed if there are cameras in here, too. The dripping sound dulls my mind as I try to focus on how to get to Max, where he could be...

A wide ventilation shaft sits high on the wall near the stairs where I entered. If I could get inside, perhaps I could scope out the other rooms without being seen. A wooden work bench stands nearby, and I drag it over to the entrance, the loud scraping sound shattering the atmosphere as it crosses over the uneven stones. As quickly as I can, I leap on top of the table, then unscrew the cover from the hole, the cover easily falling off.

Hoisting up, I'm just able to fit on my belly and squirm down the length, which heads in the direction of the right hallway. As I near a light entering from the next room, screams from a man in agony ring loudly through the shaft, my pulse racing so violently, it makes my vision blur. I'm able to shimmy closer for a better look while holding my breath.

Through the lines of the metal cover, I spot Max's bare body bound to a stockade. A sharp inhale cuts across my lips when I see the skin of his back peeled opened in several bloody slashes. Vladimir Strauss stands in front of him with a black leather whip in his hand. Obviously used for torture, the walls hold several pieces of bondage equipment, and other devices used to inflict his sadism are set up on a table near the side wall. A man with a red hand tattoo of a bull stands near the tools, flipping a pair of pliers in between his fingers like it's a Rubik's cube.

"You can make the call. Get Arianna here for me," Strauss says in a voice that sounds as if he's bored.

Max spits on the ground and doesn't speak, only moans.

Sliding my phone from my pocket, I send a text to Echoes and ask her to get in touch with Max's hackers. I alert Markus and Jakob as well.

I'm able to scrunch into a ball to position my feet over the ventilation cover. It's easy then to slide my knife out of my boot and grasp it for my next move.

"We could always just fuck your wife."

"No!" Max manages to yell, blood flying from his mouth as he does.

Shoving with all my might, the cover flies off, and I explode from the exit of the shaft, dropping to the floor with a thud.

Strauss's wide eyes take me in with shock, and I bounce to my feet while he's stunned, then split leap toward him, knife in hand. Max growls like a bear and breaks the wood of the stocks enough that he shakes himself free. His large body stumbles back in a daze, but he grabs a plank before he falls. The man with the hand tattoo spurs into action, grabbing a blade from the table and waltzing toward me.

Max swings with a mighty roar and nails the guy in the back of the head until he slumps forward, eyes rolling into his head. Like a jet stream, blood sprays from the wounds the injury caused, gathering on Max's face, giving him an even more terrifying appearance. Vlad snatches both of my wrists and holds me at arm's length while I slash at him by swinging my hand in erratic circles. Max snatches the blade from the downed man and takes two broad steps toward Strauss.

While my eyes move to my husband, Strauss manages to twist my arm and body into a lock, pressing my own knife to my throat. My legs squirm, but he takes a leg and splits mine, trapping one with his own. If I move, the blade will stab me directly in the artery. My eyes meet the darkness settled within Max's as he realizes the danger we're in. He crouches into his fighting stance, as if to pounce at any moment.

Strauss lets out a loud laugh in my ear, his hot breath sending tremors of disgust down my spine.

"If I were you, I wouldn't move one more inch, Frei-denberg. Or else..." Strauss takes my elbow and digs the knife point into the skin of my throat. Despite trying to contain it, a whimper escapes my mouth at the sensation as my pulse pounds against the pressure of the knife's sharp tip. Max's shoulders raise to his ears.

"I'm going to enjoy tearing you limb from limb." Max's voice is hoarse, but he gets the point across, despite being an idle threat. My man is naked, beaten, and operating only on the last of his adrenaline reserves. His knees shake as much as the wooden board he's holding in his hands, and from the ashen pallor of his normally olive skin, I know he's barely holding on. Strauss has him bested with me in his arms. I cannot move. It's hopeless.

A triple knock, followed by two, then one sounds through the solid wood door to the hall. One of the secu-rity guards who greeted us when we first came to the

Strauss mansion enters in a hurry. "Sir, there's a woman here to see you."

"Why the fuck would I care about a woman coming to see me? I'm a little busy." Strauss nods to my husband.

The man enters the room as Max stumbles backward, almost falling over, dropping his weapon. Out of his holster, the guard pulls a gun and points it at Max's slumped body.

"This one says she's Arianna Freidenberg."

I feel the smile that creeps onto Vlad's face, pressed firmly next to my own. The nefarious grin can be heard in his voice when he says, "Oh? Well, this is someone I definitely want to see. Bring her down. And tell her to hurry. I get impatient sometimes and may kill these two for their insubordination."

Max lifts his head. "Baby, I won't let him touch you. He'll lose his hands if he does."

Strauss tightens his grip on me, and I try to hold in my scared cry, but I can't. My tears fall freely as Max continues to gaze into my eyes. It feels like years before there's shuffling outside the door and the guard returns. Behind him are Arianna and Jakob. And then three more of Strauss's guards enter, each holding a gun toward Max, Jakob, and me.

Small fasciculations in Strauss's muscles make his hold relax slightly when he sees the beautiful Ari. Innocence radiates off her, dressed in a white frilly dress, accentuated with dewy makeup and soft curls in her hair. If he slips again, I could twist out of his grasp.

"Max!" She runs to her brother first, after surveying

the situation. Kneeling in front of him, she strokes a hand against his face while he tries to hide his body from her. Jakob takes off his coat and throws it over him, but Max grimaces from the pain on his back. "Please, sir. Please, let them go," Ari cries, lifting her head toward the man still holding my life in his hands.

"Miss Arianna... It is such a pleasure. These were not the circumstances I had planned for our first meeting. But your brother and Miss Von Dovish have disobeyed my orders. The businesses were to be kept clean. Neither asked for my blessing for their clandestine marriage, either. So... my beautiful darling. I need you to choose which one will live and which one will die."

"No! Please, don't hurt them." Large droplets fall from her big brown eyes as she pleads with Strauss. Her fingers reach out to touch him, as if to stop him from hurting us.

"What would you have me do, my pure-hearted darling? They deserve punishment."

Sucking in a thick bottom lip, she swallows, then slowly answers. "I'll marry you."

"No!" Max yells, the volume causing a screwdriver to fall off the table nearby.

I gasp, and my blood freezes in my veins. My tears stop flowing.

She knows.

Arianna knows.

She must have read the will, about our parents' wishes. She's not nearly as innocent as Max thinks...

Briefly, I sort out if she has spoken with Ace yet or not. He would only agree to marry her if he wants revenge on Max for killing his sister, for us killing his necro.

Arianna is choosing the lesser of two evils. It's not ideal, but we will have a much easier time controlling Ace than the bull. Now, if I can just get Max to calm down, we can get out of here without Strauss getting suspicious.

"Lion—" I yelp as Strauss tightens his grip on me. "Lion. I think she's right. This is the only way."

Arianna bends to brush her brother's face with a gentle palm, then walks over to us. Her fingers glide over Strauss hand, and I feel his heart rapidly accelerate through his ribs pressed into my side.

"Please, sir. I will marry you. Is-is that what you want?" With a slight flutter of her eyelashes, she produces a pink flush to her cheeks as she asks. Damn, she's good.

Max's eyes squint with agony, but I catch his attention and give him a sly wink, hoping the gunmen don't catch on. *Remember the plan,* I try to say to him with my mind. His face falters for a moment, but I sense a change in him. He understands me.

"Yes, my darling. I have such glorious plans for our future."

"Then, please, Mr. Strauss, let my brother and sister-in-law go."

Strauss's grip loosens. As I contemplate darting away, I stop myself; he could still hurt me if I make too sudden of a move. His men are still aiming their guns at each of us.

"Get the minister and the certificates."

Arianna slides closer to Vlad, grasping his hand off my arms. He allows her to take him in her grasp, and I feel his body tremble, as if her touch was what he was waiting for all along. As she inches her way next to his body, I move out of his reach and toward my husband. Two steps and I kneel to hold him in my arms.

His sweat and woody scent envelop me as I wrap around him. A hiss clips out of his mouth as I accidentally rub against a wound, but I can't not touch him. Instead, I run my fingers through his hair and let his head drop to my shoulder.

Arianna gets quite close to Vlad. "I will marry you, but you have to let them go first. And-and I'd like to plan a wedding. I-I want a wedding, please. It will be my only one."

Vlad seems taken aback, but schools his expression quickly. "Yes, my darling. We shall have a wedding. As big as you want. We'll invite the entire town."

"But my brother and sister, you need to let them leave."

Strauss clasps her hands in his and sniffs them for a long time. Peering into her eyes, he says, "I swear to you, I will let them go." As he places his lips on the back of one of her hands, none of us move. My nerves are on edge. Of course, he'll try something crafty, and I won't rest until we're all safely back at our manor. Jakob helps Max to rise from the floor, holding him up under a shoulder, and I stand beneath the other.

The cold, gray eyes of Vlad scan the room before landing back on Arianna's. "But, my darling. You must stay here as payment."

"No!" Max and I shout at the same time.

Arianna's thick lips curve into a sly smile. "Sir, I understand. I'm offering myself, and I know the consequences of disobeying your orders. But I am…" She glances around the room, then drops her voice lower. "I'm a virgin. And it wouldn't be *right* for me to be here during our engagement. I would feel safer with my own people until then." Lowering her eyelids, she peers up at him through her long, black lashes. "Please, let me go home with my family, and I'll return for our wedding."

"Or I'll just kill everyone in Freidenberg Manor to get you if you don't come. You understand that, my darling? I will slaughter everyone you love to bring you here to be with me."

Arianna inhales quickly, and my pulse races. She nods. "Yes, sir. I understand. I will return for our wedding."

"Give me one kiss, and I'll allow you to leave."

Keeping calm, Arianna's brown hair falls over one shoulder as she peers up into Strauss's cold, gray eyes. "And my brother and sister?"

The corners of his lips lift into a small grin. "And your brother and sister, yes."

Max cringes and buries his face into my neck. I run my fingers through his hair, letting my nails scratch his scalp, trying to soothe his discomfort. For him, I know this will be just as painful as the lashes on his back to watch. He grips my shoulder tighter with his large hand.

Arianna snakes her arms around Vlad and presses her lips to his. As if he had been using all his restraint, he releases his hold on his discipline and envelopes her, kissing her back desperately, his head dipping to capture as much of the youngest Freidenberg as he can. Ari eventually peels back to take a breath, then steps back. Vlad's eyelids are half closed as he stares at her with hunger. He wants more of her, and she just left him wanting... taking control.

"May we leave, please?" she asks, barely above a whisper.

Vlad nods, and my fingers reach out, waving for Arianna to move closer to me. I want to make sure she gets through the door first. The hem of her white dress swishes as she hurries out as Jakob and I try to lug Max with us. My lion stumbles, but is able to shuffle his feet.

Before we turn as a unit toward the door, Vlad strolls to his guard and grabs the gun from his hip holster, then shoots Jakob directly in the head, blood spraying across my face like a warm spritz of salt water from the ocean. My ears ring from hearing myself scream "No!" even after it happens.

He lied! Max trips as the body crashes to the cold stones in front of us.

Arianna's shrill shriek echoes around the room as she covers her face with both hands, her brown eyes filled with terror.

"I said you three could leave. Not him." Vlad tosses the gun back to his guard and wipes his hands together before straightening his sleeves. It is just another day for him. Another day and another dead body. "You're excused."

Max's muscles tense under my shoulder like he's ready for retaliation. "No, lion," I growl at him. "Move." We're in grave danger. He can't try to get vengeance now. Arianna sobs as she takes up Jakob's position underneath her brother's shoulder. The three of us step over the tank's body before reaching the hall, stunned silence running between me and my husband.

"Oh, wait." We freeze at Vlad's instruction. He lopes to the body and digs in his pockets for a key fob, tossing it to me. "Here. You'll need this to leave."

We make it outside and dump Max into the back of the SUV Jakob drove to bring Ari here. None of us speak as I punch the gas and almost barrel down the gates blocking the entrance of Strauss's estate. They open at the last moment, enough for me to squeeze the vehicle through.

Once we reach town, I pick up two cars following us, but by the time we arrive at the manor, one splits off, and the other continues inside the gates with us. The lanterns from the fenceposts illuminate the same car Aries had earlier. As soon as we pull in front of the house, Markus stands, ready to help us, his arms at his sides, tugging lightly on his shirt. When I park, I leave Max for him to gather up and jump out, on a mission to get answers from our wayward spy.

"What the fuck? Are you a fucking mole? Where *were* you? Your master was almost killed, and I saved him." Pummeling my fists into his chest one after the other as rapidly as I can, Aries takes it without moving, his sternum feeling like granite beneath my hands. He's still wearing a black mask, but breaks my fight by using his hand to take it off. The skin on his right cheek has several deep slashed scars running through it, almost as if claws have shredded his skin. Other than those, he has no descriptive features. He could be anyone with light brown hair and eyes.

"I made the deal with Ace personally. If he agreed to marry Arianna, we could get Max back. She came up with the plan herself, and I came back here for her, to make sure Ace didn't touch her." As if I weren't seething with fury, he answers me with a calm, still voice.

"Why did he agree?"

Finally, a small movement of his eyes to the side shows a bit of vulnerability in his answer. "We promised we would tell him who killed his sister."

And he probably wants to abuse poor Ari if he thinks the Freidenbergs did it. "But it wasn't us."

"No... but your brother knows who it was." His lips flatten into a grimace.

"What? Cal? He *does*?" This is knowledge to me. Of course, my brother seems to know everything and keeps many secrets. I shouldn't be so surprised, but how could he hide something that big from me for all these years.

Aries nods. "I-I think he wants to torture Max... by marrying her."

Sucking in a large gulp of air makes me relax as I say, "Yeah. I figured." My shoulders shrug with a loss of any ideas on how to fix that problem. "We'll have to deal with that later. She needs to marry him before Strauss starts putting pressure on her." Turning on a heel, I sprint toward the house. A little glance over my shoulder shows the spy has already disappeared, leaving the car sitting in the drive.

Racing upstairs, I make it to our new bedroom where Maggie *and* the other healer I met last week, Charles, have my husband laid on his stomach on a massage table. There is sage burning in the room, and Charles takes his time soaking each wound carefully with something that smells of a strong astringent. Maggie works on setting up supplies on our dresser for suturing.

Kneeling, I crawl over to my husband and slide under the head hole to see him.

The corners of his eyes crinkle, pupils tiny. His voice comes out sluggishly slow, and a bit slurred, heavy with the drugs they've given him. "Baby, I'm okay. I love you. You saved me."

"You've saved me tons, Max. I love you." Reaching up, I tilt my head back so I can capture his lips with mine. My kiss is desperate, his soothing. And we exchange that energy until we pull back and stare at each other for a long moment.

"We saved each other, foxy."

Epilogue

MAXIMILLIAN

Sleeping on my stomach every night has made things pretty awful, except that I feel like I'm blissed out of my mind lying next to my wife. When I can't sleep, sometimes I just watch her. Maybe even sniff that exotic amber scent she coats on our sheets. It's my favorite smell to wake up to in the mornings when I drag her across the bed to snuggle with me.

So when I reach for her this morning and meet a cold bed, my heart throbs hard in my chest with panic as my eyes rip open and glance around. Where the fuck is she? Sitting up with a groan of pain from my back stitches, I snag the phone on my bedside table to call her, but relax with a heavy sigh when I see her text.

FOXY

> Don't forget: I've got my healer appt this am with mags

That's right. Some woman checkup thing. Rolling to

my side to get off the bandages stuck all over my back, I smile to myself, happy she feels comfortable using the Freidenberg healers now that she *is* one of us.

The only thing we need to deal with is Ace. Hopefully, he comes through with his half of the bargain, and Cal, too. Sliding out of bed, I toss on the same pair of sweatpants I've worn the last few days since Livia saved me from Strauss. It's nice not having to wear shirts around the house under the guise of still healing.

After my morning routine in the bathroom, I make my way downstairs, looking forward to some of Mrs. Kroft's bacon and eggs. She'd made me a tray in my room for the last few mornings until yesterday when she said she'd had enough of my "laziness" and to "get out of bed if you want some breakfast," clearly done with me being master of the house. Now that Livia oversees household staff, I'd been put out to pasture in our cook's eyes. She only asked "Mrs. Freidenberg" what to cook, going over the weekly menus and barely heeding me notice, other than to yell once when I grabbed an orange from the bowl in the kitchen, saying she was "getting ready to use that!"

Still, I don't mind her antics if there is bacon. And today, despite me coming down late, it sits there on the sideboard in all its gloriousness. Slightly cold, but crisp. Arianna must have already eaten, as I dine alone. Markus rounds the corner with his harried face, trying to tuck the bottom of his forever loose flannel inside his strained waistband. Clearing his throat, he nods briefly in his greeting.

"Morning. Egon got the Barracuda back safely,

tucked in the garage. We have some men over to fix the damage."

A bright smile hits my face. This day couldn't get any better. "Excellent. Of course, everything could have been avoided if he and Gemini did their jobs."

"Aries stated that the two were held up by Halcyon and Lark, although..." Markus stands still, then moves as quickly as I've seen him toward the chair next to mine. Swallowing, he leans on a large arm, lowering his voice. "Aries said that Egon was held up by, um, a woman in a hooded cloak with an owl mask."

Scrunching my brows, I repeat back to him, "An *owl* mask?" Markus nods, reconfirming it like he didn't just say something bizarre. "Who was it?"

"So, uh, apparently, he and Gemini stumbled upon some meeting they weren't supposed to with the cloaked figure and a man in a tuxedo. A man the woman called 'John.'" Sitting back, he widens his palms, showing that's all the information he has.

"John? John who?"

"We don't know."

Something just doesn't sit right with me, despite the belly full of bacon. Moving my jaw around, I ponder what must have been so important to Egon and Gemini to leave their master alone in Strauss's dungeon. "What does Aries say about it? About them leaving me?"

"Aries says the two were slowed by the meeting and trying to gather some intel, but were then snared by Halcyon, who called in Lark as backup. You know how

Strauss's spies are." Taking off his glasses, he pulls out the soft cloth to wipe them like what he said was explanation enough.

"No, I don't. I don't know anything about them, except their names, from what Aries told me." Shoving my plate away, I frown. I've lost my appetite for the rest.

"Well, they're both formidable foes. Like their master, sadistic to the core. Your men are lucky to have gotten away." Sliding his glasses back on, his gray eyes peer at me accusingly. "Not like Jakob."

And the happiness of the morning has now vanished. "No. Not like Jakob." Turning my head, I stare out at the vast ground covering the back forty acres. I was so cocky, arrogant when I started. Now, I'd lost good men. Maybe that's why I always needed my fox to help me. Her brains and my brawn could do this city a lot of good together. Hopefully, that includes overthrowing the consort and never allow Derichs's death or Jakob's to be in vain. We could instill some real changes...

We're gearing up for war, and I feel it in my bones. If only we could collaborate with Ace now that he's agreed to take Arianna's hand. It seems our parents were right, that our combinations could create peace. It's just going to take a lot of violence to get there.

"Max! Max! Lion!" My breathing stops at the sound of Livia's panicked voice before the front door slams, causing the mirrors on the walls to shudder. Jumping from my chair, it tips over in my hurry to grab my wife.

"What is it, baby? What's wrong?" Reaching her, I

grasp her waist and tug her into me, scanning her body for any hurt, bruise, broken anything... She's safe, though, and a large smile paints her face.

"Lion... My lion." Snaking her fingers through the back of my scalp, she pulls me closer and presses her full lips against mine in a warm morning greeting. "I need to tell you something."

"What? You're killing me, what is it?" Sliding a hand down my arm, she grasps my fingers, tugging me toward the stairs. "Livia, seriously, what."

"Come on."

"If it's dick you need, I'm down for it, but just tell me." Biting her lip, she smiles coyly and continues to pull me toward our new bedroom. When we get in, I press her against the back of the door to close it and lift her up so we're face to face. "Foxy. Please..."

"Maggie gave me a checkup today." Her face beams with something I've only seen when we exchanged vows at the courthouse.

Heart thudding against my ribs, I try to will my pulse rate down. "Yeah?"

"She thinks I could be pregnant." Stunned, my chest stops rising. "Max?"

"Wha-what?" I hear my voice come out shaky, but it seems so far away.

"She says it's too early, but I had her test my hormones about a month ago. She says there's nothing wrong with them, that perhaps there never was. Are you okay? Are you... fainting, Max?"

My vision starts to go blurry, but I maintain a grip on

her. "Repeat. What just happened? I don't understand. You rejected me because you said you couldn't have children. And I said I didn't give a fuck if you could or not. I'm confused."

Carrying her over to the bed, I place her on it and squat in front of her as she places her hands on my shoulders, her legs surrounding my torso. "Maggie. She looked at the old charts I had from that specialist I went to five years ago, the one who told me I couldn't have children. He never even commented on infertility in his note. She even showed it to me. When she looked up his credentials, that doctor didn't exist, but Maggie knew a *healer* who worked with *Strauss* by the same name. Says she even *trained* under him."

"I thought healers didn't play our games, Livia." Rubbing her thighs, my mind races with a thousand questions. "Did he have his healer tell you a lie to-to, what? Keep you from me?"

Despite the gravity of what happened, she still can't shirk a small smile. "Maggie says she believes so. She went over everything with me, saying there was nothing in there that would mean I couldn't have children. That my hormone levels from the lab results back then were completely normal and my irregular cycles were from iron deficiency anemia."

Brushing the tail of her hair over her shoulder, I gaze into her smiling eyes. "And she thinks you're pregnant now?! We've only been together... maybe a couple months?"

Lifting a shoulder, she looks a bit worried, her

eyebrows stitching together. "I was never on birth control. Didn't think I needed to be. And I've never had unprotected sex until you *took* me."

Fuck yeah, I did. Maybe my sperm can break barriers, heal her womb, and cure cancer. Lifting my palm to her face, she rests against it as I finally allow myself to believe. Could she be carrying my child? Our child? Our heir? "Foxy... how do you feel? What are your thoughts?"

"I-I guess I had given up on the possibility, so I'm shocked. Obviously, I want to kill Strauss, and we will. I know that. But I don't feel that rage right now as much as really excited." Looking at her lap, she pauses. "Mainly, though, I'm scared, Max. What if I get my hopes up and it's not true? I can't take another time of feeling broken all over again. I just can't."

Grasping her in a tight embrace, I place my lips over her ear. "You're not broken. Not at all. I don't want to hear you talk about my wife like that. You're Mrs. Freidenberg, and you're mine. You're part bear now and bears aren't weak. *You* are not weak, Livia, never have been. You can face this. And this time, instead of taking that news alone, you have me with you to lean on. If you can't have faith, I'll hope for the both of us. If you can't handle the disappointment, I'll take your pain. Whatever the answer is, I'm here with you."

When I pull back to look at my beautiful wife, tears flood her golden eyes and pour onto her flushed cheeks as she smiles. Grabbing her lips with my mouth, I meld into her body, letting her know we're one now, that I'll be strong when she can't handle something, just as I know she has done for me. She pulls back to take a shaky breath and wipe her eyes.

Leaning her forehead against mine, she says, "My-my pregnancy test was positive. She ordered a blood test, and we're waiting for the results now."

"When will we know?"

"Could be today, maybe in a day or two. Ugh, I seriously can't wait." Scooping her in my arms, I lay her gently on the bed and settle next to her on my side. Some of my bandages tear, but I barely notice, the irritation replaced with anticipation of something new.

"Meh, it'll give us time to murder Egon, Gemini, and Strauss. And whoever that healer is. Basically, baby, that kill list is growing. You and I will destroy every one of them." Lacing our fingers together, we continue to study each other's eyes, our dazed smiles mirrored. "Baby..."

"Yeah?"

"I mean..." Nodding to her stomach, she smiles broadly. "Baby. You could have my baby."

"I could—" Before she can finish her sentence, her phone rings from her pocket, and we both freeze. That call could bring her joy and some peace, but it may also cause her to crumble. Either way, I'm there and will hold her. My head bobs toward it, encouraging her to answer. She inhales deeply, then slides it out of her pocket and lies on her back. "Hey, Maggie. What's up?" she says, attempting to sound casual, but her voice shakes.

Licking my lips, I strain my ears to hear, but can't make out anything.

"Oh? Wow. And, you're sure. You-you don't need

more tests? Should we test, um, my hormones again or anything?" Daring a glance at me, she quickly flicks her eyes back to the ceiling. If I thought my heart couldn't beat any faster, I was wrong. Wiping a sweaty palm down my pants, I lean up on an elbow to study her face closer to get any read off it. "Okay..." Her voice completely breaks. "Thank you." Ending the call, she puts her arm down and squeezes her eyes closed, those drops of joy or pain escaping freely down the sides of her temples. Scrunching every muscle in her face, she sobs.

"What? What did she say?" Brushing the wetness away with my fingers, I hover almost on top of her. "Livia, foxy..."

"I'm pregnant. I'm pregnant, lion. We're having a baby."

The words don't even seem to make sense to me before a wave of ecstasy hits my soul, radiating pure light and warmth through me. Is it possible to die from happiness? "We are? Are you okay? Are you—What do you feel?"

"I'm so happy, I can't stand it, Max. I'm terrified and overwhelmed, and filled with joy. It's weird! How are you?"

My face brightens when I see all those emotions reflected in her eyes, the same ones now inside of me. "Me, too. Me, too." Laughing, I play with her hair as she starts giggling with me.

"I love you, lion."

Placing a small kiss on her cheek, I lean into her more. "I love you, foxy."

And despite the bliss we're distracted by at the moment, somewhere inside, I know the road ahead will be fraught with tense battles. If I was ready to burn down the Crimson Angel for my parents, nothing will stop me from scorching the lands for my wife... and child.

To be continued...

Seep into the next installment in The Compass Series:
Rawest Venom.

Past Poisons Veracious Passions

Dating life is deadly in Gnarled Pine Hollow. Especially when all of my men end up mutilated, their parts delivered to my doorstep. Eyes track my every move.

And then there's the masked man chasing me through the park, forcing my terrified screams to turn into tantalizing sighs. Are they all connected?

Drawn into some type of game, I feel I'm being herded into a trap.

Like a cat and a mouse...

Yet which of us is which?

Acknowledgments

To my amazing editor, Mackenzie. Thank you for asking all the right questions to bring out the best in me. And thank you for putting up with my giggling fits when I nerd out. I could *not* have done this without you.

Of course, my amazing critique partner and friend, M.A. Cobb. This book wouldn't be possible without you. Your work continues to inspire me to do better just so mine could be in the same realm as yours. You helped push me from not going far enough, to embracing the five senses with gusto. Thank you for patiently reading every word twelve times at least.

To my best friend, Jen, who reads everything at least four times, thank you. As always your encouragement to do the wrong thing has lead me to where I am today. And I love you for that.

Thank you to my beta reading team: Virginia, Wishy, Katie, Denise, Lana, and now Colleen. You all are the absolute best cheerleaders and criticizers because you say it all with such care. I don't even think you understand how much I enjoy our daily chats, laughing together, and you saying, "Please don't hate me, but..." before you give me some needed piece of advice. Keep up the excellent work!

And to you. You made it through the first book of The Compass Series, reader. I want you to know that I understand if you're still angry with me for what happened in the book. The beta team didn't speak with me for two days after the, um, incident, and I think my editor also disappeared after she read it. I get it, but hang with me...

The endings may be bitter, but there's still that comfort of sweet to it, too.

Thank you. Yes, you there right now reading this. Thanks for reading!

About the Author

Kitty King is a bestselling romance author that gave up being a psychiatrist in order to entertain readers with dirty stories. She is the author of the International bestseller *Red Night: Xavier's Delight*. Kitty enjoys reading, listening to ASMR, and building houses with her mind (or in Sims). She first learned to use a compass probably around age six on a family camping trip.

And, much like Max, she loves bacon.

http://authorkittyking.com

Manufactured by Amazon.ca
Acheson, AB

13880875R00224